ACCLAIM FOR *PRIVATE DANCER*

'The best book regarding relationships with bargirls that you can ever
read. This should be compulsory reading for all first-timers to Thailand'
Pattaya Mail, Thailand

'A gripping, highly readable thriller that cleverly intertwines the stories
of the main two protagonists—bargirl and naked pole dancer Joy
and her British, travel guide writing customer/lover Pete'
The Asian Review of Books, Hong Kong

'With its conversational, almost confessional style of writing,
this novel will have you rushing through it in one night to reach
the climatic ending'
The Straits Times, Singapore

'Because of all of its local wisdom, *Private Dancer* ought to be made
available to every tourist at port of entry'
The Bangkok Post, Thailand

STEPHEN LEATHER
Private Dancer

monsoon

monsoonbooks

Published in 2019 (10th edition)
by Monsoon Books Ltd

No.1 The Lodge, Burrough Court,
Burrough on the Hill, Melton Mowbray LE14 2QS, UK
www.monsoonbooks.co.uk

First published by Monsoon Books, Singapore in 2005.
First published in Thailand in 2005 by Three Elephants.

ISBN: 978-981-05-3916-0

MIX
Paper from
responsible sources
FSC® C018072

Printed and bound in Great Britain by Clays Ltd, Elcograf S.p.A.
21 20 19   10 11 12

BANGKOK 1996

The Year of The Rat

PETE

She's dead. Joy's dead. Joy's dead and I killed her. I can't believe it. I killed her and now I don't know what I'm going to do. I don't know what I'm going to do without her and I don't know what's going to happen to me when they find out she's dead. They'll know it's my fault. I trashed the room, my fingerprints are going to be everywhere. The manager of the building saw me storm out. The guy in the room, he'll remember me, too. Her friends knew that we were always arguing, and they know where I live.

The taxi driver keeps looking at me in his mirror. He can see how upset I am. I have to keep calm, but it's difficult. I want to scream at him, to tell him to put his foot down and drive faster but we're sitting at a red light so we aren't going anywhere for a while. Ahead of us is an elephant, swinging its trunk at a guy carrying a basket of bananas. A group of tourists give the guy money and he hands them fruit so that they can feed the elephant.

"Chang," says the driver. Thai for elephant. I pretend not to understand and keep looking out of the window. A typical Bangkok street scene, the pavements lined with food hawkers and stalls piled high with cheap clothing, the air thick with fumes from motorcycles and buses. I see it but I don't see it. All I can think about is Joy.

It's as if time around me has stopped. Stopped dead. I'm breathing and thinking but everything has frozen. She's dead and it's my fault. They'll see my name tattooed on her shoulder and they'll see my name carved into her wrist and they'll know that it's all my fault. I'm not worried about what the police will do. Or her family. There's nothing they can do that can make me feel any worse than I do right now as I sit frozen in time at a red traffic light, watching overweight tourists feeding bananas to an elephant with a chain around its neck. I know with a horrible certainty that I can't go on living without her. My life ends with her death because I can't live with the guilt. Joy's dead and I killed her so that means that I have to die, too.

BRUCE

I always knew it was going to end badly. Joy was a sweet thing and whether or not she'd been lying to Pete, she didn't deserve to die, not like that. Sure, she was a bargirl, but she was forced into it, she'd never have chosen the life for herself, and I know she wanted Pete to take her away from the bars. I was in shock when I heard what happened. Now I don't know what's going to happen to Pete. It's like he's on autopilot, heading into oblivion. I've got a bad feeling about it, but it's out of my hands. He's going to have to come to terms with what he's done, her death's going to be on his conscience for the rest of his life. To be honest, I don't know how he's going to be able to live with himself.

BIG RON

Joy's dead, huh? Can't say I was surprised when Bruce told me. Do I care? Do I fuck. I'm not going to shed any tears about a dead slapper. It's not exactly a long-term career, is it, when all's said and done, what with the drugs and the risks they take. Slappers are dying all the time. Overdoses, suicides, motorcycle accidents. And the way Joy fucked Pete over, I'm surprised he didn't top her months ago. She was a lying hooker and she deserved whatever she got, that's what I say. As for Pete, I don't know what'll happen to him. If he's smart he'll get on the next plane out of Bangkok.

PETE

I don't know if it was love at first sight, but it was pretty damn close. She had the longest hair I'd ever seen, jet black and almost down to her waist. She smiled all the time and had soft brown eyes that made my heart melt, long legs that just wouldn't quit and a figure to die for. She was stark naked except for a pair of black leather ankle boots with small chrome chains on the side. I think it was the boots that did it for me.

I didn't know her name, and I couldn't talk to her because she was already occupied with a fat, balding guy with a mobile phone who kept fondling her breasts and bouncing her up and down on his knee. She was a dancer at the Zombie Bar, one of more than a hundred go-go dancers, and between her twenty-minute dancing shifts she had to hustle drinks from customers. I kept trying to catch her eye, but she was too busy with the bald guy and after an hour or so she changed into jeans and a T-shirt and left with him. They looked obscene together, he must have been twenty stone and old enough to be her father.

I was with Nigel, a guy I'd met in Fatso's Bar, down the road from the go-go bars of Nana Plaza. Nigel was a good-looking guy with a shock of black unruly hair and a movie-star smile and a pirate's eye-patch. First time I met him I thought he was wearing it as a joke and I kept teasing him about it, but then it turns out that he lost an eye when he was a teenager. Stupid accident, he says, climbing through a barbed-wire fence on his parents farm. He's got a false eye but he still wears the eye-patch. Reckons it gives him an air of mystery, he says. Makes him look like a prat, if you ask me.

It was Nigel's idea to go to Zombie. It was one of the hottest bars in Bangkok, he said. It was my first time, I'd only been in Bangkok for two days, and I hadn't known what to expect. It was an eye-opener. Two raised dance floors, each with more than a dozen beautiful girls dancing around silver poles. Most of them naked. Around the edge of the bars were small tables, and waitresses in white blouses and black skirts scurried around taking orders and serving drinks.

"She's beautiful, isn't she?" I said to Nigel as the girl walked by holding the bald guy's hand.

"They're all beautiful," he said, winking at a girl on the stage.

"No, that one's special," I said. "And I don't just mean the boots."

Nigel drank his Singha beer from the bottle and wiped his mouth with the back of his hand. "Pete, let me give you a bit of advice. From the horse's mouth. They're all hookers. Every one of them. Pay their barfines, take them to a short-time hotel, screw your brains out, then pay them. But whatever you do, don't get involved. Trust me, it's not worth it."

I watched the girl and her customer disappear through the curtain that covered the exit to the plaza.

I asked Nigel how it worked, how you got to go out with one of the girls. He explained how the barfine system worked. You paid the money to the bar—it varied between four hundred baht and six hundred baht depending on which bar you were in, and the girl was then free to leave with you. What you did was pretty much up to you, but usually a customer would take the girl to one of the numerous short-time hotels within walking distance of the plaza. How much you paid the girl depended on what she did and how generous you were, it could be as little as five hundred baht, as much as two thousand baht, more if you wanted to spend the whole night with her.

Nigel waved at the two stages, crammed with girls. "Go on, pick one," he said.

I shook my head. There was no one there I wanted.

NIGEL

It's funny watching the faces of the first-timers when they walk into a go-go bar. Their mouths drop and their eyes go wide, then they try to be all cool as if it's the most natural thing in the world to be confronted by dozens of naked girls. Pete was no exception. He sat drinking gin and tonic, his eyes flicking from side to side, trying to take it all in. I've been in Thailand for more than five years so I'm pretty blasé about it. I've seen pretty much everything here. Full sex, lesbian sex, homosexual sex, sex with a German Shepherd once, and now nothing shocks or surprises me.

Pete seemed a nice enough guy. Bit quiet, a bit serious, but a few months in Bangkok would loosen him up. He'd been sent to Thailand to update a travel book, one of those guides you always see in the hands of backpackers looking for a cheap place to stay. It was his first time in

South East Asia, so I took it upon myself to show him around the sleazier parts of Bangkok.

There are three main red light areas: Nana Plaza, Patpong and Soi Cowboy. The Plaza's my favourite. Soi Cowboy is too quiet, the girls are almost never topless and they don't do shows. Patpong is full of tourists: the shows are good but there are too many touts trying to pull you into their bars. Nana Plaza is where the expats go. It's more relaxed and, in my humble opinion, the girls are prettier. There are a couple of dozen bars on three floors, all overlooking a central area where there are outdoor bars. The outdoor bars are good for a quiet drink, but the real action takes place inside. Zombie is the best, but I'm a big fan of G-Spot and Pretty Girl, too. As soon as we sat down, Pete started eyeing up this girl. She was dancing naked, except for ankle-length boots. Nice body, lovely long hair. Face was okay, too, but I never look at the mantelpiece while I'm stoking the fire, if you get my drift.

I could see he was keen but he couldn't even get eye contact with her. She was working a big German guy, smiling and flashing her tits to keep him interested. It was driving Pete crazy. He was practically grinding his teeth when she left with the German. I figured he'd get over it. I mean, there are plenty more fish in the sea, right?

PETE

I went back several times to Zombie but she was always busy, usually with overweight Germans. They'd sit next to her, paw her, buy her drinks, pay her barfine and take her off to a short-time hotel. Eventually, on my fourth visit, she was free. I smiled at her while she was dancing, and she smiled back. She wasn't a particularly good dancer, she just stood by a silver pole, holding it with her right hand, the little finger extended as if she were drinking from a tea-cup. From time to time she'd reach up with her left hand and brush her long hair away from her face. When her dancing shift finished she scuttled off the stage and wrapped a leopard-patterned shawl around her waist. She came over to me, glancing down shyly and extending her right hand. We shook hands, the formality almost ludicrous considering that she was still topless. "Hello," I said. "How are you?"

"I'm fine, thank you," she said. "And you?"

I smiled at her stilted English and patted the seat next to me. She sat down, her leg pressed against mine.

"What's your name?" I asked.

"Joy," she said.

I asked her what she wanted to drink and she said "cola." I nodded and she pulled my chit from its holder and went over to the bar, returning with a small glass of Coke. The chit kept a running total of the drinks I'd bought.

"Cheers," she said, and we clinked glasses.

Her English wasn't good, but it didn't seem to matter. We sat together for almost an hour, watching the dancers. Then she stood up. "I must dance now," she said.

"How about I pay your barfine?" I offered.

"You want go short time with me?" she said.

It wasn't what I'd meant—I'd just wanted to keep her next to me for a while—but I didn't argue with her. Besides, if I didn't pay her barfine, I was pretty sure someone else would. "Okay," I said.

She held out her hand and I gave her five hundred baht. She went over to the cashier, handed over the money and then mimed putting on a shirt and pointed to a door that I guessed led to the changing rooms. Ten minutes later we were in bed.

To be honest, the sex wasn't that good. I mean, it was great being with her, she was drop dead gorgeous, and she did everything I asked, but she wouldn't initiate anything. It was all too passive. I shouldn't really have been surprised, I suppose, because I'd only known her for an hour or so and there we were, naked in a short-time hotel.

The hotel had been her idea. It was on the first floor of the Nana Plaza complex, less than fifty yards away from Zombie. I was staying at the Dynasty Hotel in Soi 4 but I didn't want to take her back there as I knew that the staff would only gossip. There was an old guy at reception reading a Thai comic book and he charged me four hundred baht for the use of the room for two hours and ten baht for a condom. He didn't even look up as he took my money. Joy took the key and went straight to the room. She'd obviously been there before.

Afterwards, when it was all over, she rushed into the shower, and when she came out she was wrapped in one of the two threadbare towels that the hotel supplied. I wanted to lie with her, to hold her in my arms and talk to her, but she seemed more interested in getting back to the bar. I could understand why—she was working and I was a paying customer—but I wanted to be more than that. I wanted her to care about me, the way I cared about her. I asked her about her family, about where she went to school, how long she'd worked in the bar, but her English wasn't good and my Thai was virtually non-existent, so mainly she just smiled and nodded, or smiled and shrugged.

She sat on the bed and waited until I'd showered, and we went back to Zombie together. I didn't want to go inside the bar, so we sat outside and I bought her a cola. I explained that I was going to Hong Kong the following day. I had to see the regional editor of the book I was updating. She looked suddenly concerned.

"So I not see you again?"

I was touched. Maybe she did care, after all. I told her I'd be back in a week or so.

She shrugged. "I not believe you," she said. "I think you not come back."

I had an idea. I took off the gold chain I was wearing around my neck. It was worth about a hundred pounds. I put it around her neck. "There," I said, "now you know I'll have to come back, to get my gold."

She grinned and threw her arms around my neck, and gave me a Thai kiss. Not with her lips, that's not the Thai way. She put her nose close to my cheek and sniffed. She smelled fresh and clean, like she'd been out in a field, but I knew that it was the cheap soap that had been in the bathroom.

"I hope you come back to me," she said.

JOY

To be honest, I never thought I'd see him again. He was a bit drunk, I think, and even though he gave me his gold chain I thought he'd forget about me as soon as he left Bangkok. A lot of farangs are like that: twenty minutes after they've met you they start saying they love you and want to marry you. They say it but they don't mean it. A Thai man would never say he loves you that quickly. I don't think my father ever told my mother that he loved her, right up until the day she died. I'm not saying he didn't love her, he did, but he never actually said the words. Farangs are the opposite. They say it, but they don't mean it.

He looked okay, I guess. He said he was thirty seven but he looked younger. He wasn't fat like most farangs who come in the bar, and he wasn't losing his hair. He wasn't especially good looking but he had a kind face and really blue eyes. It was his eyes I remembered most, I think. They were blue and soft.

He was a bit drunk when he left, and I guess I figured he'd forget about me as soon as he got on the plane. I remember being disappointed that the chain wasn't bigger.

The sex? I don't even remember doing it with him. I try not to think about what I'm doing when I'm in bed. I blot it out, just think about the money. It's not making love, it doesn't even feel like sex, if you know what I mean. I'm there, on the bed, and there's a farang with me, but I just let them do what they want. Tender or rough, it doesn't make any difference to me, I just want it to be over. Ten minutes is the most it usually takes. Some of the girls moan and groan, they reckon that makes a man come quickly, but I don't do that. I don't want to do anything, I want it all to be their doing. Usually I just lie on my back. I hate it when they want me to go on top because then they expect me to move, to do the work, and I don't like that.

He didn't ask me how much he was supposed to pay, and before we left the room he gave me a thousand baht. I told him it wasn't enough. He looked confused. I suppose one of his friends had told him that a thousand baht was the going rate. Most of the girls will do it for a thousand, some will even go short-time for five hundred, but I never do it for less than fifteen hundred. And if they want me to stay all night, that's three thousand. Anyway, I told Pete that he had to pay me fifteen hundred, and he did.

ALISTAIR

Pete's been working for the company for more than five years, and he's a good operator. Fast, reliable, and accurate. He did our London guide and assisted with the guides to France and Spain. I've known him since he joined the company; in fact I was on the panel that interviewed him. He used to be a journalist on a small paper in the West Country, then got into travel writing and he was freelancing for some of the nationals when we hired him. I get on well with him, professionally and on a personal level, too. When we were looking for someone to revamp our South East Asian editions, I had no hesitation in putting Pete's name forward.

His predecessor had a bad experience in Thailand. For a start, he'd gone a bit native on us. His name was Lawrence and he was an Australian. He'd been working for us at our head office in Perth, and about ten years ago he requested a transfer to Bangkok. Initially he worked well, did a great job on the third edition of our guide to Thailand, but he soon began missing deadlines and turning in shoddy copy. He was called back to Perth for an arse-kicking and he was okay again for a few months but then he married a local girl and he started getting slapdash again.

Lawrence was sent a couple of written warnings but it didn't make a blind bit of difference. The company asked me to fly over to have a word with him. He was living in a tiny house near a foul-smelling canal, no air-conditioning or hot water, with a girl about half his age. She was a pretty little thing and it was obvious that Lawrence loved her to bits. From what I could gather, he did everything for her. Cooked, cleaned, took care of the baby. They had a son, I think he was six months old when I saw him. Cute as a button, though to be honest he looked completely Thai. Lawrence doted on the kid, though, so I didn't want to burst his bubble by telling him that there wasn't much of a resemblance. "Don't you think he has my nose?" he kept asking.

Anyway, a couple of months after I went over to give him a character reading, Lawrence went up to the Golden Triangle to check out a new casino complex that had just opened. He got bitten by a mosquito and caught Japanese encephalitis. Almost died. They rushed him into hospital in Chiang Rai and had him on a life support machine. His wife came up to see him, had a word with the doctors, and vanished. He never saw her or the kid again. She sold the house, took everything that wasn't nailed down, and went back to her village.

Lawrence's parents flew over and took care of him. They got him back to Australia as soon as they could. He's still in a wheelchair and he can barely speak. Last I heard was that the doctors had done all they could and that brain damage was irreversible. A real sad fuck. And no sign of his missus or the kid.

Not that I think Pete's going to go the same way. He's too level-headed for that. Plus he's already been married. He got divorced just before he started working for the company, amicably by all accounts. They sold the house, split the profits and divided up the contents. I think the only argument was over who should keep the cats, but as Pete was travelling a lot that wasn't a serious problem. Anyway, I didn't think that he'd be keen to rush into marriage again, so he was the perfect choice for Bangkok.

Pete came to Hong Kong for a few days so that we could work through the chapter headings of the new Thailand guide. We wanted to jazz up the format to appeal to the younger crowd, more photographs, more info on the nightlife, stuff like that. Head office had also decided to maximise the use of the information we already had by producing a series of city guides. In Thailand that meant Bangkok, Chiang Mai, Udon Thani, Pattaya and Phuket. They'd also come up with an idea for a totally new book, a sort of cookery book crossed with a travel guide so that people could cook the dishes they'd eaten on holiday once they got home. I'd asked Pete to edit the book and he was enthusiastic. He'd obviously have to compile the Thai recipes but that wouldn't involve much extra work because part of his brief was to visit as many restaurants and cafes as he could, so all he'd have to do is collect recipes as he went around. Our correspondents around the region had been instructed to do likewise, and then Pete would collate them and then intersperse them with travel tips and hotel stuff which we already had. It would be an upmarket book at the top end of the spectrum to our backpacker's guide to the region and I was sure Pete would make a real go of it.

He stayed with me and we had a couple of nights on the town but Pete's mind seemed to be elsewhere. I think he was just keen to get started.

PETE

I got back to Bangkok early evening, dropped my stuff off at the hotel and rushed around to Zombie. Joy wasn't wearing the gold chain, or anything else for that matter, just the boots. She grinned and waved when she saw me and I ordered a gin and tonic and waited for her dancing shift to come to an end.

She wrapped the leopard-print shawl around her waist and rushed over, giving me a big hug and kissing me on the cheek. I bought a cola and put my arm round her.

"I not think you come back, Pete," she said.

I couldn't stop myself grinning. She'd remembered my name. "I said I would."

"I think I not see you again."

I asked her where the gold chain was and she averted her eyes. She looked like a schoolgirl who'd been caught with her hand in the cookie jar. "I sorry, Pete," she said. "I no have money."

My heart sank. The gold had no sentimental value, but I'd hoped that by wearing it she'd be thinking of me. "Did you sell it?" I asked.

She shook her head. "Not sell," she said. She made a gesture with her thumb, pressing it down. Nigel had told me that bargirls often pawn their gold and they leave their thumb print instead of their signature. She'd pawned it. She smiled brightly. "If you give me three thousand baht, I get back for you."

She glanced down, suddenly shy, and my heart melted. There was no way I could be angry with her.

"Okay," I promised, "I'll give you the money."

She grinned and gave me a quick kiss on the cheek. Her bare breasts brushed against my arm. Some of the girls danced naked, like Joy, while others wore full bikinis. Some wore bikini briefs but danced topless. I asked her why she took off all her clothes when she danced.

She explained that girls who kept their clothes on were paid less than those who took their tops off, and the best paid were the ones who danced naked. Joy needed the money, she said. She said she had to send it back to her family. I felt suddenly protective. It wasn't fair. Joy was bright, she was smart, yet she was reduced to taking her clothes off and sleeping with men because that was the only way she could earn decent money. It was a form of economic rape: if Joy had been born in Europe or America she'd probably have been at university or working in an office. I paid her barfine. I hadn't liked the short-time hotel we'd been to before, so I asked her if she knew of another place we could go to. She suggested one called the Penthouse, a short taxi drive away from Nana Plaza.

It was a hotel used by Thais, a sort-of drive-in place where you could park in front of a room and the staff would pull a curtain around your car, shielding it from prying eyes. The room was clean enough with large mirrors on the walls and ceilings. A Thai teenager switched on the aircon and told me that it was three hundred baht for short-time or five hundred for all night.

"All night, okay?" I asked Joy.

She smiled and nodded. I paid the guy and he left us alone. We showered and made love and then she fell asleep in my arms.

In the morning I gave her fifteen hundred baht. She shook her head. "All night, three thousand baht," she said. My heart fell. I'd sort of hoped that she felt that I was more than just a customer. I gave her the extra money.

"What about your gold?" she asked. I gave her another three thousand baht.

She put her hands together as if she were praying and pressed her fingertips to her chin. It was a 'wai,' a Thai gesture of respect or thanks.

Any annoyance I felt at her demands for money evaporated. She looked so cute, so childlike, that I just wanted to gather her up in my arms and protect her from the world that had forced her to sell her body.

JOY

I was quite surprised to see him again. Actually, I'd forgotten all about him. I'd pawned the gold chain the day after he gave it to me and used the money to pay the month's lease on the motorcycle I was buying. Luckily I was dancing when he walked into the bar because I'd forgotten his name. I asked a couple of my friends if they knew who he was but they didn't. I had to wrack my brains but eventually remembered. Pete. He was a writer or something. Anyway, as soon as I was finished dancing I ran over and made a fuss of him. I made sure I used his name, that always makes farangs feel special. He noticed right away that I wasn't wearing the gold and I told him I didn't have it any more. I told him I could get it for him if he gave me three thousand baht. He did, too. And he gave me another three thousand baht for staying all night. He obviously earned a lot since he didn't argue about the money.

He kept saying that he liked my hair. Most farangs do. I reckon that eighty per cent of farangs like long hair. I'm always surprised at the girls who cut their hair. Working in the bar is all about attracting farangs: you can't make enough money just dancing, they have to buy you drinks and pay your barfine. My sisters Sunan and Mon dance in Zombie and they both have hair down to the waist. Farangs like to see us dancing naked, too. We get paid more for dancing naked, but that's not why I do it. The thousand baht extra a month means nothing, what's important is that they're more likely to pay your barfine if they see you naked. I reckon eighty per cent of farangs prefer girls who dance naked. It starts them thinking about sex straight away. Some girls are too shy to take off all their clothes, but I tell them they're stupid not to. Once a guy sees you naked, he wants you. Eighty per cent of them anyway.

The other thing farangs like is for you to laugh at the stupid jokes and to flirt with them. They like their girls to be cute. Not too cute, because then it looks like you're acting, but you have to keep smiling at them, put your hand on their leg, look them in the eye when they talk to you, that sort of thing. And you have to keep smiling at them when you're dancing, let them think that they're the most important man in the bar. Some of the girls, they just slouch in the corners when they're not dancing, or they smoke or they go into the locker room and chat. They don't seem to understand that they're in the bar to work, and working means getting the farangs to like you. To want you.

Sunan's the best at it. Her English isn't so good, but she has a way of making men want her. She looks at them, she really looks at them, deep into their eyes, and even though she doesn't always understand what they're saying she knows when to laugh and when to smile. It's like being an actress. We're all actresses, and the bar is our stage and the farangs are our audience.

NIGEL

It's the Pretty Woman syndrome, that's what it is. Remember the movie with Richard Gere and Julia Roberts? He's a rich guy, she's a Los Angeles hooker, they met on the street, they fall in love and live happily ever after. Yeah, right. Never happens. Hookers hook, that's what they do, and they don't fall in love with the clients. Period. If the guy pays the girl for sex the first time, the relationship can never be anything other than on a hooker-client basis. Every time he looks at her, he's going to remember that she was a hooker when he first saw her, he's going to imagine the faces of all the guys she went with. And whenever she looks at him, she's going to remember that he was looking for a hooker when they met.

The movie was a fairytale. An urban myth, a work of fiction. It never happens. It doesn't happen in LA and it doesn't happen in Thailand. It certainly doesn't happen in the go-go bars. That movie's got a lot to answer for. It raises expectations that you can find love with a prostitute. Well you can't. I never have, anyway. And I don't know anyone who has. I do know dozens of guys who've married bargirls. Some of them took the girls back to the UK, some of them set up homes in Thailand. Without exception it's ended in disaster. Not just broken hearts, but major financial losses, too. You can't trust them, you really can't. You can't leave them alone for a minute: they'll sell you out without a second thought. There isn't a Thai bargirl alive who can't turn around a piece of land or a property within forty-eight hours. I've warned Pete countless times but I can see it's going in one ear and out of the other. I wish there was some way I could explain to him how dangerous it can be getting emotionally involved with a bargirl, but like all of us he's gonna have to learn from his own mistakes.

One of her friends came over to her . . . . and Joy . . . showed her the photograph. I sat there stunned. It was the first time Joy . . . said that she loved me, and she did it in such a matter-of-fact way that it sounded totally genuine. You . . . .

PETE

The thing I really liked about Joy was that no matter what she was doing, no matter who she was talking to, as soon as I walked into Zombie she'd come over and hug me. All the time I was in the bar I had her undivided attention. I suppose she was still being barfined by other guys, but I never saw her. Out of sight, out of mind, I suppose. Sometimes when I went to the bar she wasn't there. The other girls would say that she hadn't come in that day, but I think they were lying to save my feelings. I never asked Joy. It wasn't my business. She was a bargirl, I understood that, and she had a living to make. It wasn't as if she was my girlfriend or anything. I mean, I know she liked me, and I certainly had feelings for her, but at the end of the day I still had to pay. I bought her drinks, I paid her barfine, and if I took her to a short-time hotel I gave her fifteen hundred baht. Sometimes more if she had rent to pay or she wanted to send extra money to her family in Si Saket. Even if we didn't go to a short-time hotel, I still gave her money. I guess I thought that if I gave her money, she wouldn't go with other farangs. I never said that to her, that would have been pathetic, but I sort of hoped that she'd realise for herself that she could get everything she needed from me, that she didn't have to sell her body.

A couple of days back I was sitting with her in the bar when a guy went around offering to take pictures with a Polaroid camera at forty baht a go. Joy asked me if I'd get a photograph of the two of us together, then she went to a lot of trouble to pose the two of us, my arm around her, her hand on my knee, both smiling at the camera. She went around the bar, showing the photograph to all her friends. Today, when I went to the bar, she made a big thing of putting her wallet on the table, something she'd never done before. Then she opened it so I could see what was inside. The photograph was there. I looked slightly drunk, Joy was smiling at the lens, her hand on my leg.

"I want everyone know I love you," she said.

One of her friends came over to borrow a hundred baht from her and Joy showed her the photograph. I sat there, stunned. It was the first time she'd said that she loved me, and she did it in such a matter-of-fact way that it sounded totally genuine, completely uncontrived.

Extract from
CROSS-CULTURAL COMPLICATIONS
OF PROSTITUTION IN THAILAND
by PROFESSOR BRUNO MAYER

Estimates vary as to the number of prostitutes in Thailand. The general consensus appears to be that at any time there are between 300,000 and one million women engaged in the activity, which has been illegal in the country since 1960. It is difficult to ascertain a more definite number as there is a high degree of transience in the activity, with girls moving into prostitution for a short time as and when they require money. A high proportion come from the north east of Thailand, the region known as Isarn, forced from their villages by a depressed labour market and low wages. Many come to the capital, Bangkok, in search of work, often in the hope of supporting their families back in Isarn, but find that employment prospects in the city are not much better than at home. Prostitution offers relatively large amounts of money, particularly for those women who are able to work with tourists.

The girls who work in the farang bars are in effect the elite of the country's prostitutes. Their standard of English is generally better than that of the girls who service the Thai clientele, and because they are paid more for each sexual encounter, they tend not to have as many clients. A prostitute in a Thai massage parlour or bar could service as many as a dozen men in a day. A girl in a go-go bar might only go with one or two men a week, or perhaps even latch on to a particular customer who would pay her barfine for the length of his stay in Thailand. The girls become a temporary girlfriend, where the line between prostitution and holiday romance becomes blurred. The girls very quickly become adept at convincing the men they meet that the encounter is more than just a pecuniary one, that they care about them and not just the money they give.

Obviously, the girls do not arrive in the city with the necessary skills to begin working with foreigners. These have to be acquired, and there is a learning process which can take several months. The older girls instruct the new intake in how to apply Western-style make-up, how to dress in a manner deemed to be attractive to Westerners, and enough basic English to be able to converse with foreigners. Those girls who are not able to acquire the necessary skills either return to their villages, or, more likely, seek employment in the massage parlours, cocktail lounges and karaoke bars frequented by a Thai clientele.

PETE

One evening as we were having dinner, Joy asked me what Chinese horoscope sign I was. I told her I was a monkey. She was a rabbit. She frowned. "Big problem," she said solemnly.

I asked her why.

"Rabbit and monkey always have big problem," she said. "Rabbit is very soft. Likes things gentle. Quiet. Not changing. But monkey always changing. Never the same. Rabbit cannot trust the monkey."

"Because the monkey will pull the rabbit's ears?"

She nodded. "Big problem, Pete. Really."

There was no doubting her sincerity. I asked her what farang star sign she was and she was a Libran, same as me. Our birthdays were only ten days apart so I suggested that we had a joint birthday party. She seemed thrilled by the idea, and said she'd get her family to come down from Si Saket, a ten-hour bus ride. I wasn't sure where to hold the party, so she said she'd book the VIP room at the Chicago Karaoke Bar. That was where Joy had worked when she'd first arrived in Bangkok. I'd been there with her a few times. It was in a district called Suphan Kwai, literally Buffalo Bridge, a down market entertainment area frequented by Thais. Joy was an excellent singer, she'd sit next to me, gazing into my eyes as she sang, and even though I couldn't understand all the words, the sentiment was clear. The karaoke bar wasn't doing that well so there usually weren't more than a few people there, but her singing always generated applause and cheers. She'd only worked there for a couple of months because the money wasn't good. She was paid two thousand baht a month as a hostess and hardly anything in the way of tips. She told me that she didn't go with customers, so she barely earned enough to live on. Sunan and Mon had persuaded her to join them in Zombie, but she liked to go back to see her friends there. Having a birthday party there would give her lots of face.

It was a great party, as it turned out. I arranged for a big cake, with Garfield and "Happy Birthday to Joy and Pete" written in pink and blue icing. I went to Zombie with Nigel and I paid barfine for Joy, Mon and Sunan. I gave Joy her birthday present, a gold bracelet made of interlinked hearts that had cost almost ten thousand baht. She was so pleased, but she gave it back to me and told me to give it to her at the party, so everyone could see.

There were already a dozen or so people in the VIP room when we got there, mainly Thai men in their twenties. Two of them were Joy's brothers, the rest were cousins, she said. They were introduced to Nigel and me, but they seemed more interested in the bottles of Johnnie Walker Black Label that Joy had ordered. I was older than all of them but none waied me and I wasn't sure if that was a sign of disrespect or because they thought that as a farang I wouldn't expect it. Joy's father arrived after an hour and I waied him. He seemed surprised and I got a half-hearted wai in return. Joy had said that he was sixty but he looked older, a thin, wizened man with bony arms. He sat in a corner and one of Joy's cousins handed him a tumbler of whisky.

A waitress came in with a menu and Joy ordered food for everyone. Lots and lots of food. There was Tom Yam Gung, the hot spicy shrimp soup that's Thailand's most famous dish, shrimps in batter, spicy beef salad, omelette stuffed with pork and vegetables, catfish curry, deep fried oysters, steamed crab claws, the food just kept on coming. So did the booze. By the time midnight came we'd gone through half a dozen bottles of whisky and a couple of crates of Heineken. More and more of Joy's friends kept turning up. Most of them didn't even acknowledge Nigel or me, the only two farangs in the room. Not that it mattered, Nigel was fondling Mon most of the time, and I was getting quietly drunk. Joy was as attentive as usual and kept singing love songs to me. Mon had brought her daughter, Nonglek, three years old and as cute as a button.

At midnight Sunan lit the candles on the cakes and Joy and I blew them out. Joy kissed me. "The bracelet," she whispered. "Give my bracelet now."

I took the gold out of my pocket and gave it to her. She held it above her head so that everyone in the room could see it, then made me put it on her wrist. Mon cut the cake up and everyone had a piece. I'll tell you what was weird, though. There was only one piece left at the end of the night. The piece with my name on it. I asked Joy why they hadn't eaten it and she shrugged. "I don't know," she said. Later I asked Nigel what he thought. He reckoned it could have been a sign of respect. Or contempt. It worried me for quite a while.

At two o'clock in the morning there were no signs of the party breaking up. Bottles of whisky kept coming and everyone was taking it in turns to sing. People kept coming and going, friends of Joy and her sisters, but no one offered to pay for drinks—I guess Joy had told them that I was paying for everything. I wasn't annoyed, it was a joint birthday party after all, but it would have been nice if they'd brought a bottle with them, some indication that they were prepared to contribute. And no one had a present for Joy. No presents and no cards.

Nigel said he had to go because he had work in the morning. I was tired and fairly drunk, so I said I'd go with him. I paid the bill. It came to more than ten thousand baht. I got up to go. No one said goodbye. No one said thank you. Joy took us outside and helped us find a taxi. Nigel got into the taxi first. Joy kissed me on the cheek. "Thank you for everything you do," she said.

I gave her a thousand baht so that she could buy more whisky for her family and friends. Her face fell. "What's wrong?" I asked.

"Whisky very expensive," she said. "My family drink a lot."

I gave her another five thousand baht. She waied me. I got into the taxi. "Great party, Pete," said Nigel.

"Yeah," I said. We drove off. Joy stood on the pavement, waving until we were out of sight.

JOY

We all had a great time and I had a hangover for two days afterwards. We didn't finish until seven o'clock in the morning, and that was only because we ran out of money. We switched to Thai whisky after Pete and Nigel went because that's cheaper, but we ordered more food because everyone was hungry again, and Bird had some marijuana and we started smoking that. Everyone loved the gold that Pete had bought for me and made jokes about the fact that it was made up of hearts. They reckoned I'd stolen Pete's heart and they thought it was really funny that he'd gone so early. They wanted to know how much money the party had cost, and how much money Pete earned. I said he earned millions of baht every year and I showed them the bill. They were all impressed, even Sunan, and Sunan has a lot of money.

Park waited outside until Pete and Nigel went. I saw him sitting on his motorcycle when I went out to get a taxi for the farangs and he started pulling faces, trying to make me laugh. I met Park the first week I worked in Zombie. He's one of the DJs, he's twenty-five and he comes from Udon Thani. His sister works in Spicy-a-go-go and she's become quite a good friend of mine. Park's really good-looking and he's got a great body. He and his friends work out at a gym during the day and they're always comparing muscles. It's really funny when they get competitive about their looks, they're as bad as girls sometimes. His stomach is really hard, like a turtle's shell, and his skin is really smooth. He was going out with another dancer when he met me but he chucked her and said he wanted to go out with me instead. At first I said no but he kept after me, pestering me until I said okay. The reason I said no was because he had a bit of a reputation. Mon warned me about him, she said that Park made a beeline for any new girl if she was pretty and young, but he told me that I was different, that he really liked me. He didn't try anything on the first time we went out, either. We went for a meal after work. He didn't have any money so I had to pay, but I didn't mind that. The DJs earn even less than the waitresses, and besides, I'd been short time with an old Swiss guy and he'd been really generous so I had two thousand baht.

Park made me laugh a lot, he told me lots of stories about the crazy things that happened in the bars, and he told me about his family.

I didn't sleep with him until the second date, and it was amazing. He was so gentle with me, not rough like the farangs, he'd kiss me all over and whisper stuff to me until I'd go all tingly.

Anyway, Park went up to the VIP room with me and we sang duets together and everyone applauded. He saw the piece of cake with Pete's name on it and made a big thing about eating it. I fed it to him and then kissed him in front of everyone. I showed him the gold bracelet that Pete had given me and he wanted me to give it to him to sell. Every month he had to pay five thousand baht for his motorcycle and he was behind in his payments. I told him that I couldn't sell the gold because Pete would get angry, but I promised that I'd give him the money the following day and he said that was okay. He'd bought some yar bar tablets with him and I swallowed a couple because I was starting to get tired. They perked me up a treat.

After we left the karaoke bar, Park and I went back to his room and passed out. It was a great night, my best birthday party ever.

PETE

Let me give you an example of the sort of girl Joy is. A month after the birthday party, I walked into Zombie to find her bursting with happiness. She was grinning from ear to ear, giggling, and bouncing up and down in her seat. I bought her a cola and asked her what she was so happy about. She held out her hands and showed me a gold chain. She told me it was almost two-thirds of an ounce of Thai gold, 23 carat, and worth about ten thousand baht.

Joy explained that she'd had a customer who'd paid her barfine so that he could take her to dinner.

"Are you sure it was only dinner?" I interrupted.

She raised her eyebrows and sighed in mock annoyance.

"Pete, why I lie to you? Only dinner, okay?"

She started grinning again, and continued her story. After dinner the man realised that he didn't have enough money for the one-thousand-baht tip he'd promised her. She held up the chain. "But he had this around his neck and he gave it to me. He said he wanted to sell it, but didn't know how. Pete, he said I can sell it and keep half. He's coming here tomorrow for the money." She leaned forward, her eyes wide. "Pete, I can keep five thousand baht."

She spent the rest of the evening showing the gold to all her friends and relating the story of her good fortune. She was like a little kid who'd been told that Christmas was coming early this year.

The next evening I went back to Zombie and found her sitting in a corner, her eyes red from crying. She grabbed me tightly and put her tear-stained cheek against my neck. "Why farang lie?" she asked me between sobs.

"What do you mean?" I asked. She felt so small in my arms, small and soft and vulnerable.

"Gold not real," she said, hugging me around the waist.

She'd taken the chain to the gold shop and the woman there had laughed in her face. It was fake, not worth more than fifty baht. It wasn't even gold-plated.

"Why farang lie?" she kept repeating between her sobs. I paid her barfine and took her out for dinner at the German restaurant in Soi 4 and kept telling her silly stories until her smile returned. I didn't take her to a short-time hotel that night because I could see she was still upset, so I gave her two thousand baht and let her go back to the bar and her friends.

I went back to the Dynasty Hotel to work on the book. It was going really well. During the daytime I was visiting hotels and getting their details, checking rooms, facilities and prices, and in the early evenings I was checking out restaurants, usually eating in one and getting menus from several others. Then I'd go and see Joy. Most evenings I'd pay her barfine, but we didn't always go to a short-time hotel. Sometimes we'd just sit at one of the outside bars and talk, or go for a late-night Thai snack. She was introducing me to all sorts of dishes I'd never had before, the real hot, spicy food that most farangs don't get to experience.

I still hadn't taken her back to the Dynasty. Joy was very pretty, but she dressed like most of the girls who danced in Nana Plaza—tight jeans, high heels and a T-shirt—and she had just a bit too much make up. To put it bluntly, she looked like a hooker, and I didn't want the staff at the hotel to see me taking a hooker back to my room. She didn't seem to mind.

JOY

I should have known better than to trust a farang. I'm not the first girl to be conned and I won't be the last, but I learned my lesson, that's for sure. He was from Switzerland, an old guy, big and fat like they all are, and he smelled like he hadn't showered for a week. He had a thick gold chain around his wrist and the big one around his neck, the one that he gave me, so I figured he had money. He bought me five colas and when I put my hand on his crotch I could feel that he was hard already so I knew he'd want to pay bar for me. I figured Pete wouldn't be around until ten and it was only eight so I gave him a couple of rubs and asked if he wanted to go short-time.

We went to Uncle Rey's Guest House, it's only a five-minute walk from Nana Plaza. He wouldn't shower or anything, just stripped off and lay down on his back like a huge beached whale. He was covered with hair, grey and curly, and he lay there playing with himself while I undressed. His prick was huge, and thick, and it seemed to get bigger and bigger as he played with it. I wanted to shower but he said he didn't want me to. He said he wanted me to suck him. I shook my head and said I didn't do that and I tried to get on top of him. He pushed me down and tried to force me, but I kept turning my head away. It stank, like old fish. He kept trying to force me, but I wasn't having any of it. Eventually he sat up and took off the gold chain. He told me that he wanted to sell it, and that if I sold it for him I could keep half. It looked real enough, and it felt real, so I put the chain around my neck. It wasn't as bad as I thought it would be, but I kept my eyes closed and concentrated on not being sick. He started to thrust himself in and out and I almost choked. I could feel him start to come so I tried to pull my head away but he put his hands on the back of my head. I actually didn't resist too hard because I figured I was getting five thousand baht. Anyway, he came in my mouth and then held me there until I swallowed.

I dressed and rushed out of the room while he was still on the bed because I didn't want him to change his mind and ask for his gold back.

When I got home that night I gave the chain to Park. He put it on and made love to me all night. He looked really good in it and I suggested he keep it but he said that no, we needed the money. I wanted to keep it all but Park said it would be better to play the Swiss guy along, give him his five thousand baht share and then get him to keep paying my barfine and taking me short-time. We'd get the five thousand baht back within a week, with more to come. The old ones are the easiest, they're so quick to fall in love. All it takes is a few sweet words.

Park went to the gold shop first thing in the morning, and when he came back he was furious. He slapped me, hard, and said that the woman in the shop had threatened to call the police. She thought he was trying to con her. Park punched me in the stomach and threw me to the ground, then spat at me, calling me a stupid whore and a bitch and water buffalo, then he kicked me until Sunan came in from next door and told him to stop.

I was sore, but there were no bruises. Park was good at that, at hitting without leaving a mark. Sunan helped me up and Park stormed out. He didn't come back for two days, and that hurt a lot more than the beating.

We got our own back on the Swiss guy eventually. I told all my friends what had happened and a month or so later I got a phone call from a girl in the Suzie Wong Bar in Soi Cowboy. Park and five of his friends went around on motorcycles and waited until he came out. They attacked him with pieces of lead pipe, broke both his arms and knocked out most of his teeth. Park stole the man's wallet and we all went to the Chicago Karaoke Bar and drank three bottles of Black Label between us. It was a great night.

PETE

One night when I arrived at Zombie, Joy had three red slashes on her left wrist. I could see them from more than ten feet away, and Joy made no move to conceal them. She smiled and waved and as soon as her dancing shift was over she rushed down from the stage and sat next to me. I held her arm and looked at the cuts. They were deep gashes, a vibrant red against her brown skin. She smiled.

"Why?" I asked.

She shrugged as if a suicide attempt was of absolutely no importance.

"Come on, Joy. What happened?"

"My brother crashed motorcycle," she said.

"Was he hurt?"

She shook her head.

I nodded at her mutilated wrist. "Why did you do that?"

Tears brimmed in her eyes. "Motorcycle hurt a lot," she said. "Very expensive."

"How much?"

She sniffed. "Six thousand baht," she said.

I was astonished. "You cut your wrist because your motorcycle needed repairing?"

"Pete," she said. "I have no money."

I put my arms around her and hugged her and her tears fell on to my jeans. I couldn't make sense of it, why on earth would she cut her wrists because of a bike? Besides, she'd said the bike was still up in Si Saket.

"How did you know what had happened?" I asked.

"My brother telephone me. He say he very sorry but he have no money." The tears started again.

"Joy, don't worry," I said. "I'll give you the money."

She sat up and looked at me in astonishment. Then she threw herself at me and wrapped her arms around me. She stayed like that for several minutes, her soft, wet cheeks pressed against my neck.

I bought her a cola and then went down the road to the Bangkok Bank ATM. I withdrew seven thousand baht on my Lloyds Visa card and gave six thousand to Joy. She dashed off to her locker and didn't come back for ten minutes. When she did return, she'd redone her make-up and the tears had gone. She squeezed up next to me and put her hand on my thigh. I was happy that I could make such a difference to her life. A relatively small amount of money to me, but to Joy it was a month's wages. It was worth it to see her smiling and laughing with her friends.

I took her arm again and looked at the cuts. There were no stitches, but they weren't as deep as they'd looked at first sight. Next to the fresh cuts were three old scars. I ran my finger along the raised scar tissue. "When did you do this?" I asked.

"When I fifteen," she said.

"Why?"

"I not happy," she said.

I smiled at the simplicity of her reply. Her honesty was sometimes so childlike that I had an overwhelming urge to protect her from the world. Of course she'd been unhappy, why else would she have tried to kill herself?

"Why weren't you happy?"

"My mother die. I want to be with my mother," she said.

"Why did she die?"

Joy patted her own stomach. "Something wrong inside," she said.

"Cancer?"

She frowned, then nodded.

"Wow," I said. "I'm sorry." I put my arm around her shoulders. A stocky Thai guy with pockmarked skin thrust a bunch of roses in front of me but I shook my head. "My mother died when I was young," I said.

She looked at me, horrified. "What happened?"

I tapped the side of my head. "A brain tumour," I said.

"I not understand," she said.

"Brain tumour," I said. "Something wrong, in her head."

Tears brimmed in her eyes again. "Pete, I sorry for you," she said.

I paid barfine for her, and we went for dinner. She came back to the hotel, but all I wanted to do was to hold her in my arms, to show her that I cared.

Extract from
CROSS-CULTURAL COMPLICATIONS
OF PROSTITUTION IN THAILAND
by PROFESSOR BRUNO MAYER

Self-mutilation is a common phenomenon amongst the girls involved in prostitution. Many have scars on their wrists, not from serious suicide attempts but from superficial cuts, usually carried out in a rage under the influence of drugs or drink. For much of their lives the girls have little or no control over their environment or their relationships. Women are generally subservient to men in Thai culture, and throughout their childhoods they are under strict control as to where they can go and what they can do. In the poorer areas of the country, especially in rural communities, sexual abuse is common. Many are abused by their brothers or fathers or by male relatives, actions over which they have no control. Often the girls themselves are unwilling to complain of the abuse, accepting it as the norm.

Even when the girls leave the environment of their village and move to Bangkok, the family continues to exert control on them with requests for financial assistance. No matter how much the girls earn, they are often unable to save because of the family's ever-increasing demands. In an effort to establish some sort of meaningful relationship, the girls often become involved with Thai men working in the bar environment—DJs, waiters, and touts. Often these men have been working in the bars much longer than the girls and tend to be older and more experienced. As a result, they are adept at getting the girls to give them money and early on in the relationship they begin to exert control over them. The girls then find themselves trapped between the demands of their family and the demands of their newly-acquired boyfriend.

To aggravate the situation, the Thai boyfriends usually refuse to wear condoms, which frequently results in pregnancy. If the girl keeps the baby, as many do, she has yet another demand on her, emotionally and financially. All through her life, the girl has little or no control over her surroundings, and as a result anger and resentment builds up until it cannot be contained any longer. But when it is finally released, it is often directed inwards, at herself. The girl feels that she is worthless, that in some way she is responsible for her own predicament, and as such she tries to hurt, to punish, herself.

JOY

Pretty much all the girls in my family have cut their wrists at some point or another. Except Sunan, she never loses her temper. Everything Sunan does is thought out in advance. Me, I'm totally different, I do all sorts of crazy things on the spur of the moment, especially if I've been drinking or taken a yar bar tablet. Like the time I got back to the room early and found Park in bed with Daeng. Daeng's a little slut, she's only seventeen but she'll have sex with anything in trousers. She's a nymphomaniac and she's barfined every day that she works, sometimes two or three times a day. But twenty-odd farangs a week isn't enough and so she decides she's going to seduce my man. Pete had come into the bar just before eight and had paid my barfine. We'd gone to dinner, but he wasn't saying much. I did my best to lift his spirits but there was something wrong with whatever book it was that he's working on—to be honest I was having trouble understanding him because his Thai is awful—but I nodded and sympathised and tried my best to make him feel better.

He didn't want to go short-time so he gave me a thousand baht and we got into a taxi and I dropped him off at the Dynasty Hotel. I thought about going back to Zombie but it was Park's day off so I thought I'd go home and surprise him. Take him out for a meal, or maybe go and see a movie. He was surprised all right. He was lying on his back with Daeng on top of him. She was screaming so much that they didn't hear me open the door.

I could have killed her. In fact, I almost did. I took off one of my high heels and belted her across the head with it. Park didn't notice at first because his eyes were closed and she was making so much noise in the first place, but I slapped her again with the shoe and this time I almost broke her nose. I started calling her all the names under the sun. Park leapt off the bed, throwing Daeng against the wall, but it wasn't him I wanted to hurt, it was her. Park should have known better but when it comes down to it he's a man and men think with their dicks. If it's offered to them on a plate they're not going to turn it down.

I kept hitting Daeng until she ran out, stark naked. I threw her things after her and told her that if she set foot in my room again I'd kill her. Park was laughing, so I started shouting at him, waving my shoe and threatening to hit him with it. He just laughed in my face, said that she wasn't important, that it was only sex and what did I expect, I was out working, he was a man with needs, what else was he to do? I really lost it then. I threw my shoe at him and told him what a lazy, ungrateful pile of buffalo shit he was. Who did I give my money to? Who paid for his clothes, his drugs, his motorcycle? He earned five thousand baht a month as a DJ, that wasn't enough to pay for his booze. I paid the rent on the room, I paid for everything we had. The more I shouted, the more he laughed, and eventually he walked out.

I went into the bathroom and cut my wrist, three times. I'd done it before just after my mother died, and no, I wasn't trying to kill myself, I just wanted to show how angry I was. There was a lot of blood so I wrapped a towel around it and held my arm up in the air.

Sunan had heard the noise and she came around and helped bandage my wrist. She told me how stupid I was, that Park was a good man, that I had to understand that sometimes men strayed, that was their nature. She said that Park cared about me, that he loved me, loved me a million times more than the farangs who paid my barfine. The farangs would come and go, farangs would always lie to me, but Park was Thai, Park was my man.

Park didn't come back for two days. When he did he had a red rose and he gave it to me and said he was sorry, that Daeng had led him on, that he didn't know what he was doing and he'd never do it again. He made love to me so tenderly that I started to cry, and he kissed my bandaged wrist and told me that he loved me and that I was never to hurt myself again.

PETE

I bumped into Nigel in Fatso's Bar, nursing a Singha beer. I told him about Joy cutting her wrist and he was really dismissive about it, said that bargirls were always cutting themselves, usually after they'd had too much to drink.

I wanted to tell him that Joy was different but I could see that he was drunk so I didn't bother. She was a bargirl, but she wasn't a bargirl from choice: the life had been forced upon her by circumstances. She was making the best of a bad job, that was the way I looked at it.

The one thing I wasn't sure of was what she thought of me. In many ways she behaved like a girlfriend. She telephoned me pretty much every day, just to chat, to ask what I was doing, how I was getting on with the book. I'd found a copy of the guide to London that I'd written a few years earlier and I'd given it to her. She'd been thrilled and had gone through it, looking at the pictures and asking me questions. My picture was at the front and she'd giggled at it, telling me that I looked much younger in real life. She kept asking when the book on Thailand would be finished and if I'd be writing about her.

Sometimes we'd go out together during the day, usually to one of the Robinsons department stores. She never asked me to buy her anything, but I always did. Usually clothes, or a music tape. Once I got her a CD player. She never pestered me, though, she wasn't like some of the girls I saw with farangs, dragging them by the hand to the jewellery or perfume counters. Sometimes we'd go and eat ice cream together, and a couple of times we went to the movies. But she always had to leave by 5pm because she had to go home and shower and get ready for work. If I didn't want her to go to work, I had to pay her barfine. Always. Joy explained that if her barfine wasn't paid, the mamasan would take the money off her wages. I knew she didn't earn a great living working in the bar, and it didn't seem fair that she should be penalised for going out with me, so I paid. I didn't feel good about having to pay her each time I made love to her, but I knew that she needed money. That was why she was in the bar in the first place. I kept asking her if she loved me or my money, which was a stupid question, right? She'd laugh and she'd say "I love you number one, Pete, but number two I love your money." I really do believe that if I stopped giving her money she'd still see me, but I knew that that wouldn't be fair. It'd be the equivalent of me writing and not getting paid. I mean, I might do it for a friend, but I'd still have to work, I'd still have to find someone to pay me for what I did. So I guess I justified it to myself by thinking that if she was working as a prostitute, it was better that it was me who was giving her money and not a succession of strangers.

The thing is, it didn't feel like prostitution. It didn't really feel like I was paying for sex. Well, I mean I was, but it was never as if she demanded money, or withheld sex if she didn't get it. But I'd always give her money after we left the short-time hotel. Sometimes two thousand baht, sometimes one thousand, but usually fifteen hundred, the amount she'd asked for the first time I'd slept with her. When I gave her less than fifteen hundred baht she never complained, but she always seemed extra pleased when I gave her more.

I'd never paid for sex before I went to Thailand. The thought had never crossed my mind. It's not that I'm against prostitution, because I'm not. I believe it should be legalised everywhere, legalised and regulated. There are plenty of men around, the crippled, the old, the ugly, who probably have a tough time finding a sexual partner, so doesn't it make sense that such people should be able to purchase sexual gratification from medically-examined professionals? And wouldn't it give potential rapists and the likes a safe outlet for their urges? That's what I believed, though I never thought that I'd be the one to be paying for sex.

With Joy, I didn't feel as if I was going with a prostitute, it felt as if I was helping a girlfriend who didn't have as much money as I did. I'd helped out girlfriends in London, paid their dental bills if they were short of cash, picked up the bill in restaurants and so on. I'd lent money to a couple—one had needed money to attend an interview in Glasgow, another never told me why she needed the money but said it was a matter of life and death—and both times I'd handed the cash over not expecting to see it back. Sure, I'd never handed them money after sleeping with them—God, I could only imagine what an English girl would do if I did that—but then they weren't as strapped for cash as Joy.

And Joy never made me feel like I was a customer. She didn't hustle me for drinks, in fact sometimes when I offered she'd refuse. Generally I'd buy her three or four because part of her earnings came from commission, and obviously if she was sitting with me she was giving up the opportunity of earning money elsewhere. She never pestered me to pay her barfine, either, though she was always pleased when I did. I guess on average I barfined her twelve to fifteen times a month. Often we'd just go and eat, or visit another bar so she could see her friends. Sometimes I'd go and have a drink in another bar before going to Zombie, usually if I was with one of the guys from Fatso's: Jimmy, Rick, Nigel, Bruce or Matt. Whenever I did, girls would always come over and wag a finger at me and accuse me of being a butterfly, of being unfaithful to Joy. I'd always laugh and deny it. I knew better than to barfine another girl in Nana Plaza—there was an underground communication system that worked at something approaching the speed of light. Early on in our relationship I'd gone into Spicy-a-go-go and bought drinks for a girl called Mai. She had the longest hair I'd ever seen, longer even than Joy's, and I guess I was thinking about paying her barfine, out of curiosity more than anything, but before I could take it any further, Joy appeared in the bar with her friend, Apple. Joy was wearing a long green cocktail dress that she often wore to work. Apple saw me and said 'sawasdee ka' but Joy didn't seem to notice me. Actually, I was pretty sure she was pretending not to see me. She did a quick circuit of the bar and then left. I paid my bill, said goodbye to Mai and hurried over to Zombie. As soon as I went in Joy came over and hugged me. She'd already changed into her dancing gear. I bought her a drink and asked her what she'd been doing in Spicy-a-go-go.

"I go see my friend," she said and smiled sweetly. She'd known all right, someone from Spicy-a-go-go had called her and told her that I was getting friendly with another girl and she'd moved to protect her interests. I was flattered. If she was jealous, it showed she cared.

I was jealous, too, but I didn't know what to do about it. I liked her, I liked her a lot. It was more than like, it was almost love, but I was holding myself back because of what she did, of what she'd done. She was a hooker, for God's sake, and whenever I felt myself falling in love with her I tried to pull myself back to reality. The guys were always telling me horror stories about farangs who got involved with bargirls. Most of the girls had Thai husbands or boyfriends, they said. Most spent their money on drugs or gambling. And no matter how much you thought you could trust them, they'd rip you off eventually. I'd look at Joy and I'd think no, she was different, but at the back of my mind was always the worry that maybe she was lying to me, that I was only a customer and it was only my money she cared about. Part of me wanted to ask her to give up work, because I hated the thought of her going with other men and I hated the fact that she danced. Early on in the relationship I'd started paying her a thousand baht a month to keep her knickers on while she was dancing. Sunan and Mon still danced naked, and I know Joy was happy that I'd made the gesture. I knew she'd be even happier if I gave her enough money to not have to work at all, but that was going to cost me tens of thousands of baht a month and I was still wary of making that sort of commitment.

I was pretty sure she didn't take drugs. I'd asked her several times and she'd always denied it vehemently, and there were no needle marks on her arms. She said she didn't have a Thai boyfriend. She said she'd had one in Si Saket, but that had ended when she'd moved to Bangkok. I guess I believed her. She was in the bar working for eight hours a night and she didn't finish until half past two in the morning, and she telephoned me most days so I couldn't see how she'd have time for a boyfriend or a husband. Plus she always had my photograph in her wallet and I couldn't see how a Thai boyfriend could put up with that.

One thing that did worry me was that she'd never let me see her room. She said it was in Suphan Kwai, not far from the Chicago karaoke bar, and that it was a slum. Sa-lam is the word in Thai. Almost the same. She said to get to the building where the room was, she had to walk down a narrow alley and that it would be dangerous for me. And she said the room was small and dirty and that she was ashamed of it. "I not have money, Pete," she said. "I not have nice room. I shy, Pete."

I told her time and time again that I didn't care, that I wanted to see where she lived, but she always refused. She said there was no phone in the room, so I couldn't call her there. There was a phone in the building, though, and she used that to call me sometimes, but I couldn't use it to contact her, she said.

I asked her why she didn't find herself a room in a nicer part of town if where she was staying was so bad. She'd shrug and say that she didn't have any money. I could never understand that. I'd been taking Thai lessons at the American University Alumni School and I knew that the teachers there earned less than Joy, but they all seemed to have quite a high standard of living. They earned about twelve thousand baht a month and all were well dressed, lived in decent apartments, and several had cars and mobile telephones.

Joy's salary was about five thousand baht a month. Six thousand including the money I gave her so she didn't have to dance naked. The bar gave her a hundred baht each time I paid her barfine, so that was another thousand baht a month, minimum. She normally got five or six drinks a day, so that was another four thousand baht a month. That meant that from the bar alone she got eleven thousand baht, almost the same as the teachers earned. But I gave Joy another fifteen thousand baht a month. Even if no one else paid her barfine, Joy was earning twenty six thousand baht a month, more than a nurse, several times more than a policewoman, not much less than a doctor. So where did the money go?

Asking her just resulted in shrugs and shakes of the head. She didn't know. Bangkok was expensive. She had to get a taxi to and from work, and each journey cost more than a hundred baht. Six thousand baht a month in taxi fares? That was crazy, I said. Why didn't she get the bus? She said a bus would take too long, and it would be dangerous at night. I asked her why she didn't get a room closer to Nana Plaza and she said that all her friends were in Suphan Kwai, and so were her sisters. She had to pay for a motorcycle, she said. Five thousand baht every month. And she had to send money back to Si Saket to help her family. Discussions about money always seemed to go around in circles, getting nowhere. One thing was for sure—she never had enough, no matter how much I gave her.

JOY

I don't know where my money goes, I really don't. It slips through my fingers like water. I tried explaining to Pete, but he doesn't understand me. How could he? He's a rich farang, he can't know what it's like to be from a poor family, to have nothing. How much did he have to pay for his ticket from England? Twenty thousand baht? Thirty thousand? And it costs him a thousand baht a night to stay at the Dynasty Hotel. That's thirty thousand baht every month. And he spends money in the bars every night. Hundreds of baht. One night he sat down with a pen and paper and asked me to tell him how much I earned and how much I spent, like he was an accountant or something. I was really offended but I didn't say anything, I tried to make a joke of it. He told me that I'd be better off if I lived closer to Zombie, but that would mean I wouldn't be near my friends. I think he wants me to sit in a room all on my own, waiting for him. He's crazy. He kept asking me why I wasn't saving money. Saving what? I have to pay for my room, I have to pay for taxi fares. There's food, make-up, shampoo, clothes. Bangkok's an expensive city.

And Pete doesn't understand my family commitments. I've three younger sisters, all at school. They need money for clothes and for books. My father owns a little land but it's not good land and not much grows there. My father makes charcoal from the trees that grow there but it's hard work and he doesn't make a lot of money. My grandmother's old and she needs medicine and my brothers don't work, they've always been lazy and they won't lift a finger to help my father. If it wasn't for Sunan, Mon or me, my father would have to sell the house or the land.

The other thing Pete doesn't understand is that when you've got money, people are always asking you for it. Friends who can't pay their rent, a few baht for food, a pack of cigarettes, maybe. My friends know that Pete is giving me money and so when they're short they'll ask me to help them out. What's a girl to do? They'd help me if they had money and I didn't, we always do, we help each other. We have to. When I first moved to Bangkok, friends would let me sleep on their floor, they'd share their food, their cigarettes, they lent me clothes and make-up until I could start earning enough to take care of myself. Last week Apple was sick and couldn't work and her landlord put a padlock on her door and wouldn't let her back in until she paid her telephone and electricity bill, almost two thousand baht. She didn't have the money so she asked me. Of course I helped her. She's my friend. But if I told Pete that, he'd get angry. He keeps saying that he wants to help me, not my family and friends. I don't know if or when Apple will pay me back, but that's okay. What goes around comes around. The day might come when she's got a rich boyfriend and I haven't, then I'll be able to ask her for money.

I wish I was more like Sunan. Sunan saves a lot of her money, and she's got a really nice room and a television and a stereo. Next month she's going to buy a Toyota pick-up and Bird is going to be driving us around. Sunan works really hard. She goes short-time every night, and sometimes she goes with farangs several times a night. She doesn't play cards like a lot of the girls, and she doesn't smoke or drink. I smoke a pack of Marlboro a day and sometimes I drink beer. Sunan's older than me, she's twenty-six, and she's been working in Zombie for about two years. She used to send money to me when I was in Si Saket, and she bought our father a motorcycle. I've got a motorcycle, too, it costs me five thousand baht a month. It's up in Si Saket. Pete keeps trying to get me to sell the motorbike, he says I don't need it because I'm working in Bangkok. He doesn't know what my house is like, it's miles from Si Saket and even the nearest village is tiny. What does he expect me to do? Walk?

Sunan has a farang who sends her money every month. His name is Toine, from Denmark. He met her last year and he said he didn't want her to work so every month he sends forty thousand baht to her bank. He gave her a mobile telephone, too, and that cost ten thousand baht. Toine has a wife in Denmark and he only comes to Bangkok twice a year. Sunan's so lucky, I wish I had a farang like that. Toine keeps saying he's going to divorce his wife and marry her, but Sunan doesn't believe him. All farangs lie, she says.

PETE

I got a call from Nigel saying that he wanted to get together for a drink. He had an early meeting at an office in Silom Road so he suggested Patpong. There's a bar he likes in Patpong One called Safari. It's a ground floor bar so the girls aren't allowed to dance naked and they play good music, lots of Sixties stuff. The one snag is that the ceiling is really low over the two dance floors so the go-go dancers are virtually midgets. Nigel was already there when I arrived, sitting with a small bald guy with a bushy grey beard who looked like an elf out of uniform, sharp pointy features and mischievous eyes. He wasn't much taller than the go-go dancers. He was a nice guy and I liked him almost immediately. His name was Bruce and he'd been in Bangkok for eighteen months, running a leather handbag factory for a Thai businessman. He and Nigel had obviously been there for a while because there was a thick wad of blue chits stuffed into the plastic mug in front of them.

We stayed in Safari for an hour or so, then Bruce suggested we go to one of the upstairs bars. Patpong One is a narrow road linking two major

Bangkok thoroughfares, Silom Road and Suriwong Road. I could never work out why it had remained as a red light area. All around it were high rise office buildings and up-market department stores so I would have thought it would have made economic sense to demolish the bars and redevelop the area.

There are bars on either side of the road, filled with stalls selling fake watches, cheap clothes and tacky souvenirs. The bars on the ground floor are mainly go-go bars, each with at least a hundred girls. The first floor bars have dancers too, but they also put on shows. The girls in the upstairs bars danced topless or naked, which strictly speaking is illegal but the bars have lookouts on the ground floor. Whenever the police pass by the lookout hits an alarm button and red lights start flashing in the bar, signalling to the girls that they're to rush off and get dressed.

The shows are what pull the punters up to the first floor bars. They have girls pulling razor blades out of their fannies, bursting balloons with darts fired from blowpipes in their fannies, writing with felt tipped pens stuck into their fannies. They have shower shows, candle shows, where the girls drip hot wax over their bodies, and full sex shows. The first time I went into one of the upstairs bars I was amazed by what I saw, amazed at the sort of things girls would do to their bodies for money. Now I hardly even notice what's happening on the stage. Even the full sex show is a disappointment. According to Nigel, the same guy's been doing it for at least ten years. He's tall and thin and not particularly well-endowed, and he makes love to his wife five times a night at five different bars. He starts at ten o'clock and performs every thirty minutes, usually with the same woman, his wife. I once saw him do the business with a different girl and was told that it was his wife's sister. Apparently his sister-in-law's happy to step in when the guy's wife doesn't feel up to it. A real family business.

Bruce stopped outside a bar I hadn't noticed before. There was a sign saying "Dream Bar" and a flight of stairs leading up to a closed door.

"What do you think?" asked Bruce.

"Never been before," I said.

"Give it a go?"

"Sure." There were two Thai teenagers standing at the bottom of the stairs holding laminated cardboard signs. One of them shoved the sign in front of us. It was a menu of sex shows.

"Have you got the wine list?" asked Bruce, but the teenager didn't get the joke.

"Fucking show," said the teenager.

"Fucking great," said Bruce, in his broad Newcastle accent. "Lead on MacDuff." He twisted around and beckoned to Nigel. "In here, mate!" he yelled.

"Any cover charge?" I asked the teenager.

He shook his head. "Come inside," he said, pointing his sign towards the door.

"How much for a Heineken?" I asked.

The teenager pointed at his sign. A Heineken was eighty baht.

I nodded at Bruce. "Seems okay."

"Pete, you worry too much," he said, slapping me on the back and running up the stairs two at a time. Nigel and I followed him in.

Bruce had ordered two beers and a gin and tonic and was sitting at a table close to the raised dancefloor where two girls were gyrating unenthusiastically to a Thai pop song.

"Quiet, isn't it?" said Nigel. There were only half a dozen other drinkers scattered around the bar.

"It's midweek," said Bruce.

The dancers scurried off the stage and were replaced by two girls who went through the motions of a lesbian act.

"Where's our chit?" I asked. Normally the waitress would put a beaker containing a running total of the bill on the table.

"It's coming," said Bruce. "Relax."

Nigel began bitching about his job. He sold advertising space for a company that produced trade directories and most of his wages were commission. He hated the work and I got the impression that the only reason he stuck it was because he couldn't get anything else.

The lesbian act finished and a middle-aged girl with horrific cellulite climbed onto the stage. She began to pull a string of plastic flowers from between her legs.

"I'm getting a bad feeling about this, lads," I said.

Two heavy-set Thai men were standing by the door. They kept looking over at us.

"What do you mean?" said Nigel.

"It doesn't feel right," I said. "There are hardly any girls. And too many Thai guys. And where the hell's our bill?"

"What are you getting at?" said Bruce.

"I don't know. But let's go somewhere else."

"You just want to go to Nana," said Nigel. "You're missing Joy."

I gestured at a waitress. She ignored me.

One of the men at the door came over. He had a tattoo of a leaping tiger on one of his forearms. "Yes?" he said.

"The bill," I said.

He pointed at the far end of the bar. "Over there," he said. He went back to stand by the door.

"We're in trouble, guys," I said.

Nigel and Bruce exchanged looks. "What, come out without your wallet, did you?" said Bruce. "Anyway, it's my round."

He and Nigel started giggling like a couple of schoolboys. They were drunk. They really didn't seem to appreciate the spot we were in. I went to the end of the bar. I didn't see a cash register or anything, but then I noticed that there was a corridor leading off to the right, out of sight of where we'd been sitting. At the end of the corridor was a group of five Thai men standing around a cash register. I walked towards them. They were big men for Thais, and most of them had tattoos or scars. My heart was racing. This was like no other go-go bar I'd ever been in.

I asked them for the bill and I was given a slip of paper. Two beers, one hundred and sixty baht. One gin and tonic, ninety baht. Three shows, three people, one thousand eight hundred baht. Total, two thousand and fifty baht. About fifty quid, and we'd only been in the bar for ten minutes. I turned to go back to the bar but a hand gripped my shoulder.

"Where you go?" asked the biggest of the men.

I smiled. You always have to smile in Thailand, no matter how angry or scared you are. "I'm going to speak to my friends," I said.

The five heavies followed me back to the table. I showed the bill to Bruce and Nigel. "Bloody hell, we're not paying that," said Bruce, getting to his feet.

The heavies moved apart.

"Two thousand baht!" said Nigel. "They're trying to rip us off!"

"Gosh, really?" I said. "Get a grip, Nigel."

Bruce began speaking to the men. I was surprised at how good his Thai was. The men shook their heads then one of them went off to fetch another man who I guessed was the manager.

Bruce spoke to him for several minutes, occasionally nodding at Nigel and me. Eventually he handed over three hundred baht and we were ushered out of the door.

"What happened?" I asked as we made our way down the stairs.

"I told him that we weren't tourists, that we worked in Bangkok. He wanted to know what we did, how long we'd been here. Chit chat."

"And he let us off the bill?"

"He knew I knew the score," said Bruce. "If push had come to shove I'd have just paid and then come back with the Tourist Police. They're not here to rip off locals, they just want to screw tourists who don't know any better. All I had to do was smile and tell him it wasn't fair. Eventually he asked me how much I'd pay in a normal bar and I said three hundred baht, max. He said he'd be happy with that."

"Speaking to him in Thai probably helped," I said.

"Let me tell you about Thais, Pete," said Bruce, patting me on the back. "Sometimes you think you're in trouble when you're really not. And sometimes when you think everything is hunky dory, you're in so much shit they'll need a submarine to find you. Nothing is as it seems, grasshopper."

BRUCE

I meant what I said about Thais. They're easy to rub up the wrong way, but if you handle them right, they're genuinely nice people. Take taxi drivers, for instance. The first time I came to Bangkok, I was always getting into arguments with them. They'd either get lost or not want to take me or they'd refuse to use the meter. Now I can speak a little Thai and I understand them a bit more. For one thing, Bangkok's huge, with twice as many people as London, and for another, the road naming and numbering system is crazy. Roads meander all over the place and at times the numbering of houses seems almost random. It's not like England where the houses on one side are consecutive odd numbers with the even numbers on the other side. In Bangkok the numbers relate to the plot of land, so unless you know exactly where you're going, it's dead easy to get lost. And maps aren't part of Thai culture, either. Most people haven't a clue how to relate a map to their surroundings. You never see Thais using them. Now I almost never get into confrontations with taxi drivers because I know how to handle them.

Take last week for example. My car was in for a service so I was using taxis to get around. I was on the outskirts of the city and it was close to rush hour and the first four cabs I stopped just didn't want to go to Sukhumvit. I knew why: at rush hour it can lock up solid. Anyway, I got into the fifth taxi that stopped and told him in English where I wanted to go. Then I sat looking out of the window, ignoring his protests. Okay, so eventually he starts driving. Half an hour later, the car judders to a halt. He starts up again, we drive a few hundred feet, and we shudder and stop again. "Car no good," he says.

I lean forward and watch as he starts the car again. The engine stalls. Why? Because the bugger's slipping his foot off the clutch, that's why. I don't say anything, because Thais hate criticism. Loss of face and all that. He gets out of the car, muttering to himself, and lifts up the bonnet. Stands looking at the engine and shaking his head. I tell you, this guy was the Robert De Niro of taxi drivers. Oscar material. He fumbles with the battery leads, mutters again, then slams the bonnet shut. He opens the passenger door for me. "Car no good," he says, sincerity dripping from every pore. "I get new taxi for you. Sorry."

So I get out of the taxi and he walks to the back and starts trying to flag down another cab. Now, I know full well what's going on here. He plans to get a taxi to stop, then he'll tell the driver to keep me talking while he drives off. Then taxi driver number two will refuse to take me, and he'll drive off as well, leaving me stranded. I know this is what he intends to do, but I don't argue with him because I know that's not going to get me anywhere. I just smile and nod, and then when he's not looking I climb into the driver's seat. The silly sod had left the keys in the ignition. I start up the car, put it in gear and drive off.

This is where I played it just right. If I'd made off with the car he'd have got together with some other taxi drivers, beaten the shit out of me and then handed me over to the cops. So I drive off real slowly, just above walking pace, watching him in the mirror. He sees what I'm doing and comes haring after me, waving his arms and shouting. I let him run for a hundred yards or so, then I pull up and wind down the window. I smile. A big, big smile, Thai style. I give him a thumbs up. "Car okay," I say. "I car doctor. I fix."

He looks at me. He smiles. He knows that I know. I know that he knows that I know. But I don't confront him with it, I don't rub his face in it. "Car okay?" he says.

"Oh yes. No problem now. I fix."

I get out of the driver's seat, and move into the back. He gets into the driver's seat, puts the car in gear and drives off. He smiles. "Okay now," he says, nodding approvingly.

We drive all the way in without any more hassles. Now, the guy was right, of course: we hit traffic and it took us more than hour to cover three miles. And when he did finally drop me off, I gave him a huge tip. He smiled. I smiled. Face was saved on both sides. A situation that could have turned really nasty became an object lesson in how to get what you want in the Land of Smiles.

Anyway, I liked Pete. He was a pleasant change from the expatriates you normally run into in Bangkok. Face it, most of the guys who choose to come to Thailand are thinking with their dicks, not their heads. It's different if they're sent here, then they come on a full expat package: accommodation, flights home, all the perks. But anyone who chooses to live here has to work on local terms, and that means shit money. Guys like Nigel. He pretends he's a wheeler-dealer, he's always on the verge of setting up his own company that's going to make him a fortune, but when all's said and done he's just here to get laid. I doubt he has much luck with women back in the UK because of his missing eye, but out here he can get laid every night of the week for the price of a decent bottle of Scotch. Pete was sent out by his company and that makes all the difference. You can see from the way he behaves in the bars, he barely notices the girls, he's more interested in what I have to say. Nigel can't sit down without shoving his hand down some bird's bikini and he spends more time fondling them than he does drinking.

I'm the same as Pete. I was running a handbag factory in Newcastle, and we'd started subcontracting some of our manufacturing to a couple of suppliers in Thailand. One of the Thai guys came over to see us and we got on like a house on fire. Saravoot his name was. Before he went back, he offered me a job running one of his factories outside Bangkok. I was divorced and the kids were grown up, so I thought what the hell.

I'm still not sure how things are going to work out here. Saravoot's a nice enough guy, but sometimes he's a bit strange. I'm not quite sure how to explain it, but I can give you an example. His factory was way overstaffed. There's a feeling out here that the more people you have working for you, the more important you are. Staff equals status. So Saravoot would take great pride in the fact that he had almost five hundred people working for him, even though the same amount of work could have been done by half that number if they worked efficiently. Now, one of the reasons that Saravoot brought me over to Bangkok was that he'd seen how we operated in Newcastle, and one of the first things I did was to draw up a proposal to restructure the sewing side that would pretty much double productivity. We had to let thirty people go, all of them women, and it was like pulling teeth. I had to keep pressing Saravoot for months until he agreed to put my proposal into action.

So then he goes to see a fortune teller, and the fortune teller tells him that I was good for the company, but that I shouldn't be involved in the day-to-day running of it. The fortune teller used my date and place of birth in his calculations, but it sounded like hocus pocus to me. Anyway, it effectively meant that I was on sabbatical for six months, and when I went back we had even more staff than before. And things he promised just didn't materialise. He said I'd get a BMW, but the delivery date kept changing and I had to make do with an old Toyota. Then a Beamer arrived, but Saravoot said it was for his wife and that he'd ordered me a

Range Rover. I'm still waiting.

And he told me I'd be getting business class flights home. But whenever I get tickets, they're always economy. There's always an excuse: they booked too late, the travel agent made a mistake, but that's bollocks. There's no point in confronting him because that doesn't work with Thais, they pretend not to understand or they just walk away. So I just grin and bear it.

The business in Dream Bar was typical Thailand. It was a rip-off joint, but by adopting the right attitude, by not showing aggression, everything was sorted. If we'd shouted or sworn at them, they'd have got violent, guaranteed. And you can't win a fight against Thais because they never fight one on one, they're always mob-handed. For a start there were half a dozen of them in the bar, but even if we'd got past them, there'd have been another ten outside, probably tooled up. There's no shame in Thai culture about ganging up on someone, no Queensbury Rules or anything like that. But fighting is always a last resort. Handle yourself properly, show the requisite amount of respect, pay a little money, smile a lot, and you can talk your way out of any situation.

Anyway, we walked out of Patpong and caught a taxi in Silom Road. The guy wanted two hundred baht at first but I spoke to him in Thai and he agreed to use the meter.

Pete wanted to go to Zombie in Nana Plaza—he'd mentioned it two or three times while we were in Safari. I'm not a big fan of Zombie, I prefer Spicy-a-go-go on the opposite side of the plaza. As soon as we walked into the bar, Joy came running over to Pete and practically threw herself at him, hugging him around the neck and kissing his cheek. She was a pretty thing, long hair, quite curvy, terrific breasts. She sat next to Pete and he introduced her to me. She shook my hand. That always makes me smile. There they are, sitting there topless but holding their hands out like we were at a business meeting. Come to think of it, I suppose it was a business meeting at that. Pete had to buy her drinks and she wanted him to pay her barfine, so it was all about money.

It's practically impossible to know if the girls in the bars really like us or not. They are working, after all. But I think there's a difference between the way they treat us long-term residents and the way they act with tourists. They know we're going to come in week after week, so I guess they know they can't get away with stinging us. But did Joy love Pete? Tough call. She was very attentive, hanging on his every word, pouring his tonic into his gin, rubbing his leg, leaning her head against his shoulder, but those are standard bargirl tricks. I'm sure she'd act exactly the same way with any other customer. Pete was definitely infatuated with her, though. He couldn't take his eyes off her. And we'd only been there a few minutes before he asked her to go off and put on a bikini top. That was funny, because when we went in she was stark bollock naked, except for a pair of black ankle boots. Must be love, huh?

Joy's two sisters came over to join us. Sunan and Mon. Sunan was a hard-faced girl in her late twenties, tall with a tight body but cold eyes. She sat next to Nigel and almost immediately asked him to buy her a drink. I hate it when they do that. I don't mind offering, but I don't want to be pushed into it, you know?

Mon was different. Actually, she looked a bit like Joy. She was older, she said she was twenty seven but I think she's probably about thirty. You could tell from the stretch marks on her stomach that she'd had at least one kid, but she had a beautiful face and a great figure. She was cuddly, you know. A bit like my ex-wife. She didn't hit me for a drink but I bought her four colas and we had quite a decent conversation. Her husband had cleared off not long after her daughter had been born, she said, and she'd had no choice but to work in the bars. She was saving like mad and as soon as she had enough money she was going to go back to Si Saket. I felt sorry for her and when I left I gave her a thousand baht. Pete stayed on. He'd paid Joy's barfine and she'd gone off to change. I went along to Fatso's Bar for a nightcap.

BIG RON

I get to see all sorts in Fatso's Bar. The works. That's one of the reasons I enjoy running the bar: all human life is here, and a fair sprinkling of sub-human specimens, too.

There's the tourists: they come here for a couple of weeks, screw themselves stupid and then head back to England or Denmark or Germany or wherever they're from and dream about the wonderful time they had. Most of them reckon it's a sexual paradise, they can't believe what's on offer here. They sit at the bar with stupid grins on their faces, get tanked up and then head on down to the Plaza. The ones I feel sorry for are the ones who fall in love. They meet a girl the first night and they think it's the real thing. They spend every night with the same one, and by the middle of the holiday they're hooked. They fall for whatever line the girl gives them—the sick mother, the younger sister's school uniform, the bank foreclosing on the family farm, the dead water buffalo, there's a million sob stories and I've heard them all. Sometimes they bring the girls here, like they're on a date or something. They sit at the bar, all lovey dovey, holding hands and making eyes at each other. God, it's enough to make me puke. I've given up saying anything. They don't want to be told, they want to believe that they're a knight in shining armour and that the girl doesn't want to work in the bar, that she's only doing it to help out her family. Bollocks. They're hookers and they know exactly what they're doing. I see the same girls in here week after week with different farangs.

The mainstay of Fatso's Bar are the regulars, though. We serve good, solid English food in the restaurant upstairs or at the bar. Fish and chips. Roast chicken dinners. Gammon steak and chips. None of the Thai crap. Food you can get your teeth into. Our breakfasts are a big puller, too. We've plenty of regulars pop in for a feed before heading off to the office.

I don't encourage tourists, to be honest. It's all about repeat business so I want guys who live in Bangkok, guys who'll come in four nights a week or more. The guys who have been here, done that and got the fucking T-shirt. Guys like Jimmy. Been here for more than fifteen years now, runs a chain of furniture shops by fax. You won't catch the likes of Jimmy falling in love with a Thai girl. Same with Rick. Been here almost ten years. Sells condom-making machines, does a roaring trade. Doesn't believe in them himself, none of us do. I've fucked more than two thousand women and a fair amount of katoeys too, and never got anything more serious than NSU. Well, there was the genital warts, a bugger to shift they were, but I don't really count them.

Rick's the same as Jimmy and me: we go to the bars, choose a girl, and screw them. No attachments, no relationships, they're slappers, pure and simple. That's the only way to treat them.

In fact, the longer a guy stays here, the more he's likely to go with katoeys, because you know where you are with a katoey. A katoey's a transsexual. But don't get me wrong, it's not like going with a guy in a dress. They're fucking lovely here. Drop dead gorgeous some of them. They take hormones to grow breasts, or have implants, and then they have their dicks cut off. Sex with them is something else, I can tell you. For a start, they give the best blow jobs. That's a fact. You've never had a blow job until you've had a katoey go down on you. You see, a guy knows what a guy likes. You don't have to fuck them, though Jimmy and Rick do it all the time, whether or not the geezer's got a dick. I don't screw them much, what with me being thirty stone and all, but I always fuck one up the arse on World Aids Day. Point of principle.

The ones who get into real trouble are the ones who fall between the tourists and the guys like Jimmy and Rick. They've been here for a few months, maybe longer, and they think they know it all. They think they understand Thais, they probably learn to speak a bit of the language, and they let their defences down. That's when they get fucked. There was a Jap guy we knew, came over to work for Toyota. Fell in love with a Thai girl, bought her a house and some land up near Chiang Mai. Gave money to her family, even bought them a pick-up truck and a couple of motorcycles. The girl must have been the screw of the century because the Jap decides he's gonna marry her. He goes up to Chiang Mai, and there's a huge wedding party. Food, booze, the works. The whole family gets legless, a great time is had by all. In the middle of the festivities, a Thai guy goes up to the Jap. "You can go now," says the Thai.

"What do you mean?" says the Jap. "This is my wedding."

"No," says the Thai. "This is my house. On my land. And that's my wife. Now you can fuck off."

And that was that. The Jap came running back to Bangkok with his tail between his legs. Went back to Japan a few months later, a

56

broken man. He'd been ripped off from Day One. I've heard a million stories like that. And they're all true.

PETE

Every night at eleven o'clock, all the girls in Zombie, those who hadn't had their barfines paid, had to go up on one of the two stages and dance for about ten minutes. It was a hell of a sight, more than a hundred girls, most of them naked, dancing so close together that they were almost touching. It was a way of showing the customers what was available, I guess. I used to hate it. It was like a cattle market. Joy always used to stand next to her sisters and if I was there she'd grin and wave, but I never felt comfortable watching her. And if I didn't go to the bar, I always had a sick feeling in the pit of my stomach at eleven, knowing that she was up on the stage and that guys were ogling her.

After the mass dancing, there were a few shows. Nothing to compare with what went on in the upstairs bars in Patpong—a lesbian show and a show where one of the girls would paint another with luminous paint.

One night, as Joy sat next to me watching the lesbian show, she put a hand on my thigh. "What you think, Pete?" she asked, nodding at the stage. Two girls, both friends of Joy, were writhing on a blanket. On the other stage, two girls were doing a similar show, trying in vain to synchronise their movements with a slow Thai love song.

"It's okay," I said, not sure what she meant.

"Mamasan want me do," said Joy.

"The lesbian show? Why?"

Joy beamed. "She say I very pretty. Farangs want to see girl with long hair do lesbian show. She want me do with Wan."

"What does Wan think?" I asked.

"She need money. She want to do."

"How much do they pay if you do the show?"

"Ten thousand baht."

I was surprised. That was a lot of money, more than a good secretary would earn in a month working for a multinational company in Bangkok. "How many shows?" I asked.

"Lesbian show every night. Then go upstairs to G-Spot for shower show. What you think, Pete? If you not want me do, I not do."

She looked at me earnestly, waiting to see what I'd say. I felt flattered because it was clear she was serious. It really was up to me. I watched the two girls on the stage. One was lying on her back while the other licked her breasts and fondled her between the legs. "You can do that?" I asked Joy.

She nodded. "Easy," she said.

Two fat Germans were leaning forward, leering at the girls. I didn't like the idea of Joy performing, but it was just a performance. Acting. And I figured that the more money she earned from 'legitimate' work, the less incentive there'd be for her to let someone pay her barfine.

"What you think?" she asked.

"I'm not sure," I said. I explained my reservations about farangs watching her with another girl.

"Same dancing," she said.

I wasn't sure if it was. When she was dancing she was always with other girls, often more than a dozen. Doing the lesbian show put her centre stage.

"Do you want to do it?" I asked.

"Up to you," she said.

The girls on the stage changed position, one squatted over the other, balancing herself by holding one of the silver poles, and began to moan with simulated pleasure as the other used her tongue. The Germans leered and leaned forward for an even closer view.

"You wouldn't be shy?" I asked.

She shrugged. "It not real," she said. "Same movie star." She was right. It was acting, a show for the tourists.

"Okay," I said. "Why not try it? See if you like it."

Joy nodded. "Okay, Pete. I do for you."

Two days later it was Joy's first appearance as a 'special artist'. Her new role also meant that her barfine had increased—before midnight it now cost a thousand baht to buy her out because if she wasn't there someone else would have to be found to take her place. After midnight, her barfine dropped to seven hundred baht.

The lights dimmed and Joy and Wan skipped up onto the stage. Wan was a cute nineteen-year-old with shoulder length hair and an upturned nose that had cost her twenty thousand baht from one of Bangkok's top plastic surgeons. She was one of Joy's closest friends and they often arrived at Zombie together.

Wan spread a tartan blanket over the dancefloor, then the two girls took off their leopard-print sarongs and bikinis to hoots and cheers from the farangs. The slow music started and Joy and Wan went into an unconvincing clinch. Joy reached up and held on to two of the silver poles, while Wan began to plant small kisses over Joy's breasts. Joy looked across at me and began to giggle. In fact she giggled throughout the show. Wan did, too. They knew all the moves, but it was clear that they weren't taking it seriously. At one point the mamasan, a fifty-something old bat with a hairy mole on her left cheek, shouted something to the girls and they began to fake orgasms, but after a few minutes they both collapsed into giggles again.

When the show was over, Wan gathered up the blanket and Joy pulled on her bikini and shawl and scampered over to where I was sitting. "What you think?" she asked.

"You kept laughing," I said.

"Jug ga jee," she said. Ticklish. "You can come to G-Spot with me?" she asked. "I have to do shower show and I shy go alone."

G-Spot was one of the upstairs bars. Along one wall was a glass panel behind which were a number of shower heads. I'd been up a few times to see the shower shows, but basically all you're looking at is a line of girls getting wet. It wasn't much of a turn on, though tourists and first-timers seem to get a kick out of it.

I paid my bill and Joy took my hand and led me out of Zombie. Several heads turned to watch us go. Joy was one of the sexiest girls in Nana Plaza and in her green bikini top and with her leopard-print sarong tied around her waist, she was drop-dead gorgeous. I was proud to be seen with her, and even prouder that she wanted me to go with her.

Joy stood by me while she waited to be called for the show. I bought her a cola and she sipped it through a straw. G-Spot wasn't an especially popular bar: most men preferred to stick to the ground floor. I don't know if it was because they couldn't be bothered with the stairs but for most visitors to Nana Plaza, the upper floors were undiscovered country. As a result, the prettiest girls tended to work on the ground floor where the bars were busier. I could tell from the way Joy was preening herself that she thought she was a cut above the girls who worked in G-Spot. Maybe that was why she'd brought me with her, to show to the girls that she had a farang boyfriend, another sign of her status.

Several guys tried to make eye contact with Joy but she pointedly ignored them. She leaned against me, then turned and kissed me on the cheek. "Sorry," she laughed, wiping away the lipstick with her thumb.

Half a dozen girls made their way to a curtained door. Joy patted me on the thigh. "Okay, I go now," she said. She tottered across the bar on her impossibly high heels. She turned and waved before disappearing through the curtain.

A few minutes later the main lights dimmed and spotlights came on, illuminating the showers. Water began to spurt out of the shower heads, then one by one the girls came out in single file. There was laughter all around me. Guys were pointing and shaking their heads and the bargirls were jumping up and down and shrieking. Joy was wearing a shower cap. The girls took bars of soap and began lathering themselves. Joy followed their example, but did her best to keep her head out of the water.

The farang manager of the bar went over to the shower screens and rapped on the glass. He pointed at Joy and mimed for her to take off her cap. She smiled and did as she was told to a round of applause.

After the girls were all covered with soapy suds, they paired off and simulated lesbian sex. Joy was with Wan again. This time, though, Wan leaned against the wall while Joy kissed her all over. At one point she got soap in her mouth and she stopped what she was doing to rinse her mouth out. She grinned at me and gave me a small wave. Ten minutes later, it was all over. Joy came back through the curtain, towelling her hair dry. "What you think?" she asked.

"I think you were great," I said. "The prettiest girl there."

She smiled. "You sure?"

"I'm sure," I said.

We went back down the stairs to Zombie. "My hair take long time to dry," she said.

"I know. That's why you wore the cap."

"No, that was for fun," she said. "I know the manager go crazy. Funny, huh?"

I hugged her. She was funny. Cute, too. She sat by me in Zombie until it was time to dance again and made such a fuss of having to dry her hair that I paid her barfine so that she didn't have to work.

She only stuck at being a showgirl for ten days. Joy hated getting her hair wet and didn't like having to redo her make-up. She decided that the extra money wasn't worth the trouble. I didn't argue. I hated seeing the way men grabbed at her when she came off stage. The lesbian show was a turn on, more so than straight-forward dancing, and guys were always offering to pay her barfine, and wanting to take Wan along, too. Every man's fantasy, I guess, two beautiful girls at the same time.

One night, about a week after she'd started doing the shows, I'd popped into Zombie late at night, just before closing time. I'd been over at Fatso's Bar with Bruce and the lads and decided to say hello to Joy before going back to the hotel. She was there all right, sitting with Wan at the bar, wearing a black wraparound skirt and a T-shirt. She saw the look of surprise on my face. "Farang pay bar for me and Wan," she said hurriedly. She'd been drinking beer, from the bottle, and was grinning lopsidedly. She pushed the bottle away as if it wasn't hers.

The news hit me like a sucker punch. She'd always insisted that no one else could pay her barfine, that she was my private dancer. "Why, Joy?"

"No, Pete, you not understand. Farang have birthday, he want see me and Wan do lesbian show. He pay two thousand baht to me and two thousand baht to Wan, just for show."

"Where?" I asked. This didn't sound right.

"We go Penthouse Hotel."

The Penthouse was one of the short-time hotels I went to with Joy. Mirrors on the walls and ceilings, blue movies on the television, condoms by the bed. "Come on, Joy. Why go to a short-time hotel? If he wanted to see the show, he could see it here."

Joy waved Wan over and spoke to her in Khmer. That was something I'd noticed before. Joy could speak reasonable English, certainly enough to make herself understood, and my Thai was good enough to talk to her. She and Wan usually spoke to each other in Thai, but whenever there was something she didn't want me to know, Joy would use Khmer. It had a totally different vocabulary to Thai but with many similar sounds, so there was no hope of me eavesdropping.

When Joy finished speaking, Wan smiled at me. "Farang have birthday today. He say he want private show, he want see me and Joy do lesbian show for him. He just watch and drink beer."

She looked across at Joy for approval and Joy nodded.

Joy raised her eyebrows at me as if she'd proved her point.

"Joy, you said no one could pay your barfine. How do you think I feel?"

"I don't know," she said, lowering her eyes.

She looked so sad I wanted to put my arms around her and hold her. I guess she was only trying to earn a little extra money, and if a guy wanted to pay her to see what he could watch for free in Zombie, I suppose she'd be a fool not to take advantage of him.

"You angry at me?" she asked.

"No, I'm not angry at you," I said. I wasn't, either. But I was still glad when she decided to quit doing the shows.

JOY

Some of the girls in Zombie won't work with another girl. They're too shy, they say they don't want someone else to see them having sex. Think of the money, that's what I tell them. You're having sex with one guy, right, so if there's two girls, it's half the work. Half the time, too. Most farangs come really quickly with two girls, they can't control themselves, especially if you know what to do. Sunan showed me, once. A French guy paid barfine for Sunan and me a few days after I started work in

Zombie—he was turned on by the idea of making love to sisters. He paid barfine and gave Sunan and me two thousand baht each. We went to Uncle Rey's Guest House, just around the corner. Fifteen minutes later, we were back dancing in the bar. With the farang's money.

Sunan made me get on top and then she kissed him while I had sex with him. He wanted to pull out and have sex with Sunan, but before he could, Sunan began to moan and groan. "You fuck my young sister," she said, then she reached behind me and started playing with him. He came like a rocket. Easy money. He started saying he wanted to do it again, but Sunan said he'd only paid to come once and we left.

Once I started doing the lesbian show, farangs were always asking to barfine me and Wan together. Wan was up for it because she needs the money: her boyfriend has a major heroin habit and she's just bought a pick-up truck for her father. I knew I was taking a risk, because if Pete found out, he'd hit the roof. If Pete had already been then I was reasonably sure I'd be okay, but if he hadn't popped in I had to brief the girls to say that I'd just gone out to get something to eat. I only got caught once and that was Wan's fault. She'd talked me into having a couple of beers before we did the show, then a farang bought me and Wan another beer each before asking if he could pay our barfines. Now, I knew it wasn't a good idea because I had a feeling that Pete was going to pop in, but I was feeling a bit tipsy and he was offering more money than usual. Three thousand baht each. The lesbian show had really turned him on. Anyway, Wan talked me into it, but I said we'd have to be quick. It got me out of doing the shower show, and he had to pay the extra barfine because they had to find two more girls to go upstairs to G-Spot. We changed and went to the Penthouse Hotel. I wanted to go somewhere closer, but the farang insisted on the Penthouse because the rooms have mirrors everywhere.

The farang was a bit drunk and it took almost an hour before we could get him to come. Wan and I did the full lesbian show, then he got on the bed with us. I tried to make him come quickly but he'd obviously done it with two girls before and he knew how to control himself. He'd ordered more beer from the boy who let us into the room, and by the time we'd finished I was really drunk. And sore.

When we got back to Zombie I had another beer and that's when Pete came in. He wasn't happy but I think I managed to convince him that nothing had happened. Sometimes farangs can be so stupid.

BRUCE

He's a character, Big Ron. For a start, he tips the scales at something like twenty-four stone. If he's in a bad mood he sits on his specially reinforced bar stool like Jabba the Hutt, the slug-like thing in *Star Wars*, glowering at everyone. Mind you, he has to put up with a lot. He's in the bar for something like fifteen hours a day, has to be because he knows that the staff would rip him off given half the chance. He was an accountant for a big bank in South Africa for years but left when Mandela took over. Made a fortune, mind, doesn't have to work again. In fact, I think he came to Thailand for a holiday, then stayed on, then decided to invest in a bar. Doesn't have much of a life outside Fatso's, it has to be said. When the bar closes he walks down to Nana Plaza, barfines a girl and takes her back to his hotel. Never lets the girl stay the night, he kicks them out once they've done the business. Not much romance in Big Ron's life.

He runs a great bar, that much I'll say. It's quite small with a horseshoe shaped bar in the middle. On the two longer sides there's just enough room for a line of bar stools, but there's more space where the door is. Big Ron sits there with his back to the door, facing the bar. All around the walls are hundreds of photographs of the regulars. He keeps a couple of cameras behind the bar and the girls are under strict instructions to photograph anyone doing anything stupid. There are pictures of guys being sick, guys unconscious, guys baring their chests or worse, guys with girls, guys with guys.

I'm in half a dozen photographs. Most of them were taken during Thai New Year when everyone goes crazy. The Thais reckon it's good luck to sprinkle each other with water—good news because it takes place in April which is just about the hottest time of the year. We've raised it to a whole new level, though. We get tooled up with state of the art water pistols and it's like open warfare. We drench people. Soak 'em. I led a few raids into the Siegfried Bar, down the road from Fatso's. Went in with a bucket of water and played havoc with the Germans. Just like the SAS, that's me. Short and stupid. No sense of humour, the Germans. You'd think we wanted to start World War Three the way they went on. The owner came out and tried to read the riot act, but we soaked him. Then a couple of German tourists came out to complain and we got them, too. Bloody funny.

Big Ron really got into the spirit of the festival. He had a big drum of water outside the bar and we dumped people in it as they arrived. He covered anything important with sheets of polythene and let the girls wear swimsuits. Bloody brilliant.

The Fatso's girls are something else. For a start, they all speak good English, which is unusual in Thailand. They're all lookers, too. I mean, they're not bar girls or anything, you'd get a slap across the face if you tried to pay their barfine, but Big Ron has them in short black skirts and tight-fitting red jackets. Bloody gorgeous. They remember your name and what you drink, and they make a bit of a fuss of the regulars. I always make sure I give them a big tip. The last of the big spenders, me. It pays off, though. There's a tradition in Fatso's called Big Glassing. If you have four untouched drinks in front of you, they're poured into one of those long glasses they use for a yard of ale, then topped up until it's full. Then you have to drink the whole lot in one or lose face. It's a bugger if you're drinking vodka and Coke, I can tell you.

There's an old ship's bell hanging close to where Big Ron sits, and if you ring it once you buy everyone in the bar a drink. Two rings and you include the staff, three and you include anyone upstairs, too. It can get really competitive some nights as we all try to get each other Big Glassed. But whenever a Big Glass gets put in front of me, I know the girls'll have done their stuff. It's almost pure Coca Cola, no alcohol, so I can drink it without any effects. Well, I burp like crazy for an hour or so, but I don't fall down dead drunk like the rest of the guys. That's the way it works in Thailand. So long as you keep shelling out the bucks, everything goes your way. It's a great country.

PETE

I think the turning point in my relationship with Joy came after I'd known her for about six months and we went to Isarn for four days. It all happened by chance, actually. I was in Fatso's Bar and I got talking to a German guy called Bruno. He was in his sixties, bald as a coot with a beer-drinker's paunch and he seemed to know a hell of a lot about Thailand. He was a visiting professor at a German university and his field of expertise was tourism and hill tribes. He'd been coming to Thailand for more than twenty years and had a Thai wife, Pam. She wasn't with him in Fatso's; he said she'd let him off the leash for the night and nudged me in the ribs, hard. "She's Thai, she understands men," he said.

He was writing a book on Thai arts and crafts and was planning to drive around Isarn visiting factories and workshops and attending a craft festival near Si Saket, where Joy was from. Bruno offered to take me along with him. I was keen to go because I would soon be working on the section of the book devoted to the north east of Thailand, and I could cover a lot more ground if I was with Bruno. Plus, he clearly knew a lot about the area and would be able to answer many of the questions I had.

Later, when I was in Zombie, I told Joy that I was going to Isarn and she started bouncing up and down on her seat. "Bai duey," she kept saying. "Go with." She told me that the places I was going to were dangerous, and that I'd be safer if she went with me. I explained that my friend Bruno's wife was also from Isarn and that she'd be able to look after us. Joy changed tack then, saying that she wanted to see her father. I relented and said okay. I figured it would be a good way of deciding exactly what my feelings for her were. I'd seen a lot of Joy, but virtually all our time together was spent in Zombie, the outside bars in Nana Plaza, restaurants nearby or short-time hotels. In fact, I'd rarely seen her in daylight; the entire relationship was skewed to the night. It was totally unnatural, so I was keen to see how we'd get on if we were together twenty four hours a day.

On the day of the trip we arranged to meet Bruno and Pam outside a big shopping mall close to the airport. Joy turned up with a change of clothes in a plastic carrier bag. I'd asked her not to wear so much jewellery or make up and she looked pretty. She looked young, too. Joy was twenty and I was thirty-six, but in the bar I never noticed the age difference. Standing outside the shopping mall I felt suddenly old and it seemed that all the Thais walking by were turning their heads to look at us.

When Bruno arrived in his Landrover, I realised why he'd been so keen for me to go with him. Pam was driving but she'd sprained her wrist and had trouble changing gear. Bruno didn't have a driver's licence, but I did. For the next four days I did most of the driving. Bruno sat next to me and talked hour after hour as if he were addressing a lecture hall. Actually, that makes it sound worse than it was because he did have an incredible knowledge of the country and its people; it's just that he spoke in a hoarse whisper and often his English was twisted into German grammar which made it hard to follow what he was saying.

We drove across to Khorat and then up to Udon Thani, about eighty kilometres from the border with Laos, then cut across to Nakon Phanom to visit a ceramic factory he'd heard about, then down to Ubon Ratchathani, close to Cambodia. On the way we stopped off at several temples that hadn't been included in the earlier editions of my company's guide book, and Bruno took me to restaurants that were well off the normal tourist trail.

As I drove and Bruno talked, Joy and Pam sat behind us, gossiping away in their own language. It seems that Pam's village was in the same part of Isarn as Joy's and they got on like a house on fire. Pam was in her forties, darker skinned than Joy and plumper. Each night the four of us would eat together, then Joy and I would go walking around whichever town we were in. She seemed happy to be away from Bangkok and the pressures of the bars. She told me about the food that was sold at the roadside stalls, told me stories about her childhood and tried to teach me words of Khmer. Thai was her first language, but she spoke Lao and Khmer almost as well. With English she spoke four languages, and I couldn't help thinking how different her life would have been if she'd been born to a rich family in Bangkok instead of poor farmers in Isarn. She had a natural intelligence and a quick sense of humour, and a sensitivity to my moods that I'd never experienced in a girlfriend before. When I wanted to be quiet, she'd be quiet, too, but she seemed to sense when I was bored and would start to entertain me, teasing and joking until I couldn't help but laugh at her. She was deferential to Bruno, pouring his beer for him at mealtimes, offering him water while we were driving, also referring to him as Pee-Bruno, a sign of respect.

At night she slept in my arms, kissing me on the neck whenever she woke up and whispering "chan rak khun." I love you. "Chan rak khun ja dai." I love you to death.

On the way back from Ubon Ratchathani to Bangkok we detoured to Joy's village, to the south of Si Saket. She got more and more excited as we got closer, pointing out landmarks to me and telling me the names of the villages we passed.

The roads got progressively worse until we were bucking along a road that was barely wide enough for two vehicles to pass. The fields on either side of the road had few animals and what crops there were seemed ill-tended and spindly. I asked Bruno why the farmland was so poor and he said that Isarn got less rainfall than the rest of the country, and because the crops were generally of poor quality the farmers didn't have the money they needed to invest in fertilisers and pesticides.

We stopped off at a small market so that Joy could buy a large fish and some fruit as presents. I'd given her five 1000-baht notes so that she could give some money to her family. I knew how important that was to her. She'd waied me in the hotel room when I'd given it her, a gesture that I always found incredibly moving, far more so than if she'd just said thank you or kissed me.

Joy's house was about fifty feet from the road, a two-storey wooden house with a pitched roof. There were no windows, just shutters, there were big pottery barrels connected to drainpipes which Bruno said would be the house's only water supply. Electricity came from an overhead cable from a series of poles that ran along the roadside that I'd assumed were telephone poles. Bruno laughed at that, telling me that the nearest phone would probably be a mile or so away.

We got out of the Landrover and walked towards the house. There was no hard path, just a track worn across the threadbare grass. There was litter everywhere, polythene bags, pieces of newspaper, chocolate bar wrappers and there was a general air of neglect about the place. The wooden siding was rotting in places and one of the window shutters was hanging on one hinge.

Sunan and Mon came out to greet us. I was surprised to see them because Joy hadn't said that they'd be there. Sunan was in her bargirl's uniform of tight black T-shirt and blue Levi jeans and Mon was wearing a long pink dress and high heels. Mon was carrying her daughter, Nonglek. Joy introduced them to Bruno and Pam and we went to sit on a low wooden platform at the side of the house. Joy took the food into the house while Sunan gave us glasses of water. I couldn't see whether the water had come from one of the rain barrels but I didn't want to offend her by asking so I just drank it. Pam, Mon and Sunan were soon deep in conversation.

Inside half a dozen young men were sprawled on plastic sofas watching a flickering portable television. They didn't seem in the least bit interested in our arrival. The ground floor consisted of one large room with an old dresser against one wall and wooden chairs scattered along the length of another. There was a poster of the King and Queen of Thailand on the wall behind the television, and hanging next to it a garland of yellow and red flowers.

"This is typical of this part of Thailand," said Bruno. "The girls are the wage-earners, the men spend most of their time watching television and drinking. The girls are brought up in this environment and assume that it is normal behaviour." He nodded over at Sunan and Mon. "Mon is the oldest so she presumably started work first. Then she'll have encouraged Sunan to join her, and then Joy. The men live off the girls' money, the girls in turn get a feeling of worth by providing for their families."

Joy came out of the house and sat down next to me. "What you think about my house?" she asked.

"It's nice."

"You want see my bedroom?"

"Sure."

She took me inside. It was gloomy and smelled damp. To the left of the living room was a door that led to a small kitchen. Plastic bags of foodstuffs were hanging from nails, presumably to keep them away from insects. There was an old stove connected to a gas cylinder. It was caked with dirt and grease, as were the two woks that lay on the floor next to it.

Joy led me up a flight of wooden stairs. Leading off a short hallway were three rooms. Joy's contained a three-drawer cupboard and a rack of clothes which was covered with a sheet of polythene. In the corner were two rolled-up sleeping mats. There were two posters on the wall, one of the present King of Thailand and one of King Rama IV. Joy stood in the middle of the room, watching to see how I'd react.

"It's pretty," I said, and she beamed.

"Really? You like?"

"Sure." I nodded at the sleeping mats. "Who sleeps here with you?"

"Mon."

"And no mosquito nets? Don't you get bitten?"

"Sometimes."

I couldn't believe how primitive the place was. The floorboards were warped with big gaps between them, and bare lightbulbs hung from the ceiling. What little furniture there was in the house was as shabby as the building itself. Home repairs and decoration clearly didn't rate very highly on the family's list of priorities. It was as if they didn't care about their surroundings. It certainly wasn't a matter of not having the time or manpower—there were six men downstairs watching television at four o'clock in the afternoon.

Joy took a step forward and kissed me softly on the cheek. "Thank you for coming to my house, Pete," she said. "Chan rak khun." I love you. "I sorry my father not here to see you. He want see you very much." Joy explained that her father was away working and wouldn't be back until later that night. Mon disappeared into the kitchen and after half an hour reappeared with bowls of Thai noodles which we ate outside. One of Joy's brothers brought out a bottle of Thai whisky and a large bottle of Coke.

We still had a long drive back to Bangkok so we didn't stay long. Before we left I saw Joy slip Mon a handful of banknotes. It was the money I'd given her, pretty much all of it. I took lots of photographs of Joy and her sisters and her house.

I did all the driving on the way home because Pam's wrist had got worse. Joy sat behind me, stroking the back of my neck as she talked to Pam. It was a good trip. I learnt a lot about Isarn, and I learnt a lot about Joy, too.

BRUNO

I enjoyed Pete's company during our drive around Isarn. He was a good listener and an intelligent conversationalist, something one doesn't often come across in Thailand. Joy was a pretty enough girl, a bit coarse I thought, but she had lovely hair and a nice figure. As soon as she opened her mouth I could tell she was from Isarn. She was polite enough, but there was a roughness about the way she spoke. In many ways she reminded me of Pam when I first met her some twenty years ago. Pam has put on a lot of weight since then, of course, but she's still a good-looking woman. They got on very well together, Pam and Joy, chatting away as if they'd known each other for years. That's often the way it is with Thais, especially when they come from the same part of the country.

Pete obviously likes the girl, and I can understand why. She was very attentive, very affectionate, but it was interesting to hear what she was saying to Pam. Joy kept on talking about all the things Pete had given her, the clothes, the jewellery, the presents. She said he appeared to have a lot of money and that he was very generous. And she said "khao long rak chan," he fancies me, several times. It was the typical attitude of a bargirl, seeing the customer as a source of financial rather than emotional support, but I really think that Pete believed the relationship involves more than that.

When I got back to Bangkok I sent Pete several papers I'd written, including one that I thought might be helpful to him: 'Cross-Cultural Complications of Prostitution in Thailand.' He never mentioned it so maybe he didn't read it, but if he had I think it might have set alarm bells ringing.

It's virtually impossible to have a true Western-style relationship with these girls. Take Pam, for instance. She doesn't love me, not in the Western sense, and I'm reasonably sure that she has a Thai husband or boyfriend who stays away while I'm in Thailand. After all, I'm only here for three months a year, six if I can arrange a sabbatical, I can hardly expect her to be celibate for the rest of the time. She'd had three children by the time I met her. Pam's husband had gone off with another woman and she worked in the bars to support her family. Now I take care of her, and she's a great help to me in my work, but the relationship is not love. It's more like a friendship with sex.

Do I love her? Of course not. I love my wife in Germany. She's the mother of my children, and family is very important to us Germans. Thai women can be great fun if they are handled properly, but I fear that Pete will have a problem if he tries to make Joy conform to his Western ideal of a relationship.

I must say I found the three sisters a fascinating case study and I wished that I could have spent more time with them. I'd like to do a paper analysing the Western perception of the morality of the situation. An initial perspective from an outsider would be that the three sisters were somehow morally deficient, selling their bodies to foreigners, dancing naked in a go-go bar, surrounded by all the worst vices, smoking, alcohol, drugs. One might be surprised that they could behave in such a manner without attracting the scorn and derision of the rest of the family. And yet, a closer examination would show that the male members of the family were more than happy to take advantage of the situation. The money provided by the girls allows them to live a life of relative luxury. So who is in the morally superior position? The prostitutes or the family members who live off them? I think it would be a fascinating study. It would also be interesting to contrast the Western perspective of morality with that of the Thais. From a Western point of view, the girls would appear to be morally deficient, but so far as the sisters are concerned, by helping their families they are storing up merit which will lead to them gaining status in a future life. Far from doing anything wrong, they see themselves as occupying the moral high ground when compared with the farangs to whom they sell themselves. Once I have the time, I intend to do more research on the subject.

PETE

There was a definite change in Joy after the Isarn trip. She began telephoning me at the hotel, sometimes two or three times a day, and she became more protective whenever I was in Zombie. I'd offer to buy her drinks but she'd refuse and tell me to save my money. I still had to pay her barfine, and I still gave her money whenever we slept together, but she seemed reluctant to take it, as if it were a reminder that we still had a bargirl–customer relationship. The crazy thing was, I was actually faithful to her. I hadn't barfined anyone else for months and it wasn't because I was frightened of Joy finding out. It was because I didn't want to. Nana Plaza was full of gorgeous, available girls, but I honestly wasn't interested in any of them. Joy was the only one I wanted. Whenever I went out shopping, I was always looking for things to buy her. A handbag. Shirts. I always wore a Garfield watch and I found a lady's version that looked similar, and she wore it all the time. "You and me same," she'd say, and giggle.

So why didn't I just go the whole hog and ask her to move in with me? Because there were still nagging doubts. Small things, sure, but I never had the feeling that she was being one hundred per cent honest with me. She still wouldn't let me see her room, kept insisting that it was dangerous, even though I'd said that I'd go during the day. And a couple of times she hadn't been in Zombie when I'd popped in. Her friends had said it was her day off. I asked her why she didn't tell me when she had a day off because then we could go out without me having to barfine her, and she said that she never knew in advance when her day off was. That didn't make sense to me. I asked her to call me next time she knew she was taking the day off but she never did. And sometimes, when we were with a group of girls, I got the feeling she was talking about me. My Thai was getting better, but most of Joy's friends were from Isarn and they spoke a dialect that I couldn't follow, sort of a cross between Lao and Thai. The girls would laugh and look at me and I'd ask Joy what they were saying and she'd say something innocuous but it never sounded convincing. Like I said, it was just a feeling.

There was one incident that really worried me, though. She had a red wallet in which she kept her money and her ID card. There were also a couple of photographs of the two of us. I was always proud of the fact that she had the pictures, I guess because it showed that I was special. Once, when I picked up the wallet, she went crazy, trying to get it away from me. When I opened it, the photographs weren't there. There was a photograph of a Thai man instead, in his twenties and wearing a baseball cap. I was annoyed and stormed out of the bar. I calmed down after an hour or so and went back. Joy wasn't there. Her friend Apple came over and said that Joy had started crying and had gone home.

Joy telephoned me the following day and said that she'd switched the pictures to see how I'd react. I asked her who the guy in the picture was and she said it was the brother of one of the dancers and that he was a lady boy. A lady boy isn't the same as a katoey—a lady boy hasn't had a sex change and doesn't dress like a girl—but they talk and act girlishly and sometimes wear make up. The guy in the picture hadn't looked like a lady boy to me. I asked her where she'd got the picture from and she said her friend gave it to her before I went to the bar.

You see, I know that was a lie. A definite, undeniable, lie. Quite often, when Joy and I went to a short-time hotel, I'd go through her bag while she was in the shower. I'm not particularly proud of it, but I told myself I was doing it because I loved her, because I wanted to know if she really loved me. What was I looking for? Money, partly. I knew that if I found a thousand baht note that she'd been short time. Business cards that other farangs had given her. If I found any, I'd throw them away. Once, during the first few weeks when I'd been seeing her, I found a fifty-dollar bill in her purse. I felt like shit when I found it, but at least I knew what she was up to. Sometimes there'd be a condom in the bag and that made me feel even worse, but at least I knew that she was taking precautions and in a crazy way that made me feel better. Usually though, all I'd find would be a small amount of money, her ID card and cards I'd given her with my address in London and the hotel in Soi 4.

Anyway, the week before we went to Isarn, I found two photographs in her wallet, tucked in behind her money. They were both the same, the guy in the baseball cap. So when she said she'd only just been given the picture, I knew she was lying. I confronted her, too. And she denied it, right down the line, until in the end I was almost convinced that I'd imagined it. Almost, but not quite. It was the same photograph. I couldn't understand why she'd lie. I mean, she was a bargirl, if she wanted someone else, all she had to do was to tell me. Why lie?

Anyway, about a week after we got back, I took her to the karaoke bar with two of her friends. I had to pay barfines for all three, but I knew that Joy enjoyed herself more if we went as a group and they could take it in turns to sing. I ordered food and we all drank beer. When one of the other girls was singing, Joy leaned over and kissed me on the neck.

"Pete, I love you too much," she said. "I not go with farang any more. Only you, Pete."

I asked her what she meant. She told me that she'd decided that she wasn't going to allow anyone else to pay her barfine. "If anyone ask, I tell them I have you," she said solemnly.

I was surprised. Really surprised. I'd never asked her to stop working, I didn't think I had the right.

"I serious, Pete," she said. "Now I have you, only one."

ALISTAIR

Pete's appointment was one of the best I've made. He was working hard, much harder than Lawrence even before Lawrence had gone native. The stuff he did on Isarn was brilliant. He's got a real flair for writing but what really impressed me was his insight into Thai culture and customs. Considering he'd only been in Thailand for a couple of months, I think he'd developed an amazing understanding of what made the people tick. His copy was peppered with tidbits of information that was totally new to me, and I've been in South East Asia for the best part of ten years. He was prolific, too, and had totally revised the section on the Isarn region. I sent him a congratulatory memo and suggested to head office that we increase his Christmas bonus.

He was so far ahead of schedule on the Thailand book that I asked him to spend a month with me in Hong Kong to help me update the regional backpacker's guide. The information I had on Macau, South Korea and Taiwan had come from stringers the company uses and frankly it wasn't up to the standard of the rest of the book. I figured that Pete could work his magic on the copy, plus he could help me with the selection of pictures and maps. When I asked him he was reluctant at first, saying that he still had a lot of work to do on his own book, but I offered him a business class ticket and told him about the bonus I was pressing for and after a bit of arm twisting he agreed to come out for three weeks.

PETE

I really didn't want to go to Hong Kong. I actually felt that Alistair was taking advantage of me. I guess I was a victim of my own success: if I hadn't worked so hard on the Thailand book, he wouldn't have asked me to bail him out. It wasn't my fault his stringers had let him down, but I was going to suffer for it. He practically blackmailed me into agreeing to go, telling me that he was sending a memo to head office recommending a big bonus. The unspoken threat was that if I didn't do what he wanted, a second memo could be winging its way to Australia. He wanted me to go for a month but I managed to get him down to three weeks. And he said that I could stay with him but that he'd sign off a daily hotel rate so I'd make a stack of money on the job.

Joy was really unhappy that I was going. She gripped my arm when I told her as if she were scared that I was going there and then. "You sure you come back, Pete?" she said.

Her anxiety was so cute. I assured her that I'd be back and told her that I'd phone and write as often as I could.

"I write to you too, Pete. Every day. I miss you too much." I gave her Alistair's address and telephone number.

That night I paid barfine and we went to our favourite German restaurant in Soi 4. Afterwards I took her back to the Dynasty Hotel. It was the first time I'd taken her back to my hotel, and I could see she was pleased. She stayed all night and in the morning I gave her five thousand baht and told her I'd see her in three weeks and that I wanted her to be a good girl.

"Of course, Pete," she said, looking shocked. "What you think? I have you, only one."

On the day I left, she went to the airport with me, and there were tears in her eyes when I kissed her goodbye. I gave her five thousand baht and she promised to write every day.

JOY

Five thousand baht? How was I supposed to live for three weeks on five thousand baht? I didn't say anything to Pete but I didn't wai him. Five thousand baht? I couldn't understand why he was being so stingy. He asked me to write to him every day and to phone him. Phone him? He's no idea how expensive it is to phone abroad. And I had to pay another monthly installment on my motorcycle, so that was five thousand baht right there. I'd promised him not to go with any other farangs, didn't he understand that he'd have to take care of me? Sometimes farangs can be so stupid. But Pete should know better, he's lived in Bangkok for months and he's writing a book about Thailand so he must know the way things are. What does he think? That I should stop going with farangs and live on rice and water?

PETE

Alistair and I worked flat out on the book, pretty much fifteen hours a day for the whole three weeks. We only broke to eat and sleep. He was right, four weeks would have made more sense but I didn't want to be away from Bangkok too long. After the first week I began checking Alistair's mail box every morning but there was never a letter from Joy. And she didn't phone. I couldn't call her so it was up to her to contact me, and I was hurt that she didn't. I wondered what had happened. Maybe she'd lost her wallet with my address. Maybe her handwriting was bad and the postman couldn't read it. Maybe she'd put the wrong stamp on it and it was coming by surface mail in which any letters she sent would take several weeks to get to me. I'd told her that she could phone me by reversing the charges, but maybe she hadn't understood. There were so many 'maybes' that it was ridiculous. The one maybe that I wouldn't consider was that maybe she'd forgotten all about me.

Three days before I was due to fly back, she sent me a fax. "Pete, I love you too much. I cannot dance." That was all. Nine words. It was typical of Joy, I guess. Faxes cost a set fee per page. Something like four hundred baht. She could have sent me a thousand words on the page for the same price. Having said that, what she wrote really touched me. Alistair thought it was really funny, but he's got no soul.

When I did go back to Bangkok, I checked into the Dynasty Hotel again. I don't know why I hadn't moved into somewhere more permanent, guess I was just lazy. I had a big room and cable TV and room service, and I was paying a thousand baht a day, about seven hundred quid a month. The company was paying me an accommodation allowance of a thousand pounds a month, and for that I could get a decent sized apartment. I'd have to sign a long-term lease and put down deposits for the utilities, and Thailand being Thailand, I preferred the convenience of a hotel, for the time being at least. Plus, they were happy to keep stuff in storage for me while I was away so I didn't have to keep the room on.

Anyway, as soon as I'd checked in and got my things out of storage, I walked around to Zombie. Joy was dancing and she grinned and waved when she saw me. She had to wait until her dancing shift finished before coming over to hug me. I paid her barfine straight away so that she didn't have to dance again. She went off to change and came back in blue jeans and a tight black top. I bought her a cola and told her that I hadn't got any letters.

"Pete, I write to you too much," she said.

"Are you sure?"

She looked offended by my doubts. "Pete, why I lie to you? How much does a stamp cost? Twelve baht? I go post office too much."

I didn't know what to say. For the three weeks I was away there had been no letters and no phone calls.

"You get my fax?" she asked.

"Yes, I did," I said. Despite what she'd written in the fax, she didn't seem to have any problem dancing. In fact, before she'd seen me, she was gyrating around a silver pole as sexily and enthusiastically as the first day I'd laid eyes on her.

"You like?" she asked.

"Sure." Actually, I suddenly got the feeling that she'd sent the fax for my benefit rather than hers. She'd done it because she knew that's what I wanted. And the message about her not being able to dance, that's what I wanted to hear, too. It was as if she was pressing my buttons. I remembered something Big Ron had once said to me: that girls regard farangs as ATM machines. They press the right buttons and money comes out. And if one ATM machine is shut down, they can easily find another one. Was that what Joy was doing, pressing my buttons for cash? I noticed that the gold bracelet I'd given her for her birthday was missing.

She saw me looking at her wrist. "Pete, I sorry, I have no money," she said. She made a pressing motion with her thumb, the sign Thai use to show that they've pawned something. "I have to pay my rent and I have no money."

I was stunned. The bracelet had been made of interlinked hearts. I'd spent ages choosing it in the jewellers, it was something that I felt showed what I felt about her. I had given her my heart. And she'd sold it, the first chance she got. I stood up. She caught hold of my arm. "Pete, I want you understand me," she said.

I shook her away. "It was a birthday present, Joy. If you'd needed money, you could have asked me.".

"You not here," she said. Her chin was up in defiance. She wasn't sorry, she was angry. She felt that it was me who was in the wrong.

I wanted to tell her that I'd checked the mailbox for a letter from her every day, that most of the time I'd been in Hong Kong I'd been thinking about her. I wanted to tell her how much I loved her, but the look on her face stopped me. She'd sold the gold I'd given her and she didn't care. The fact it was made up of hearts, the fact that I'd given it to her on her birthday, the night I'd paid for her party, all of that meant nothing compared with the money she'd got for selling it. She'd said pawned, but that was the same as selling it. If I wanted her to wear it, I'd have to buy it back. I'd have to pay for it twice. And who was to say that she wouldn't sell it again the next time she needed money?

I felt angry and frustrated, I'd come racing back to see her, she'd been all that I'd thought about while I was on the plane, while I was queuing at immigration, while I was in the taxi from the airport. She didn't care about me, all she cared about was my money. I shook her hand off my arm and rushed out of the bar.

JOY

What did he expect? He'd left me with five thousand baht. I had bills to pay, Park was pestering me for money and Sunan said I had to send money back to our father. The bar was really quiet so what was I supposed to do? It's okay for Pete, he's a farang, he's got lots of money. He keeps telling me about his apartment in London that he still owns, it's worth almost seven million baht, he said. And I know he's got money in the bank because whenever we go out he goes to the Bangkok Bank ATM. He doesn't know what it's like to have no money, to have to live from hand to mouth.

A few of my friends came over after he'd rushed out of the bar, wanting to know what was wrong. I said he didn't feel well. I didn't want them to know that he was angry at me. I waited for half an hour, and when he didn't come back I changed back into my bikini and started dancing again.

NIGEL

Pete came into Fatso's with a face like thunder. I was on to my sixth pint of lager so I was feeling no pain. Jimmy and Rick were doing their best to Big Glass as many of the regulars as they could so I was knocking them back as soon as they arrived. Pete ordered a gin and tonic and drank it down in one. Jimmy rang the bell and Pete drained his second drink almost as fast as the first. I asked him what was wrong and he told me that Joy had sold the gold bracelet he'd given her for her birthday. I wasn't surprised, and he shouldn't have been either. Gold equates to money in Thailand. In fact, that's how you buy it, according to weight. They sell it as one baht, two baht, three baht, and so on, with each baht equivalent to fifteen grams. The price you have to pay is fixed each day and the jewellers often put the price in their window. Two prices, actually: a buy price and a sell price. I don't know what it is today. Typical Thailand, that, giving the unit of weight the same name as the money. Actually, thinking about it, we do the same in England, don't we? Pounds and pounds.

Anyway, when you buy a gold chain, they multiply the daily price by the weight, then add on five hundred baht or so for the design, but basically you're paying for the gold, nothing else. It's not like in England where you pay hundreds of pounds for a tiny piece of gold. When a Thai bargirl admires another girl's gold, she's not interested in what it looks like, all she cares about is the weight. The value. I heard Joy and her friends talking about the bracelet at the party. "It's only two baht," she said. Pete didn't hear her, his Thai isn't that good, and I didn't say anything to him because I know how he feels about her. What I'm saying is, to her it was just money she could wear on her wrist, but to Pete it was a token of his love.

"Forget it, Pete," I said, "she's just a hooker."

"Fuck off, Nigel, you don't know what you're talking about," he said.

"She's a bargirl."

He glared at me. "She's a dancer. She's stopped hooking."

"Yeah, right," I said.

Rick rang the bell so I drained my glass before the next one arrived. So did Pete. Noo put a tequila and orange in front of Alan which meant he had four untouched glasses so they were taken away and poured into a big glass. Alan was up in the loo, so he had a nasty surprise waiting for him. He'd drink it, though. He always did. He'd drink it in one and then rush outside to throw up before the alcohol got into his system. Smart guy, is Alan. He's an analyst with a big stockbroking firm, a Japanese one I think, and he earns a fortune.

"What do you mean, yeah right?" asked Pete. He looked at me sideways. More of a stare than a look. Baleful. Like he wanted to smash his glass into my face. Whatever Joy had said to him, she'd really screwed him up.

"Nothing."

"Come on, what do you mean?"

"You don't want to know."

Jimmy and Rick were openly listening. Big Ron winked at them. He knew what I knew and I could see that he was bursting for me to spill the beans.

Pete turned to face me. "Don't fuck around, Nigel. If you know something, tell me."

I hadn't been planning to tell him, I really hadn't. I knew how he felt about Joy, and I knew that if I did tell him he probably wouldn't believe me. But now that she'd sold his gold, he'd be more receptive. I just hoped he wouldn't want to kill the messenger.

"She went out with a customer. When you were in Hong Kong."

Pete closed his eyes and swore under his breath.

"I wasn't going to say anything ..." I started, but he cut me off with a wave of his hand.

"Are you sure?" he said.

"Big, fat, German," I said.

"Was she holding his hand?"

Big Ron chuckled but turned it into a coughing fit when Pete glared at him. I could see Big Ron's point. It didn't really matter if he was holding her hand, did it? Not compared with what they'd be getting up to in a short-time hotel.

"Yeah, I think she was."

"When was this?"

"Hell, Pete, I don't know. About a week after you went."

"Did she see you?"

"She walked right by me, but she didn't say anything."

"Shameless hussy," said Rick, and dissolved into a fit of laughter.

Alan came down the stairs and groaned at the sight of the big glass.

"Just the once?" asked Pete.

"I wasn't in Zombie much, to be honest," I said.

Pete put his head in his hands. "Fucking hookers," he muttered.

"I'll drink to that," said Jimmy.

I ordered another drink for Pete. So did Rick. Then Big Ron rang the bill and Pete had four drinks in front of him so he was Big Glassed with gin and tonic. Just over two pints, and Pete drank it down in one. He was legless by the time the bar closed and Rick and Jimmy had to help him back to his hotel.

PETE

I woke up with a hell of a hangover, but I was barely aware of how badly I felt because all I could think about was Joy. I tried to work, but it wasn't any good. I wanted to confront her with her infidelity, but I knew there was no point. Nigel had seen her leaving with a customer. End of story. And she'd sold the heart bracelet I'd given her, the bracelet she'd so proudly displayed to her friends and family. I spent most of the day pacing around the room. I didn't even want to go to Fatso's Bar: I ordered a club sandwich from room service but hardly touched it. I kept looking at my watch, wondering why she didn't phone. She must have known how angry I was.

I tried to get some work done, but failed miserably. Every time I switched on my laptop computer all I could do was stare at the screen. The words wouldn't come. At seven thirty I became really depressed because I knew she'd be arriving for work at Zombie. She'd be changing into her bikini and tying her jungle print sarong around her waist, strutting around in her high heels looking for farangs to fleece. If she was working, she wouldn't phone. And if she was angry at me, maybe she'd let someone pay her barfine to get back at me. Thoughts of her kept running through my mind, thoughts of her flirting with another man, walking out of the bar with him, screwing him in a short-time hotel, doing everything with him that she'd done with me. Thinking of her with someone else made me sick to the stomach, but I couldn't stop, I kept tormenting myself.

Eight o'clock passed. Nine o'clock. I tried watching television but I couldn't concentrate. All I could think about was Joy.

I kept picking up the telephone, to check that it was working. Once I got an outside line and dialled the hotel's number, to reassure myself that there was nothing wrong with the switchboard. When I heard the operator say "Dynasty Hotel" I hung up, feeling stupid. She hadn't called. She wouldn't call.

By the time ten o'clock came I was so wound up that I couldn't stay in the room any longer. I didn't feel like going to Fatso's because I was sure Nigel had told everybody what Joy had done. And I couldn't bear going to Nana Plaza, knowing that Joy was there, either dancing or in a short-time hotel. I went out of the Dynasty and flagged down a motorcycle taxi. I told the guy I wanted to go to Patpong. There wasn't much traffic and he drove so fast that my eyes were soon streaming with tears. He dropped me at the Silom Road end of Patpong and I threaded my way through the tourists and touts. I wasn't sure where I wanted to go, I just wanted to find some way of blotting Joy out of my mind. I wanted noise, I wanted alcohol, I wanted a girl who wasn't Joy. I wanted to go straight back to Soi 4 and confront her, to tell her that I knew she'd been with another farang, that she'd betrayed me, but I knew there was no point. She'd only deny it.

I stopped outside the Takara Massage Parlour. It was on the third floor and the entrance was via a lift which opened on to the street. I'd been there a couple of times with Bruce and Nigel, and while it wasn't a place I particularly liked, I wanted to get off the street, to get away from the tourists.

The lift doors opened into a reception area, and to the left was a small bar. I sat down and ordered a gin and tonic, a large one. I drank half of it and then turned around to face the large window that was set into the wall. Behind the glass were twenty or so girls in evening dresses, each with a small blue numbered badge pinned to their chest. Most were young, in their early twenties, but there were several older women, too. A few were smiling at me, their backs arched and breasts thrust forward to make the most of their assets, but the majority of the girls were watching a small television set in the corner. Some of the girls were crying and they were passing around a box of tissues.

"See anything you like?" asked the mamasan, a fifty-something woman with permed hair and a mole in the middle of her chin.

I drained my glass and ordered another from the girl behind the bar. "Not yet," I said. "But give me time." I asked her why the girls were crying and she said that they were watching a Thai soap opera and that one of the characters was dying of Aids.

I drank my second gin and tonic. Then a third. I stared at the girls. None looked like Joy, but maybe that was a good thing.

Two farangs stepped out of the lift and went over to the window. They were drunk and began making faces at the girls. The mamasan went over to them and encouraged them to choose, recommending two girls who had only recently arrived in Bangkok.

"Very young," said the mamasan. "Their ID say they eighteen, but I can tell you they younger." She leaned forward and in a stage whisper, said, "Number twenty-three only sixteen. Almost a virgin."

I had another gin and tonic while the two drunks selected girls. The older of the two men with a beer gut hanging over the waistband of his trousers, chose number twenty-three. The mamasan rapped on the window and mouthed the numbers to the girls. They stood up and a few minutes later came out of a side door, each carrying a shopping basket containing liquid soap, talcum powder, KY Jelly and condoms.

The girls went upstairs with the tourists, chatting to themselves in Thai. My Thai was just good enough to follow what they were saying. Number twenty-three was complaining about her customer being fat and ugly. Think of the money, said the other one.

"You decide?" the mamasan asked me.

I was feeling light-headed, as if my mind were slightly out of kilter with my body. I pointed at a slightly plump girl with shoulder-length hair. She looked nothing like Joy: she was very pale skinned and had a long nose, probably the result of plastic surgery. Lots of girls paid for plastic implants which made their noses look more like farangs. "Her," I said.

"She Jo-jo," said the mamasan, waving at the girl.

"I don't care," I said. Jo-jo wasn't a Thai name. She was just using it when she worked with farangs. But I meant what I said. I didn't care about her name. I just wanted to use her to blot Joy out of my thoughts.

Jo-jo came out with her shopping basket. She was wearing a long electric blue dress with a low-cut cleavage that emphasised breasts that were obviously as false as her nose. I asked her what she wanted to drink and she said whisky and Coke so I bought her one and another double gin and tonic for myself. I told her I wanted to go upstairs straight away. The rooms containing the showers and baths were on the fourth and fifth floors. I paid the cashier five hundred baht for a full body massage and Jo-jo and I went to the fifth.

I sat on a massage table while Jo-jo set the airconditioner and turned on the bath taps. She switched on a red light and turned off the main fluorescent lights, then slid off the dress. She wasn't wearing any underwear and had a good, full figure. She helped me undress, checked the temperature of the water, then helped me into the bath. I lay back and she slid in between my legs, facing me. She washed me, humming quietly to herself, cleaning everywhere, even between my toes. I leaned over and picked up my gin and tonic and drank it as she worked.

She climbed out of the bath and used a lump of soft soap to lather up a bowl of water which she poured over a thick blue plastic mat on the floor. I got out and lay face down on the mat, my head on a thick rubber pillow. Jo-jo used her body to massage me, rubbing herself up and down, along my back, between my legs, slowly at first and then more vigorously. I had my eyes closed and I kept thinking about Joy. Joy had never given me a massage, I don't think she even knew how to, but I couldn't stop imagining it was her.

Jo-jo rolled over me and told me to turn over. She knelt down next to the mat and prepared another bowl of hot, soapy water and poured it over me, concentrating the flow over my groin and thighs. She lowered herself on top of me and began rubbing herself against me, her large breasts against my chest, her thighs against my groin. I felt myself growing hard and she moved more sensuously as if she were making love to me. Jo-jo was a professional, though, and there was never any chance of my accidentally entering her without a condom.

"You want fuck me?" she whispered.

I opened my eyes. "Huh?"

"One thousand baht, you can fuck me." She ground herself harder against me and parted her lips in what she must have thought was a sexy pout. She looked like a goldfish gasping for air.

"Okay," I said.

She pushed herself up against me and groped in her shopping basket for a condom. After ripping the packet open with her teeth she took out the condom and slid it on to me. It was something she'd obviously done hundreds of times before, totally mechanical movements devoid of any sensuality. Thoughts of Joy suddenly flooded through my mind and I felt my erection start to subside.

Jo-jo realised what was happening and she began to caress me. "You very handsome man," she said, straddling me. I reached up for her soapy breasts and stroked them. She gripped me tighter and I felt myself respond, then she quickly slipped me inside her.

She rode me the way she might ride a horse, pressing her thighs against me and holding on to my shoulders as she pushed down. My back slid along the wet mat with each thrust until my feet were pressing against the tiled wall.

"Jo-jo?" I said.

"Yes?"

"What's my name?"

She frowned. "I don't know," she said. She moved faster, pounding against me. "I not care. You handsome farang."

I closed my eyes. Joy was so much gentler, so much more sensitive to how I felt, changing her pace, varying her movements to make the love-making more sensual. Jo-jo was riding me, trying to get me to come as quickly as possible so that she could get back behind the window again. I didn't want to be with her, I wanted to be inside Joy, I wanted to make love to a girl I loved, not have paid-for sex with a girl who didn't even know my name. I stopped moving. A few seconds later, so did Jo-jo.

"You come already?" she said.

"Yes," I lied.

She reached down to my groin, held the condom, and lifted herself off. She slipped the condom off and examined it with a frown before wrapping it in a tissue and putting it in the basket.

I got back into the bath and she rinsed me off, then herself. "You want massage?" she asked, nodding at the table.

I said no, I had to go, and I dressed while she dried herself and sprinkled talcum powder over herself. I gave her a thousand baht and left while she was still dressing. I felt like an unfaithful husband, I felt as if I'd betrayed Joy, and that was crazy because she was the hooker, she'd been the one who'd left Zombie with a farang, she was the one who let someone else pay her barfine. It wasn't me who was being unfaithful. I wasn't the one in the wrong.

I went down in the lift, and out into the crowds of Patpong. Despite the bath, I felt dirty. Unclean. I walked along to Suriwong Road past the go-go bars. Touts kept touching me and trying to entice me into their bars. "You want see fucking show? Many girls? Free look. No cover charge." I hated being touched. Generally Thais avoid physical contact with strangers, but Patpong wasn't Thailand, it was where farangs came to ogle girls, get drunk and have sex and normal rules of behaviour didn't apply. I shrugged away the touts but didn't say anything. I'd seen touts turn on tourists before and knew how easily they could change from grinning sycophants to angry thugs. Theirs were the smiles of cruising sharks.

I found a group of motorcycle taxis, the riders wearing bright orange vests over denim shirts. They asked me where I wanted to go. Nana Plaza, I said. I wanted to see Joy.

JOY

Pete arrived just after midnight. I wasn't dancing when he came in so I went straight over to see him and threw my arms around his neck. He'd just showered and his hair was still wet. I thought that maybe he'd gone short time with another girl but he said he'd showered in his room. I told him I was sorry about selling his gold, that I really needed the money, but he still didn't smile at me. Well, he smiled, but I could see it wasn't a real smile. He was worried about something. I found him a seat and sat down next to him.

Sunan came over and said hello. I told Sunan in Khmer to rub my number off the board by the changing room. I'd been in the short-time room with a customer earlier in the evening and Pete often checked the board when he came in. If he looked, he'd see my number, 81, and STR. Pete wasn't stupid, he'd know what that meant.

He ordered a gin and tonic but he didn't ask me if I wanted a drink. I didn't ask. I know that most farangs don't like to be asked, you have to wait for them to offer.

"What's wrong, Pete?" I asked.

"Why do you think something's wrong?"

"You not happy," I said. "I can see you not happy."

"Do you love me, Joy?"

"Of course. I love you number one in the world. I have you, only one."

"And you not go with farang?"

As soon as he said that, I knew what had happened. I'd obviously been seen with a customer. Pete had a lot of friends in Bangkok and most of them knew me. There was the one with the eye-patch who was tight with money, Nigel. The short one with the beard, Bruce. And the ones called Jimmy and Rick who liked going with katoeys. I smiled and put my hand on his thigh. "Pete, you know I not want go with farang. Have you, only one."

He looked at me without speaking for a while, like he was trying to see inside my head. I waited to see what he'd say. To see how much his friends had told him. It would be my word against theirs and he didn't love them the way he loved me. I'd heard Sunan talk to her boyfriend in Denmark lots of times. He'd get suspicious when he phoned and she wasn't home, but Sunan could twist him around her little finger. It's so easy with farangs. They want to believe you, you just have to tell them what they want to hear. A Thai man would never believe the lies we tell, he'd believe what he was told or what he suspected.

"Joy, I know you go with farang," Pete said. His eyes were red and his breath reeked of drink.

I shook my head. "No, Pete."

"Somebody saw you. Somebody saw you leave with a farang when I was in Hong Kong."

"Who? Who saw me?"

"A friend."

"And what did the shit-eating dog tell you, Pete?"

"He said a farang paid your barfine."

I sighed. Sometimes he could be a real pain. "Okay, maybe farang pay my barfine so I can go eat. Sometimes farang want go eat with me, Pete. What you think? You think I want fuck farang? I not want, Pete. I want you only one."

Pete looked sad. He leant his head back against the wall.

"Pete, why I want fuck farang? How much I get? One thousand five hundred baht. You give me a lot more. Why I want to lose you? Pete, I know you. If you know I go with farang, you not love me. You not take care of me Sunan went over to the board and rubbed my number off. She turned around and stuck her tongue out at me, then crossed her eyes. I almost laughed but I kept a straight face and carried on talking to Pete. "Pete, I know you have many friends in Bangkok. I know if I not good girl they tell you. You think I stupid, Pete? You think I water buffalo?"

He opened his eyes. He looked at me for a while and then smiled.

This time it was a real smile and I knew I'd won. "No, Joy, I know you're not stupid."

"I love you, Pete. I love you, only one." I fluttered my eyelashes and he laughed. Eighty per cent of farangs like their girls to be cute.

He asked me what I wanted to drink and I went over to the bar to order a cola.

Sunan came over and stood next to me. "What's he so upset about?" she asked.

"I was seen with a farang while he was away," I said.

Sunan laughed. "Just once?"

"Yeah, lucky for me, huh?"

We both giggled and I went back to Pete. After an hour he paid my barfine and took me back to the Dynasty Hotel. He was too tired to make love so we just lay together. I left at five o'clock in the morning, I told him that one of my cousins was in my room and that she was young and I had to take care of her. He was sleepy so he didn't argue. He gave me three thousand baht and I went to see Park.

PETE

Funny thing happened yesterday. I went into a book shop to buy a couple of thrillers, and while I was browsing I came across a book about Chinese astrology. I flicked through it. There was a section on compatibility and I read through it. According to the book, the monkey and the rabbit got on just fine. I tried to remember what Joy had said. Big problems. The monkey always wants to pull the rabbit's ears. I wondered why she'd said that. Maybe someone else had been teasing her. Maybe she'd made it up. I mentioned it to her when I saw her in Zombie and she just laughed and said the book was wrong.

I paid her barfine and she left her purse on the table when she went to change. I picked it up and opened it. My photograph was there. And two of my business cards. She only had a hundred baht. She rarely had more than that in her purse. I could never work out where all the money

I gave her went. She said she didn't have a bank account and she lived in a room with two other girls so I didn't think she'd leave money there. Whenever I asked Joy what she spent her money on, "Bangkok very expensive," she'd say. "Have to pay room, pay food, shampoo."

"Shampoo?" I'd say and she'd laugh.

"You like my hair long, Pete. Every day I have to wash. I use a lot of shampoo."

Sometimes I'd sit down with her and try to work out what her outgoings were. She said the room she shared cost four thousand baht a month, but that the other two girls often didn't have any money so she had to pay their share, too. Electricity cost another thousand baht a month. Then there were her taxi fares, another two hundred baht a day. I asked her why she didn't get the bus, because buses in Bangkok are very cheap, just a few baht, and pretty efficient, too. She said she didn't want to go on the bus dressed for working in the bar because everyone would know she was a prostitute. She didn't want everyone looking at her, she said. I kept asking her why she didn't move closer to Nana Plaza—that way she could save six thousand baht a month in taxi fares. She said that all her friends lived in Suphan Kwai, but conceded that I had a point. "Okay, Pete, you very clever. Maybe I get a new room." She never did.

She spent another hundred baht a day on food, she said, and that seemed expensive. A bowl of noodles on the street would cost twenty baht, chicken and rice the same. If she was eating with the other girls, they'd be buying food together which would make it even cheaper. Whichever way I played with the numbers, Joy shouldn't be paying more than seventeen thousand baht a month. And that was if she was paying all the rent.

Pretty much every time I saw her, I'd give her a thousand baht, sometimes more. I figured that if she had enough money, she wouldn't be tempted to let anyone else pay her barfine. I guess in all I gave her sixteen thousand baht a month, maybe a bit more. The bar paid her six thousand, plus there was the commission she got from the drinks punters bought for her. That was probably another four thousand baht or so. So what did she do with the rest of her money? I didn't get the feeling that she sent any back to her family in Si Saket. She should have been saving at least nine thousand baht a month. I wondered if maybe she was still paying for her motorcycle, the one her brother had crashed, but the payment book had disappeared from her purse and she insisted she'd sold it. She knew I thought the bike was a waste of money, it always seemed crazy to me that she was living in Bangkok and paying for a bike in Si Saket, but I knew that to her it had been a status symbol, it gave her face when she went back home to her village.

I pulled out her identity card and smiled at the photograph. It had only been taken a year or so ago but she looked impossibly young, smiling at the camera with no make up and her hair tied back. She'd changed a lot since the photograph had been taken, and most of the change was down to her having worked in Nana Plaza.

I put the card back. There was something behind the business cards I'd given her. I groped with my fingertips and pulled it out. It was a condom. My heart fell.

"What you think, Pete?"

I looked up. Joy was standing there, looking at me. She'd changed into a tight black tank top and flared denim jeans. Her face was a stone mask. She took the condom off me.

"What you think?"

I didn't know what to say. I didn't know how I felt. There was no reason for her to be carrying a condom, not if she was telling the truth when she said she wasn't going with customers.

"Pete, it not mine," she said, sitting down next to me.

"It was in your wallet," I said. I wanted to walk away, to get the hell out of the bar. I wanted to tell her how angry I was, how betrayed I felt, but at the same time I wanted to hear what she had to say because maybe, just maybe, there was an explanation for it. I wanted to give her the benefit of the doubt, I wanted her to tell me that everything was all right, that she really did love me. So I sat there with some Thai pop song blaring out of the wall-mounted speakers, surrounded by half-naked hookers and sweating farangs, and waited for the love of my life to explain why there was a condom in her wallet.

"This belong to Apple," she said. Apple was dancing and making eyes at a small, bald guy in the corner. Joy shouted over at Apple and waved her over.

Apple scampered off the stage and tottered across to where we sitting. She held out her hand. "Hello, Pete, how are you?"

I told her I was fine, even though she could see from the look on my face that I wasn't.

Apple looked at Joy. Joy spoke to her quickly. I don't think it was Thai because I didn't recognise any of the words. It was probably Khmer, Apple and Joy were from the same village, fairly close to the border with Cambodia and they spoke several dialects. Joy knew that my Thai had been improving, and while I couldn't always make out what she was saying, I could at least follow the gist. But Khmer was a closed book to me, and Joy knew it.

Joy waved the condom as she spoke and Apple kept looking at me. When Joy stopped speaking, Apple nodded furiously. "Condom for me," she said. "Condom not for Joy."

"Why did you give it to Joy?" I asked her.

"I not have key for locker. Joy take care my money and my condom."

"Money?" There'd only been a hundred baht in Joy's purse.

Joy spoke to Apple quickly. Snapped at her, almost. Apple flinched, then smiled hurriedly.

"But I spend money already." She patted her stomach. "I eat rice soup. Aroi mark." Delicious. There were a number of food stalls at the entrance to Nana Plaza and one of them sold rice soup. Thais often ate it for breakfast, but it was a great late-night snack and the guys from Fatso's could often be found sitting at the side of road slurping bowls of it after the Plaza had closed. Jimmy and Rick swore it was the perfect hangover cure, but Big Ron reckoned it was a sure-fire way of getting salmonella poisoning. I liked it, and had even included the hawker's recipe in the guide book.

Joy gave the condom to Apple, who slipped it inside her bra then went back to the stage.

"Okay?" said Joy, sitting down next to me and putting her hand on my thigh.

"Yeah, I guess so."

She leant over and kissed me on the cheek. "I love you, Pete. Only one."

I put my arm around her and buried my head in her hair. She smelt fresh and clean as if she'd just showered.

"I don't want you to lie to me, Joy," I said. "If you want a Thai boyfriend, just tell me. If you want to go with customers, you can tell me and I'll understand."

She pushed me away. "Pete, I not lie to you."

"I know, I know," I said. "But if you want to be with someone else, or you want to go with customers, please, please tell me. You were working in Zombie when I first met you, you were dancing and going with customers, I have no right to change you, if you ..."

She pressed a finger against my lips. "Pete," she said. "Shut up."

BIG RON

Do I think Joy was lying to Pete? Fuck, I'd have been surprised if she hadn't been. She's a hooker, for fuck's sake: when he met her she was a hooker, how the fuck could he seriously expect her to change her spots just because he wanted sole fucking rights?

You know, I actually believe that generally speaking, the bargirls don't like us. It's partly a racial thing, they really do believe that we're inferior to them. Sure, we're physically bigger and we have more money, but they reckon we're not much smarter than animals. They call us water buffaloes or monitor lizards. There's no bigger insult than to say that a person is an animal, and that's what they think we are. We're a source of income, that's all. Sometimes they might take a longer term view, but it's still all about hard cash at the end of the day.

There's a guy comes in here to drink, name of Greig. Runs a restaurant and bar off Sukhumvit which is as close to being a brothel as you can get without actually having short-time rooms upstairs. Anyway, Greig got himself a Thai wife a few years back. He swears blind she wasn't a bargirl, but you can just tell from looking at her that she used to dance around a silver pole. They've got a couple of kids and he dotes on her. But I know for a fact that she doesn't love him. She doesn't even like him. He wears this thick gold chain around his neck, five baht it is, maybe six, and hanging on it are two gold Buddhas. Now, I'm not averse to wearing gold, and I've got a Buddha on my neck chain myself, but I happen to know that it's only lucky if you have an odd number of Buddhas. One or three, maybe five. Any more than that and you look like a fucking Christmas tree. But two or four, that's really unlucky. That's what they put on corpses. Now, Greig doesn't know that, he walks around with his two Buddhas like he's something special. But his wife, she's got to know the significance of wearing two Buddhas. So why doesn't she tell him? Why does she let him make a fool of himself? Because she doesn't fucking care, that's why. She's married him, she's had two kids by him, but he means nothing to her. He's a water buffalo to her, nothing more. She's probably got a Thai husband that she shags every chance she gets. But you couldn't tell Greig that. He reckons the sun shines out of her arse.

PETE

Joy phoned me one afternoon and asked if I was going to see her that night in Zombie. I said I probably was, but I asked her if she'd come and see me in the hotel first. She'd come to the hotel several times and I was no longer shy about her visiting. She said she'd come at six o'clock, about an hour before she was due to start work.

I worked on the book until she came. It was going well, I was meeting all Alistair's deadlines and I now had a reliable photographer supplying us with pictures. On average I was writing five thousand words a day, equivalent to about ten pages, and I knew it was good stuff.

I stopped writing when there was a knock on the door. It was Joy, wearing a short T-shirt that showed off her midriff and flared black jeans. She looked cute, but she looked like a hooker. I'd asked her time and time again to wear a jacket or a more respectable shirt, but she never listened to me. It wasn't that she didn't look good, she did, but respectable Thai girls didn't walk around showing off their stomachs, and the fact that she didn't have long sleeves meant that the scars on her wrist were clearly visible. Don't get me wrong, I wasn't ashamed of Joy, but I didn't like the way that Thais looked at her so contemptuously. I wanted them to look at her and think that she was a pretty girl with a farang, not a bargirl with her customer.

She fluttered her long lashes at me which she knew always made me laugh. I let her in and she sat on the edge of the bed. She nodded at the laptop computer. "So how your book?"

"Good," I said.

She was holding her red wallet.

"You have my picture?" I asked. I was still worried about what Nigel had said, that she'd left Zombie with a farang. I remembered what had happened a week or so after I'd met Joy. We'd been sitting together and a big, bearded guy came up to our table. He winked at Joy and gave her two ten by eight inch colour photographs, then left. They were pictures of Joy, smiling at the camera, wearing a black and white striped dress. I'd asked Joy who the man was and she said he was just a friend and that he'd taken photographs of several girls a few days earlier. She'd handed me the photographs and said that she wanted me to have them. I looked at them closely.

They'd obviously been taken in a hotel room. Okay, so maybe he'd invited a group of girls to his room to take their picture, but it seemed way more likely that Joy had been alone with him, and that she'd done what she usually did in hotel rooms. I didn't say anything at the time and I hadn't mentioned it since. I figured that he'd known her before I'd met her, that I had no right to question her on what had happened in her past. But now she was virtually my girlfriend, albeit one who was working as a bargirl. Now I reckoned I did have the right.

She held out her wallet and I took it. The two photographs of the two of us together were there. I closed

the wallet and gave it back to her.

"What you think, Pete? You think I not have your picture?"

"I don't know what to think, Joy. You work in a bar, you see lots of men every night ..."

"I have you only one," she interrupted.

"I know, I know. But I don't like you working in Zombie."

"I not want work in bar, Pete."

"So what do you want?" I asked.

"I don't know." She shrugged. "I want stay with you. I want go everywhere with you."

I couldn't help but smile at her. She seemed so open and vulnerable, I just wanted to wrap my arms around her and protect her.

"But I have to keep travelling to research the book," I said. "And I'm really busy now. You'd be bored with me."

She shook her head fiercely. "No. Never."

I didn't know what to suggest. I didn't want her working in the bar; I was constantly worried about what she might be up to when I wasn't there. But if she gave up work and stayed with me, I knew she'd soon be bored. I had to spend hours each day in front of my computer, I wouldn't be any company for her.

"Pete, I have an idea. Maybe I go stay with my father in Si Saket. Then I come see you when you not busy."

I was surprised. "You'd do that?" I said.

"My father very happy if I stay with him. Mon in Si Saket, too. I can help her take care of Nonglek."

I thought about it. It seemed the perfect plan. She'd be away from the bars, but she'd be able to come and see me whenever my workload wasn't too heavy. But I knew there'd be a price. "How much would you need to live in Si Saket?" I asked.

She looked at me and for a wild moment I felt like a pig being eyed up by a butcher. Then she smiled and the feeling evaporated as quickly as it had arrived. "Thirty thousand baht," she said, and smiled coquettishly.

Bruno had told me that Si Saket was in one of the poorest parts of Thailand. Thirty thousand baht would be a fortune there. "Thirty thousand baht a month?" I repeated. That would be twice as much as a teacher earned. "Come on, I want you to live in Si Saket, not buy it."

Her eyes flicked from side to side, then she looked up hopefully. "Twenty thousand baht?"

I shook my head. "I think ten thousand baht would be better,"

I said.

"Okay," she said. "When?"

"Tonight," I said. "You can stop working tonight, and go to Si Saket in a couple of days."

Joy squealed and threw her arms around my neck. "I love you too much," she said.

JOY

I wasn't surprised when Pete asked me to stop work. I knew he didn't like me working in the bar. But I thought he'd pay me more than ten thousand baht a month. He can afford a lot more. When I worked he paid my barfine maybe twelve or fifteen times a month and gave me money every time he made love to me. That comes to a lot more than ten thousand baht. I didn't complain because if I was in Si Saket I wouldn't have to pay rent, and food and stuff is cheap. And I figured I could always ask him for more later.

He went with me to Zombie and I told the mamasan that I was quitting. All the girls were really jealous. I think every bargirl wants a farang to take care of them, to give them money every month so that they don't have to work. The mamasan wasn't nice about it, though. She said that I'd be back before long, that I was crazy to give up work because farangs always lie. If he really loved you he'd offer to marry you and take you to England, she said.

I told her that Pete lived in England and that England was always cold and wet. So why didn't he want me to live with him in Bangkok, she asked. Because he was busy with his book, I said. And what did Park have to say, she asked. I told her that Park could come back to Si Saket with me. I wanted to get him out of Bangkok anyway. There were too many temptations in Nana Plaza. Too many girls.

BIG RON

See, the big mistake that Pete made was that he thought that Joy was giving up work because she loved him. She spun the same old line, that she loved him so much that she didn't want to dance in Zombie. He sat in the bar and said he was sure she was serious, because he was only giving her ten thousand baht a month and she could earn three or four times that dancing and hooking. And that, right there, is where he made his big mistake, because he was thinking like a farang. Sure, given a choice between earning ten thousand baht or thirty thousand baht, your average farang is going to go for the bigger sum. But bargirls are basically lazy, and the choice he was giving Joy was ten thousand baht for doing nothing or twenty thousand baht for dancing four or five hours a night and screwing customers in short-time hotels for more money. For the average bargirl, doing nothing is the better option.

And Pete was sweetening the pot by letting her go to live in Si Saket. Fuck it, he encouraged her to go. Now the average farmer probably only earns two thousand baht a month, and if there's any factory work going, it probably pays three thousand baht. So Pete was giving her three times the average monthly wage to go and live with her dad and the rest of her family. She wasn't giving up work because she loved him, she was just choosing the easy option.

Finding staff who'll work hard for reasonable money is the bane of my life, I can tell you. Half the girls I hire to work behind my bar don't even bother to turn up. Shit, they get seven thousand baht a month and all they have to do is serve drinks and food. They don't even have to smile at my customers, the guys come here for the food and the booze, not the female company. My girls get a free uniform, one day off a week, and two weeks holiday a year, which is a darn sight more than they get working in Nana Plaza, but a good bartender is rarer than hen's teeth.

I had one girl, pretty little thing, face like a twelve-year-old, long, long hair and a swimsuit model's body. She came in for an interview and spoke excellent English and seemed perfect. She was a bit sketchy about her previous jobs but that probably just meant she'd been living off a farang for a while and was too shy to admit it. Anyway, I arranged for her to come in the following day for a week's trial. She turned up bang on time and I gave her a uniform. She went to lean against the beer fridge and started talking to one of the other girls, Noo, I think it was. Now, we were a bit short on change and there's usually a rush just before twelve so I asked the new girl if she'd go to the bank and get some change. I gave her five thousand baht and told her to come back with twenties and fifties. She smiled, took the money and went back to the fridge and carried on talking to Noo.

Now, I didn't get upset, I just smiled and called her back over and said that I needed the change now, and asked her very pleasantly to go to the bank right away. Fuck me, she throws a fit, she does, calls me all sorts of names, says that she didn't expect to have to work like a dog and with that she flounces out, her nose in the air, and I never see her, or the uniform, again.

PETE

Joy was so cute after I told her that I didn't want her to work any more. She came back to my room with the contents of her locker in a plastic carrier bag. "Now I not Number 81," she said, referring to her badge number. "I tell everybody you not want me work. Everyone say I very lucky, Pete." I asked her when she wanted to go to Si Saket and she said she'd catch the bus the following day. I went with her to the nearest ATM and withdrew ten thousand baht, her first month's 'salary' and gave it to her. She put it in her bag. She stayed with me that night and left early in the morning, saying that she wanted to go to the bus station to buy her ticket.

I offered to go to the bus station with her but she said it was too crowded and hot and that she didn't want me to be uncomfortable. That was so typical of her, always thinking about me. She called me from the bus station and told me that she loved me, and that as soon as I wanted her to come back, I was to call her.

I telephoned Joy every two or three days. I'd tell her in advance when

I was calling, and usually she'd be by the phone, waiting. The phone box was about a kilometre from her house, she said, sometimes she walked, sometimes she drove her motorcycle. If I called at an unplanned time I'd ask whoever answered the phone if he or she knew Joy. If they said no, I was stymied, and I'd have to hang up. If they did know Joy I'd ask them to tell her that I'd called and that I'd call again in thirty minutes. Sometimes it was really frustrating, either the person who answered wouldn't understand my Thai, or they wouldn't pass on the message, but usually the system worked. She was always pleased to hear from me, asking how I was getting on with my book, when she could come and see me.

For the first few weeks I was working flat out on the book, sending each chapter to Alistair in Hong Kong as I finished it. I ran into a major problem almost as soon as Joy went back to Si Saket; the Thai photographer we'd commissioned to take photographs of Phuket turned in the shittiest set of negatives I've ever seen. Something had gone wrong during the developing and there were grains of some chemical all over them. Totally unusable. I had to find another photographer, a farang this time, and tell him what was needed.

It was more than a month before I could tell Joy to come down and see me. She caught the bus and arrived in Bangkok late on Friday night. I took her back to the Dynasty Hotel and we spent the whole weekend together.

On the Saturday night she wanted to go to see her friends in Zombie and we went together. She seemed proud that she wasn't working any more and bought drinks for her friends with money I'd given her. She seemed more relaxed and happier than when she'd been working and I began to think that maybe everything was going to work. I paid bar for three of her friends and we went to a restaurant I hadn't been to before. Joy ordered lots of Thai food including a great pork omelette that was so good that I got her to get the recipe from the chef. She loved to help me with my work and made a big show of writing it down in English in front of her friends.

When I put her on the bus to Si Saket on Monday morning, with another ten thousand baht, she kissed me on the cheek. "I love you,

Pete," she said. "I want come stay with you in Bangkok for ever."

JIMMY

I'm not sure if I'd be able to run a business in Thailand. What I've got suits me just fine, I've got three furniture showrooms around Liverpool and I keep in touch with my managers by phone and fax. Four times a year my accountant comes over and we go over the books together. Works a treat, I tell you. The time difference means I can spend the morning in bed, I have lunch, then hit the phone. Assuming there's no problems, an hour a day pretty much keeps the business ticking over. Then I have dinner, then hit the bars. Wouldn't have a lifestyle anywhere close to that if I had to run a business here.

The big problem is that you get jaded after a while. When you first come to Bangkok, you walk around with your tongue hanging out, you can't believe that all these gorgeous girls are totally available to you for a few quid. You go a bit crazy, everybody does. Hell, in my first six months here I reckon I must have slept with more than two hundred women. Well, I assume they were all women, I was pretty naive back then and I suppose there could have been a few katoeys among them. Anyway, after a few months you start to hanker for something a little different. My mate Simon, he goes for older women, sometimes as old as fifty. Another mate, Nigel, he's in search of the perfect blow job. Hasn't had full sex for more than a year, he says. Reckons the best blow jobs are from katoeys, and I can't argue with him there. No one gives a better blow job than another guy, that's what I always say. Women do their best, but a guy knows what another guy wants.

Recently I started experimenting with couples. Two girls at a time. To be honest, it's not always as good as you'd think. They talk, the girls, they talk in Thai or Khmer or whatever and you can't understand what they're saying. And when it is good, sometimes it's too good. Did you ever see that movie Saint Jack? The one with Ben Gazzara, set in Singapore. He fixes this guy up with two hookers, and when the guy goes upstairs,

Gazzara waits for him with a smirk. He knows that it'll be all over in a couple of minutes. Some of the girls prefer to work in pairs, they know that most guys will shoot their load as soon as the girls start to do their stuff. I mean, you've got one kissing you and playing with your nipples, while the other's pounding up and down on your dick. Wham, bam, thank you ma'am, was it good for you?

I had a right seeing to last week, from two deaf and dumb hookers. There's a few of them in Queen's Castle in Patpong. Geng and Hom. Cute as hell, really small but great bodies both of them. I paid barfine and took them to a short-time hotel. Now, normally when you take two, they insist on the lights being off, I guess because they're shy. So when I get into the room, first thing I do is to turn off the lights while I go into the bathroom to shower. When I come out, they've only turned the lights back on. Then I see why. They're sitting on the bed, signing to each other. That's right, they can't communicate in the dark so the lights have to stay on. Brilliant. And the other thing was, there was no chattering while they did their stuff. Just the occasional grunt. A great time was had by all. Well, I had a great time, anyway.

Extract from
CROSS-CULTURAL COMPLICATIONS
OF PROSTITUTION IN THAILAND
by PROFESSOR BRUNO MAYER

A notable change in attitude occurs in those expatriates who spend a considerable length of time in Thailand and who incur long-term exposure to the bars and the prostitutes who work there. During the initial phase of contact, farangs are attracted to the girls, and during the first few months may attempt to form friendships with them. Many farangs initially take the view that the girls are forced into the life of prostitution and that given the opportunity would prefer to have a regular boyfriend-girlfriend relationship. The girls often give the impression that this is the case, but there is an ambiguity inherent in the nature of the bargirl-customer relationship that the farang often fails to appreciate, namely that to the Thai bargirl, love and money are not separate aims. The girl believes that money is an expression of love, and that love is an emotion bestowed towards those who offer support, support being more often than not, financial. The girl sees nothing incongruous about linking money and love, but the farang, observing the relationship from a Western perspective, believes that the two are mutually exclusive. One is loved for one's money, or for one's self.

Newcomers to the bar scene tend to the belief that girls will in fact love them for themselves, and therefore try whenever they can to restrict the amount of money they give to the girl. No matter how much the girl is attracted to the man she will resent the reduction in financial support, seeing it as a lack of commitment. The girl might not express her disappointment verbally, but her actions will lead the man to realise that she is unhappy. He in turn will believe that she loves him only for his money, in which case he will try to test her by further reducing the amount of money he gives her. Such relationships always fall apart. After the farang has been through the cycle several times, he will begin to distrust all bargirls, labelling them as prostitutes who care only about money. They are unable to accept that the girls see nothing wrong in liking, or even loving, a man for himself and for his financial support, that to the girl such things are inextricably linked. The farang will stop searching out girls with whom he thinks he can build a loving relationship in keeping with his Western ideal, but instead makes do with individual sexual encounters, one-night stands if you like, with the sex paid for and no emotional attachment sought. Such farangs begin to see all women in Thailand as prostitutes, and eventually become resentful and scornful of Thais generally. Once they reach this stage, many farangs decide to leave the country, never to return.

BRUCE

Jimmy's a character all right. I don't think there's a drug he hasn't taken or a sexual perversion he hasn't tried. He staggers into Fatso's Bar, disappears upstairs to the toilet then comes down a few minutes later rubbing his nose with pupils as big as saucers. I'm not sure how well his business is doing back in the UK, but he sleeps most of the day and he's in the bars all night so I don't see that he can be getting much work done. You know what he used to do when he was a teenager to make money? He used to eat shit. I kid you not. He'd let it be known that on such and such a day at such and such a time he'd eat a turd. People used to come from miles around pay fifty pence a head to watch. And he'd do it, too. There was no faking, he'd really eat shit. He set up his first business, renovating old desks, when he was fifteen and he used his shit-eating money to do it. He cracks on he's worth well over a million now and he's only thirty five, but he's been out here for more than ten years and I can't see how he's managing to build a business the way he behaves.

He turns into an animal when we get to the Plaza. And he's got a thing about katoeys. I reckon he might be a closet gay but he's scared to admit it. I mean, when all's said and done, katoeys are men. They might be transsexuals, they might have their dicks cut off, but they're still men. And it's not regular sex he has most of the time, it's oral and anal and that smacks of homosexuality to me. How do I know? Because Jimmy boasts about it all the time, that's why. It's like he's proud of it.

Rick and Matt are going the same way. There probably isn't a girl in the Plaza that Rick hasn't been with, and now he's working his way through the katoeys. Jimmy and Rick kept telling Matt how great it was in bed with katoeys and eventually he tried one from Zombie. Now I think he's on the turn, too.

I try to steer clear of the three of them in the Plaza. They're okay in Fatso's, but I find them a bit sad when they're in the Plaza. Jimmy's too stoned to talk and Rick's chat-up technique is to stick out his tongue and lick the tip of his nose. Matt is okay, but he tries too hard to impress the other two.

I actually started getting fed up with the bars after I'd been here for six months or so. After a while they all start to look the same. And most of them play the same music. It's not unusual to walk out of one bar with a song playing and to walk into another bar to hear the identical tune.

I don't know how Jimmy and Rick and the rest can keep going night after night. The girls, too, start to look the same. Not because they've all got black hair and brown eyes, that's not what I mean, it's more their attitude. "You very handsome. Where you from? Where you stay? Buy me drink? Pay bar?" Every man is a potential customer, and once they've worked out that you're not interested, they move on.

Most of the time I don't go into the bars these days, I sit outside. It's more civilised, and there's less pressure. I sit and drink a coffee or two before heading home, it's a great way to unwind. Some of the girls have become friends, too, because they know I work in Bangkok, they know I'm not the same as the tourists and losers who just come here for cheap sex.

My favourite bar is Spicy-a-go-go. They've got a big outdoor bar with two televisions where they show all the English football matches. It's a great spot to sit, you can see everyone who comes into the Plaza and there's a hamburger stand close by if you fancy a snack. I know the owner and if he's not too busy he'll often sit down for a beer and a chat.

That's where I met Troy. Troy isn't the usual type of bargirl, she never hustles drinks, not from me, anyway, and I don't think I've ever seen anyone pay her barfine. She's pretty, just over five feet tall with shoulder length hair and eyes that always seem to be laughing. Perfect teeth. Almost all the girls you see in the bars have perfect teeth. They never seem to go to the dentist either. It must be the diet. No processed sugar or the fact that they eat lots of fruit.

Anyway, Troy used to come and sit outside whenever she wasn't dancing. She'd just sit and watch what was going on, maybe chat to another of the girls. She never approached customers, and the first time I asked her if she wanted a drink she just shook her head. It wasn't as if she was playing hard to get or anything, she just wasn't interested.

She told me later that she could live off what she earned as a dancer, and she was happy with that. She didn't dance naked, or even topless. The way she explained it to me, if she worked in a local restaurant, she could earn two thousand baht a month, maybe two and a half thousand. If she could get a job in a department store, she might get three thousand baht a month, but for that she'd need a school leaving certificate, and she didn't have one of those because she'd had to stay at home and take care of her younger brother when she was eleven. But if she danced in Spicy-a-go-go, she could earn four thousand baht a month, plus commission on drinks. Even without hustling drinks, that would give her an extra couple of thousand baht a month. Troy said she could live quite easily on six thousand baht a month, and still have money to send back to her family.

It made economic sense to me, and I respected her decision to work in the bars but not to prostitute herself. She told me that she didn't approve of what went on in the bars, but that she had no choice. She was nineteen years old with a limited education, what other choice did she have? I felt so sorry for her.

The first time I met Troy I tipped her five hundred and she couldn't believe it. She tried to refuse, but I made her take it. I told her I wanted to help her. The next night I paid her barfine and took her to dinner. She didn't even know how to use the cutlery, kept watching me to see which spoon or fork I used, and then copying. I took her to a German restaurant in Soi 4 and she let me order for her. I only realised later it was because she couldn't read the menu.

The third night I paid her barfine and took her back to my house. We talked all night and she slept in my bed. We didn't make love, we didn't even undress, she just lay curled up next to me, her arms around me as if she didn't want to let me go. When I woke up the next day she'd cleaned the house from top to bottom and had cooked me breakfast, a sort of noodle soup with chicken. She stayed with me the whole day. She wouldn't let me pay her, either, she kept saying that she was happy just being with me. Eventually I managed to persuade her to take a thousand baht.

PETE

I'd arranged to see Joy in Zombie one Saturday evening.

I'd been in Pattaya updating our hotel listing and collecting menus from new restaurants and I'd called her to say that I'd be back in Bangkok over the weekend and asked her to get the bus down.

I got to the bar just before ten o'clock and it was rocking. There were several dozen girls dancing on the two stages, most of them naked, and it seemed that every farang in the place had a girl on his arm. Or thigh. There was a whiteboard on the wall close to the girls' changing room which listed the numbers of the girls and which dancing shift they had been assigned to, and there was another column that listed the girls who had been barfined. There were more than thirty names. A typical Saturday, in another couple of hours only the oldest and ugliest girls would be left.

Joy came running up within seconds. "Pete, Mon die," she said.

I didn't understand. Die has several meanings in Thai. "What do you mean?"

"Mon die lau. She die, Pete." Die lau. Dead.

I was stunned. Mon was living in Si Saket, in the family's house. I'd seen her when I went to visit with Bruno and Pam and she looked fine. And Joy was smiling broadly, as if she was telling a joke.

"Ubat het?" I said. Accident?

Joy shook her head. "No. Mon kill Mon."

"When?"

"Last night."

She was still smiling. It was a happy, open smile, or at least that's what it seemed. It was unreal, what she was saying appeared to have no connection with the expression on her face. I kept expecting her to start laughing and for her to tell me that she was playing some sort of joke on me. "Mon kill Mon? Khar tua tai?" Suicide?

Joy nodded. "Yes. Mon khar tua tai."

"How, Joy?"

She mimed a rope around her neck and mimed pulling it up.

"She hanged herself?"

"Yes."

The smile was typical Thailand. She was doing it to put me at my ease, to soften the impact the bad news would have. I understood, but it was still disconcerting. Sunan came up and she was grinning, too. I told her how sorry I was and she shrugged as if what happened wasn't important. I'd always liked Mon. She always seemed more honest and open than Joy and Sunan. I mean, I loved Joy, I really did, but I'm not sure that I trusted her. Not one hundred per cent. But I always felt that Mon was telling me the truth. Maybe that was because I didn't know her as well as Joy, so there was less for her to lie about. That's part of the problem with Thailand, after a while you begin to think that everyone is lying to you.

I took Joy out for dinner and as we ate she told me what had happened. She said that Mon had been arguing with her husband and that she'd got upset and hanged herself in Joy's bedroom. Joy had found her hanging there and had cut her down and tried to give her the kiss of life. "I try very hard, Pete, but she dead already. I cry a lot."

It still hadn't sunk in. I remembered how Mon had smiled as she'd danced, as if it were the most natural thing in the world to be showing off her body to dozens of strangers. She had a good body, too, softer and rounder than Joy's, a woman's body rather than a girl's. She was always so alive, so full of fun, I couldn't believe that she'd taken her own life. And what about her daughter, Nonglek? She'd doted on the little girl. Surely no mother with a young child would kill herself.

"What about Nonglek?" I asked. I knew that Joy loved the little girl, too. She'd often brought her along when she saw me during the day. We'd go shopping with her or go to eat ice cream. I loved watching Joy take care of Nonglek, I could see that she'd make a great mother herself.

"Father take her to his village," she said. "He say he not want her stay with my family."

I could hardly eat, and what did pass my lips had no taste. I ordered another gin and tonic, my sixth since we'd sat down in the restaurant.

"Joy, you told me that Mon's husband had gone. You said they didn't live together."

She nodded. "I know. He come back to talk with her."

"And because of that she killed herself?"

"Yes. I think so."

"Are you sure it wasn't something else?"

She shrugged. "I don't know."

I put my head in my hands. It didn't make sense. It didn't make any sort of sense at all. This was a girl who'd worked in a go-go bar, danced naked in front of strangers, slept with men for money. She'd been married, had a child, separated. How could an argument, no matter what was said, make her kill herself?

Joy put her hand on my arm. "I miss Mon," she said.

"I miss her too," I said. And I did.

Joy smiled.

After we'd eaten, Joy came back to the hotel with me. She stayed for two days and then went back to Si Saket. I had to fly down to Phuket and wouldn't be back in Bangkok for a week. Joy wanted to go with me but it wasn't on because head office was always really tight on expenses and there'd be hell to pay if they discovered that I'd taken a girl with me. Especially a bargirl, albeit one who'd given up work.

After she'd gone, I thought a lot about Mon. I couldn't understand why she'd kill herself. There had to be something more to it than just an argument with her ex-husband.

Extract from
CROSS-CULTURAL COMPLICATIONS
OF PROSTITUTION IN THAILAND
by PROFESSOR BRUNO MAYER

The first case of Acquired Immune Deficiency Syndrome in Thailand was reported in 1984. As was the case in the Western world, the disease was initially prevalent only within homosexual and drug-talking populations of the country, but by the late 1980s heterosexual sex became the main method of transmission. Estimates of the total number of HIV-infections vary between three hundred thousand and one million, but as testing has only been carried out on a limited basis, no accurate figures are available. There are also difficulties in assessing the number of deaths caused by Aids due to the reluctance of the Thais to admit the existence of the disease. Cause of death is more often than not listed as pneumonia, cancer or opportunistic infection rather than the virus. Indeed, many sufferers refuse to acknowledge that they have Aids because of the stigma which is attached to the disease.

Realising that the large number of prostitutes working in the country could facilitate transmission to the local population, the Thai authorities instituted a programme of education during the early 1990s in an attempt to teach sex workers that it was in their best interests to use condoms. Free condoms were provided to sex workers and they were encouraged to use them at all times, even with their regular boyfriends.

Many bars and massage parlours have instituted HIV testing of their girls in addition to their regular checks for sexually transmitted diseases. Some bars will not allow girls to work unless they have a medically-certified clean bill of health, but generally the checks are voluntary and paid for by the girls themselves. As a general rule the girls are checked for STDs once a month, and for Aids every three months. There is no central collection point for statistics resulting from these tests, but anecdotal evidence suggests that the incidence of HIV infection has been rising rapidly. The bars and massage parlours are reluctant to talk about the number of HIV positive prostitutes, but it is considered to be between one per cent and twelve per cent of the girls employed as sex workers.

If a girl is known to have acquired the virus, she is dismissed, but of course there is nothing to stop the girl going to work in a bar which does not insist on its girls being tested. Generally speaking, those bars which service the tourist and expatriate community are more likely to insist on Aids testing than those which are frequented by locals. It is thought that this is partly responsible for the rapid spread of the virus through the Thai population as a whole. Statistics suggest that up to ten per cent of Army recruits are now HIV positive and two per cent of women giving birth in Bangkok's hospitals have the virus.

Because of the stigma which is attached to the disease in Thailand, those girls who develop symptoms rarely seek medical help. Instead, they choose suicide. There has been a sharp rise in the incidence of suicide among bargirls over the past five years. Suicide is common among the girls in any case because of the psychologically damaging nature of their

work and the tendency for the girls to be addicted to drugs or alcohol,
but it is believed that Aids has now become a leading cause of suicides
in Thailand.

JIMMY

Aids? It's an attitude of mind. I've been here for years and I've never
heard of a bargirl getting it. Not from sex, anyway. They test all the
girls in the bars and any that are HIV positive are kicked out. It doesn't
happen very often, and when it does it's because the girl was injecting
drugs. All you have to do is check for needle tracks and you're safe. The
idea that you can get it from sex is one of the big con jobs of the age, it's
a scare story spread by religious nuts and women who want to scare their
men into being faithful. Look, if Aids really was a problem it would have
gone through the bars like wildfire. And it hasn't. End of story.

I've never heard of a farang getting it, either. I've been screwing
without a condom here for more than ten years and I've got nothing
worse than a dose of clap. Okay, I got gonorrhoea of the throat once, but
that was my own fault. But Aids, no. I took out a life insurance policy
a couple of years ago and I had to have a blood test for that and I was
clear. No problemo.

The guys in Fatso's talk about Aids a lot, and we're all in agreement.
Poofters get it, and intravenous drug users. And there's a good chance
that a baby born to an HIV-positive mother will get it. But a good old
bonk is as safe as it's ever been. Am I sure? Hell, I'm positive.

PETE

Joy said she wanted to go home for a few days to see her father. He was
becoming a monk, she said, and she said he wanted to divide up his
belongings. I didn't quite understand what she meant. It was something

like a will: he was giving his land and the house to his children, almost as if he'd died. "Pete, I think he give house to me," she said earnestly. "Everybody in my family very angry. I not oldest, but Father love me a lot."

I tried to get her to explain why her father was becoming a monk, but she just shrugged and said that was what he wanted to do. It didn't make any sense to me. Monks didn't work, and Joy was always telling me how poor her family were. She was equally at a loss to explain why he was giving away all his worldly goods. He was only about fifty-five years old.

Joy didn't seem interested in talking about it, all she wanted to do was to celebrate her good fortune. We went to Zombie and she kept buying drinks for her friends. Well, she ordered the drinks and the chit went into the beaker in front of me, so it was actually me was who was paying.

Joy seemed to take pride from the fact that she didn't have to work any more. Girls would come up and pay their respects and every now and then she pat me on the arm and say "five minutes" and rush off to speak to someone. She was working the room, making sure that everybody knew she was there and that she wasn't working. Now she was a customer, spending money rather than earning it.

Whenever she came back she'd put her hand on my thigh and kiss me on the cheek, marking out her territory, I guess. And whenever another girl sat too close to me or started flirting, she'd speak sharply to her in Khmer. I was flattered by the fact that she appeared to be jealous, and I tried to tell her that there was no need, I only wanted to be with her.

We stayed until the bar closed and then we walked around to the Dynasty Hotel. We made love, but her heart didn't seem to be in it, and later, when she lay in my arms, she began to cough. I got her a drink of water but it didn't seem to help. "I sorry, Pete, I sick," she said.

She rolled away from me and curled up into a tight ball. I put my arms around her again and held her. She kept coughing. I asked her if she wanted some tablets, I had some left over from the last time I had 'flu, but she said no, she had her own medicine in Sunan's room. I told her that I didn't want her to go, that I wanted her to stay the whole night and she said okay, she'd stay. The coughing continued, and you want to know the weirdest thing? I think she was faking it. It didn't sound like a genuine cough, you know? And all evening, when she'd been drinking and smoking and talking with her friends, there hadn't been a single cough.

As I lay next to her, I couldn't get the thought out of my head that she was pretending to be sick so that she didn't have to stay with me. But that didn't make any sense. If she didn't want to be with me, why come and see me in the first place? If there was somewhere else she wanted to go, all she had to do was to say so and I'd go with her. It couldn't be that she wanted to sleep in Sunan's room, because she said it was a slum, and my room in the Dynasty costs a thousand baht a night.

I turned and looked at her. Her thick black hair tumbled over the pillow and she'd pulled the sheets up around her neck. Her body shook as she coughed again and I stroked her shoulder through the sheet.

"I sorry," she said.

"That's okay." I cuddled up to her and tried to sleep. It was impossible. Every two minutes or so she'd cough. Then she started tossing and turning. I tried to ignore it, but her coughs just got louder and louder. Eventually she sat up.

"Pete, I want go Sunan's room," she said. "I think I sick."

I offered to take her home, but she shook her head. "No, I want you to sleep." She slipped off the bed and wrapped a towel around herself. "I phone you tomorrow, okay?"

I watched as she pulled her knickers on under the towel. She turned her back on me and put her bra on over the top of the towel. It always made me the smile the way she became suddenly shy when she got dressed. Being naked never seemed to worry her when we were in bed or making love, but afterwards, of after she'd showered, she insisted on covering up as much as possible. Once she'd fastened the bra she pulled the towel down, turning so that her back was to me. She put on her jeans and shirt before facing me again.

I got out of bed. "I'll go back with you," I said.

Joy shook her head. "No. You sleep. I want go alone."

I didn't know what to say. Did she mean that she wanted to go alone because there was something there she didn't want me to see. Someone? Or was she being considerate? I couldn't tell, I really couldn't tell, and that's what worried me. If she loved me, why didn't I trust her? And if she didn't love me, why couldn't I tell if she was lying or not?

She walked over and put her arms around me, then rested her head against my shoulder. I stroked the back of her head. "Why can't I come with you, Joy?" I asked.

She coughed. "Sunan's room very small, Pete. Have many people sleep there. Sunan. Apple. Bird. My cousins. Friends of Sunan."

"Who's Bird?"

"Brother."

"Same mother, same father?"

Joy nodded. Thais have a tendency to be vague about family relationships. Any close male relative was a brother, and even a second cousin could be referred to as a sister. Bird wasn't a name that she'd mentioned before.

"Sunan's room very small and sok-ka-prok," she said. Sok-ka-prok. Dirty.

"But I want to see where you stay," I said.

She shook her head determinedly. "When I have nice room, you can come stay with me," she said. "You can stay with me all the time." She hugged me, tightly. "I go now, okay?"

"Okay," I said. It was pointless arguing with her. She kissed me on the cheek and I opened he door for her.

"I see you tomorrow, okay?"

"Okay."

She coughed again and waved as she waited for the lift to arrive.

The next day I got a phone call from Alistair that knocked me for six. The guy who was doing the editing of the London edition had left the company. Apparently he'd been offered a big jump in salary by some American operation and he was only giving Alistair a month's notice. The fact that he had more than double that in holidays owing meant that he left immediately, and that had given the company a major headache. The edition had to be with the printers within the next eight weeks and the guy hadn't exactly been working overtime, and Alistair wanted me to fill the hole. I argued with him for almost half an hour but there was no shifting him. He wanted me to go, and the company wanted me to go. The only one who didn't want to go was me and nobody seemed to be taking any account of how I felt.

Mind you, after I'd hung up the phone and thought about it, it did make sense. I still had my flat in London, and I knew the city probably better than anyone else in the company. It would have been difficult to throw someone else in at the deep end, so I guess Alistair was doing the right thing. I'd done the first London edition about five years previously, so most of the work would involve updating my own copy. I doubted that it'd take a full two months, though I didn't tell Alistair that.

I'd arranged to see Joy in Zombie at nine and when I got there she was drinking Heineken with Sunan, Apple and Wan. I told Joy I needed to talk to her and we went to a German restaurant down the road from Nana Plaza. She sat and listened as I explained that I had to go back to England to work on the guide book.

She reached out and held my hands. "You not come back?"

"Of course I'll be back," I said. "Two months, that's all. Maybe not as long as that."

"I want come with you," she said.

"Impossible," I said. I would have loved to have taken her with me, but it would have taken months to arrange. The embassies don't make it easy for Thai girls to get visas. They have to have a sponsor, they have to show that they are gainfully employed and have money in the bank, and that they have family. Basically, they have to prove that they'll be coming back to Thailand. It would take three or four months, and Alistair wanted me in London by the end of the week. Even if I applied for a visa that day, I'd be back in Bangkok before her application was even considered, never mind approved. According to Big Ron there were people who could arrange it, for a "fee" of twenty thousand baht or thereabouts, but even that would take several weeks.

"I'll telephone you every day," I promised. "And I'll write to you."

"And I write to you every day," she said. She held my hands tightly. "Pete, I not want you go."

"And I don't want to go, but I have to. It's work."

Her lower lip trembled. "I think you forget me."

"Never," I said. "I'll never forget you, Joy."

"When you go?"

"Two days."

Tears welled up in her eyes. "I think you not love me any more."

I moved around the table so that I could sit next to her and hold her hands. I told her that she was the only one that I loved and that there was nothing for her to worry about.

"What you want me do, Pete?"

I said that I wanted her to go back to Si Saket and stay with her father until I returned to Bangkok.

"Okay, I do for you," she said. "I get bus tomorrow."

I kissed her on the cheek. "Don't worry," I said.

"What I do for money?" she asked.

I told her I'd give her ten thousand baht before I went

and I'd send her another ten thousand baht in a month.

"I have good idea," she said. "You can give me two months money now. Then maybe I can do business in Si Saket."

"Business?"

"Maybe buy something. Then sell."

"Like what?"

She shrugged. "Shampoo. Clothes. I can buy Bangkok and sell Si Saket. Make profit."

I thought about it for a while, then shook my head. "I know you, Joy. If I give you two months money today, you'll spend it all tomorrow. Then you'll have no money. Better I send it to you when I get to London."

For a moment I thought she was going to be angry at me, but then her face broke into a grin. She began to laugh.

"What?" I asked.

She gripped my arm with both hands and rocked backwards and forwards as she laughed. "Pete, you know me too well," she said. "You know what I do."

"Yeah, I know. When you have, you spend. If you have ten baht, you spend ten baht. If you have a thousand baht, you spend that."

She laughed even louder and people at other tables turned around to look at her. She put her hands over her mouth and tried to stifle her giggles.

"What time do you want to go tomorrow?" I asked.

"Have many buses to Si Saket. Ten o'clock. Midnight."

"Which one do you want to get?"

"Midnight VIP bus, I think."

"Okay. We'll come here tomorrow and have dinner, and I'll give you ten thousand baht."

"Thank you, Pete," she said, and brushed my neck with her lips. "Thank you for everything you give me."

We went back to my room at the Dynasty Hotel and this time there was no coughing fit after we'd made love. She'd stayed the whole night, her arms wrapped around me as if she was scared that I'd be the one to disappear.

ALISTAIR

I wasn't being completely honest with Pete when I told him that he was the only one who could sort out the problems we were having with the London edition. There were plenty of guys we could have sent in, but I recommended Pete because I thought it would do him good to get out of Thailand for a while. I'm not saying he was going the same way as Lawrence, but I just had the feeling that the place was starting to get to him. He was meeting all his deadlines, just about, but his work didn't have the same flair. His prose was flat, it was as if he was going through the motions and when I spoke to him about it he got all defensive. I figured a few months back in England would do him the world of good.

He kept talking about his girlfriend, Joy. Joy did this, Joy did that, and he didn't seem to be ashamed of the fact that she was a dancer in a go-go bar. I can't imagine anyone in Hong Kong admitting that their girlfriend was a dancer. They'd be too embarrassed. Pete kept saying that she didn't go with customers anymore, but even so. I mean, she was a hooker, effectively, and he was talking about her as if she were the girl he was going to marry.

Anyway, I recommended to head office that we send Pete to plug the hole in London. Didn't tell them why, of course, just said he was a hard worker and pointed that as he still had his old flat in London we'd save money on hotel bills. All we'd have to do is pay him a per diem allowance, we'd save money and Pete'd make a few quid to boot. Everyone's happy, and hopefully by the time he gets back to Bangkok he'll be over Joy and back to his old self. We'll see.

PETE

Joy left my room just before midday. I packed my suitcase and arranged for the hotel to put the rest of my things in storage. Joy phoned me about an hour after she left. "I want tell you I love you," she said. "Not forget me, Pete. Please not forget me."

I told her not to be silly and that I'd see her in the German restaurant that evening.

"Not forget my money," she said.

"I won't forget you, and I won't forget your money," I promised.

"I love you too much," she said.

I went around to Fatso's Bar for lunch. Big Ron does a great roast chicken dinner, stuffing, roast potatoes, thick, lumpy gravy, just like Mum used to make. He was an accountant, Big Ron, number two in one of the biggest foreign banks in South Africa, but somewhere along the line he learned to cook and he's forever popping into the kitchen. Quality control, he calls it, but I reckon most of the quality control takes place in the bar. He eats at least five full meals a day. Fish and chips. Gammon steak, fried egg and chips. Liver, bacon and onions. Now he's so big, taxi drivers won't take him because they think he'll damage their suspension. Charng, they call him down Nana Plaza. Elephant. Actually, what they say is 'Ay Charng', which means 'fucking elephant'.

I told him that Joy was going back to Si Saket while I was in London and he bellowed with laughter.

"Check the fucking postmarks," he said.

"What do you mean?"

"Standard con," he said. "Page one of the hooker's handbook." He pushed away the remnants of his apple pie and ice cream and belched. One of the girls whipped the plate away. "You find a farang gullible enough to pay you to stop work. You tell him you're going to stay with your family, help them plant rice, pick pineapples, get boy scouts out of the buffalo's hooves, whatever. Farang goes home, satisfied that his girl is doing the decent thing. Hooker fucks off to Pattaya or Phuket, anywhere where she's not going to bump into gullible farang should he arrive back unexpectedly."

"No," I said. "Not Joy. Joy's different."

"Bullshit."

"I'm only giving her ten thousand baht a month," I said. "She could earn five times that in Zombie."

"You're forgetting one thing, Pete. Bargirls are basically fucking lazy."

"So what did you mean by check the postmarks?"

He belched again and put his hands on his massive stomach like a pregnant woman checking that all was as it should be within. "To keep the gullible farang happy, you write to him, right? But the girls aren't stupid, so if they have jumped ship to Phuket or wherever, they send their letters back to the village and get someone there to forward them to gullible farang. Farang checks the postmark and is satisfied that his girl is doing the decent thing. He writes back to her at the village, and her mate sends the letter down to Phuket."

My roast chicken dinner arrived and I started eating. "I phone her, too," I said.

"She's got a phone up country?"

"Communal phone. A phone box at the roadside. I call up and whoever answers goes and fetches her. Her house is about ten minutes away."

"Call forwarding," said Big Ron. "New technology."

I told him to fuck off. Joy wasn't lying to me, she wanted to stay with her father, and she didn't want to work in Nana Plaza.

"Whatever you say, Pete," he said.

Jimmy came down the stairs, rubbing his nose. His eyes were bloodshot and running as if he were getting over a cold. He groaned as he saw the three glasses of Tequila and orange lined up in front of his stool. "Which of you bastards did that?" he yelled.

Alan was sniggering into his lager.

"Don't you Big Glass me, you lanky streak of piss," said Jimmy. He picked up one of his drinks and drained it in one gulp. "I'm on a mission tonight. I'm going to barfine the geezer at Zombie."

The geezer was a striking katoey who had started working in Zombie two weeks earlier. Matt and Rick had both barfined her and swore blind that she was the best they'd ever had.

When I'd finished eating I paid my bill and walked down the road to a Bangkok Bank cash machine where I withdrew ten thousand baht for Joy. One month's salary. I went into a newsagents nearby to buy an envelope to put the money in, and while I was there I saw a rack of stamped airmail envelopes. I bought seven, figuring that if I gave them to Joy she'd be sure to write to me once a week.

I went back to the hotel and wrote my London address of each of them. Joy knew my address but I wasn't sure how good her handwriting would be.

JIMMY

As soon as Pete had left Fatso's, Big Ron started taking the piss out of him. He's merciless, is Big Ron. No one's safe. Mind you, he had a point with Pete. Pete's been in Bangkok long enough to know how these girls work. They don't start working in the bars because they want to meet the man of their dreams, they do it because they want to earn money. That's all farangs are to them, a source of income. It's like Big Ron says, we're like money machines to them, ATMs. Joy's pressing Pete's buttons and he keeps paying out. He's asking to get ripped off. There's only one way to find out if a bargirl likes you, I mean really likes you, and that's to stop giving them any money. You'll find out soon enough what their real feelings are. They're gone like the fucking wind. But there's no mystery with Joy. She's even sold the gold he gives her. That there should show him what she thinks about him. He reckons he's giving her jewellery, she sees it as money.

I stopped trying to have a relationship with the girls long ago. It always ends in tears. Now I just pay 'em and screw 'em, simple as that. They're happy, I'm happy, no one gets hurt, and that's how it should be. It doesn't mean you can't have fun with them, you can. I'm not like Big Ron, there's an anger when he does it. I think he doesn't even like the girls he screws. Receptacles for jism, he calls them, and he usually does 'em two at a time. Nothing wrong with it, but it's the way he badmouths them that I don't like. I mean, I came in this morning and he was fuming. I asked him what was wrong.

"Got a right fucking pervert last night," he scowled. "Wouldn't even let me come over her face."

See, there's an anger in him, you can see it in his face when he talks about them. I reckon a bargirl shafted him badly some time in the past, and now he hates them all. That happens a lot with guys who try to get close to the girls they barfine. They try to treat them like regular girlfriends, and they get all resentful and bitter when they get burned. Better to not even try to get involved, that's what I say.

See, that's one of the reasons I prefer katoeys. I know the guys take the piss out of me, but you know where you are with a katoey: it's a straight forward financial transaction, no emotional involvement, none of that stupid flirting, "I love you no shit", all that sort of crap. They know they're guys with their dicks cut off, I know they're guys with their dicks cut off, all I want is to come and boy, do they know how to do that. They're experts. It's like I always say, no one knows what a guy wants more than another guy. That's not to say I'm gay, because I'm not, I reckon homosexuals are sad fucks who need therapy or medication to put them back on the right track.

Katoeys don't look like guys, they look like goddesses. There's this bar in Patpong, King's Castle I think it's called, where half the dancers are katoeys. It's a great bar, one of the busiest on the strip. Now, the thing about King's Castle, is that all the katoeys are absolute stunners and they dance at the front. The girls, the real girls, are as ugly as dogs, and they dance at the back. Most of the punters don't even know that they're katoeys, they just think that the pretty girls are at the front and the dogs are at the back. Most of the guys who barfine the katoeys don't even know they're going with men. They go back home to Germany or Denmark or wherever they're from thinking they had a night of great sex with a pretty Oriental girl. Little do they know they were with a man and that they came inside a cylinder of flesh carved from a dick and sneakily lubricated with a spot of KY Jelly. Unless you really know what to look for, you'd never know. They've got tits, great legs, superb arses, and they make love the way women do in blue movies. Lots of enthusiasm, lots of noise. Your average Thai hooker does it with her head turned to the side or with her eyes closed, but katoeys do it like they love it. Okay, I know it's an act, but at least they take the trouble to fake it.

But afterwards, there's none of the lies that the bargirls tell. None of that crap about sick fathers or young sisters who need money for school or dead water buffaloes. You pay them and they leave. Strictly business. And that's the way it should be. They give you sex, you pay for it, end of story. Katoeys never phone you up to sweet talk you, or curl up next to you and tell you that they love you, only you. Katoeys don't bother with the lies, the games, the crap. You're better off with them. Trust me.

PETE

I got to the restaurant just before seven o'clock but she didn't turn up until half past. She rushed into the restaurant as if she were scared that I wouldn't be there. She gave me a big hug and kissed me on the cheek. "I sorry, theerak," she said. Theerak. Darling. I hated the word. It was what the bargirls called their customers and whenever Joy said it I'd flinch.

"What happened?" I asked.

"Have traffic too much," she said, sitting down opposite me and putting her red leather wallet on the tablecloth between us as if daring me to open it and check that my photograph was there.

I looked at my watch. "What time's your bus?" I asked.

"Midnight. I tell you before."

"Do you want to eat?"

She shrugged. "Up to you."

I ordered a few Thai dishes. I wasn't particularly hungry. I wasn't looking forward to going back to England and leaving Joy alone. I had a sudden urge to take her back with me, even though I knew it was impossible. She didn't have a passport, never mind a visa.

"What you think, Pete?" she asked.

I told her.

"I want come with you, too," she said. "I not want stay alone."

"You won't be alone," I said. "Your father's there. Your brothers."

"I not like stay my house," she said. "Mon die in my room. I scared phee too much." Phee. Ghost.

"You are going to stay in Si Saket, aren't you?"

"You want?"

"You know that's what I want."

"Okay. I can do for you."

I took the envelopes out of my pocket and slid them across the table. She inspected them one by one, then grinned.

"You think I not write to you?"

I smiled back. "No, I know you'll write. I just wanted to make it easier for you." I gave her another envelope, this one with her name on it. "Your salary," I said.

She put the envelope under her wallet without opening it.

The food arrived. Neither of us ate much. I couldn't taste anything. I wanted to tell Joy so much, that I was going to miss her, that I hoped she'd be good while I was away, but I knew that there was nothing I could say that would make me feel any better about going. And no matter what she said to me, I was always going to have my doubts. Big Ron's words kept echoing in my mind. Standard con. Was Joy different? As I watched her eat, pecking delicately at her food as if she too didn't have any appetite, I wanted to believe that she wasn't the same as the thousands of other bargirls who worked the red light areas. Time and time again I'd heard the boys in Fatso's talk about the stupid farangs who'd been ripped off, farangs who should have known better. Had I joined the legion of sad fucks, too? God, I hoped not. But the fact that Joy had given up work for me surely meant something. And when I asked her to go back to Si Saket and wait for me, she'd readily agreed. Everything I asked her to do, she did. So what was I worried about? I'm just not sure, but there was a nagging doubt at the back of my mind, a feeling that something was wrong.

"Joy?"

She looked up from her food and smiled sweetly. "A-rai?" What?

"Do you love me?"

"What you think?"

"I don't know."

"Why you not know?"

I shrugged. I wasn't sure what to say. Voicing my doubts might upset her, and I didn't want to do that only hours before I had to say goodbye to her for two months.

"Pete, I have you only one. If I not have you, I die."

I smiled and reached over to stroke her hand, the one she was holding her fork with. "You don't have a Thai boyfriend?"

Her smile froze. I'd offended her. I stroked her hand again but she pulled it away. "Why you ask?"

I sighed. "Because many of my friends say that the girls who work in the bars always have Thai boyfriends or husbands."

"I not same girls who work bar," she said.

"I know," I said.

She looked me straight in the eye as if daring me to argue. "If I not love you, I work Zombie, Pete. I not go Si Saket. I have nothing in Si Saket, but I go for you. I wait you come back Thailand."

"I know," I repeated. I wished I'd never started this conversation.

"I want you believe me, Pete."

"I do." And I did.

When we'd finished eating I paid the bill and we went outside. She flagged down a taxi and kissed me softly on the cheek. "I love you," she said. She turned and opened the door. She opened her mouth to say goodbye, but on impulse I put my hand on the door handle.

"I'm coming with you," I said.

She frowned, but before she could argue I put my hand on her hip and guided her on to the back seat and slipped in besides her.

"We go Dynasty?" she said.

I shook my head. "I'll go to the bus station with you," I said.

"Better I go alone."

"Why?"

"Bus station very busy," she said.

The taxi driver asked her where she wanted to go and she told him brusquely in Thai to wait.

"I go with you to Dynasty," she said.

"No, I want to say goodbye to you at the bus station."

Her lips went all tight and for a moment there was an icy hardness to her eyes. A horrible coldness gripped my insides.

"Where are you staying?" I asked her.

"With Sunan," she said.

"Okay, let's go to Sunan's house and get your things."

"Things?"

"Your bag. Your clothes."

"Not have."

That didn't make any sense at all. Joy was staying in Si Saket most of the time, but she had been in Bangkok for several days and I'd seen her in several different outfits. There was no way she'd come down with no clothes. If nothing else she had her make up and her hair shampoo.

I looked her, the tight feeling in my stomach getting worse by the second. She was lying, I was sure of that, but why? What was there to lie about? Why didn't she want me to see Sunan's room?

"What's wrong, Joy?" I asked her.

"I not want you go Sunan's room."

"Why?"

"I shy. Ben sa-lam." It's a slum.

I took both her hands in mine. I told her that I didn't care where Sunan lived, I didn't care how bad it was, she was all I cared about. I just wanted to spend as much time with her as possible before I went back to England. She listened to what I was saying, but it was clear from the look on her face that she still didn't want me to go back with her.

I began to get annoyed. I was giving her ten thousand baht, I'd paid for her to stop work, I was supporting her, the least she could do was to show me where she'd been staying. I'd told her why, I made it clear we'd only be there for a few minutes while we collected her things, surely I wasn't asking too much? Unless. Unless she was hiding something. I sat back in the taxi and folded my arms across my chest. I looked at her. She looked at me. I waited. Eventually she spoke to the driver in Thai. I heard the words "Suphan Kwai", Buffalo Bridge, the area where Sunan lived.

Joy didn't say a word during the drive to Suphan Kwai. She looked out of the side window, her face turned away from me. I kept trying to talk to her but all I got were head shakes and shrugs. She was sulking, big-time. That annoyed me because I hadn't done anything wrong. If she was hiding something from me, then she was in the wrong. She was supposed to be my girlfriend. She was supposed to be in love with me, and love was supposed to be based on honesty. I'd let her come around to my hotel room on many, many occasions. She'd stayed over, the girls on reception didn't even ask to see her identity card any more, they knew she was with me.

I stopped trying to get her to talk. I tried to think where I'd gone wrong. The taxi stopped on a road lined with hawkers stalls and the air was filled with the cloying smell of fried food. I paid the taxi driver. Joy was already walking away down an alley, her clumpy black shoes clattering on the concrete. I hurried after her. She refused to look at me as we walked, despite my attempts to get her to talk.

"Are you angry at me?" I asked.

She shook her head, but still she wouldn't look me in the eye.

A couple of hundred yards down the alley was a traditional wooden Thai house surrounded by a brick wall. Joy went through a doorway. An old Thai man with a towel wrapped around his waist was ladling water over himself with a small plastic bucket. He grinned at Joy, showing a mouthful of blackened teeth. Joy ignored him. We went around the corner of the house. A fat woman with her hair tied up in a bun was scraping food around a wok. She unscrewed the top of a bottle of something with her teeth and poured the contents into her wok. She said something to Joy and Joy grunted.

"Who are they?" I asked Joy.

"They live here too," she said. We went into the house and up an open wooden staircase. There were two doors at the top, one to the left and one to the right, which Joy knocked. There were several pairs of shoes and sandals outside. I waited halfway up the stairs. Joy put her face close to the door and said something, in a language I didn't recognise. Someone replied. Sunan, I think. Joy turned her face away from me as she spoke. I looked at the sandals and counted nine pairs. They were all scuffed and dirty. Some large, some small. The large ones must have belonged to men. Were there men inside? Was that why Joy didn't want me to see her room? Did she have a boyfriend? But if she did, why did she let me come back with her? Why not just refuse to tell the taxi driver where to go?

Joy said something to Sunan again, then turned to look at me. "Room dirty," she said. "Sunan want to clean."

"That's okay," I said. "I don't mind."

"She very shy."

"So I'll wait." I sat down on the stairs. Joy glared at me. Really glared. I smiled up at her.

"Better we wait outside," she said.

I smiled again. "I can wait here." Joy kept looking at me. Her eyes were hard, really hard. I kept smiling. So long as I kept smiling she wouldn't express her anger. That was the theory anyway. But behind the smile my mind was racing. I couldn't for the life of me understand why she was behaving like this. I'd paid for her to stop work. Thirty minutes earlier I'd given her ten thousand baht. All I wanted to do was to take her to the bus station, to say goodbye to her, to show that I cared. What had started as an expression of my feelings for her had degenerated into a clash of wills, mine against hers. I was forcing her to do something she didn't want to do, the height of rudeness in Thai terms. So I smiled and waited and felt like shit.

Ten minutes later I was still sitting on the stairs and Joy was standing by the door.

"Joy, I want to go into the room," I said.

She shouted something to Sunan. Sunan answered. I couldn't make out what either of them had said. "She not ready."

I stood up. "Now," I said. "If you won't let me into the room, I'm going to go home."

"Up to you."

"If I go home, you won't see me again."

She looked at me, her lips pressed tightly together.

I fought to control my anger. I wanted to take back the money I'd given her. I wanted to take the Garfield watch off her wrist. I wanted to take the gold chain from around her neck, another present. I wanted to tell her that I knew that she was lying to me and that if she was lying then she couldn't possibly love me.

"Joy, tell me everything's okay. Tell me I can go into the room now. Please."

"Why you not believe me, Pete? Why you always think I lie to you?"

"Can I look at Sunan's room?"

She didn't say anything. I turned on my heel and walked away. I hoped that she'd run after me, or shout my name, but she said nothing. I walked down the stairs and out of the house. The old couple were sitting at a rickety folding table eating their evening meal and they grinned as I walked by them. I walked across the yard and through the gap in the brick wall and down the darkened alley. I felt sick to my stomach. I didn't want it to end like this. I didn't want to walk away from her angry, not when I was due to go back to London for months. I stopped in my tracks and turned around. Joy was standing at the wall, watching me impassively. I walked slowly back. "Why, Joy?" I asked her quietly. "Why do let me get so angry?"

"I don't know," she whispered.

"Why didn't you come after me?"

"What you want me say, Pete? I not know what to say."

"I want you to tell me that you love me. That you don't have anyone else, that you only want me."

130

"You know I love you."

I shook my head in exasperation. "You say you do, but you don't act as if you do. All I wanted to do was to go into your room, to see where you stayed. That's all. I don't understand why you wouldn't let me into the room."

"The room no good. Dirty. Sunan say she want to clean."

She smiled and fluttered her eyelashes. I didn't want to laugh, but I couldn't help myself, she looked so damned cute. As my face broke into a smile she put her head on one side and fluttered her long lashes even faster.

"Okay, okay," I said. "Stop it."

She stepped forward and grabbed me around the waist. "Not fight with me, Pete. I love you, I not want fight with you."

I rested my cheek against the top of her head and breathed in the smell of her hair. I wanted to make love to her there and then, to take her, to possess her. It always surprised me how quickly anger could turn to desire, how one moment I could want to scream at her, then just as quickly I wanted to be inside her, kissing her and telling her that if I could I'd die for her.

"Pete, if you want, you can see my room," she whispered. She slipped her hand in mine and together we walked back to the house. She took me back up the stairs and knocked on the door. Sunan opened it, a big smile on her face.

"Sawasdee ka," she said, opening the door wide.

The room was about twelve feet square, with a door that I supposed led to a bathroom. There was a large fridge in one corner and a Formica table in another, and under a single window were a pile of sleeping mats. The floor was bare wood and whatever cleaning Sunan had been doing didn't involve sweeping because there were empty soft drink cans and cigarette packets scattered around. There were two suitcases by the sleeping mats. Joy and Sunan stood in the centre of the room and watched my reaction.

I smiled but I felt sick inside. I could sense their unease, they were still unhappy at having to let me in. I looked around, wondering what was making them so nervous. I knew for sure that Joy was lying: it wasn't that they were shy about the state of the room, they were hiding something else. There didn't seem to be any personal items that belonged to Joy. I'd given her two bags, a black leather backpack and a Garfield shoulder bag, and they weren't there. She had several photographs of me, some taken in Zombie, others taken when I'd visited her house in Si Saket, and she'd told me that she'd put them in frames. They weren't in the room, either. In fact, it didn't look like a room where girls stayed. There was a large poster of a Ferrari on one wall, and a poster of a girl on a motorcycle on another. They didn't seem like the sort of pictures that Sunan would want to look at. There were marks on the wall by the fridge where something had been stuck up and taken down. There were a dozen marks, and from the spacing I figured there had been photographs there. My stomach was churning. I just knew that Sunan had taken the photographs down because she didn't want me to see them.

"Okay, Pete?" asked Joy.

No, I wasn't okay. I was far from okay. I could think of only one reason why they'd made such a fuss. Joy and Sunan weren't staying in the room alone. There'd been a man there. Maybe two men. Boyfriends or husbands. If they'd been family members, brothers or cousins, there'd have been no reason to have hidden them from me. "Yeah," I said. "I'm okay."

"We go now?"

"Go where?"

"Bus station. I go Si Saket. I go now."

I nodded at the suitcase. "Aren't you going to take your clothes?"

"Not mine. They belong Sunan."

"What about your bag? Your make-up? Underwear?"

"Not have. When I stay room Sunan, I wear her clothes. Use her make-up."

It was weird. She was going back to Si Saket without so much as a toothbrush. I knew she travelled light—we'd spent four days travelling around Isarn and she'd only had a carrier bag with a couple of shirts and a wash-kit—but it didn't make sense that she had no clothes or stuff to take back. I told her that I wanted to use the bathroom. I didn't, I just wanted to make sure that there wasn't anyone hiding there. There wasn't, and there were only two toothbrushes on a shelf on the wall.

On the way out I looked down at the shoes and sandals outside the door. I tried to remember how many pairs there'd been before. I wracked my brains but couldn't recall. But I had a feeling that there was a pair of men's flip flops missing. Was that what had happened? Had there been a man in the room, and had Joy wanted me to go away so that he could get out? And if there had been a man there, who was he? None of this made any sense to me. She was staying in Si Saket, she was doing everything I asked of her, surely she couldn't have someone else in Bangkok?

We went back to the main road in silence. I didn't know what to say to her. If there had been a man in the room, then she was lying to me. If there hadn't been a man there, then I was being foolish. Either way the evening had been totally spoiled. Joy was going to back to Si Saket knowing that I didn't trust her.

She flagged down a taxi and told the driver that we wanted to go to the bus station. "What about Sunan?" I asked.

"Sunan stay Bangkok with Bird."

Bird drove Sunan's Toyota pick-up truck and Sunan gave him a few thousand baht a month. I'd seen him a few times and didn't know what to make of him. He rarely smiled and never spoke to me, usually he didn't even acknowledge my presence. Joy had said that he was jealous of farangs because they had money and he didn't. I felt suddenly sorry for Joy. She was going to be stuck on a bus all alone for eight or nine hours, then she'd be staying in Si Saket without Sunan or her friends until I came back. I was treating her like a piece of furniture, putting her into storage until I needed her again. I wished that I could take her to London with me.

She was looking out of the window and she didn't turn around when I slid my hand on to her thigh. "I'm sorry, Joy," I said.

"I sorry too," she said.

"Why? Why are you sorry?"

"Because you not happy." She finally turned to look at me, then leaned over and kissed me, on the cheek, close to my lips. I put my arm around her and stroked her hair. She smelled fresh and clean and new. "I wish you could come to London with me," I said.

"I want go with you," she said. "I want go everywhere with you."

The bus station was packed, and I appeared to be the only farang there. There were scores of buses and queues everywhere. Hardly any signs were in English and I couldn't see any departure times. People kept looking at Joy and me with undisguised curiosity. I wondered whether they automatically assumed that she was a bargirl.

Joy didn't seem to be aware that we were being stared at and talked about. She went over to a line of booths and talked to an old woman behind a glass screen above which were several lines of Thai writing and the letters VIP. Joy handed over a couple of banknotes and came back with a ticket.

"I go VIP bus," she said. "VIP bus has aircon." A Thai teenager came up and spoke to Joy. "He take us to bus," she said. We followed the youngster to a bus which was already three-quarters full.

I asked Joy if she wanted a soft drink or some food to take on her journey and she said no, she'd probably sleep all the way to Si Saket. I wanted to hug her and kiss her but Thais don't show their feelings in public and I didn't want everyone on the bus to see her in the arms of a farang.

"Joy, you know I love you," I said.

She nodded seriously. "I know, Pete."

"You'll be okay in Si Saket?"

"Not okay. I miss you too much, but I do for you."

I felt ashamed that I'd doubted her. If she didn't love me, there'd be no point in her going to Si Saket. She could earn much more than the paltry ten thousand baht I was giving her. And she'd obviously be much happier in Bangkok with her friends than stuck in a village in Isarn. I took out my wallet and gave her five thousand baht. "Buy something for your family," I said. I didn't like giving her money, certainly not in view of the gawping passengers, but I couldn't think of any other way of showing her how much I cared. She took it and slipped it into the back pocket of her jeans.

We both jumped as the bus driver sounded his horn. She gave me a quick kiss on the cheek and then scampered up into the bus. She got a seat at the back and the last thing I saw as the bus pulled out was her waving and blowing kisses at me through the window.

JOY

I was so annoyed at the way Pete behaved. I told him I didn't want him to go to Sunan's room, but he kept on insisting. What was I supposed to do? He practically pushed me into the taxi. I wanted to cry but I kept looking out of the window so he wouldn't see my tears. I thought about taking him to another room, maybe Apple's or Cat's, but I'd already said Sunan was there so if he hadn't seen Sunan he'd have known I hadn't taken him to the right room. I don't understand why he didn't just do as I asked. We could have said goodbye at the restaurant and everything would have been just fine. You see, I wasn't sure if Park would be in Sunan's room or not. He'd said that he was going to go and see his friends in Nana Plaza but when I left him to go and see Pete he was still asleep.

We'd arranged to get the late bus so I knew he'd be back before midnight, and there's no telephone in the room so I couldn't call first. I felt so trapped, it was like Pete was pushing me into a corner, trapping me.

When we got to the house I rushed upstairs and spoke to Sunan. Yeah, Park was there. I called him all sort of names through the door: if he hadn't been so lazy then Sunan could have just tidied his things away and then we could have let Pete in. Sunan was telling me to get Pete away from the door so that Park could get out, but Pete wouldn't move. He was so rude, he just sat there and waited. Then it all got really stupid, because Sunan told Park he'd have to go out of the bathroom window. He climbed up on an upturned bucket and Sunan pushed, but the window wasn't quite big enough and he could only get half-way through. Sunan started giggling and even Park saw the funny side, but I was in the hallway with Pete and I didn't think it was amusing at all. If Pete caught Park in the room, he'd stop sending me money, and then where would we be?

After five minutes of pushing and pulling, Park realised that he wasn't going to be able to get through the window, so Sunan told me to take Pete outside. I said that he wouldn't go but Sunan said we didn't have a choice. The main window in the room was welded shut and the door was the only way in and out.

Pete grew more and more impatient, and all I could say was that Sunan was tidying up. I could see that he didn't believe me, but what could I do? I could hardly drag him away, could I? Eventually he got really annoyed and told me that he didn't trust me. He stormed off. I went after him, but he was really angry. Why are farangs so quick to lose their temper? It's as if they don't have any control over their emotions.

I didn't know what to say to him to calm him down. I stood in the alley and waited to see what he'd do. I know he loves me, and whenever he's been angry before he's always come back, so I just waited. Sure enough, after a few minutes he walked back to the house and asked me if I still loved him. What did he expect me to say? "No Pete, I hate you." Is that what he expected me to say? And then what would happen? He'd get all upset and I wouldn't get any more money. It's such a stupid question. A Thai man would never ask his wife if she loved him. And a Thai woman would never ask her husband, either. It's one of the most pointless questions a person can ask. If someone stays with you, then of course they love you. If they don't love you, they'd just leave. It's obvious, isn't it? Well, it's obvious to me, but it doesn't seem to be obvious to farangs.

Anyway, he came back and that was all that mattered. I figured that by then Park would have gotten out of the room so I told Pete it would be all right to go back. Sure enough, he'd gone, though I could see Pete looking at the shoes outside the door and I wondered if he'd noticed that Park's sandals had gone. Sometimes Park can be really stupid. He should have left his sandals where they were, but I suppose he didn't think. He'd taken his things with him but he'd taken my bags too so I had to tell Pete that I'd been wearing Sunan's clothes while I'd been in Bangkok. Pete kept looking around the room like he was a detective looking for clues. I mean, what more did he want? I'd let him into the room, I'd done as he'd asked, and he still wasn't happy. I was just glad that Sunan had taken all the photographs down. Park was in most of them.

He took me to the bus station. Before we went I told Sunan to tell Park to go to Si Saket the following day. It meant I'd have to suffer the bus ride on my own but I couldn't take the risk of Pete seeing him at the bus station. He might have recognised him from Nana Plaza.

I made sure I waved to Pete as the bus left because I know that farangs like long goodbyes. They're not the same as Thais, Thais just say goodbye and that's it, we don't make a big thing of it, but farangs want lots of kisses and waves and promises that they won't be forgotten. I gave Park hell the next day when he got to Si Saket, told him he was stupid to have hung around Sunan's room. I wasn't really angry, in fact we both saw the funny side of it, him hanging halfway out of the window and Pete sitting outside the front door with a face like thunder. We started laughing and we ended up telling everybody in the village what had happened. Yeah, I guess it was funny.

I'd talked to Park about going back to Si Saket when Pete first suggested I give up working at Zombie. He wasn't very enthusiastic, but I thought it was a really good idea because it would get Park away from the temptations of Nana Plaza. He worked as a DJ in Spicy-a-go-go three or four nights a week and the rest of the time he hung around the Plaza with his friends, and I know he was always chatting up other girls. I used to give him hell but he'd slap me and tell me that what he did was his own business. I used to cry and tell him how much I loved him, and once I cut my wrists to show him how unhappy I was, but he didn't seem to care how I felt.

Anyway, when Pete offered me ten thousand baht a month to stop work, I told Park it was too good an opportunity to pass up. Park started moaning about not wanting to leave his friends in Bangkok, but I said that we could keep coming back to visit. A bus ticket was only a couple of hundred baht and so long as I was in Si Saket when Pete phoned we could do what we wanted the rest of the time. He said that ten thousand baht wasn't enough for him to give up work and that really annoyed me because the most he ever earned was three thousand baht a month. I paid the rent, I gave him money for drink and cigarettes and I bloody well paid for his motorcycle. I didn't say that to his face, of course, because he'd only have slapped me, I just smiled sweetly like I did with farangs in the bar and say that once we'd moved to Si Saket I'd tell Pete that I needed more money. Pete had a good heart, if I asked for more I'd get it. Besides, it wouldn't be for ever. A few months, then Pete would be back in Thailand and I'd tell him that I wanted to be near him in Bangkok.

PETE

I barely slept the night that Joy went to Si Saket. I couldn't get the image of the shoes from my mind. The shoes lined up outside the door to Sunan's room. Men's shoes. And the way Joy had behaved didn't make sense, not if she was being truthful, not if she really loved me. Her actions only made sense if she was lying to me. I wanted to believe that she loved me, I wanted to believe it more than anything in the world, but I could still picture the hard look in her eyes as she refused point blank to let me into the room. Why? Why? Why? I could think of only one explanation—there was somebody in there she didn't want me to see. Husband? Boyfriend? Images of Joy with a Thai man haunted me all night.

I got up just after dawn. Three cleaners were sitting in the corridor outside my door, chattering away. I opened the door and asked if they minded being quiet and they all smiled at me. They were passing around a bag of dried fish and one of the women held it up to me. I shook my head and closed the door. They started talking and laughing again as I went through to the bathroom and showered. I couldn't get Joy out of my mind. I kept picturing the way she'd cover herself with a towel after she'd showered, taking great care to conceal her body from me, despite the fact that there wasn't a part of her that I hadn't seen, hadn't caressed, hadn't kissed. Was there someone else who knew her body as well as I did? Someone else who shared her bed? Someone with her, in Si Saket?

It was crazy to torture myself like this, I knew, but knowing and stopping were two completely different things, and I knew that my imagination would torture me all the more once I got back to England. There was only one way of putting my mind at rest. I'd have to get someone to go and check on her. I couldn't do it, there were hardly any farangs in Isarn, and my Thai wasn't anywhere near good enough for me to start asking questions.

There were two firms of private detectives advertising in the Bangkok Yellow Pages. I phoned the first one but couldn't get any sense out of the woman who answered the phone. She couldn't understand my Thai and didn't appear to be able to speak English. I kept flicking through my dictionary to find the words for investigate and detective but eventually she lost patience with me and put the phone down. Typical Thailand. The advertisement for the second firm listed personal identity checks as one of the many services it offered, which included translations, visas and marriage papers. The woman who answered spoke really good English and once I'd explained what I wanted, she told me that Khun Phiraphan would definitely be able to help me.

His office was in a tower block off Suriwong Road, a stone's throw from Patpong. It seemed to be quite a large operation, there was a big reception area filled with chrome and leather furniture and an efficient receptionist who gave me a glass of iced water as soon as I sat down. I thought Phiraphan might start playing power games with me and have me wait for an hour or so before seeing me, so I was pleasantly surprised when after ten minutes the receptionist said that he was ready and took me down a long corridor.

Phiraphan was in his late forties wearing a three piece pinstriped suit and thick horn-rimmed glasses. His handshake was firm and dry and he waved me to a seat opposite his shiny black desk. I explained how I'd met Joy, and the financial arrangement I'd made with her. He steepled his fingers under his chin as I talked and he watched me over the top of his glasses with unblinking brown eyes. Initially I was a little embarrassed at baring my soul, but he didn't smile or say anything, he didn't even take notes, he just listened impassively. I told him about my suspicions, the fact that she wouldn't let me see her room, the fact that sometimes she wouldn't stay the night, the feelings I had that she wasn't being completely honest with me.

Phiraphan waited until I'd finished, then he took a slim gold pen and made some notes on a yellow legal pad. He started asking questions. About Joy. Her family. Her job at Zombie. Her friends. I wanted to ask how much it would cost, but I didn't get the chance. The questioning went on for almost fifteen minutes. "Do you have a photograph?" he asked.

I handed over half a dozen colour prints that I'd taken when I'd visited Joy's house with Bruno. There were photographs of Joy, Mon and Sunan, and of the house. I also gave Phiraphan a piece of paper on which I'd written Joy's address in Thai, and the number of the phone in Si Saket.

"Do you think you'll be able to help?" I asked.

"Absolutely," he said, examining the photographs one by one. "I have worked on many such cases."

"For farangs?"

"Oh yes. If she has a husband or boyfriend, I will be able to find out for you. Guaranteed."

"How much would it cost?" I asked.

He looked at me and I almost laughed out loud because he had the same glint in his eye that Joy had had when I'd asked her how much money she'd need to stop work. I was being weighed up by the detective, the price he was going to quote had more to do with what he thought I could afford rather than what the job was worth. That was par for the course in Thailand, and I'd dressed accordingly. I figured I was less likely to get ripped off if I wore a sweatshirt and jeans and my old Reeboks.

"You must understand, such an operation will not be easy," he said. He picked up the piece of paper I'd given him. "I know this village, it is close to the border with Cambodia and is a dangerous place. Strangers will always be noticed. I must be very cunning."

I nodded.

"I will have to drive up with two associates. It may take us several days."

I nodded again.

"I think such an operation would cost fifty thousand baht."

Ouch. That was about twice what I thought it was going to cost. I asked if there was any chance of a discount, and he shrugged. I offered twenty five thousand baht and we settled on thirty thousand. I'd brought twenty thousand baht with me so I took it out and gave it to him, with the promise that I'd send the rest when I got his report. He stood up and shook my hand and then ushered me to the door.

The next day I caught a British Airways flight to London.

JIMMY

I gave Rick and Matt a piece of my mind, I can tell you. I was livid. Bloody livid. They'd both told me that the geezer was the best screw they'd ever had. Fucked like a bunny on E, they said. A guaranteed three hole fuck who kept coming back for more. Jesus, if you can't trust your mates, who can you trust, hey? I went into Zombie and barfined the geezer, bought her a few drinks to loosen her up, then took her back to the flat. She showered, I showered, everything's hunky dory. I climb into bed with her, and we get down to business. Great kisser, lots of tongue, lots of enthusiasm. She goes down on me and gives me a blow job to beat all blow jobs. So far so good. She licks my arse, sucks my balls, runs her nails down my legs, drives me crazy. Like I said, no one knows what a guy wants better than another guy. So I pull her up and flick her over on to her back. She rolls over, says she prefers it from behind, but I want to kiss her while I'm screwing her so I keep her on her back. I put my hand between her legs and fuck me, what do I find but a dick. A fucking dick.

I stopped dead. She hadn't had the fucking operation. I was gobsmacked. The katoeys who still have their dicks usually work in the upstairs bars in Nana Plaza, they don't work downstairs until they've had their tackle surgically removed. It wasn't big, it was more of a vestigial thing, smaller than my little finger, and as soft as overcooked spaghetti. I guess it was the tablets she took to grow breasts, they make the balls and dick shrink, too. Anyway, the geezer realises that's something's wrong. She smiles at me and caresses the back of my neck. "You not know?" she says. "I thought you know."

"No," I said. "I didn't know."

I rubbed it with my hand but there was no life in it. It was like a dead thing. The geezer pulls me down and starts kissing me again. She slides a hand down my chest and grabs my dick and within seconds I'm hard again. She was sexy, all right, even though she still had a meat and two veg. I start panting and before I know what's happening she rolls on to her front and gets up on her knees. She pushes herself back against me and the next think I know is I'm up her arse, pumping away like there's no tomorrow. She's looking over her shoulder, urging me on, and I come like a fucking steam train. It was a great shag, all right, the first of many that night. But I gave Rick and Matt hell when I saw them in Fatso's. I mean, they're mates and they should have told me. The thing was, they both swore blind that they didn't know that the geezer had a dick. It just shows you how cunning katoeys can be. Masters of illusion. Which, I guess, is what it's all about. None of this is genuine, really, not when you get down to it. You're paying for an illusion. That's what Pete doesn't realise, of course. He thinks it's for real.

PHIRAPHAN

I've had a few farangs in my office over the years, and they always have the same story. They meet a girl in a bar, they fall in love and want to marry her, but they want to check that the girl is being faithful. I think they're crazy. What do they expect? Bargirls are prostitutes, why do they think a prostitute is going to be faithful? They don't become prostitutes because they want to settle down and raise a family, they become prostitutes because they want money. And most of the time they give their money to their boyfriends or husbands, or they're on drugs. Most of my clients are Thais, and I do a fair amount of marital work, and in my experience, if one partner suspects his spouse is being unfaithful, the chances are that he or she is. There has to be something to spark off a suspicion, so if a situation doesn't feel right, it probably isn't. But when it comes to farangs and bargirls, I can guarantee that the girl's lying. She's either got a boyfriend or a husband, or maybe a kid up country that she's not telling the farang about.

Most of the farangs I do work for have only been in Thailand for a week or so. They come here on holiday, meet a girl, pay her to stop working, then go back to wherever they came from and keep in touch by letter and phone. I think the distance makes the attraction all the more intense, it's as if they've fallen in love with a fantasy figure. How can they expect a girl from a different culture, who doesn't even speak their language properly, to fall in love with them after a few days? How gullible can they be?

Pete was a bit different because at least he'd been in Thailand for a while and could speak some Thai. That just made it all the more surprising that he should fall for a bargirl's charms. He showed me her photograph and frankly I couldn't see what the attraction was. She was a typical Isarn girl with dark skin and a small flat nose, not my type at all. He gave me a photograph of her house near Si Saket and the address, then asked me how much it would cost to check her out. I explained that it wasn't going to be easy, her village was close to the border with Cambodia and strangers would stick out a mile, and I told him what I'd need as a fee. He left me a deposit, gave me his address and phone number in London, and that was it. Actually, I'd have done the job for considerably less. I had a personal reason for visiting Si Saket. I have an old girlfriend who lives there and it had been a while since I'd seen her. Pete's case gave me a perfect excuse for visiting her.

PETE

It was strange being back in London after such a long time in Thailand. I hadn't seen my flat for more than six months and it didn't feel like home. Neither did London. I missed the noise of Bangkok, and the heat and the smells, the smiles of the people and the buzz of the place. There was a stack of mail in my mail box but nothing important. A friend had been sending any mail on to me every month or so, and he'd kept an eye on the place for me.

I got stuck into work straight away. The company had a small sales office in Covent Garden and Alistair had arranged for the guy who had been compiling the London guide to leave what he'd done with our sales guy. I took a cab out and picked it up. Most was on disc and I loaded it into my own desktop word processor. It was a mess and I spent the first week whipping it into some sort of coherent shape. It soon became clear that it was going to take me longer than Alistair had anticipated, three months maybe.

I pinned up several photographs of Joy on the wall around my desk, pictures I'd taken around her house in Si Saket. I wondered what she was doing and if she was missing me as much as I was missing her. I'd arranged to phone her on the morning of the second day I got back in London. Thailand was six hours ahead of England, so I said I'd call at ten o'clock in the morning which would be four o'clock in the afternoon for her. It was always best to pre-arrange calls because the telephone was a call box a mile or so from her house. If she wasn't there it would be pot luck as to who answered. If it was someone who knew Joy and who was prepared to listen to my stilted Thai, then I could ask them to go and get her and I'd call back an hour or so later. But if it was a child who answered or an adult who couldn't understand my Thai, then they'd just hang up. If I was in Bangkok, I could get a member of the hotel staff to call, but five thousand miles away in London, I was on my own so it was better to tell Joy in advance when I was going to call. I just hoped that she'd be there.

I set two alarm clocks on the day I said I'd call because I was working late into the night. The quicker I finished the book, the sooner I'd be able to get back to Bangkok and see Joy again. I paced around the flat, waiting for ten o'clock. I kept stopping to look at the photographs of her, smiling cutely at the camera.

I started dialling as soon as the second hand hit twelve and practically held my breath as it began to ring out. It seemed to take for ever but I guess it was only ten seconds or so before she answered. "Sawasdee ka. Hello?" It was her.

I almost couldn't believe it. I suddenly felt guilty for ever doubting her. She'd done everything I'd asked of her. I'd asked her to stop work. She'd agreed. I'd asked her to go and stay with her father while I went back to England. She'd agreed. I'd asked her to be at the phone at a particular time. She'd agreed.

We chatted about my book, about what London was like, and what she was doing. She said that her father was buying barrels of fuel and she was selling it at the roadside by the litre. "I very dark now," she said. "Maybe you not like me any more."

I told her not to be silly, that I'd love her whatever the colour of her skin. That's one of the crazy things about Thais, they prefer their skin to be as light as possible, whereas often they looked better when their skin was dark. There was a huge amount of prejudice, with the whiter skinned people of Bangkok clearly looking down their noses at their poorer, darker, cousins from the east of the country. Each time Joy returned from a stay in Si Saket she was always darker, but I thought she looked great.

She asked me when I was coming back to Thailand and I said probably two months. To be honest I was pretty sure I'd be working on the London book for three months but I didn't want her to be too disheartened. Twelve weeks was a long time and if she thought I wasn't coming back she might well decide to go back to Bangkok and stay with her friends.

Joy said she missed me and started blowing kisses down the phone. I felt suddenly guilty for doubting her. Of course she loved me, if she didn't love me she'd have just stayed in Bangkok.

I promised to call her in another two days at the same time. "I love you," was the last thing she said to me. When I put down the phone I was elated, almost light-headed. She loved me. I was one hundred per cent sure she loved me.

BRUCE

Did Joy love Pete? I don't know. I guess the pat answer would be, in her way. It's not as if they lived together, is it? Hell, he was paying her to stay in Si Saket, hundreds of miles away. She was a young girl, twenty-one. She needed stimulation, things to do, parties to go to. She'd worked in a go-go bar, lots of music, drugs, people coming and going. Whichever way you look at it, that's got to be more exciting than planting rice, hasn't it? Love isn't a result of paying money, is it? And that's what he was doing, really. Sure, he was taking her out for dinner, going to movies with her, sleeping with her. But he wasn't living with her, he wasn't sharing his life with her, and that's where love grows. If you ask me, he was treating her like a mia noy, a minor wife. She was only getting a small part of his life, and for a girl her age, that's not enough.

Now Troy, Troy's totally different. I know Troy loves me. I can see from the way Troy looks at me that she loves me with all her heart.

It was funny how quickly I got used to having her around. She never enjoyed working in Spicy-a-go-go in the first place, and she kept coming up with reasons not to go in. I didn't mind. I'd been spending too much time sitting outside the bar anyway when she was there. The fact she was in the house made me keener to get home. We'd eat together, she's a great cook, simple food, spicy the way I like it, and then we'd watch TV together. She liked to watch Thai game shows and chat shows and she'd explain the jokes to me. Sometimes we'd just sit and talk. Her English isn't very good and my Thai is so-so, but we managed to talk for hours. I was never bored with her. I'd tell her about my childhood, about Newcastle, about what I planned to do with Saravoot's factory. She slept in my bed, not for the sex, it really wasn't for the sex, it was just that I wanted her close by. She'd sleep wrapped around me as if she was frightened of losing me.

She brought a few clothes around, and stuff she needed for the kitchen, and I gave her one of the bathroom shelves for her wash things. She did the shopping and she'd always leave the receipt and any change on the kitchen table as if she wanted to prove to me that it wasn't about money. I gave her some, of course, because she wasn't working as much as she used to, and she had to send money back to her family. She had a baby, a two-year-old, that her mother and elder sister looked after while she was in Bangkok. Her husband was a right bastard, used to knock her around and ran off soon after the baby was born. Now she didn't like Thai men, she said.

She cooked, too. Always Thai food, she couldn't get the hang of farang recipes. The fridge was full of herbs and spices and plastic bags of things I couldn't identify. She used to make up batches of sauces and pastes, some of them so hot they could burn the roof off your mouth. Her nam prik was the best I've ever tasted. I used to love watching her cook, she was always so intense about it, as if her life depended on getting it right.

One night, as we lay in bed, I asked her what she wanted out of life. She was playing with my beard, wrapping the hair around her fingers and tugging it gently. "I want good man to love me," she said. "I want someone take care of me. I want someone to love."

I asked her if she wanted to go to school, to learn English or computers, something that would help her get a better job.

"I too stupid," she said, which fair broke my heart because if there's one thing she's most definitely not it's stupid.

I asked what job she'd like to do, if she could do anything. "I want to be your maid," she said softly. "I want to take care of you every day."

That wasn't on because I already had a maid, a woman in her sixties who Saravoot sends in to keep the place clean and look after my laundry. I offered to find her work at the handbag factory. I was pretty sure I could get her a job somewhere, either on the sewing machines or in quality control.

She didn't say anything for a while. "Your factory very far away, Bruce. How I get there?"

I knew what she wanted. She was hoping that I'd offer to let her travel in with me every day, and that would mean she'd be living with me all the time.

"Some of the people who work in the factory live there," I told her. "They have rooms, and they get their food." They were dormitories rather than rooms, but I figured that once she saw the living quarters she'd be happy. From what she'd told me, anything would be an improvement on her house in Nong Khai.

"You want me live in factory?" she said.

"It's up to you," I said. "Why don't you come in and have a look for yourself."

"Okay," she said, snuggling up against me. "If you want, I want too."

PETE

Joy was waiting by the phone in Si Saket the next time I called. And the next. On one occasion it was pouring with rain, I could hear the drops pounding off a corrugated iron roof in the distance. "Pete, I very wet," she giggled. "Have rain too much." She kept asking me when I'd be coming back to Thailand, kept saying how much she missed me. I told her that I'd be back as soon as possible, but that I had to do a lot of work on the book. "I understand, Pete," she said solemnly. "I wait for you. I be good girl for you." She told me she was spending most of the day at her roadside stall, selling fuel to passing vehicles.

I told her I'd written to her and she said she'd written many letters to me. "Maybe I write too much," she said. "Because I miss you, I want you know how I feel."

I felt bad at not trusting her, how could I ever have doubted her? Everything I ever asked her to do she did, with a smile. With love. After I'd said goodbye I went straight back to work. I wanted to get the book finished as quickly as possible so that I could get back to her.

I'd been in London just over a week when the letters arrived. Five of them, from Thailand. My handwriting on the envelope. I ripped them open and read them one by one.

July 8

Dear Pete

    I'm sorry for everything Joy make you not happy. But in my heart I love you too much. I have you only one. But I not want have big problem with you. Pete, listen to me. I want you understand me. Pete, what I do? How I do? Pete, everything I do I want make you happy heart. But every time you think I lie to you. Pete, sometime Joy no good. Sometime Joy be good. Pete, I want you know me. Every time I love you. I love you a lot. I miss you all the time.

    Joy

July 9

Hello my love

    Are you happy in England? I hope you very happy heart in your house. What do you do now? You have a little time to think about me? or you forget me? Pete, now I want see you. I want talk with you. I want kiss you. Now I lonely. I want you live in Bangkok with me all the time. I like to see you and talk with you every day. Sometimes I have a big problem but I happy because I can talk with you. I think about you and me every day. I love you and have you in my heart only one. Miss you all the time.

    Joy

July 10

From Joy

Dear Pete

Pete, where you stay now? I want to see you now. This time you have time can you think about me? For me I think about you too much. I want you come back to Bangkok now. I want you come see me, talk with me. Pete, when you with me, I very happy heart with you. I like have you stay with me all the time. I happy when I see you, I talk with you. Pete, I hope you not forget me and you love me. I cannot stop love you. I love you when I die. I love you too much.

Joy

July 11

Hello my love

Pete I want you give back my heart to me now because I think about you too much. Pete, I cannot sleep. I not want to do anything. Pete, when you come back Bangkok to see me? Pete, this time what you do? Pete, I hope your book be good, for your book I not like you have big problem. I want your book everything be good. I happy heart to you too because I not want you stay in England long time. I want see you and kiss you now. When you have my letter I want you smile and miss me. I hope you come to see me soon. Love you and miss you too much.

Joy

July 14

For my love

Hello Pete. How are you? What do you do now? Pete, when your book not have big problem? Now what you think? You tired heart or happy heart? I hope you very happy heart for your book and happy in England. Pete, when you live in England you be happy because you not have big problem every day. If you very happy heart when you live in England, I very happy heart for you too. I not want you think too much, and not have big problem everyday. I want see you, talk with you. I love you all the time. Only you. When you come to see me, I very happy in my heart.

Joy

In one of the letters she'd included a purple and white flower petal. I held it and smelled it as I reread the letters. I wondered how long it had taken her to write each one. Hours, maybe. Without a dictionary, too. She must have laboured over each one. I could picture her sitting on the bed, frowning as she struggled with English spelling and grammar. I wished I could hold her in my arms and press her against me and tell her how much I loved her. I'd only been away for just over a week but it felt like an eternity.

A week? I picked up the envelopes. She'd used the ones that I'd given her in Bangkok, addressed to me in my handwriting. I'd left Bangkok on July 8. I'd received the letters on the 17th. Mail normally took about a week to get to England from Thailand. I flicked through the letters. She'd obviously written the first one on the day I'd left. The last one had been written on the 14th, three days ago. Three days? That didn't make sense. There was no way a letter could reach me in three days. I looked at the postmarks on the five air mail envelopes. They all bore the same date. July 8. I dropped the envelopes on the coffee table and sat on the sofa with my head in my hands. She'd posted all five letters at the same time, on the day I'd left Bangkok. But each letter had been dated differently. Why? If she'd posted them all on July 8, why hadn't she put them in the same envelope? And if she'd written them all on July 8, why the different dates on the letters?

I remembered what Big Ron had said about the standard con, about the girl having her mail redirected so that she could carry on working without the farang knowing. Is that what Joy was doing? No, that was impossible, I'd been calling her every two days and she was always there, waiting for my call. It didn't make any sense. If she'd written the letters at the same time, which she obviously had, then why hadn't she put them in the one envelope?

JOY

The letters? Yeah, that was my father's fault, I guess. I was actually quite offended when Pete gave me the stamped addressed envelopes. It was as if he was saying that my English wasn't good enough, that he couldn't trust me to write his address on my own. I didn't say anything, of course. That would have been rude. So I just smiled and took them. I don't know why farangs make such a big thing about letters. They don't mean anything, not really. Most of the girls in Zombie send letters to their farangs, but they don't write them themselves. And when the farangs write back, the girls don't read them. Most of the letters they get are in English or German anyway, and besides, who cares what they say? It's always, "are you being a good girl?", or "please don't work in the bar" or "do you love me?" The only thing the girls care about is if there's any money in the letter. That's how a farang can show how much he loves a girl—send her money. Anything else is just whistling in the wind, that's what I always say.

As soon as I got back home I wrote to Pete. I actually wrote seven letters and put one in each envelope. I figured I'd get one of my sisters to post them while I went over to see my friends in Khorat. I mean, I wasn't going to say anything different, was I? It wasn't as if I was doing anything exciting, I was just helping my father on the farm, selling oil in my brother-in-law's garage, just run-of-the-mill stuff. So I wrote seven letters, telling him how much I missed him, how much I loved him, all that sort of sweet-mouth stuff that farangs like. I left the letters on the kitchen table and went outside to wash. When I came back the letters had gone. I didn't notice at first, and when I did notice I just assumed that someone had put them away. It was only next morning when the family was having breakfast that I asked where they were.

"I posted them," said my father.

"You what?"

"I posted them. I took them to the post office yesterday afternoon."

I wanted to cry. I'd spent almost two hours writing them, and it'd all been a waste of time. My father asked me what was wrong but I couldn't tell him. He wouldn't understand, he probably didn't even realise that they were all going to the same address. If anything, I suppose it was Pete's fault, really. If he'd trusted me to get my own envelopes, I wouldn't have written them all at the same time.

At least I had a week or so to work out how I was going to explain it to Pete. I was sure I'd think of something. If there's one thing I've learned during my time in Nana Plaza, it's that love makes farangs blind.

PHIRAPHAN

I took my assistant, Malee, up to Si Saket with me to add to my cover. There was no way I could breeze into Joy's village asking questions, her family would smell a rat straight away. I had fake Government credentials showing that I worked for the Ministry of the Interior and I had a briefcase full of files. We started about a mile away from Joy's house, telling people that we were acting for a new agency which was offering loans and grants to girls who'd worked in bars in the city but who'd returned to their village. The Government wanted to help girls who'd turned their back on prostitution, we said, and we'd ask if they knew of anyone who could benefit from the scheme. We were given Joy's name at several houses on the first day, but we left it two days before calling at her house. It was quite a big place, a wooden house on two floors, three bedrooms upstairs, a big screen TV and a stereo downstairs. They were obviously fairly well off. Next to the house was a large garage with several pick-up trucks which were in the process of being repaired. It was clear that Joy had already been told that we were in the area. As soon as we introduced herself she asked us in and listened intently as I gave her the pitch.

"I used to work night-time in Bangkok," she said, before I'd even finished.

"Good, good," I said. I took a form out of my briefcase and gave it to Malee.

She asked Joy for her full Thai name, her date of birth, her ID card number, her educational history. Then she asked the big question. "Marital status?"

"Married," said Joy.

Bingo. It was so easy. I wasn't surprised, I'd used the Government grant scam more than a dozen times. Malee doesn't bat an eyelid. "Husband's name?" she says.

Joy gives her the name, and his date of birth.

"Is your husband here?" I ask. "Because we could make it a joint application."

Joy calls over to four young men who were watching a boxing match on TV. "Park, come here!" she yells.

A guy in his twenties came over. He was well built as if he worked out, with a square face and slightly bulging eyes. He wasn't exactly good-looking, but he had a friendly smile and I could see from the way that Malee looked at him that women liked him. Joy introduced him and he sat down next to her. Malee asked him for his ID card number and his educational qualifications, then she asked Joy what she'd do if she was given a Government grant.

"I'd start up a factory in my village so that people here could work," she said.

Malee wrote down what Joy said, though I didn't believe it for one minute. Then she pushed the form across the table and asked them both to sign it.

I took a small camera out of my pocket. "And just to make it official, I have to take your photograph," I said. "It minimises the possibility of fraud."

Joy and Park nodded and moved closer together so that I could get them both in. I took the photograph, put the camera and the form in my briefcase, and left with Malee. Before we got in the car I took a photograph of the house and the garage next to it.

I dropped Malee at the bus station in Si Saket so that she could go back to Bangkok. I stayed on for a couple of days with my girlfriend and had a great time. I told her about Pete and Joy and she laughed until she cried. "Why are farangs so stupid?" she asked and I had no answer to that.

PETE

When I called Joy and asked her about the letters she'd sent, she started giggling. "I want send letters too much," she said. "I joking with you." I said I didn't get the joke, but she just laughed. "I want you know I miss you too much. I think funny if you get many letters together," she said. I asked her why she'd put different dates on the letters but she didn't have an explanation for that, she just kept saying it was a joke, that she wanted me to smile when I read them.

Joy asked me if I'd be back in Thailand for her birthday, August 29, and I said I'd do my best. Work was going well and if I kept working as hard as I had been, there was a good chance I'd get it finished before the end of August. "I want see you on my birthday," she said. "Everyone here want see you too much. My father, my brother, everybody. Maybe we have party, okay?"

I said, sure, we'd have a party if I could get back in time. I asked Joy how she spent her time in Si Saket. She said she worked all day and in the evening she watched television with her brother and father. I asked her if she was bored. She said she was but that she was happy because I was happy. She'd do whatever I asked. I felt really guilty at not trusting her before. I wondered what Phiraphan was doing, whether or not he'd started his investigation. I was sure he'd be wasting his time. Joy was doing exactly as I'd asked, she'd gone back to the family home to wait for me. I'd called her every couple of days and she'd always been there, there was no question of her still working in Bangkok. She wasn't trying to con me, I was certain. She loved me and she was proving it.

After I hung up I went out and bought a card for her, a view of a grinning London bobby in front of a bus, and I wrote a message to say how much I missed her and how much I loved her. I put ten thousand baht in the envelope and posted it Swiftpost so it would get to her quickly. I did miss her, more than I could explain in words. There was a cold, hollow place in the pit of my stomach, a constant reminder that she wasn't around. I missed her smile, I missed her laugh, the smell of her hair and the feel of her body pressed up against mine. I missed the way she'd reach for me in her sleep, her hand brushing against the sheet as it sought mine, her fingers slipping between mine. I missed watching her shower, watching her dress, watching her put on her nail-varnish, the tip of her tongue between her teeth as she frowned in concentration. I missed her so much that I ached and the only way I could express it was to send her ten thousand baht.

Three days after the five letters arrived, I got two more. Before I opened them, I checked the postmarks. They'd both been posted on the eighth, same as the others. I opened them. One was dated July 12, the other July 13. What on earth was she playing at? I read them, but all I could think about was that she'd written all seven letters on the same day. Why hadn't she put them in the same envelope?

July 12

To my love

From Joy, woman in the room but not have heart in her. Pete, I not understand why I miss you a lot. Pete, I want you know me, understand me. I am sorry because I give you big problem every day. I not make you happy before you go England. Pete, I hope you can give time for me. Today I no good but tomorrow I can be good for you. I want your book everything be good. I like you come see me soon. Have time think about me. From me, woman not have everything and not have heart. Pete, now I think you forget me.

Love you only one,

Joy

July 13

To my love

From me, Joy. Maybe you forget. I sorry I write to you too much. You can tell me if you not like. Pete, in England now very hot or very cool? How are you, Pete? Pete, I want you give your problem to me. I want see you. Love you in my heart, only you.

Joy

JOY

It was a real pain having Pete call me every two days. I wanted to go with Park back to his village. His parents needed help on the farm and they were pestering him to go. I really wanted to go with him because I knew that Daeng was there and I didn't want Park going anywhere near her, not after the time I'd caught him in bed with her. Daeng had managed to get two farangs to give her money every month, one guy in Switzerland and another from Germany. Park kept on teasing me about it, asking me why I had only one and why Pete only gave me ten thousand baht a month because Daeng was getting twenty thousand baht from each of her customers. Forty thousand baht a month. I told him not to be so greedy, that her customers would probably only send her money for a few months and then she'd have to go back to the bars. That was always the way with farangs. They'd come to Thailand and fall in love with a girl and then they ask her to stop work. They go back to their own countries and start sending money, but after a while the love fades and the money stops. I told Park that Pete was different, he'll be living in Thailand for a long time so he'll give me money for a long time.

Anyway, I could see that the prospect of Daeng and forty thousand baht a month was eating away at him so I did my best to keep him amused in Si Saket. I took him to karaoke bars and bought him bottles of Black Label and we went out to the cinema and treated his friends. Everything to give him face, to make him look like the big man. It meant I was spending all the money that Pete was giving me, but at least he stopped mentioning Daeng.

Sunan came up from Bangkok with Bird and she offered to drive Park and me to Udon Thani but I said we'd have to wait until I'd spoken to Pete. I figured I'd tell him that my father was ill and that I was going to stay with him in the hospital.

Sunan brought dozens of pairs of Levi jeans with her, real ones, not the fakes they sell in Patpong. She and a group of girls in Zombie had been having a competition to see who could get the most pairs. They'd tell all their customers who were going back to their own countries that they really wanted a pair of jeans. Jeans are really expensive in Thailand, but not so expensive abroad. So Sunan would tell two or three farangs every night, and give them her address. Maybe a hundred farangs every months, and about one in ten would remember, especially the ones she'd screwed. They'd been playing the game for two months and so far Sunan had more than twenty pairs, all different sizes. She'd been telling some farangs that she wanted a 26-inch waist, some 28 inches, some 30, and tell them different colours and styles. That way she'd get different sorts. We had great fun trying them all on. She gave me a blue pair and a black pair and Park got two blue pairs.

We often have competitions like that in Zombie. We did one with Barbie dolls just after I started working in Nana Plaza. I got more than fifty, but Sunan had over a hundred, from all over the world. We took them to Chatuchak Market and sold them. She's so smart, Sunan. I've learned so much from her. She has a farang in Denmark who sends her forty thousand baht a month and he only comes to Thailand three times a year. I've met him, he's about fifty with grey hair and he's got a really good heart. He always buys me presents when we go shopping together. His name is Toine or something like that and he's married with two children. He says that he loves Sunan and that he'd marry her if he could but he has to take care of his family. He writes a letter every week to Sunan and every month he sends her money, American dollars. I wish that Pete was more like Toine, it's a real nuisance having to get to the phone every two days just to sweet-talk him. He keeps on asking if I love him or if I've forgotten about him. Why do farangs always talk about love? Thais hardly ever do. If you love someone you stay with them and you take care of them, you prove that you love them every day. Park never asks me if I love him. He doesn't have to. I buy his clothes, I pay for his motorcycle, I give him money to send back to his parents if they have problems, I show that I love him in lots of different ways. But farangs, farangs always want you to tell them, as if saying the words makes it true.

I never used to tell farangs that I loved them, I thought it was stupid, but Sunan taught me that it's better to say it. You get more money. Especially if you tell them while you're screwing them, just before they come. You breathe really heavily and gasp that you love them, they really like that. And at the airport, of course, when you're saying goodbye to them. If you say you love them and cry, they give you money, it works every time. I usually go with Sunan and Toine to the airport and the first time I saw her cry I was really surprised, I didn't know what was happening. Toine gave her ten thousand baht and a big hug, and afterwards Sunan explained that she was doing it because that's what farangs do when they say goodbye. I asked her how she could cry so easily and she said she thought of something sad. That's what I do now when I go to the airport with a farang, I think about my mother dying. It works. Eighty per cent of farangs give you money when you cry.

PETE

I was sitting at my desk going through notes on up-market London hotels when Phiraphan's fax came through. The first sheet was his report and I read it as it came off the machine. Married without registration. I read the phrase a dozen times before the sheet spewed out of the machine. Married without registration. That meant they'd gone through the marriage ceremony but hadn't registered it with the authorities. But married was married, whether or not they'd done the paperwork. According to the report, Joy and her husband had been living in the house in Si Saket for the past three months. Ever since I'd started paying her a monthly "salary", in fact. Phiraphan said that the whole village knew that Joy was married, and that Joy and Park had known each other for more than a year. A year. That meant that she'd known him before she met me. It had all been a lie. Everything she'd ever said to me, her declarations of love, her insistence that she had only me, that she didn't have a husband or boyfriend, none of it had been true.

The second sheet was a questionnaire that she'd signed. There were two signatures on the form. I guessed that the second one was Park's.

The third sheet consisted of two photographs. The quality wasn't that good but the top one was of Joy and a Thai man, the other was a picture of Joy's house. It took a couple of seconds for the significance of the second picture to sink in. Then I realised. Since I'd been there an extension had been built on to the side, an extension sheltering several pick-up trucks and a motorcycle. And it was probably my money that had paid for it.

I sat down and stared at the pictures. She had a husband. A husband. She'd gone back to Si Saket with him. She was living with him. She was keeping him, with my money. She was making love to him. Sleeping with him. She loved him.

I dropped the sheets of fax paper on to the sofa and paced up and down. Maybe there'd been a mistake. Maybe Phiraphan had made it up, maybe he'd wanted to justify his fee. I picked up the sheets and read them again. Everyone in the village knew about Joy and her husband. I'd been to the village with Bruno and Pam. I'd been introduced to Joy's family and friends at the birthday party. If what Phiraphan said was true, every single one of them had known that I was being deceived, that I was being played like a one-string fiddle. I stared at the questionnaire. It was definitely her signature. It was definitely her in the photograph.

No, there was no mistake. No doubt. She was married and she'd been lying to me from the moment I set eyes on her. I wanted to telephone her there and then, to accuse her, to scream at her, to ask her why, why she'd lied to me, but I knew there was no point. First, she'd deny it. She'd try to convince me that there'd been a terrible mistake, that I was the only man she loved. And if that didn't work, she'd just cut off all contact. I'd never hear from her again and she'd find another stupid farang to subsidise her lifestyle. She was playing a game with me, the game of conning the farang. That's all I was to her, a farang to be played with. Big Ron had warned me, and God knows I'd heard all the stories myself, I knew the dangers of falling for a bargirl but I'd always believed that Joy was different, that Joy was being straight with me, that she wasn't playing a game. I'd been wrong, right from the start.

I paced up and down the flat, faster and faster, wanting to do something, wanting to react, but feeling totally powerless because she was so far away. That's what the hurt the most, the fact that I couldn't confront her with her infidelity.

I kept looking at the photograph, hoping that there had been some ghastly mistake, but it was definitely her, sitting next to her husband and smiling prettily at the camera. It was the same guileless smile she had in the photographs that Bruno had taken of the two of us in Isarn. How could she do it? How could she lie to me? How could she write the letters she'd written?

I'd told her, before she'd agreed to stop work, I'd told her that if she had a Thai boyfriend or a husband I didn't mind, I'd still be her customer. I'd still see her, I'd still give her money. But if she wanted me to take care of her she had to be honest with me. She'd looked me straight in the eye and lied. She had no one, she'd said. She only had me. Why had she lied? And what about Sunan? And her father? And all the people I'd met in her village? The girls in Zombie? They must all have known that Joy had a husband and that I was only the farang meal ticket.

I looked at the photograph again. It was the kitchen of her house, Joy and her husband sitting at the kitchen table, the table where she'd given me a cup of tea to drink. He was wearing a denim shirt that looked several sizes too big for him. I stopped pacing and stared at the photograph. I recognised the shirt. It was one of mine. I'd given it to Joy two or three months ago. She'd come back to my hotel in a tiny tank top and I'd wanted her to wear something less revealing when she left in the morning. I'd given her a pale blue denim shirt and told her that she could keep it. It looked much better on her than it did on me, but she'd gone and given it to her husband. How could he wear it? Didn't he have any shame? I was sleeping with his wife and he was wearing my shirt. Was the money that important to him? Or did Joy mean so little?

None of it made any sense to me. If he really loved her, why didn't he take care of her? Why didn't he get a job and ask her to stop work? How could he live with himself, knowing that his wife was sleeping with another man? How could he wear the fucking shirt? Didn't it remind him of what his wife was doing? And what about Joy? Didn't she think about me every time she looked at the shirt? Didn't it remind her of the time we spent together? Didn't it remind her of me? Or was it just a shirt she'd conned out of the stupid farang? Maybe it was a trophy of sorts.

I looked at the photograph more closely. She wasn't wearing the Garfield watch I'd given her. She always had it on in Bangkok, it matched the one I wore and she always made a big thing of showing them to her friends. Now she was back in Si Saket, she wasn't wearing the watch. What did that mean? The shirt was okay but the watch wasn't?

It was as if I was involved in some weird game but that I hadn't been told all the rules. I didn't even know how I could win. If I stopped giving her money, Joy would just go and find some other farang to support her and her husband. She had nothing to lose and everything to gain.

I wanted to win, I wanted to show her that I wasn't the same as all the other farangs who were being fleeced in the bars. I wanted to show her that I was different. I paced around my apartment, wracking my brains. If I was going to get my own back I was going to have to take my revenge Thai-style. I was going to have to think like a Thai.

NIGEL

Pete telephoned me one evening and told me that Joy was married. Can't say I was all that surprised, I mean most of them have husbands or boyfriends. Why wouldn't they? They don't work in go-go bars because they want to meet the man of their dreams, do they? They work for money, it's just a job like any other so of course they don't cut off all their relationships. Did he really expect a hooker to be faithful to him? Well, maybe he did, but that's his own fault. I'd told him enough times the way things were, and so did the rest of the guys in Fatso's. I made sympathetic noises but I couldn't say too much because there was a pretty little thing from G-Spot lying next to me and although her English wasn't too hot a lot of these girls understand more than they let on. Pete kept saying that he wanted to get his own back and I tried to talk him out of it. "It's a bloody game to them," he said. "And I want to show them that I'm a better player than they are. I'm not going to let them win," he said.

He's wrong. It isn't a game to these girls, that's the whole point. It's a way of life. It's how they earn their living. I don't reckon he should have tried to punish her for doing what comes naturally. She was a hooker, hooking, and he had no more right to punish her for that than to take revenge on a spider for catching flies. I didn't tell him that, though. In fact, I barely remember what I did say to him because half way through the conversation the girl I was with started to get a bit jealous and began trying to get my attention. She succeeded, too. I told Pete I had to go and that I'd speak to him later.

PETE

I knew the one thing I couldn't do was to confront Joy with what she'd done. She'd deny it, for sure. And if I told her that I had a signed confession and a photograph, she'd do whatever she could to avoid any further conflict. She'd just put the phone down and not speak to me. Thais hate being confronted by their mistakes or lies, it's not in their culture to accuse people of falsehoods or to rub their noses in their errors. It's all about face, and if I told Joy I knew that she'd lied to me, she'd lose face. But in her mind, I'd be the one in the wrong because I'd behaved badly by pointing out that she'd lied.

It was game, and if I really wanted to win the game, I was going to have to play by the rules. No conflict. No arguments or name-calling. I had to punish her with a smile.

I kept calling her, and she was always there. "I love you, Pete. I want you come to Thailand see me." Now that I knew the truth, I could see that she was almost working to a script. She'd tell me she loved me, but at some point she'd always manage to bring up that she was short of money. She never actually asked me to send her any, she never said the words, but I always got the message. I tell you, if I hadn't known the truth, if I hadn't received Phiraphan's report and photographs, I'd have been convinced that I was the centre of Joy's life, that she loved me with all her heart. But I did know the truth and for all I knew her husband was next to her at the phone box, sitting astride the motorcycle I was paying for, grinning at his lovely wife as she ripped off the farang in another country.

I couldn't concentrate on the London book. Every time I sat down at the word processor, I found myself looking at the photographs of Joy that I'd put up on the wall. Even when I took them down and put them in a drawer, I couldn't get her out of my mind. Alistair sent me an email asking how I was getting on and I told him everything was fine. It wasn't, I was falling behind schedule, but I was sure that I'd be able to get back on track once I'd sorted out the Joy thing. I figured that once I got my revenge I'd be able to get on with my life.

Joy had made me look foolish, and to win the game I reckoned that I had to do the same to her. I had to make her lose face in front of her family and friends. And her husband.

I baited the trap early on, about a week after I'd received Phiraphan's fax. I told her that work was going well and that I hoped to be back in Thailand before her birthday. And I told her that my boss had given me a big bonus and that I thought I'd be able to buy her a pick-up truck as a birthday present. She asked me if I was sure and I said yes, I'd bring the money with me. And I said that we should have a big party on her birthday, like we'd done the year previously. Maybe we could go to the same place, the Chicago Karaoke Bar in Suphan Kwai. Joy sounded so happy that I felt guilty, so after I'd hung up I read through Phiraphan's report and looked at the photographs until the anger returned. She'd asked for it, I told myself, she'd lured me into the game and she only had herself to blame if she got hurt.

Two days later I phoned her again. Joy said she'd talked to her father and they'd decided that we should either get a Toyota or an Isuzu pick-up. I didn't believe for one minute that it was her father she'd discussed it with. It'd have been her husband, for sure. I could picture the two of them sitting at the kitchen table, going through brochures, deciding how to spend the gullible farang's money. I asked her what her father thought we should buy. "He say Toyota best, but Isuzu not so expensive if something go wrong."

I had a sudden urge to hug her and to tell her that I knew she'd been lying to me but that I didn't care, I still loved her. She was so damn cute. I was offering her a pick-up truck and she was worrying about how much it'd cost to repair.

I said okay, we'd get an Isuzu. I asked her what colour she wanted. "Up to you," she said. "What you like?"

"Red," I said.

"Okay, I want red, too."

I told her I'd call her again in two days and she blew kisses down the phone to me before she hung up.

Two days later when I rang, she told me that everyone in her village was excited about the pick-up. "Pete, my father say we should buy Isuzu SLX. It has air, has everything."

I said sure, the SLX would be great. I asked her if she'd told her father about the party because I'd like him to go. And Sunan, and Bird, and all her family. The previous year about thirty people had turned up at the karaoke bar, this year I wanted more. Joy said that she wasn't sure if everybody could come because they couldn't all afford the bus fare from Si Saket to Bangkok. I told her not to worry, that I'd reimburse them all when I got there. I felt like a poker player who was sitting on four aces, gradually raising the stakes to keep the players in, knowing full well that he was certain to keep the pot.

I kept up the charade for more than a month, calling her every couple of days, sending her a card every month, telling her how much I missed her and loved her. When she asked me about her "monthly salary" I said that as I was coming back I'd give it her when I saw her because I didn't like the idea of sending it through the post. She said that was a good idea and that she'd borrow some money from Sunan.

About a week before her birthday I told her that I'd bought my ticket back to Thailand and that I'd be arriving early in the morning. She said she'd meet me at the airport, and that Sunan would be with her. I asked her if all her family would be going to the party and she said yes, and that they were all excited. "They want see you, too much," she said.

I asked her if she'd arrange a birthday cake, similar to the one we'd had at the previous year's party. I'd gone to the cake shop in the Peninsula Hotel and ordered a huge cake with Garfield on it and "Happy Birthday Joy and Pete" in icing letters. "Good idea," she said. "I get for you."

I said that we'd go and buy the Isuzu on the day of her birthday and that we'd drive it back to Si Saket. It was Joy who brought up the matter of a deposit. She said that if I wanted to buy a red Isuzu SLX they'd have to order it in advance and they wouldn't do that without a deposit. It was brilliant, she was raising the stakes herself. The perfect game. I said there was no way I could get the deposit to her in time, but that I'd be bringing the money with me in US dollars. "I have idea," she said.

Her idea was to pawn the gold that I'd given her and to use that money as the deposit. When I got back to Bangkok I could give her the money to get the gold back. I said it was a great idea.

After I'd hung up I started to feel guilty again. I found myself wishing that there'd been some sort of mistake, that she did love me, that she wasn't being unfaithful. But I knew I was only trying to fool myself because I had the evidence. The application form Phiraphan had sent me was in Thai and I'd worked through it with my dictionary, checking every answer she'd given. There was no doubt, no mistake, no misunderstanding. When she'd been asked for her marital status, she'd written "married". End of story. Whatever happened from now on, it was her own fault.

NIGEL

I got a phone call from Pete at about seven o'clock in the morning. I was knackered, I'd only been in bed for about four hours and for most of that time I'd been occupied with a girl from the Rainbow Bar, a cute little thing I've known for years. She's a great lay but I've got to use a condom with her because she injects heroin. I always insist that she doesn't bring any gear back to my room because the cops would love another farang to put behind bars for fifty years or so. She says she never shares her needles but you can't believe a word bargirls say so I always use a condom, and a British or American one at that.

Anyway, Pete starts jabbering on about the game, about how he was going to win. I told him he'd be better off just forgetting about her and finding another girl. I mean, it's not hard in Thailand, there's millions of them. There must be over two thousand hookers working out of Nana Plaza alone, you're spoilt for choice. But there was no talking to him. He asked me if I had a pen and then had me write down the number of a mobile phone.

"It's Sunan's," he said. "She and Joy should be at the airport, I want you to call them and tell them that my flight's been delayed and that I won't be getting into Bangkok until late tonight. Tell them that they're to start the party without me."

He had to repeat what he'd said because it didn't make any sense, and then he explained the whole plan to me. I had to admit, it was bloody funny, the thought of two dozen of Joy's friends and relatives coming down on the bus for a party, pawning their gold for a pick-up truck they weren't going to get, and then turning up at the karaoke bar to wait for him.

Anyway, I did as he asked, I called Sunan and said that I wanted to speak to Joy. They were both at the airport, just as Pete had said. I told Joy that Pete would be late. She sounded disappointed but I told her that we'd meet her at the karaoke bar in the evening. She said she wanted to wait at the airport but I said we weren't sure what time he'd be getting in. She asked me if I was going to the party and I said sure, I wouldn't miss it for the world. That seemed to reassure her. Did I feel bad about deceiving her? Not really, I've been lied too so many times by bargirls that it was a pleasant change to be on the other side of the fence for once. I mean, yeah, Joy was a cute girl, but taking money off Pete and giving it to her husband is just taking the piss. Joy asked me if I wanted to go to Si Saket with her and Pete. Pete was going to buy her an Isuzu she said. A red one. Pete really had spun her a line. I hope he never gets the hump at me.

I was wide awake by the time I'd hung up so I shook whatshername and gave her a good seeing to before getting up. Bitch insisted I gave her an extra two hundred baht but what the hell, she was worth it.

PETE

I spent pretty much the whole day staring at my watch. Bangkok was six hours ahead of London and I figured that Joy and her family would probably get to the karaoke bar at about nine in the evening. At three o'clock in the afternoon I poured myself a gin and tonic. I pictured them all sitting around the VIP room, same as we did last year, ordering bottles of Johnnie Walker Black Label and knocking it back like there was no tomorrow, figuring that the farang would be along to pick up the bill. Joy would be singing. She loved karaoke, and she had a good voice. I drank my gin and tonic and remembered how she used to sing to me, holding my hand and looking into my eyes. I wondered if her husband had gone to the karaoke bar with her, and if he was there with her now. Had he been there a year ago, sitting with the group of the guys in the corner as Joy entertained me and Mon did the bargirl thing with Nigel?

The phone started ringing just after five o'clock in the afternoon. I left the answering machine switched on and it took the calls. The first time she didn't say anything but I could hear music in the background and Thai voices, laughing and singing. She called again about half an hour later. She didn't leave a message but I could hear her talking to Sunan.

After she'd hung up, I played back the tape. I couldn't believe what I was hearing so I played it several times. There was no mistake.

"Man mai yoo," said Joy. "Ben khrueng chak."

"Man poot a-rai?" asked Sunan.

I couldn't make out much more, but that was enough. What they'd said was innocuous enough. Joy had said I wasn't there. There was a machine. And Sunan had asked what I'd said. But it was the way they'd referred to me that made my heart sink. When Thai people talk about each other, they usually use their names rather than pronouns. When they do use pronouns, however, they're used to denote status. If it's someone older or more respected, they'd say "pee" for he or she. If younger, "nong". Between equals they'd use "kao" for he. But Joy and Sunan had used "man" as the pronoun, and man wasn't used for people, "man" was used for animals. It meant "it", but "it" doesn't convey the contempt implied when a Thai uses it to refer to a person. It's a huge insult. It was how they really felt about me. I was nothing, I was a source of money and that was all.

I poured myself another gin and tonic, put my feet up on the coffee table, and waited.

She called three more times before six o'clock, but still didn't leave a message. I wondered if they'd cut the cake. I wondered how many bottles of Black Label they'd ordered, and if they'd brought enough money to pay for it. I wondered if they realised that I wasn't coming, that they'd have to pay for their party out of their own pocket, and that they'd lose the deposit on the gleaming red Isuzu SLX. I wondered if Joy realised she'd been caught out and that I knew she had a husband.

She called for the last time at eight o'clock in the evening, which was two o'clock in the morning in Bangkok. She was on Sunan's mobile but it sounded as if she were outside. Her voice was soft but she didn't sound upset. "Pete, where are you?" she said. "Why you not here with me, Pete? I love you, only one."

That was it. No anger, no recriminations. I felt like shit. I wanted to call her back, to say that I was sorry, that I still loved her no matter what she'd done, no matter what lies she'd told, but I kept staring at the photograph of her and her husband and convinced myself that the only way to win the game was never to talk to her again.

I wanted her to know, though. I wanted her to know that I wasn't just one of a thousand stupid farangs. I wanted her to know that I knew, that I'd won the game, that I was smarter than her. I made copies of Phiraphan's report and photocopied the photographs and put them in an envelope addressed to Joy at her home in Si Saket. I was about to seal it when I had a thought. I got all the photographs of her, the ones taken in Zombie and the ones from our trip to Isarn, and I tore them all up and put the pieces in the envelope, too. I took the envelope to the Post Office and got stamps. At the last minute I almost baulked, I stood at the post box and I couldn't let go of the envelope, I stood for what seemed like hours with it half in and half out of the slot. Then I took a deep breath and opened my fingers. The instant it dropped through the slot I wished I hadn't done it, but it was too late then. I wondered how she'd react when she opened it and saw for herself the evidence of her betrayal.

JOY

How did I feel when Pete didn't turn up? How do you think I felt? He was a farang, and farangs tell lies. Eighty per cent of farangs lie. They say they love you when they don't mean it, they say they want to take care of you and then they don't. I think the way he lied was terrible, though. My father and two of my brothers and almost a dozen cousins came all the way from Si Saket to celebrate our birthdays, his as well as mine. They were all very angry at Pete but I told them that he'd had a problem back in England. Sunan lent me some money to pay for the party but she made me promise to pay her back. I didn't know what had happened, whether he'd been delayed or whether he'd decided not to come.

Park said I was stupid to believe anything a farang said. He said they come to Thailand for only one reason and that was to fuck Thai girls and that we should just try to get as much money from them as we can. He says they're not people, they're dogs. He didn't go to the party, he went to see his friends at Nana Plaza, but he came around to the karaoke bar when Nana closed. Park was annoyed about the Isuzu, but he had no reason to be because it was me and Sunan who had pawned our gold as the deposit. Why did Pete do that? Why did he make us spend money if he never intended to buy the pick-up truck. I never asked him to buy me the truck, it was his idea. Okay, I'd always said that I wanted one and that it'd be good for our family to have one, but I never told him to buy it for me. There was no need, I can earn enough to buy one in less than a year. Same as Sunan, she bought a Toyota for Bird and she's almost paid it off already. A girl can earn good money in Nana Plaza, giving farangs what they want.

We all had a good time at the party, anyway. My father got drunk and started to cuddle me but I pushed him away. I'm too old for that now, I told him. They all sang happy birthday to me, just like farangs, and everybody said it was even better than last year because there weren't any farangs around.

Afterwards, when Park had come, we went back to Sunan's room. Park and I had a big fight because I could smell perfume on him. He'd been with some slut, I was sure of it, but he denied it. I said that Thai men lied as easily as farangs and he slapped me, hard, across the face. Two, three, four times, until Sunan told him to stop. I was right, though, it's not just farangs who lie. Thais lie, too. Eighty per cent of them.

PETE

Joy called several times the day after the party and once on the day after that. "I love you, why you not come see me, Pete?" she said on the answering machine. "I go back Si Saket. I wait for you in Si Saket."

I felt like shit. I didn't feel like I'd won. I kept picturing her with the cake, waiting for me. I wanted to telephone her and say that I was sorry, that it had all been a mistake and that I was coming after all. But at the same time I wanted to call her and gloat, to rub her nose in what I'd done to her.

I'd imagined that after the party, after I'd got my revenge and everything, I'd be able to walk away, that I'd never give her another thought. I was wrong. I was so fucking wrong. If anything, now I wanted her even more.

I tried to take my mind off her by playing games on my computer. Most of the time I played Risk, a war game, a game of strategy where the aim is to conquer the world. I played for hours every day. But half my mind was still on Joy. I still wanted her. I still wanted to be with her. I propped the photograph of Joy and her husband against my VDU to remind me of what she was and what she'd done. I couldn't concentrate, I couldn't work on the book, all I could do was to play Risk and pace around my apartment. I barely slept and I didn't want to eat. I didn't shower and I didn't shave. I lost about two kilos in a week and I looked like shit.

I played Risk so much that I began to win every game against the computer, even when it was set at its most competitive level. I played on autopilot, barely considering each move. I knew how to win, I knew exactly what to do so that no matter how the game started I would win. And once I'd reached that stage, the game stopped being fun any more.

I played. I won. Where was the satisfaction in that? It was the same with Joy. I'd played the game and I'd won, but it didn't mean a thing. I was older than her, I was better educated, I had a well-paid job and the freedom to go wherever I wanted. Of course I'd won the game. I was better equipped to play. One afternoon I closed the Risk file and started writing. I wrote about Joy. How I'd met her. How I'd fallen in love with her. How she'd betrayed me. And how I got my own back. I wrote through the afternoon and late into the night. I didn't finish until three o'clock in the morning. I'd written almost four thousand words.

That night, for the first time, I slept without dreaming about her. When I woke up, I read through what I'd written. Parts of it made me smile, and parts of it made me miss her so much that I wanted to phone her up there and then.

I emailed what I'd written to Alistair in Hong Kong and a couple of hours later he emailed me back: "Pete—what a sad fuck you are! Great piece. Why don't you try and sell it? Esquire or GQ would snap it up. How's the book going?"

I messaged him that the book was on schedule, even though it wasn't. I'd spent so much time pining for Joy that I'd have to work night and day for the next month or so if I was going to meet his deadline.

ALISTAIR

Hiring that private detective was the best thing Pete could have done. Joy was driving him crazy and his work was suffering. I tried to be subtle about it because I was so far away, but he was missing deadlines left, right and centre. I was under pressure from head office to put a rocket under Pete, but the times I mentioned it to him he didn't seem to be listening. All he'd talk about was Joy and how she'd lied to him. For a week or so he seemed to stop working completely. I wasn't sure what to do. To be honest, he sounded like he was close to a nervous breakdown and I thought that if I gave him a hard time I might push him over the edge. Looking back, maybe I was being too soft on him. Maybe what

Pete needed right then was an almighty kick up his arse.

He emailed me this story he'd written about the whole Joy saga. I was livid. Four thousand words. Four thousand fucking words. He was supposed to be working flat out on the London guide and there he was typing four thousand words on a Thai hooker. I was lost for words. I sent him some bland reply saying he should try and place it with a men's magazine, but what I really wanted to do was to grab him by the throat and bang his head against a wall. I mean, what the fuck did he think he was playing at? Who pays his wages? We do. Who's he responsible to? Us. But he was several thousand miles away and I needed the guide finishing so I couldn't sack him there and then, that would have been cutting my own throat. I was the one who'd recommended Pete for the London job and if he fucked up then it'd reflect badly on me, too.

JOY

I was so shocked when I got the copies of the questionnaire I'd filled in and the photographs. I realised why Pete hadn't come to Thailand, and why he hadn't been in touch. Why are farangs so devious? Why couldn't he have been more honest? And why had he torn up all the photographs he'd taken of our time together in Si Saket. Did it mean so little to him?

I thought at the time that there was something not right about the man who came to our village. He was too smooth, and I didn't like the way the girl who was with him looked at me. Sort of contemptuous, like she was better than me. I thought it was because my family was so poor and she was from the city, but it was obviously because they were detectives working for Pete. It was a nasty thing to do, to promise me money and then not give it to me.

Park was furious when he saw the photograph of him sitting with me. He slapped me and said that I was stupid, that we should have stayed in Bangkok. He stormed off and didn't come back for a week. I think he went to see that bitch Daeng, but when he came back he wouldn't say where he'd been.

I cried and I cried and I didn't eat anything for two days. I wanted to die, that's what I kept telling Sunan. I was bored with my life, with everything. Pete wouldn't love me, he wouldn't take care of me, I'd have to go back to Nana Plaza to work and everyone would know that Pete had stopped giving me money. All the girls would laugh at me behind my back, they can be really cruel. I've done it myself, so I knew what to expect. It happened to my friend Cat last year. A customer of hers from France promised to take care of her so long as she went back to her village and kept away from the bars. He gave her twenty thousand baht and said he'd send her money every month until he came back to live with her. She had a big party and brought herself a mobile phone, walked around Nana Plaza as if she owned it. She went into Zombie every night, buying drinks and showing off. Two weeks later she'd run out of money and had to start dancing again. We all said how stupid she was. How easily she'd be duped by the farang. I didn't want the girls in Zombie to laugh at me, but what could I do?

Sunan gave me some tablets to take. She said they'd make me feel better but they just made me crazy. I started laughing and I got the razor that Sunan used to trim her hair and I slashed my wrists. I wanted to hurt myself, to show everybody how angry I was, but I didn't cut myself too deep, not down to where the veins are. I wanted to hurt myself but I didn't want to die. I wanted Pete to know how much he'd hurt me. I got a knife from the kitchen and I used it to write a letter with the blood. Sunan was laughing at me, telling me that I was crazy. She doesn't understand me. I don't think anyone really understands me. Park, maybe, but even he doesn't understand why I cut myself. I get so angry sometimes, but there's nobody I can get angry at. If I shout at Park he just slaps me, if I shout at Sunan she hits me too. The only person I can really get angry at is myself, and when I do hurt myself I feel better for a while. Not for long, but for a while at least, and that's better than nothing. I wish my mother was still here. When I was little and I was upset I could always go to her and she'd pick me up and cuddle me and everything would be okay. But now I don't have a mother. Besides, I was a child then and now I'm an adult. I have to take care of myself.

PETE

About two weeks after I'd sent Phiraphan's report to Joy, I got an airmail letter from her. The letter inside was child-like and at first I thought it was written in brown paint. Then I realised what it was. Blood.

Pete. I love you. I want go stay with you in England. I want you come in Bangkok. For you.

Love Joy

And just in case there was any doubt where the blood had come from, there was a small picture, drawn in blood, of a cut wrist and drips falling from it.

Underneath, in green ink, she'd written: "I want see you now."

I stared at the letter, wondering if she'd really done it, if she'd really cut her wrist for me. I knew she'd done it before, she had the scars from where she'd cut her wrist when her mother had died, and she'd done it again when her brother had crashed her motorcycle. But had she cut her wrists because of what I'd done?

It was the last thing I'd expected her to do. I thought that maybe she'd have written me a letter saying she never wanted to see me again. Or maybe a letter saying that she was sorry for lying to me. But I guess what I really expected was for her to cut off all contact, to admit that the game was over and for her to walk away, to go back to her previous way of life, fleecing farangs in Nana Plaza. But her letter was just a declaration of her love, saying that she wanted to be with me. It didn't make any sense. She had a husband. She was with him, spending her money—my money—on him. How could she want to be with me? How could she think that I'd believe that she wanted to be with me? I thought I understood Thais but her letter made no sense to me at all.

I'd won, I'd proved that she had a husband, that she'd been lying to me. There was nothing she could do to turn back the clock, so why mutilate herself?

I wondered how she'd done it. Had she got drunk, or had she done it when she was angry, with a knife or with a razor blade? And of all the things she could have done to prove that she was sorry, why cut herself? I sat with the letter in my hands and tried to get inside her head, but it was impossible.

The day after I got the letter in blood, I received another envelope, this time containing a six-page letter, written in green ink, half in English, half in Thai. She repeated over and over how much she loved me, how much she missed me and how much she wanted to be with me. Nowhere in the letter did she mention the fact that she'd lied or that she had a husband. It was as if the whole private detective incident had never happened, total denial.

I put both letters in the top drawer of my desk. I don't know why, but I couldn't throw them away. I'd accepted the fact that I'd never see her again, that it was over, irrevocably over, but I wanted to keep the letters.

I started working on the London book, fifteen or sixteen hours a day, and I didn't shave or shower for days on end. I got up, I worked, I ate, I slept, and I got up and started work again. Joy didn't call and there were no more letters. As the days passed, I spent less and less time thinking about her, and when I did it didn't hurt as much. The anger faded first, and then I stopped missing her, and after a few weeks I could laugh about what had happened.

ALISTAIR

Pete really buckled down to work and tore through the London guide book. I was getting revised chapters every two or three days, and he did the complete index in forty-eight hours. He was the Pete of old, fast, accurate and writing with flair, showing all the qualities that had led me to recommend him for the job in the first place. I was well pleased with his performance and so were head office. I actually put through a memo recommending we increase his Christmas bonus.

I was looking forward to getting him back to Bangkok. There was still work to be done on the travel-cookery book—*Cooking Across South East Asia* we'd decided to call it—and head office had decided they wanted books on Cambodia and Laos. There were sections on Cambodia and Laos in our South East Asian guidebook but they were becoming increasingly popular as tourist destinations and justified their own volumes. Pete was the perfect choice as editor, now that he'd put the Joy thing behind him.

PETE

Bruce phoned me up a couple of days before I was due to go back to Bangkok. He'd been offered a better job with another company and he'd decided to accept. Apparently Saravoot had been pissing him about something rotten. He hadn't delivered the company car that he'd promised, and he'd stopped paying the rent on Bruce's house. The reason Bruce had phoned was that as part of the package the new company had put together, he was going to be living in a large three-bedroomed apartment in Soi 23, a couple of miles down Sukhumvit from Fatso's Bar. He asked me if I wanted to share and I said that I'd give it a try. It'd been years since I'd lived with anyone, and almost twenty years since I'd shared with another guy, but I'd always gotten on well with Bruce and figured we probably wouldn't get on each other's nerves. He'd be out at work all day, he said, and most nights we'd be in the bars anyway. He said he'd fax me directions, then asked how Joy was.

I told him what the private detective had discovered. "Bloody hell, mate," he said. "You must be shattered."

I said I was okay, that I'd half expected that she had someone else, then I told him about the birthday party. He pissed himself laughing and said that he couldn't wait to tell Big Ron and the boys. To be honest, it sounded as if he was laughing at me, not with me, like he didn't understand that it had all been a game and that I'd won it.

BRUCE

To be honest, I wasn't surprised that Joy had a husband. Why should she give up everything for him? Pete's always been an optimist, he's the sort of guy who goes to a greyhound racing track and asks if he can bet on the rabbit, you know? Joy's a bargirl, he should have known what to expect. And it's not as if he was as pure as the driven snow. He'd paid barfine for dozens of girls, why should he expect her to be faithful to him? Okay, I guess it was a bit much for her to have an actual husband, but it's not as if Pete had ever asked her to live with him. He took her back to his hotel, sure, but he never really treated her like a girlfriend, never mind a wife.

I kept telling him that if he really loved her, if he really wanted to have her in his life, then he should just offer to make an honest woman of her. Tell her that she could live with him, spend twenty-four hours a day, seven days a week with her. He'd soon have found out whether or not she really loved him. This business of paying her to live in Si Saket with her father never made any sense to me. He never gave her the chance to show if she was serious about him. These people, they have nothing, they're poorer than the poorest families back in the UK. Of course Joy is going to hold on to someone who offers her any form of security, and if she can't get that from Pete then I can understand why she'd latch on to a Thai man. She had no way of knowing if Pete would really come back to Thailand, or if he'd keep on supporting her. She knew he'd been screwing around, too. The girls talk, they always do. How did he think Joy would feel, knowing that he'd barfined another girl? Probably the same as Pete felt when he discovered that Joy had a husband.

And I thought the business of the party was really petty. It was a nasty thing to do. I mean, she's hardly got any money, and he makes her spend it on a party and a deposit for a pick-up truck. I know he was hurt, but he should just have walked away. That's what I would have done, anyway. Just walked away and never spoken to her again. I think that by going through with that whole revenge thing, he was lowering himself to their level. And I think he's underestimating their capacity for revenge. If he made her look foolish in front of her family and friends, she's going to hate him for ever. And she'll get her own back. We'll see. I hope I'm wrong.

SARAVOOT

I don't understand what it is with farangs. They all seem to go crazy when they come to Thailand. It's as if they hand in their common sense when they get off the plane. I was very impressed with Bruce when I met him in Newcastle. He was well groomed, always immaculately turned out, and his factory was the same. He was a hard worker, in at eight, often putting in a twelve hour day. I used to call him from Bangkok and it seemed that he was always in the office. I used to joke about him not having a home to go to.

I spent many hours in Bruce's company. I liked him. He knew everything there was to know about the handbag business, and he took pride in his factory and workforce. When I raised the possibility of working with me in Thailand, at first he was reluctant. I got the feeling that he hadn't travelled much and I suggested he come over for a week's holiday, at my expense, so that he could see for himself what Thailand was like. I showed Bruce around the factory and he immediately came up with ways that we could improve our productivity. I offered him a position as my factory manager at a salary half as much again as he was getting in Newcastle. He accepted and six weeks later he flew over to Thailand.

I rented a house for him, a four-bedroomed mansion on the outskirts of Bangkok. It was on a private estate with its own security guards and a communal swimming pool. Cost me almost a hundred thousand baht every month, but I wanted him to be comfortable. The house had everything: cable TV, video recorder, stereo, a fully equipped kitchen, top-of-the-range Italian furniture. It was beautiful. And I arranged for one of my maids, Lek, to go in every day.

The first few weeks were fine. Bruce spent most of his time meeting the staff and getting a feel for the business. But then he started dressing down. First his suit jacket went. Then his tie. Then he started coming to work in jeans and polo shirt. I mentioned it a couple of times, but he didn't pay any attention. He didn't seem to understand that the suit and tie commanded respect. He was a farang, he was a manager, and it was important to keep standards high. I don't always wear a suit, in fact I often go into work dressed casually, but always designer clothes. Versace shirts. Armani pants. Bally loafers. He was wearing counterfeit Lacoste shirts that he'd bought in Patpong. He seemed to take great pleasure in telling me how little he'd paid for them. Less than a hundred baht.

Then he started coming in late. I got the feeling that he was staying out in the bars, drinking. He'd complain of headaches and sit in his office, drinking black coffee and telling his secretary not to put calls through to him. That's no way to run a business. Not my business, anyway. And girls began telephoning the office wanting to speak to him. One in particular, a girl called Troy. Several of the office girls complained to the office manager about the girl. She was impolite, demanding to speak to Bruce, saying that he was a friend.

The crunch came when Lek went into the house and discovered that Troy had moved in. Troy apparently told Lek that she was Bruce's wife. Lek was horrified. Bruce didn't seem to appreciate that no self-respecting Thai woman would want anything to do with a bargirl. Lek walked straight out of the house and refused to go back. And if that wasn't enough, I caught him showing the girl around the factory. It seems Bruce had some idea of hiring her to work in the office. I couldn't believe how stupid he was being. I'd have had a revolt on my hands. She was a bargirl. A prostitute. A coarse, ugly, impolite girl, young enough to be his daughter. She was wearing tight jeans, high heels and a T-shirt that showed off her midriff—everything about her screamed prostitute. And he had the audacity to introduce her to me. She waied me and averted her eyes. She knew how annoyed I was but Bruce didn't notice. He had to go. He'd lost everyone's respect. He'd become a joke.

I wasn't looking forward to searching for a replacement. It's so difficult to find decent farangs. Most want to come to Thailand for the wrong reasons. They don't want to come to work, they want to sleep with young girls. If I could, I'd prefer not to have any farangs working for me. Thai managers work hard and always consider how their behaviour affects the company, they have a loyalty that you can depend on. Farangs are lazy and untrustworthy. That's my experience, anyway, and I don't think I've been especially unlucky. Most of my friends who run companies tell me that they've had bad experiences, too. When farangs first arrive in Thailand they work hard, but then they become lazy and start spending all their evenings in the bars. Then they get involved with bargirls and forget why they came to the country in the first place. It's as if all they can think about is sex. If you want to do business in Europe or America, you have to have some farangs working for you because Westerners always seem to feel happier if they can deal with their own people. But sometimes I wonder if they're worth the trouble.

PETE

As soon as I'd wrapped up the London guide, I flew back to Thailand. Bruce had faxed me the address of his apartment but he'd have been better sending me a map because the taxi driver drove past the correct road half a dozen times before we found it. It was a brand new building and by the look of it most of the apartments were empty. Bangkok was in the middle of a property slump and rather than sell at a loss or drop their rents, most Thai landlords preferred to leave their properties empty.

The flat was on the twelfth floor. I knocked on the door and to my surprise it was opened by Troy. Bruce was lying on the sofa but he jumped up when I walked in. He'd shaved off his beard since I last saw him. He must have seen me looking at his chin because he grinned and rubbed it. "Troy's idea," he said. "She reckons it makes me look younger. What do you think?"

I thought he looked better with the beard but I didn't say so, I just said, yeah, it took years off him. He helped me carry my cases into the bedroom.

It was a huge flat, more than two hundred square metres, and the sitting room was about the size of a basketball court. There were three bedrooms. Bruce had taken the master bedroom but mine was big with its own bathroom. "That's Troy's room," said Bruce, nodding at the room opposite his.

"How long's she staying here?" I asked.

"I figured we'd need a maid," he said. "What with all our laundry and everything. I said we'd give her three thousand baht a month."

"Plus her rent, right? She's living rent free, isn't she?"

He looked at me without saying anything for a few seconds. "Is that a problem?"

I wanted to say that yes, it was a problem. I wasn't sure that I wanted to share the apartment with a hooker. She'd be answering the phone, she'd be in and out of my room, she'd be there most of the day when I was working. Bruce should have told me he'd planned to move her in before he offered to share with me. It was one thing for two guys to share an apartment, it was something quite different for two guys and a hooker, albeit one disguised as a maid. "No, it's not a problem," I said. "I just wish I'd known, that's all."

"She works hard," he said. "Wait till you see what she does with your shirts."

Troy was in the sitting room, watching a Thai variety show. She was wearing hot pants and a tight white T-shirt that left nothing to imagination. I knew she was twenty-one but she looked much younger.

It was about ten o'clock in the morning and Bruce suggested we go down to Fatso's Bar for breakfast. I asked him if he didn't have to go to work but he just shrugged and said he'd call in sick.

In the taxi he asked me if I'd been in touch with Joy. I told him I'd no idea where she was.

"Are you going to look her up now that you're back?"

I shrugged.

"I'll give it a week," he said. "You'll be back with her."

BIG RON

Was I surprised that Joy had a husband? Was I fuck. It's her instinct to lie, to get as much from a farang as she can. It's like the story of the scorpion and the frog. You heard that one? There's this frog sitting down at the edge of a stream. A scorpion comes up and asks the frog if he'll carry the scorpion across the stream. Scorpions can't swim, you see. Now, the frog's not stupid. "If I let you on my back, you'll sting me," he says.

"Why would I do that?" asks the scorpion. "I want to get across the stream. If I sting you, you'll die and I'll drown."

The frog thinks about it and then says okay. So the scorpion climbs on the frog's back and the frog starts to swim across. As they reach the midway point, the scorpion stings the frog. With its dying breath, the frog says to the scorpion, "Why did you do that? Now we'll both die."

As he disappears under the water, the scorpion shrugs and says, "Instinct, I guess."

It wouldn't matter how much Pete loved Joy, how much he gave her. It wouldn't matter if he meant to marry her and take her away from the life that had pushed her into prostitution, no matter what he did or what he promised, she'd follow her instinct.

It's like we say here. You can take the girl out of the bar, but you can't take the bar out of the girl.

PETE

I left it a week before going to Nana Plaza. I'd been in Fatso's, but Rick and Jimmy were playing silly buggers, Big Glassing anyone who went to the toilet. Bruce was doing his old trick of getting the girls to pour his away when no one was looking, but I couldn't be bothered playing that game.

I sat outside and had a gin and tonic. It tasted as foul as ever. It came out of a Beefeater bottle but whatever it was, it didn't even taste like gin. It was always a shock to the system because Big Ron served large measures of the real stuff, but once you stepped inside the Plaza you had no idea what you were drinking. Most of the guys stuck to bottled beer in the Plaza, because at least a Heineken was a Heineken.

One of the dancers came out and sat down next to me. It was Wan, the girl who used to do the lesbian show with Joy. I bought her a cola and she clinked glasses with me. I asked her if she'd seen Joy but she shook her head. "She go back Si Saket," she said. "Pete, why you not go party?"

I told her that I knew Joy had a husband and that she'd lied to me. Wan looked at me with wide eyes and denied that Joy was married. I wouldn't have expected her to say anything else. Joy was her friend and I was an outsider.

I don't know why, but I told Wan the whole story. About the private detective, the photograph, and how I wanted to get my revenge. She sat and listened, sometimes smiling, sometimes shaking her head sadly. I asked her what she thought.

She shrugged. "I don't know," she said in a sing-song voice.

I asked her if she thought Joy loved me. A stupid question, and I hated myself for asking it.

Wan looked at me earnestly. "Joy love you too much, Pete. She have you only one."

JIMMY

We all thought what Pete did was a hoot. The farang bites back. But I think he made a big mistake because it meant a serious loss of face for Sunan and Joy, and I don't think Pete appreciated what that means. Thais will wait years for revenge if they have to, but they never forget an insult.

They can be very creative when it comes to getting their own back, too. The big thing here with unfaithful husbands, is for the wives to get a bit handy with the old kitchen knife. The unkindest cut of all. But they don't do it in anger, they wait, they wait until the husband thinks he's gotten away with it, then slash! Blood on the sheets and the guy has to use a pair of tweezers to piss. It happens so often in Bangkok that the hospitals here have got really proficient at sewing dicks back on. Micro-surgery, they call it, they reconnect all the vessels and nerves and stuff and apart from a ridge of scar tissue around the base of the thing it's as good as new. The doctors are now so good that, providing the dick is wrapped up in a pack of frozen peas or suchlike, there is more than ninety per cent chance of repairing the damage.

Now, once the wives realised that the doctors could sew the dick back on, they started to dispose of the organs. Up country, they throw it to the ducks. The birds fight like fuck for them, apparently, must be a delicacy. Or maybe there's a revenge element, too, a chance for the ducks to eat humans for a change. Anyway, there aren't too many ducks in Bangkok, so the wives there started throwing them in the street. If a truck rolls over it, a cut off dick can be squashed flat until it's the size of a saucer. No bloody use to anyone, that. Or there's another variation—putting it in the blender. Thirty seconds at high speed and there isn't much left. Prick puree.

There was a great one in the Bangkok Post a while back. A woman in Khorat had found that her husband had a second wife. That's what they call mistresses here, mia noy, second wife. They're not married or anything, and it's usually only a temporary thing, but the whole Thai marriage thing is a mystery anyway. So this woman waits for a couple of months until her husband has a dose of the 'flu, and she gives him a couple of tablets before he goes to bed, telling him that they're for his headache. Well, they're not, they're sleeping tablets, and he wakes up with a pain in his groin and blood all over the place. He goes apeshit, searching high and low for the bit she'd cut off, but she just keeps screaming at him that it serves him right. He checks the fridge, the back yard, the toilet, but there's no sign of it. He begs her to tell him what she did with it. She goes out into the garden and points up at the sky. Seems she'd tied it to a helium-filled balloon and let it go. Brilliant, huh? Guy's still with his wife, you know. Didn't press charges. I guess he realised that with a one-inch dick, he's not going to be able to get himself another woman.

She probably makes him satisfy her with his tongue. See, that's what I mean about the Thais and revenge. They have a knack for it. Pete better watch his step.

PETE

I'd been back in Thailand almost a month before I saw Joy again. At first I didn't recognise her—she was wearing a big white T-shirt and black flared jeans that I hadn't seen before and she'd cut her hair so that it now reached to just below her shoulders. She'd dyed the front, too, red streaks that she'd tucked behind her ears. She was with Sunan and they got out of a taxi and walked into the Plaza together. I was sitting outside Zombie, watching a rugby match on one of the overhead televisions. Can't remember who was playing, and to be honest I wasn't even concentrating on the game, I was thinking about Joy. Everything about Nana Plaza reminded me about Joy. The girls, the music, the noise, the smells. That's what was so funny, really, I was thinking about Joy but when I saw her I looked right through her. It was only when I saw her face harden that I realised it was her. It was the hair, I guess, she looked totally different with shorter hair.

My heart sort of turned over and I smiled. She smiled then, as if she'd been waiting to see how I'd react before she betrayed any emotion. Sunan said something to Joy, then walked through the curtain into Zombie. Joy slipped on to the stool next to me. She was carrying her red purse and she let me take it off her. She didn't say a word, just kept looking at me and smiling. I opened the purse. The photograph was there. The photograph of the two of us sitting in the bar, taken more than a year ago. I was stunned. It was the last thing I'd expected. There was no way she could have known that I'd been in Nana Plaza, no way of knowing she was going to see me, so why the hell was she carrying my photograph.

"So, how are you?" she asked, the first thing she'd said since seeing me. Her first words and she was asking how I was. Again, it was the last thing I expected. I thought maybe she'd be angry, bitter, resentful maybe, but it was as if we'd never been apart. She sat next to me, her hand in my lap, smiling as if I were the most precious thing in her life.

I took her left hand in mine and turned it over so I could see her wrist. There were three red razor scars there, alongside the old scars from the cuts she'd made when her mother had died and her brother had crashed her motorcycle. There were other marks running down her wrist, small black cuts. I frowned as I examined them. She turned her wrist so I could see them better. Letters. P. E. T. E. Oh Jesus, she'd carved my name into her flesh. I traced the letters with my finger.

"I do for you, Pete," she said quietly.

"Why, Joy? Why?"

"Because I want you know I love you."

I didn't know what to say. I'd seen the photograph of her and her husband. Hell, I'd sent her a copy of it so she knew that I knew she was married. And she knew that I'd seen the questionnaire she'd filled in.

"What you want me do, Pete?"

I didn't know. I didn't know what to do and I didn't know what to say. I took her back to the flat and we made love. Afterwards we sat on the balcony, looking across the city. Joy chain-smoked and told me what she'd been doing, planting rice on a farm in Khorat, she said. She'd lost weight and she said that was because she'd been smoking marijuana. "Because I think too much," she said.

I asked her what she wanted to do and she said she didn't want to work as a dancer. "I not same before, Pete, now I good girl. I be good girl for you." She was going to speak to the mamasan in Zombie and ask if she could work as a waitress. "What you think, Pete?" she asked, leaning her head against my shoulder. "You think good idea?"

I said yeah, I thought it was a good idea.

JOY

Wan phoned me to say that Pete was back. I'd been dancing in a bar in Soi Cowboy but business wasn't good. The police in Soi Cowboy don't allow topless or naked dancing, or any shows, so most tourists go to Patpong or Nana Plaza. The men who go to Soi Cowboy are usually working in Bangkok, they've been there for a long time so they're tighter with their money, you can't con them into paying five thousand baht for a night. I'd only been working there for a few days when Wan called, so I quit straight away.

I went to Nana Plaza three times before I saw Pete. The first two times he wasn't there and I ended up going to a short-time hotel with an American guy who used to barfine me when I danced in Zombie.

Pete looked terrible, like he'd been staying out too late and drinking too much. He looked old. He kept asking me where I'd been, what I'd been doing. I wanted to tell him it was none of his business because he hadn't sent me money for months.

He took me back to the apartment he was sharing with Bruce. It was huge. Three big bedrooms, a sitting room that was almost as big as Zombie, and a balcony. Every bedroom had its own bathroom. Six Thai families could have lived there but Pete and Bruce were staying there on their own. It was too big, I felt I was lost and I'm sure there were ghosts there.

Pete kept asking me what I wanted to do. I didn't know what to say to him. I wanted him to take care of me, to give me enough money so that I didn't have to work, but he didn't offer to do that. Dancing was the best way of earning money, but I knew he didn't want me to dance, so I said I'd work as a waitress. He seemed to like that idea. I explained that waitresses were paid only half what the dancers earned and Pete said he'd pay the difference. Big deal, huh? Last of the big spenders.

PETE

Joy started work as a waitress. She looked really cute in her uniform—a white shirt with a thin black tie and a long black skirt. She worked really hard, serving drinks, emptying ashtrays and cleaning tables. She seemed to enjoy it, too. I guess she was happier because she didn't have to bare all in front of the customers.

Every time I went in she'd make a big fuss over me, hugging me and kissing me, and whenever she wasn't working she'd stand next to me and talk to me. Waitresses could have their barfines paid, same as the dancers, but I never paid it. I told her that I wouldn't treat her like a prostitute again. I'd see her before work, or after, and on her days off, but I wasn't prepared to pay money to the bar so that she could leave work early. She said that she understood, that she wanted to prove to me that she could be a good girl. To be honest, I'd have preferred to have her working in a shop or a restaurant or a regular bar like Fatso's, but I knew that she could earn more working in Nana Plaza.

I went in pretty much every night to see her. Sometimes I'd stay for an hour, sometimes for a lot longer. And every time I left, she'd walk me to the door and kiss me goodbye as if to let all the other girls know that she was mine. Or that I was hers. Whatever. Sometimes she'd call me at three o'clock in the morning, just after the bar had closed, and she'd ask if she could come and see me. Half an hour later there'd be a timid knock on the door to the apartment and she'd be there, smiling shyly, still wearing her waitress uniform, and she'd spend the night asleep in my arms, pressed up against me, barely breathing.

I was trying to get some work done, but she was all I could think about. I don't know why I loved her, I really don't. If I drew up a list of everything I liked about her, and compared it with a list of why she was totally unsuitable, there'd be no doubt about which would carry more weight. She was a former bargirl, she'd slept with God knows how many men. And it's not as if she was forced into it: I'd seen Joy with lots of different men in Zombie and she was always vivacious, full of life, enjoying herself while she worked. I hated to think about it, but I knew she'd be the same with them in bed. Sex was just something she did, enthusiastically and with flair, and I had no illusions that she was only that way with me.

She was a liar, too. She'd lied to me so many times that I'd lost count, and even taking into account the Thai propensity for telling you what you want to hear, it was still impossible to base any long-term relationship on lies. The big lie was her husband. She'd insisted that he was only in her house for a few days, that he wasn't in her life any more, but prior to my detective uncovering what was going on, she'd always denied that she had anyone. It wasn't just the emotional betrayal, it was the fact that she'd been making love to a Thai while she'd been sleeping with me. That was a big thing all right because we didn't always use a condom.

It happened almost by mistake, a couple of months after I'd starting paying her barfine. I was with her in a short-time hotel and the condom broke. That happens a lot with condoms made in Thailand, they must use cheap rubber or something. Anyway, I felt it break and I pulled out. It had torn apart and I took it off. It was the last one I had. I knew I could go out to reception and buy one off the guy there for ten baht, but Joy held on to me. "Pete, I not sick. I not have Aids, I not have anything. I make love to you, only one." Then she pulled me back down and I finished making love to her without a condom.

Since then I'd rarely used one, and I'd never caught anything. I always figured that Joy was being faithful, but once I'd discovered that she had a Thai boyfriend, I'd started using condoms again. Initially, anyway. Then Joy had asked me not to, she said she wanted a baby, she wanted to have children with me to show me how much she loved me. I told her that I was scared of getting sick but she told me that there was no need to worry, Park had gone, she only made love to me, and she'd gone for an Aids test when she got back to Bangkok. I did as she asked, but at the back of my mind was the thought that maybe she was still lying to me.

So how could I continue a relationship with such a deep level of mistrust? I don't know, I really don't know. It was her looks, partly, but it must have been more than that because the bars of Bangkok are packed with beautiful girls, all willing, all available. Okay, so Joy had the sort of hair I loved and a body to die for, and I think she's the prettiest girl I've ever seen, but that wouldn't be enough on its own to make up for the betrayal.

It was a thousand small things she did. The way she spoke softly to me on the phone, the way she giggled, and the way the giggle would turn into a loud raucous laugh if she heard something really funny. It was the way she was always looking at me to see if I was happy, the way she'd ask me if everything was all right whenever I looked glum. I loved the way she sat with her back arched, as if she'd been groomed at a Swiss finishing school. The way she brushed her hair behind her ear.

I loved watching her dress. She'd spend several minutes checking herself in the mirror, looking over her shoulder to see that her shirt was just right at the back.

Some of the things she did were so damn cute. Thais have a thing about heads and feet. The head is the most important part of the body, the feet the worst. So it's bad manners to point your foot at anything, or to touch something with your feet. And it's equally impolite to make contact with another person's head, even by accident. When Joy wanted to touch my hair, even if it was just to brush it away from my face, she'd wai first and say 'khor thot ka', excuse me.

Her religion was so important to her, too. Whenever she entered or left Nana Plaza, she'd pass a shrine and she'd wai it. I guess it's the equivalent of a Catholic crossing herself when she goes into a church. It can be done automatically, a gesture with no thought, or it can be done with care, with reverence. With Joy it was the latter. She meant it, she respected the shrine, despite the fact that it was at the gateway to a red light area, a den of iniquity. It was as if she was untouched by what was going on around her.

She was always telling me that she loved me. One time I asked her why. She looked deep into my eyes, right into my soul. "Because I same you, Pete. Your mother die when you were young. My mother die when I was young. We the same. I understand you, Pete." When she said it, it took my breath away. I was expecting one of the standard Thai bargirl responses. "Because you good looking, because you fun, because you take care me." I didn't expect such an emotional appeal and I was lost for words, all I could do was to reach out and hold her.

She'd never asked me to explain why I loved her, and if she had, I wasn't sure what I'd have said. Words like "cute" and "pretty" weren't enough, not compared with the way she'd explained her love for me. Anyway, trying to rationalise it never made any sense to me. I'd just keep going around in circles. I loved her, but I could never trust her, and without trust was it really possible to love? So if it wasn't love, what was it? I don't think infatuation would have gone on for so long, and I don't think infatuation would have withstood her lies and betrayal. Obsession, maybe.

Bruno had an explanation; one that sounded ridiculous when he told me, but one that I'd come to think might possibly be true. He said that Joy's village was close to the Cambodian border, and that many parts of her culture were closer to Khmer than to Thai. The Thais believe that Khmer witchdoctors have strange powers, especially involving love and sex. The Thais believe that Khmer girls can ask the witchdoctor to give them a tattoo, an invisible tattoo, somewhere on their body. The tattoo is magic, and once a man touches it, his heart belongs to the girl for ever. It doesn't matter whether or not she loves or wants him, it doesn't matter how she treats him, he's hers and will be forever.

I laughed when Bruno told me the story, but the more I thought about it, the more it had a ring of truth. There was something inexplicable about the way I felt about Joy, and magic seemed as good a way of rationalising it as any. I had asked Joy about the invisible tattoo and she'd thrown back her head and laughed until she'd cried.

JOY

It's true about Khmer girls and the invisible tattoos, but I'm not Khmer, I'm Thai. Thai girls don't need magic to get farangs to do what they want. It's technique, it's something you can learn to do. You have to know what farangs want, and be prepared to give it to them. And what do farangs want? Some just want sex, and they're the easiest to satisfy. Sex is easy. You just lie back and open your legs and let them get on with it. Some farangs who come to Thailand on holiday want a temporary girlfriend. They want sex, but they want someone to show them around, take them to the Grand Palace, that sort of thing, then wave them off at the airport. They're easy to deal with. Some farangs want you to love them, and that's easy to fake, too. It's not magic that Thai girls use to keep farangs, it's psychology.

Sunan and Mon taught me how to do it, and now I teach the girls who come down from our village. The first thing you have to teach them is not to be scared of farangs. I tell the girls to think of them as water buffaloes. They're big and they can be intimidating, but they're basically stupid and very easy to lead by the nose. And it doesn't matter if you don't speak very good English. The farangs will always play stupid games with you, and they'll speak really slowly and mime. All you have to do is to be sweet to them. When you first go up to them, you shake their hand or wai, and then you ask them if it's okay to sit down next to them. And you never ask them to buy you a drink, they have to think it's their own idea. That's the big trick, to make them think they're giving, rather than you taking. I never ask a customer to pay my barfine. I wait for them to ask. Some of the girls are really pushy but eighty per cent of farangs hate pushy girls. And if a customer doesn't ask me if he can pay my barfine, then there are plenty of other buffaloes in the fields.

I quite enjoyed working as a waitress. It wasn't difficult, and I could spend time talking to my friends. I got lots of drinks, too, and tips. A lot of farangs seemed to think that because I was a waitress I was a good girl. It became more of a challenge, I think, because they thought waitresses didn't go with customers, so they'd buy me lots of drinks and didn't paw me as much as when I was a dancer.

Pete came to see me every day, which was great, because every time he came in he'd give me money, sometimes as much as a thousand baht. The rest of the girls were so envious. They really admired me, too. Pete had found out about Park, he knew that I'd lied to him, but he still came back and gave me a thousand baht a day. They wanted to know how I'd done it, how I'd stopped him from finishing with me. I just laughed and said I had a Khmer tattoo.

PETE

Bruce went up country for a few days with Troy. The morning after he got back he knocked on my bedroom door. "Pete," he said. "Can I have a word?"

I opened the bedroom door but he'd gone back into the living room. He was pacing up and down. "What's up?" I asked.

"Look, I'm not accusing anybody, but has anybody been here?"

"Been here?"

"Visitors. Have you had any visitors?"

I was still half asleep. "Err, Joy. That's all. Why?"

"There's a watch missing from my room."

I was staggered. Joy had never, ever stolen anything from me. She'd never taken anything without asking first, and more often than not I had to press her to accept something as simple as a shirt or a photograph. There were three watches in my room, and more than ten thousand baht in a drawer. There was no way she'd have taken a watch from Bruce.

"Where was it?" I asked.

"On the dressing table. It was there before I went to Nong Khai. And my business cards have gone."

"Your business cards?"

"I only just got them. There was a box of business cards on the dressing table. Okay, I don't care about them, but the watch was expensive."

"Bruce, what are you saying? You think Joy stole a box of business cards? Why would she do that?"

He shrugged. "Maybe she didn't know what they were?"

I sighed in frustration. "If she didn't know what they were, why would she steal them?"

"They were in a wooden box. Maybe she thought it was a pretty box. Anyway, it's the watch I'm more concerned about."

I sat down at the dining table. "Look, she was never out of my sight, Bruce. She was with me all the time. There's no way she could have got into your bedroom."

We went backwards and forwards like that for almost ten minutes, me saying that she wouldn't have and couldn't have, Bruce insisting that the watch had gone, and so had the business cards. The thing was, I'd been in Bruce's bedroom several times to use the phone while he was away, and I hadn't seen the watch or the cards. There was some other stuff on the dressing table, including some photographs of him and his family, but no watch and definitely no business cards.

Eventually Bruce went to work. Nothing I'd said had swayed him from his conviction that Joy had stolen from him.

JOY

I couldn't believe it when Pete told me what Bruce had said. I'm not a thief. I've never stolen from anybody. Even when I was small and my family had nothing, I never stole. Pete should have known better. He's left me alone with his wallet and I never even looked inside it, which is more than can be said for him. I know he goes through my bag, checking to see if I've got any photographs of other men or extra money. I never said anything to him about that, and he should have showed me the same respect. He should have just told Bruce that I never steal, and left it at that. Pete kept pressing me, telling me that he wouldn't get angry if I had taken the watch so long as I gave it back. That was as good as accusing me. I was so angry, but I didn't show it.

I mean, how many watches can I wear? I have the Garfield watch that Pete gave me, why would I want another one? And the business cards? That was just stupid. I said to Pete, "How much would I be able to sell the cards for? A million baht? Two million baht?" It was crazy. If I was going to steal anything, I'd have taken money. Pete and Bruce always have money lying around, and I'm sure they wouldn't have noticed if I took a few hundred baht. But I'm not a thief. Pete should know that. If I wanted money, I could get a farang to give it to me. I could go short time and get two thousand baht, and if I flirt with a guy I can get a big tip without even having to have sex with him. There's no need for me to steal a watch. Or business cards.

What made it worse was that Pete said I couldn't go back to the apartment any more because Bruce was worried that I might take something else. I felt so insulted. Whether or not I go to his apartment isn't important, it's not as if I have to pay if we stay in a short-time hotel, but I just feel so angry at being treated like a criminal. I'm not a thief and Pete should know that. Bruce, too.

BRUCE

I don't know why Pete is making such a big fuss about the watch. There's no bloody mystery. I went to Nong Khai with Troy, and before I went my business cards and the watch were on the dressing table. When I came back, they'd gone. I told Pete that Joy had fucked up big time because I had five hundred dollars in travellers cheques in the bottom drawer. I reckon what happened is that she nipped into the room while Pete was in the shower and grabbed the first thing she could lay her hands on. It stands to reason, right? I didn't steal them. Pete didn't steal them. Pete says that the only visitor while I was away was Joy. You don't have to be Hercule fucking Poirot to work out who the guilty party is. But Pete wouldn't have it. Kept insisting that I must have put the watch somewhere and forgotten about it. Bloody ridiculous.

I think the world of Joy, and Pete should have done the decent thing by her months ago, but you've just got to look at her. She's not in the same league as Troy. I know I can trust Troy: many's the time I've had a few drinks too many and I've given her my wallet, and she's never taken so much as a twenty-baht note. Troy is totally honest. I reckon Joy's more than capable of stealing, though. Look at the way she lied to Pete about her husband, even when he had photographs of them together and everything. She denied it right down the line. And Pete's caught her out in countless other lies. So why does he think he can believe her when she says she didn't take the watch?

The day after I mentioned it, he helped me search the apartment. We went through all the rooms, checked all the drawers, even went through the kitchen. Nothing. Then he started asking me if I was sure I hadn't brought anyone back to the flat. Bloody cheek. Then he wanted to know if I'd taken the watch anywhere with me, when was the last time I'd seen it. I got fed up with him in the end and told him he'd be better off interrogating Joy. He stormed out of the flat. The sad fuck.

PETE

Joy called me and asked me if I wanted to go and eat before she started work. She said her step-sister and three cousins had come down to Bangkok from Si Saket and they all wanted to meet me. We said we'd meet at the German restaurant in Soi 4 at six o'clock. I was supposed to get the edited proofs of the Bangkok guide to the courier service I used but I figured Alistair wouldn't mind waiting an extra day. I was already a week past deadline so I figured he'd changed the schedule anyway.

I'd had a couple of gin and tonics by the time Joy arrived. She was already wearing her waitress uniform and had her numbered badge clipped to her belt. Server 127. She waied me and introduced the girls. There was her step sister, Dit, who like Apple was a younger, slightly chubbier, version of Joy, and her cousins, Ning, Moo and Wandee. They all stood slightly behind Joy as if they were frightened of me, but Joy encouraged them to wai me.

We sat down at a table by the window and ordered drinks. I had a gin and tonic and all the girls had orange juice. Ning, Moo and Wandee were looking around the restaurant and pointing at the pictures and the place settings, and I got the feeling that it was their first time in a Western restaurant.

I gave Joy a laser pointer I'd bought for her in Patpong. It was on a keyring and could flash a laser beam more than a kilometre. I figured she could have fun with it in the bar. She showed it to the girls and they examined it curiously.

I let Joy order the food and she told the waitress what she wanted. The younger girls watched as Joy ordered and I could see that Joy was taking pride from the fact that she was in control.

Joy asked me what I'd been doing and I explained how the book was getting on. She translated to the other girls, and again I could see that she was enjoying showing off her English skills. She kept using the word "farang" rather than my name, but I wasn't offended because "Pete" probably wasn't a name they'd heard before.

I asked Joy how long the four girls were staying in Bangkok and she surprised me by saying they'd come to work. In Zombie. I could imagine Dit in a bar, but Ning, Moo and Wandee seemed too shy.

"Working as waitresses?" I asked.

Joy shook her head. "Dancing, same me before," she said.

Dit nodded enthusiastically. She seemed to be the brightest of the four and she'd been listening intently to the conversation Joy and I had been having and occasionally interrupted to ask Joy something, presumably for a translation. The other three girls were talking to each other in hushed Thai.

"Have they danced before?"

Joy giggled and said no, they hadn't.

"Aren't they shy?" I asked.

"No, not shy. They want money too much," she said.

The food arrived and Ning, Moo and Wandee examined the dishes like surgeons preparing for an operation.

Joy nodded at Dit. "What you think?" she asked me. "Pretty?"

Dit smiled at me showing beautifully straight, white teeth. She'd probably never sat in a dentist's chair but she had a perfect mouth. Her hair was as long as Joy's had been when she was dancing, thought it was slightly wavy. Her face was virtually identical to Joy's, though Dit had a small mole to the right of her nose.

"Suey mark," I said. Very pretty.

Dit giggled and put her hand over her mouth. It was a gesture I'd seen Joy do a thousand times.

"Same father, different mother," said Joy.

While we were eating, Joy took a piece of paper from her purse and gave it to me. It was a letter, addressed to me. It wasn't Joy's writing, the letters were all capitals and down the margins were childlike scrawls of hearts and flowers. It was a love letter, but the sort that an eight-year-old might write. I read it, with Joy and Dit watching my face intently, looking to see how I'd react. It was signed "Joy" but it wasn't her signature.

"Who wrote it?" I asked.

"Friend Joy," said Joy. "What you think?"

"Lovely," I said. "Why didn't you write it?"

"Her writing better. I tell her what I want say to you and she write for me."

I put the letter in my back pocket. I wasn't sure what to say. Joy was perfectly capable of writing to me, she'd written dozens of letters. So why had she asked a friend to write to me?

Ning, Moo and Wandee were tucking into the food. Joy put prawns on to my plate, and then poured more tonic water into my gin. She said something to the girls, not in Thai but in Khmer, I think, and all the girls nodded. I got the feeling that she was telling them what she was doing and why.

When the bill came I paid with cash. Joy said something to the girls and they all waied me. She'd obviously told them to thank me.

Joy asked me if I'd go over to Zombie with them. It felt strange walking into Nana Plaza with Joy and four very young girls, as if I were a teacher taking a class on a field trip. Dit looked about nineteen, the same age as Joy when I met her for the first time, but Ning, Moo and Wandee all looked as if they were under eighteen. They held hands as they walked past the touts and the neon lights advertising the bars, huddled together like frightened rabbits.

We went into Zombie and Joy sat everybody down and went over to get drinks for us all. Then she stood in front of the girls and began talking in Thai, pointing out various parts of the bar, the toilets, the changing rooms, the short-time room, the dancing stages. The girls sat wide-eyed, sipping their orange juices and hanging on her every word.

The next day they were all up on the stage, dancing naked around the silver poles. A six-foot-tall Scandinavian guy paid barfine for Dit and she left holding his hand, Joy smiling proudly like a parent at a graduation ceremony. How did I feel? Uneasy, I think. Like I'd been witness to a coming of age in a culture I didn't understand. Or didn't want to understand. Dit was a bright, pretty young girl from the country but she'd taken on the life of a Bangkok bargirl without a moment's hesitation.

JOY

Wandee had to go home after a week. She wasn't working out. She couldn't dance, in fact she could barely walk in high heels. That wasn't the problem, though, a lot of the girls just stand and hold the pole and jiggle around, it's not as if the farangs actually go into a bar to watch girls dance. The problem was that she wouldn't talk to customers, even if they approached her. She wouldn't smile, either, it was as if she was paralysed with fear. I tried to get her to relax, I'd sit with her and help her make conversation, but she was too nervous. Only one guy wanted to pay her barfine, an old Swedish man, but he came back to complain the next day. He told the mamasan that Wandee lay on her back with her legs pressed together and her arms folded across her breasts. He demanded his money back and the mamasan gave it to him.

The mamasan wanted to beat Wandee, but I said no, that I'd talk to her. I sat her down and explained what she had to do, but she just kept on shaking her head and saying that she couldn't do it. I asked her what the problem was, because it wasn't as if she was a virgin or anything. She'd had a boyfriend back in Si Saket, and I think she first had sex when she was fifteen.

It was farangs, she said. She didn't like the way they looked, and she didn't like the way they smelled. I said that hardly anyone does, but you had to think of the money. You can do anything if you think of the money. I used to work in a factory for a few thousand baht a month. You can earn that in one night, so isn't a few minutes of discomfort worth it? She started crying and I put my arms around her. Some girls just can't do it, and I guess Wandee is one of them. I gave her enough money to get the bus back to Si Saket and sent her on her way.

Sunan was furious. She'd paid for clothes and shoes for Wandee and she'd given her spending money. She was expecting to get a commission from the money Wandee earned. She's a smart businesswoman, is Sunan. She brings lots of girls down from Si Saket and then takes ten per cent of what they earn for the first year. Sunan wouldn't talk to Wandee after she'd said she wanted to go home. Wandee kept saying that she was sorry and that she'd pay Sunan back, but Sunan just ignored her.

Dit was totally different, she took to working in the bar like a duck to water. She was going out with farangs every night, and she was in the short-time room a lot, too. Dit loves sex and I don't think she cares who she does it with. Her husband came with her to Bangkok and he encourages her to screw as many farangs as possible. She gives most of her money to him and he's already bought a motorcycle.

Dit's a good dancer, and a quick learner. I showed her a few moves and she learned them really quickly. She's got a good body, long legs and big breasts. Eighty per cent of farangs like girls with big breasts. Her English is getting better every day, too. She can make farangs laugh and she knows what to say to make them like her. She reminds me of myself when I was her age.

I think the only difference between us is that she likes sex and I don't. I hate it. Except with Park, of course, but then it's not sex, it's making love. What I do with the farangs is just sex, in and out until they come, and I hate that. They'd never know, of course, because I know how to smile as if I'm enjoying it and I make the right noises. Just like the lesbian show I used to do with Wan. It's all a big act.

PETE

Joy had been working as a waitress for almost two weeks when I saw him. I actually wasn't sure it was him, so I kept looking at the booth where the DJs worked. He was wearing a baseball cap so I couldn't see how short his hair was, but there was no mistaking the bulging eyes. Joy kept coming over to me, as attentive as ever, leaning against me, rubbing my shoulder, pulling faces to make me laugh. "What are you looking at?" she asked eventually.

"That guy. The one playing records."

She didn't look around, she just kept looking at me. "What about him?"

I took a deep breath. "Joy, he looks just like your husband."

She frowned, then turned and stared at the DJ, her hand resting lightly on my thigh. She made a soft, snorting sound. "Him? No," she said. A teenager walked by carrying a tray and she grabbed him by the arm. "My husband looked more like him," she said, nodding at the surprised waiter.

I looked back at the DJ's booth. If it wasn't him, the resemblance was amazing. Joy released her grip on the waiter's arm, and slid her arms around my neck. "Pete, I not lie to you," she said. I looked into her eyes and wanted so much to believe her.

"It looks just like him," I said.

She took a step back and looked at me admonishingly. "Pete, he only work here one week."

"What's his name?"

"I don't know," she said. "You want me ask?"

I nodded. She sighed theatrically and walked over to the DJ's booth. She climbed up on to a seat and called over the top of the glass partition. "What's your name?" she shouted in Thai.

"Gung," he called back. It means 'prawn' in Thai and is a common name for both men and women.

She walked back to my table, swinging her hips prettily. She raised her eyebrows. "Gung," she said. "His name's Gung. Are you happy now?"

I smiled and put my arm around her. She smelled fresh and clean, despite the smoky atmosphere. I kissed her on the neck and she pressed herself against me. "Yeah," I said. "I'm happy."

Something about the way she smelled worried me. I'd smelled it before, but for the life of me I couldn't remember where.

BRUNO

Love is blind. It really is. It's not a cliche, it's a truism. There's an experiment that demonstrates the fact perfectly. You show a film to a group of volunteers. It can be about anything. The one I've seen is a robbery, three men steal some money from a security van and are thwarted by two passers-by. Then you tell the volunteers that they're going to be asked a series of questions about what they've seen. They're told to answer specific questions truthfully, and to lie when they answer others. Now, you get three types of people to ask the questions. The questioners, of course, haven't seen the film. You get a stranger, a friend, and a marriage partner to ask the questions, and they have to assess whether or not they are being told the truth or a lie.

Now, what do you think the results of the experiment would be? The layman would assume that the partner would be most likely to spot the lies. But in fact, the exact opposite occurs. The strangers are most likely to spot when they are being lied to. The partner is the least likely. And the friend is somewhere in the middle, depending on how close a friend he or she is.

What does this tell us? There are a number of possible conclusions to be drawn. It could be that people find it easier to lie to those who love them, that they learn to hide the non-verbal cues that give away untruths. It's far more likely, however, that we as human beings prefer not to believe that those we care for would lie to us, so we fool ourselves, we force ourselves to overlook the telltale signs of deceit. Love truly is blind.

PETE

I could sense there was something wrong as soon as I walked into Fatso's Bar. Big Ron was sitting there with a big grin on his face, jiggling in his specially reinforced chair like a volcano all set to explode. I sat down and ordered a gin and tonic.

"Joy's at it," he said.

I felt cold inside. I knew what was coming. I could tell by the smug look on his fat face.

"She was barfined last night."

"Impossible," I said. "I was in there at ten."

"Yeah, but what time did you leave?"

"About eleven. Then she came around to the apartment when she'd finished work."

Big Ron giggled like a schoolgirl on her first date. "Better speak to Matt, then."

I pretended that I couldn't care less, but my heart was racing. Matt was an American guy and a regular visitor to Nana Plaza, where he'd recently started barfining katoeys. He walked into Fatso's about an hour later and sat down on the stool next to me. He grimaced. "Big Ron told you?"

"Yeah," I said, swirling the ice cubes around my drink with my finger. "You're sure?"

"No question. I was with Jimmy, and Jimmy tried to barfine her. She said no, but about twenty minutes later she left with an American."

"Do you know who he was?"

Matt shook his head.

"And there's no doubt, Matt? She couldn't have been going out to buy cigarettes?"

He shook his head again. I guess we both knew I was clutching at straws. "I know the difference between a girl going out for cigarettes and a girl who's had her barfine paid, Pete. She'd changed into her jeans, for a start."

Yeah, he was right, of course. I tried not to show how upset I was, rang the bell to buy everyone a drink, and ending up getting pissed out of my skull.

I went around to Zombie just after midnight. Joy was there, playing with the laser I'd bought her. She grinned and ran over and gave me a big hug. "I think about you too much," she said.

"I love you, Joy," I said.

"I love you, too much," she said.

"Don't ever lie to me, Joy," I said, hating myself for sounding so pathetic.

"You drunk," she said. "I never lie to you, Pete. I love you, too much."

JOY

I told Park it was a stupid thing to do, that Pete was sure to recognise him if Park started working in Zombie. Park slapped me and told me he didn't care, that he wasn't going to allow a farang to dictate his life. I said that he was being dumb because Pete had his photograph, but Park slapped me again so I stopped arguing.

Sure enough, Pete spotted Park and I was the one who had to cover up. My heart was racing as I walked across the bar to shout up to Park. I nearly burst out laughing when he said that his name was Gung. Prawn? Park hates prawns. Calls them sea insects. Pete believed me, though, so maybe he's as stupid as Park seems to think he is. I told all the girls to say that Park was Gung if Pete asked them, but I don't think he did.

Park kept pressing me to go with other farangs, even though I warned him that Pete's friends all drink in Zombie and one of them would be bound to see me. Park didn't care, but he said that if I was worried about getting caught I should take the farangs into the short-time room. I told him how much I hated the short-time room—it smells and the bed's got ticks, all the girls complain about getting bitten, but Park wouldn't listen to me. Sometimes he can be so stubborn.

It's not as if we needed the money. Pete was giving me about four thousand baht a week, and I was earning at least five hundred baht a day in tips. I was paying for our room, and our food, and I was giving Park money for beer and cigarettes, and I was paying for his motorcycle. Sometimes men can be so ungrateful. I mean, Park was only getting three thousand baht a month for playing records. It's not even a real job. The DJs don't get to choose their own music, the farang who owns the bar, Damien, he decides what they play. Most of the time he just puts on one CD and lets it play right through. The farangs don't care, they're in the bars for the girls, not the music. I know the real reason Park wanted to work as a DJ again: it was so that he could be around the girls. I saw him making eyes at Wan and I gave him a piece of my mind. There's no way any man of mine is getting away with being a butterfly, not in front of my friends.

PETE

I left it until the end of the month before going around to Zombie to see the owner. I'd gotten his name from Jimmy. Damien Kavanagh, his family are big in double-glazing back in the UK, that's what Jimmy had said. But there were other versions of his life story floating around Fatso's, too. Bruce had heard that he'd once been a barrister in Belfast but had done a runner with clients' money. Rick said that Kavanagh wasn't his real name, that he'd changed it by deed pole after he'd been convicted on fraud charges a decade ago. Big Ron was sure that he'd spent time in a Thai jail for trafficking women into Europe. No one seemed to know for sure. Whatever the truth about Kavanagh's past, I found him in a cramped little office off the back of the room where the bargirls changed. He was crouched over a computer keyboard, peering at the screen through thick-lensed spectacles. He was a shifty-looking man, in his fifties, I guess, with thinning grey hair and a habit of licking his lips when he listened, like a frog contemplating its next meal. I introduced myself and told him what I wanted to know, and he just grinned and shook his head.

"Why didn't you just walk away?" he asked.

I shrugged. "She wants to change. She doesn't want to dance any more."

Damien chuckled and pushed his glasses up his nose. "Pete, Pete, Pete, these girls are here for one reason, and one reason alone. They're hookers, and they're hooking."

"Joy's different ..." I began but stopped when he started shaking his head.

He leaned forward as if about to share a secret with me. "You're wasting your time," he said. "And what's more, you know you're wasting your time."

"Okay, but I need to know for sure," I said. "I need to see her card."

The card was the key. Sure, I knew there was no reason for Matt and Jimmy to lie, but if Joy's barfine had been paid, it would have been recorded on the card that she used to clock in each day. The cards were stored in a rack by the side of the lockers.

"You used to be a journalist, yeah?" he said.

"That's right."

"Well, me showing you a girl's card would be the equivalent to you revealing a source," he said smugly. "I just couldn't do it. I'd have a revolt on my hands. The girls wouldn't stand for it."

"But Joy said ..."

"They'll say anything so long as they can get money out of you. Why can't you just accept that? They're hookers."

"She says she loves me ..."

He started laughing again and I felt my cheeks go red. He took his glasses off and began to polish them with a grubby handkerchief. "Pete, that's what they all say."

I wanted to slap his smug face, but I didn't. I tried to reason with him. I explained that she could earn much more money if she was dancing and going with customers, that it had been her idea to work as a waitress.

"The waitresses go short-time, too," he said. "Some of the waitresses get screwed more than the dancers. It's the black and white uniforms, makes them look like schoolkids. Big turn on, that."

"But Joy's ..."

"Different," he finished for me. "Yeah, you said."

"Look, Damien, I know what you're saying, but do you know for sure that Joy has had her barfine paid? Have you looked at her card?"

"I don't have to," he said. "Look, have you any idea how many guys like you come into this office and tell me exactly the same story as you've told me? I had a Danish guy here last week. He'd fallen in love with a girl, Need, the one with big knockers. Now, Need's been hooking since she was twelve years old and she's almost thirty now. She's got three kids and a Thai husband who hits her around. But this Danish guy, he comes in here convinced that she's the Virgin bloody Mary. Says he's going back to Denmark and wants Need to work as a waitress while he's away. So Need winks at me and I say, sure, fine, whatever. He gets back on the plane, she takes off her kit and starts dancing again. He'll probably send her money every month and she'll give it to her old man so that he can go out and get drunk and slap her around."

I started to say that Joy was different, but even before the words left my mouth I could see him start to grin.

"Look, you've more than a hundred girls working here, do you actually know which one Joy is?" I asked him.

He put his glasses back on and blew his nose on his handkerchief. "Saw her a couple of weeks ago and I asked the mamasan who the pretty new waitress was. She said it was Joy, that she used to dance."

"But it's not as if you know her personally?"

"She's not one that I've fucked, if that's what you mean."

"No, that's not what I mean. I mean, maybe, just maybe, she's keeping her side of the bargain. Maybe she hasn't had her barfine paid."

He shook his head.

"Look, do me a favour," I said. "Just have a look at her card. You don't have to tell me what's on it, but maybe when you've looked at it you'll realise that she is different. And if her barfine has been paid, all you've got to say is that your advice to me hasn't changed."

He sat back in his chair. "Suppose I do that," he said. "What do you plan to do?"

"I'll walk away," I said. "If I'm sure that she's lied, I'll walk away."

"You won't be able to," he says. "You'll tell her that I showed her the card, and she'll give you any one of a hundred excuses why she went out. She was sick and paid her own barfine, she went out to eat with friends, blah blah blah. She'll convince you that you're mistaken, then I'll have a riot on my hands when she tells everyone that I let you see her card."

"I promise you, Damien, on my life, that I won't tell her."

He picked up a chipped mug and sipped something brown. He put the mug down. "If I look at her card, I want you to promise me something."

"Anything."

"If I see what I know I'm going to see on that card, I want you to never talk to her again. Forget about her."

"No problem," I said. "I've got to go to Cambodia next week. Phnom Penh. I just won't tell her when I'm getting back."

He looked at me for several seconds and I thought he was going to change his mind, then he pushed himself up out of his chair and went over to the rack of time cards. He ran his finger down them. "What number is she?" he asked. "There are a few Joys here."

"Server 127," I said.

He found the card and sat down. He studied it, then turned the card over. He put the card in the top drawer of his desk as if he was scared that I'd make a grab for it. My heart was racing, but I tried to look as unconcerned as possible. "Pete, I don't see anything on Joy's card that changes my opinion."

For a few seconds I couldn't breathe, it was as if a steel belt had been tightened around my chest. I forced a smile. "Right," I said.

"I'm sorry," he said.

I didn't want his pity. "Nah, it doesn't matter. I guess I knew anyway."

I laughed but the sound caught in my throat. I don't know why but I started telling him about the DJ, about how I thought it was Joy's husband but that she'd denied it. Damien nodded. "That's him," he said. "The mamasan said he came back to Bangkok with her."

I stood up. "Yeah, I knew I shouldn't trust her. It's like you said, they're all hookers."

He scribbled something down on a piece of paper and gave it to me. It was an address. He leered at me. "When you're in Phnom Penh, try this place. They've got the prettiest Vietnamese hookers you've ever seen. All of 'em under fourteen. Great place Phnom Penh, real Wild West. Like Bangkok was thirty years ago."

I smiled, trying hard not to show how upset I was inside. I shook his hand and left.

DAMIEN

That Pete, what a sad fuck. He'd obviously fallen for the girl in a big way and when he came into the office he was wound tighter than a watch on a wanker's wrist. I could see it in his eyes. He was trying to be cool, trying to pretend he wasn't that worried, but he kept fidgeting in his seat and a couple of times I thought he was going to cry.

I didn't know Joy, I've more than a hundred girls in Zombie alone, probably up to a thousand working for me in Nana in total. Me and my partners have seven bars, and Zombie is just about the biggest and most profitable. The girls there are the best, they're the prettiest and the hardest working. I didn't know Joy personally, though I'd seen her. Beautiful girl, great body. Had that young, unsullied look that I go for, but her skin was too dark for my taste. Her sister I know, Sunan. One of the hardest working girls in the Plaza, is Sunan. Two or three times a night, every night. Her sister, Mon, was another good worker. They were a good source of new girls, too. Every few months they'd go back to their village, show off their new clothes and their gold, and they'd come back with three or four new girls who wanted to work in the bars. Sunan would teach them how to dance, how to put make up on, how to talk to customers. Some of the girls we get are so shy they wouldn't say boo to a goose, they dance all right but then they sit together in groups talking to their friends. But the girls Sunan brings down know how to go up to a customer and introduce themselves. It doesn't take much, all they have to do is smile and say hello. The customer'll do the rest. Sunan tells them how to act with customers, how to get them to pay the barfine, and how much to ask for afterwards. I tell you, Sunan should think about starting up a bargirl school. She'd be a great mamasan, too. I've asked her a few times but she knows she can earn more dancing. How much does she earn? The bar pays her about six thousand baht, she earns another six thousand or so from her share of bar drinks, and her barfine gets paid an average of thirty times a month, I guess, so she gets another three thousand from that. So there's fifteen thousand baht right there, which is more than a teacher gets. Plus there's the money she gets from the punters themselves. I doubt she does it for less than fifteen hundred baht, so that'd be another forty-five thousand baht. That means Sunan's probably pulling in sixty thousand baht a month, which is about ten times the national average wage. Pretty good, huh.

Now, one look at Joy's card and I could see that she'd been at it. Her barfine had been paid five times during the previous month, and she'd been to the short-time room twice. I've never understood why anyone would want to take a girl into the short-time room, but it gets used half a dozen times a night. It's a horrible place, a room without windows or aircon, a single bed with no pillow and a sheet that gets changed once in a blue moon, and a wastepaper basket for the used condoms and tissues. We charge four hundred baht every time the room's used, and punters seem happy to pay it. They could go down the road to the Penthouse and for the same amount of money have a night in a decent room with a TV and clean sheets and mirrored ceilings. The girls love it, though, because it's quick and easy money. They don't even have to get changed.

Pete was asking for trouble trying to change Joy. She's a hooker, she was born a hooker and she'll die a hooker. The best thing for him to do is just to accept that fact. Pay her, screw her, and let her go home to her husband. When he gets bored with her he can find another regular girl. No one gets hurt.

He promised me that he'd walk away, but I'd bet my bottom dollar that he doesn't. We'll see.

JOY

I was fourteen when my father had sex with me for the first time. I didn't know what was happening or what he was doing. I thought that a ghost had got inside him and was making him do it, but the next day I told Mon and she said that he did that to all his daughters. Except for Sunan. Sunan wouldn't let him. He beat Sunan black and blue but she never let him. Once he hit her so hard that she couldn't get up and she lay on her sleeping mat for four days and couldn't eat anything. There was blood in her urine but our father wouldn't let her go to the hospital. I was twelve then, it was the year after our stepmother had died. She had cancer and was sick for a long time.

I hated it, but I didn't ask him to stop because I remembered what he did to Sunan. I just turned my head to the side and let him do whatever he wanted to do. That's what I used to do with farangs, too, until I learned that I could get more money if I pretended to enjoy it.

My father never said why he did what he did. I guess maybe he missed our stepmother because he never did it when she was alive. He'd come into my room about once a week, and he always smelled of drink, same as the farangs do. He wasn't rough, though, and he never asked me to do the sort of things that farangs ask me to do. He just had sex with me in silence, then went back to his room.

My elder brother started having sex with me about three months after my father took my virginity. My brother was rough and he wanted me to do other things for him, too. I cried because I didn't understand why he was doing it. I could understand my father because he didn't have our mother but my brother had lots of girlfriends. I tried to stop him but he was too strong. He'd hit me if I didn't do what he wanted. I'm not as tough as Sunan, I couldn't stand up to him, so I just let him do it to me.

My father stopped fucking me when I was sixteen. He'd moved on to Dit by then. Dit was like me, she never said anything, though I heard him stumbling along the corridor to her room at night. I was just glad that he wasn't coming to my room.

My brother carried on, though, and he made me fuck his friends as well. He used to charge them twenty baht a time and he'd beat me if I didn't let them do it. He did the same to Dit, too. Practically ran a brothel out of our house, but he was always careful to make sure that our father was away in the fields. After a while I stopped complaining. I told my brother to give me half the money and he decided that it was fair and so he did. Small money, but at least I didn't feel as I was being raped. It was work. That made it seem all right.

PETE

I had a major drinking session in Fatso's. Drunk as a skunk. I was well behind schedule on the travel cookery book but my heart wasn't in it.

Most of the guys had gone around to the Plaza, so I sat with Big Ron and poured my heart out. I told him about Joy's card and her husband working as the DJ. "She's playing a bloody game," I said, "but she's not going to win."

That's what it was to Joy. A game. The rules were simple. Say whatever you have to in order to get the stupid farang to part with as much money as possible. Tell him what he wants to hear, lie if you have to, and keep taking the money. She'd been playing a Goddamned game with me, but now I knew what the rules were and I was going to show her who was the better player.

I had a plan already, so I rang the bell to buy Big Ron and the girls drinks and explained it to him.

Several of the girls had tattoos on their shoulders. Usually butterflies or animals, though sometimes they'd have their name tattooed. I was going to persuade Joy to get my name tattooed on her shoulder. That way she'd never forget me. Whenever she saw the tattoo she'd think of me. And more importantly, so would her husband. Then I'd dump her, and the tattoo would be a constant reminder to the two of them that I'd won the game.

It took me almost a week to persuade her to get the tattoo. I didn't want to press it too hard because she'd have suspected that I was up to something. I'd sit with her in Zombie and point out girls with tattoos, saying how pretty they were. I asked her if she'd like one and she said sure, she thought they looked good. After a couple of days I asked if she'd have a heart with my name on it, and she said yes. I asked her how much it would cost. She asked one of her friends, Cat, and Cat said she'd had one done for seven hundred baht. I gave Joy a thousand baht and said she should get one.

The next day when I went in to Zombie, she said she'd been to the tattoo parlour with Cat, but that it had been closed. I shrugged, playing it cool, and pretended that I didn't care.

The next day, she said she and Cat had spoken to the tattoo artist, but that he'd said that the best days for girls to have tattoos done were Tuesday and Thursday, something to do with fortune telling or religion, she couldn't explain which. I figured she was just making excuses, and I told her so. She denied it and said she'd get it done in two days, on Tuesday.

On Monday night when I went in to Zombie she'd already drunk four bottles of Heineken lager and was giggling. She was drunk. She didn't get the tattoo done the following day because she said she had a hangover. I kept putting on the pressure, slowly but surely, smiling all the time, making it a game. When I told Big Ron what I was doing, he called me a callous, unfeeling bastard, but he was laughing as he said it. I didn't feel guilty about what I was doing, because every time I was in Zombie, Joy's husband was up in the DJ's booth. Any guilt I felt evaporated when I looked up at the booth and saw him and his tight T-shirt and stupid baseball cap. If they wanted to play the game, they couldn't complain if they got burnt.

Eventually she ran out of excuses. She telephoned me at midday and I could hear a buzzing noise in the background. Joy was at the tattoo parlour with Cat and she wanted to know if I wanted my name in the heart or both our names. I said it was up to her.

Four hours later she was ringing the doorbell of the flat. She stripped off her shirt and showed me the winged heart on her left shoulder. In the middle of the red heart, my name. Big Ron had said that Joy would probably try to get away with a painted tattoo, one that would wash off after a few days. I rubbed it with my thumb and she yelped. It was genuine. "You not believe me, Pete?" she asked, a look of despair on her face.

I hugged her and said no, I believed her, I knew that she'd never lie to me. I held her close to my chest and breathed in the smell of her hair. I'd won. I'd won the game but I didn't feel good about myself. I sat with her in the bar for most of the night as she proudly showed her friends the tattoo. When the bar closed I took her to the Penthouse Hotel and we spent the whole night together. I stroked and kissed the tattoo as I made love to her.

"You happy now, Pete?" she asked, and I said I was. It was a lie. I felt like shit.

I had one more thing to do. The day after she had the tattoo done, I bought a return ticket to Phnom Penh. Alistair had been on my back for a while, telling me that I had to go over to Cambodia to do the research for the Cambodian guide, but I'd been putting him off. Once I'd bought

215

the ticket, I packed my bag and then telephoned Joy. I told her that the DJ had stopped me outside Nana Plaza and that he'd told me that he was her husband and that he'd said I wasn't to go to Zombie any more.

"Why he say that?" asked Joy. She didn't deny that he was her husband, I noticed.

I warmed to the story, telling her that the DJ said his name was Park and that he was jealous, that he didn't want me to give her any more money, that he wanted me to stay away from her.

"Pete, he lie to you," she said. "I not know why he say that, but he wrong."

I said it didn't make any difference, that if she had a husband I didn't want anything to do with her. I put down the phone and caught a taxi to the airport. Four hours later I was in Phnom Penh.

BIG RON

Pete's going to have to watch himself because if he carries on the way he's going, it's gonna be payback time. And it won't be Queensbury Rules because out here they always fight mob-handed and tooled up, pieces of wood, knives, guns even. Happened in the Plaza six months back, a farang had got up the nose of one of the mamasans. Called her a water buffalo and stormed out without paying his bill. Two weeks later three guys caught up with him and started knocking him around with pieces of lead pipe. Stan his name was, big bugger too, lifts weights and works out. He got one of them and smashed his head into a wall. The other two ran off.

Anyway, Stan figures he's got away with it and starts getting cocky. Eventually they got him again, walking down the road. Four of them, with knives. They slashed him across the face, damn near blinded him. The doctors saved his eyes, but he's going to be scarred for life. Always was an ugly bastard, was Stan, so I don't think he's worrying too much. Girls here don't turn down customers because of a few scars. Look at me, for God's sake. I'm twenty-eight stone and pig ugly and I've never been turned down.

That's what I can't work out about Pete. What is this with him and Joy? There are thousands of them out there, thousands of Joys, and they all screw for peanuts. Receptacles for jism, that's what I call them. Fuck 'em, pay 'em, and move on, that's what I say. Pete should just walk away, forget about this revenge thing. He won't win. They won't fucking let him win.

JOY

I don't understand Pete. If he doesn't want to be with me, why doesn't he say so? It's as if he just wants to cause me problems. Why did he ask me to get his name tattooed on my shoulder? Doesn't that count for something? And he lied about talking to Park. Why did he do that?

Park was in my room when Pete telephoned. I asked Park what he was playing at, and he said he didn't know what I was talking about. I got angry then and said that he'd spoiled everything. He had no right to talk to Pete, he was my customer. Park got really angry then and slapped me. I slapped him back and he hit me really hard. Almost blacked my eye. He wouldn't talk to me at work, he turned away every time I went up to him, and he didn't come home with me. I was so embarrassed, all the girls were talking about me. Cat had told everybody about the tattoo and Park had told somebody about Pete finding out that he was my husband. The girls put two and two together and they thought it was hilarious. Why did Pete do that to me? I kept telephoning Pete but he either wasn't there or he wasn't answering the phone. Bruce came into Zombie just after midnight with Rick and Jimmy, the guys who like to fuck katoeys. Bruce said Pete had gone to Cambodia and didn't know when he was back. I burst into tears and went to the toilet.

Dit came after me and asked me what was wrong. I told her and she said she'd go and speak to Park for me. It didn't do any good. Park said he was through with me. I went to see the mamasan and said I couldn't finish my shift. She was really horrible and said that if I went early I'd have to pay my own barfine. I begged her to be kind-hearted but she said no, rules are rules. I borrowed six hundred baht off Dit, flung it at the mamasan, and went home.

I sort of hoped that Park would come after me, but he didn't. I sat on my bed and cried my eyes out, then decided to go back to Si Saket. The money I'd been saving was under my mattress. I got it out, had a quick shower then I got a motorcycle to the bus station and got on a VIP bus. I pretty much cried all the way home.

PETE

I spent two weeks in Cambodia and hated every minute of it. I kept thinking about Joy, about what I'd done to her. I called Sunan's mobile phone but there was no answer. I called the phone box in Si Saket but the old woman who answered said Joy wasn't there. It wasn't that I wanted to save the relationship, I'd accepted the fact that it was one hundred per cent over, but I wanted to know that she was all right. She'd cut her wrists after the birthday party that never was and I hoped she hadn't done the same again. To be honest, I spent so much time worrying about Joy that I didn't get everything done that I should have done. My hotel bill was horrendous, too, what with all the calls to Thailand and everything, but the company would reimburse me. I was more worried about what Alistair would say when I told him that I'd have to go back to Phnom Penh.

Bruce was lying on the sofa reading a book when I got back to the flat. He seemed to be spending less and less time in the office and I figured it wouldn't be too long before he got the push. I mean, what's the point of paying him an expat salary if he's going to spend most of his time in the flat or the bars? He put down the book and grinned at me. "Have I got a story for you," he said. "You are not going to believe this."

BRUCE

It was one of life's great coincidences, the sort of thing that makes you think there is some sort of order to the universe. Practically a mystical experience, it was. I was sitting in this outdoor restaurant close to Soi Cowboy, waiting for a guy who was going to sell me a health insurance policy. He was late but that was no surprise because the traffic was really bad and he was driving. I never take the car out at night, I stick to motorcycle taxis. They're faster and cheaper, though you do take your life in your hands every time you climb on.

Anyway, I was sitting at the bar wondering whether I should order food or not, when this Thai girl sits down next to me. I couldn't work out what her game was because she wasn't dressed like a hooker but she started up a conversation with me and regular Thai girls wouldn't dream of doing that. She was a bit overweight and her skin wasn't too good, but she spoke excellent English. She said she worked in a beauty parlour in a hotel in Silom Road and that her name was Tukkata. That's Thai for doll, she said.

I bought her a drink—whisky and Coke she wanted, another sign that she wasn't a regular Thai girl because whisky and Coke is very much a bargirl's drink. I couldn't work her out because she was flirting but she never asked if I'd take her back with me. She said that a friend of hers had a problem and she wanted to ask my advice. I thought that maybe she was going to sting me for money, but that's not what happened at all.

Seems that two months ago she'd met this American guy, Vernon, in the beauty parlour where she'd worked. He'd come in for a haircut, and as Tukkata cut his hair, he told her that he'd just married a Thai girl. A girl who'd been working in a go-go bar. He'd only met her ten days earlier, but he was sure that she was the love of his life. He'd gone back with her to her village, met her family, had a proper Thai wedding, and now he was planning to get her a visa and fly her over to San Diego, where he lived. Since then, this guy Vernon had flown back to the States. According to Tukkata, he was starting to have second thoughts about the girl. She was writing to him, but sometimes when he phoned her late at night she wasn't there. He wondered if she was working in the bar again.

He sent her money every couple of weeks but she was always asking for more. Tukkata asked me what I thought. Well, what I thought was that it was yet another example of a stupid farang being ripped off by a bargirl, but I didn't say that. I just smiled and shrugged and said that it was difficult to say because I didn't know the girl.

Yeah, she agreed. It was difficult. "I've spoken to Sunan, and Sunan says she loves Vernon, but I'm not sure if I believe her."

I nearly fell off my bloody barstool. I mean, how many girls can there be called Sunan? I asked her what bar she'd worked in and Tukkata said she wasn't sure of the name of the bar but that it was in Nana Plaza. I asked her if it was Zombie. Tukkata frowned and said yes, that sounded familiar. And did Sunan live in Si Saket? Her jaw dropped like I was a mind-reader or something. I couldn't believe it. Of all the bars in all the world, I have to sit next to a girl who knows a guy who married Joy's sister.

Pete couldn't believe it, either. Tukkata had Vernon's phone number in San Diego and I gave it to Pete. "You've gotta call him," I said. "You two have just gotta talk."

VERNON

Meeting Sunan was like a fairy story, it really was. I'd never been to Thailand but it seemed like a fascinating place. I don't know when I first thought about having a Thai wife, I guess it was some time after my Mom died. Mom always took real good care of Dad, even when he got sick with cancer. She nursed him and never stopped loving him, right up until the end. She worshipped the ground he walked on, did everything for him. Girls today just aren't the same, not American girls, anyway. They're too busy with their careers, with their lives. All they ever want to talk about is themselves, what they're doing, how they feel. I don't hold with all that stuff about keeping a wife barefoot and pregnant, but I want someone who loves me and wants to take care of me, someone who'll make me feel special.

I joined one of those Asian dating clubs. Found an advertisement in a supermarket tabloid and sent off a cheque for fifty bucks. Back came a catalogue of photographs, passport photos really, of hundreds of girls. There was a paragraph describing each girl, how old she was, her measurements, her job, what she wanted out of life. Some of the girls were pretty enough, but I didn't see anyone that I was attracted to. At the back of the catalogue was an advertisement for a series of video cassettes about life in Thailand, and since I'd never been to the country I thought it might be a good idea to buy one. I sent off another cheque and a couple of weeks later it arrived.

The first part was general touristy stuff, the temples, the river boats, the markets, but then there was a section on Bangkok's night life and that was when I saw her. She was one of four dancers interviewed, and as soon as I saw her, I knew that she was the girl that I wanted to spend the rest of my life with. She was gorgeous with long, long legs and a great smile, and big brown eyes that seemed to be on the verge of tears.

I called the director of the video and he told me that Sunan danced in a bar called Zombie in Nana Plaza. I had three weeks vacation time and I took it at the end of the month, got a cheap flight to Bangkok and went, just like that.

It was unreal. I walked into Nana Plaza and the bar was in the far corner. I sat outside and ordered a Coke. The outside bar was circular with half a dozen girls in the centre, serving drinks and talking to the customers. There was a curtain hanging across the door to the main bar. I could hear rock and roll music blaring out, the Rolling Stones, I think, and every now and again a girl in a bikini would come and peer around the curtain. I was so excited that I could hardly breathe. I'd had a Polaroid photograph taken from the video and showed it to one of the girls behind the bar. Yes, she knew it was Sunan, and yes, she was working that night.

The girl went behind the curtain and five minutes later, Sunan was there, sitting next to me, every bit as beautiful as she'd been in the video. Her skin seemed a little darker and her hair was a bit longer, but it was her. She even had her name and a number on a little badge pinned to the wraparound skirt she'd put on over her bikini. I was so nervous, I remember my voice was trembling when I told her who I was and that I'd flown all the way from San Diego just to meet her. I said I wanted to take her for dinner, just to talk to her, to get to know her, and she explained about the barfine system. The girls have to work all night unless someone pays their barfine, about fifteen bucks. I paid it and we went out. I kept wanting to pinch myself to make sure that I wasn't dreaming.

SUNAN

It happens all the time. Some farang will say he wants to pay my barfine so that we can go and eat or sit in a bar and talk. It's fine by me, though to be honest I always prefer to just go to a short-time hotel. There are load of hotels within a five minute walk, and I can make a guy come in about ten minutes at most, so I can be back dancing within half an hour of having my barfine paid. I charge fifteen hundred baht minimum for short time, two thousand if they want me to stay all night, but again, I try not to stay the night unless they insist. My boyfriend likes sex a lot and if I'm not there to see to him, I know he'll go on the prowl, so I try to get home by 3am whenever I can.

I didn't think much of Vernon the first time I saw him. He looked like he was fifty because his hair was grey and he had bags under his eyes and I thought he was bullshitting when he said he was forty. His body was okay, he was quite tall and thin, but his teeth weren't good, they weren't white at all, almost yellow. That surprised me because most Americans I've met have really white teeth.

He didn't smoke so maybe it was all the coffee he drinks.

He took me to one of the restaurants in the Landmark Hotel. A lot of farangs like to go there with girls, it's not far from Nana Plaza and the waitresses are nice to the girls. Some places don't like to serve bargirls, they turn their nose up at us, but the Landmark's okay. He talked to me non-stop for almost four hours. Wouldn't shut up. He'd seen the video I'd made about a year ago. An American guy had barfined half a dozen of the girls and taken us over to the Nana Hotel. He'd paid us five hundred baht each to talk to us while he filmed us, what we thought of Bangkok, what the bars were like, stuff like that. I was lucky that Vernon didn't see the other video the guy made. Two of the girls went back to Nana Plaza but the rest stayed behind and the guy paid us two thousand baht each to do lesbian scenes. Pretty raunchy stuff it was, too. He'd brought a stack of sex toys with him, things we'd never seen before. We kept laughing, it looked so ridiculous, and the guy ended up getting really angry with us.

Anyway, Vernon spent four hours telling me that he thought I was the love of his life, that it was fate that brought us together, that he thought he could spend the rest of his life with me. Why are farangs always so quick to fall in love? It happens all the times in the bars, a farang comes to Bangkok on holiday, meets a girl in a go-go bar, and decides he loves her and wants to marry her. How can you possibly love someone you've only just met? Crazy. So Vernon keeps telling me that he sees something in me he doesn't see in other girls, that I'm not like the girls in America. To be honest, I could only understand twenty per cent of what he was saying because my English isn't that good, and I spent most of the time wishing that he'd take me to a short-time hotel and screw me.

PETE

I telephoned Vernon right away. I told him I was Joy's boyfriend, and he said he knew who I was because when he'd gone to Si Saket Sunan had shown him a photograph of Joy and me taken outside the house. But Vernon had been told that I was Joy's husband, not boyfriend. Sunan had told him that we'd been married for two years, but that we'd not been getting on well and had decided to get a divorce.

I put him straight, I told him about Phiraphan and Joy's husband and the way I'd been lied to. I told him about bargirls and how they couldn't be trusted. He listened in a stunned silence. "Wow," he said eventually. "That's unbelievable."

I asked him how much he was giving Sunan and he said he'd agreed to send her a thousand dollars a month, plus he'd paid Sunan's father a four-thousand-dollar dowry. And he said he'd bought a ring for Sunan that had cost two thousand dollars, a blue sapphire ring similar to the one that I'd got for Joy. I interrupted him and asked what he meant. The most expensive thing I'd ever bought Joy was the gold bracelet I'd got for her on her birthday, and that had only cost three hundred and fifty dollars at most. Vernon told me that he'd met Joy in Bangkok before the wedding and that she'd been wearing a sapphire ring, and that Sunan had told him that I'd paid two thousand dollars for it. It was an engagement ring, Sunan had said, and she'd taken him to the same jewellers to buy a similar one for her.

I almost pissed myself laughing. I knew the ring he was talking about. Joy had bought it herself in Patpong. Three hundred baht it had cost. I asked him what else they'd said about me. Vernon said that he'd been told that I'd bought an apartment in Bangkok and that Joy lived with me, but that we'd now decided to split up and were sleeping in separate bedrooms.

He explained how he'd seen Sunan on a video and flown to Bangkok to meet her. She'd told him that she'd only been working in the bar for a couple of months and that she hated it. That was pretty much the same story Joy had fed me when I first met her. I put Vernon right and told him that Sunan was one of the hardest working girls in Nana Plaza and that she'd been hooking for years. I couldn't believe that he'd fallen in love with Sunan. She wasn't even particularly pretty and anyone who saw her couldn't not notice how hard her eyes were.

I asked Vernon if Joy had been at the wedding, and he said no, she hadn't. In fact, the only relatives at the ceremony were her brother Bird and her father, and a few cousins whose names he couldn't remember. I asked him if he thought it was possible for Sunan to fall in love with him so quickly. She could barely speak English, after all.

It was like soulmates meeting, he said. As soon as he saw her he knew that she was the love of his life. I told him he was making a big mistake, that Sunan cared only about money. His money. She'd take him for everything he had and then she'd dump him.

"Oh no, you're wrong," he said. "Sunan's different. She's not like the other girls."

I told him that they were all the same, that love didn't even come into it. I asked him if he didn't have doubts himself and he went quiet for a while. I waited for him to speak. When he did, he told me a story so bizarre that if it had happened anywhere else but Thailand I wouldn't have believed it.

VERNON

It was the night before the wedding. I was staying at Sunan's house. There were lots of people there, and I didn't know who most of them were. I'd been introduced to them all, of course, but they had such weird and wonderful names that I couldn't be expected to remember them all. Sunan's father was upstairs and so were some of the older people, Sunan's uncles and aunts or great uncles and aunts. Sunan and I were sleeping on mats in the big room on the ground floor, along with her brother Bird and half a dozen other people. One of Sunan's aunts, a woman called Nit who must have been in her late fifties, was giving us all massages. She's a professional masseuse, apparently, a medical one, not the sort that works in the massage parlours in Bangkok. She was doing everybody, massaging them until they fell asleep. We were all sleeping in our clothes, I guess that must be Thai style.

So eventually it's my turn. I was the last to get a massage, everyone else was asleep. I was a bit embarrassed, actually, even though I was wearing a T-shirt and jeans. I was lying face down and she knelt beside me, rubbing and probing. It wasn't all that relaxing, to be honest, she prodded a lot and I just wished that she'd stop. I decide the best way to get it over with would be to pretend to fall asleep, so I closed my eyes and started to breathe heavily. After a couple of minutes of fake snoring, Nit stops. The next thing I know, she's reaching into my back pocket and pulling out my wallet. I couldn't believe it. I didn't know what to do. I was being robbed by Sunan's aunt. On the night before the wedding. I froze. I heard her rifling through the bills. There was more than a thousand dollars in cash in the wallet, plus twice as much again in travellers cheques.

I pretended to wake up and I rolled over. Nit dropped the wallet and scampered over to the far side of the room. I put the wallet back in my pocket. I didn't mention it to Sunan the next day. Didn't mention it to anybody.

On the day of the wedding Nit helped get Sunan ready and she smiled broadly whenever she saw me. I began to think that maybe I'd imagined it, that maybe I'd actually fallen asleep and dreamed that she'd taken my wallet. But in my heart I knew that it hadn't been a figment of my imagination.

Two days after the wedding my watch and my wallet were stolen from the house while I was outside with Sunan and Bird. I reckon it must have been one of the men who always seemed to be hanging around the house. I think they work for Sunan's father. I'm sure it was nothing to do with Sunan. She was really upset when she'd heard what had happened. She said she'd find out who'd done it and get everything back. She never did, but I know she tried. You get thieves everywhere in the world: Thailand's no worse than America, Si Saket's no more dangerous than San Diego. I was just unlucky.

PETE

Unlucky? Vernon just doesn't get it. Of course they stole his watch and wallet. They were lying to him every step of the way. About Joy's ring. About how long Sunan had been dancing. Hell, she probably already had a Thai husband herself. I told Vernon everything that had happened to me, but it's like he wasn't listening. He asked me if I'd seen Sunan dancing in Zombie during the past few weeks and I said that yes, of course I had, and I'd seen her leaving with customers. He kept asking me if I was sure. I mean, does he think I was making it up or something? He kept saying that if he was sure, absolutely sure, that Sunan was lying to him then he'd be able to walk away, but I didn't believe him. Anyway, I told him to get

VERNON

I couldn't believe what Pete was telling me. The Sunan he was describing bore no relation to the girl that I'd fallen in love with. Sure, I had my suspicions that things weren't right, but I think that happens with every long-distance relationship. It's always difficult when you have to depend on the phone for contact. It'll be different once Sunan is in San Diego with me. I tried explaining that to Pete, but he wasn't listening.

Sunan wrote me the most loving letters you could imagine. Almost childlike they were, telling me how much she loved me and how happy she was to be married to me and how much she was looking forward to living with me in America. The letters were great. I used to reread them all the time. I could smell her perfume on them, too. She'd tell me how hard her life was and how poor her family was, and how happy everyone was that I was sending money to help them. There were lots of little scribbles in the margins, flowers and hearts and stuff like that. And once she sent me a purple and white flower, some sort of orchid. I keep it pressed between the pages of my diary.

The thing that worried me most was that sometimes when I called Sunan's room's late at night, she wasn't there. I know Thais do stay out late at night, but now that she's my wife I'd expected that she'd stay home more. I suppose I can't expect her to wait for me to call all the time, but it did bother me. I wasn't sure that calling the private detective was the best way to go, though. If I met a girl in San Diego, I wouldn't get a detective to check up on her, would I? You have to trust people. And Sunan wasn't just people, Sunan was my wife. She'd married me and she'd promised to come and live with me in America. She wouldn't do that if she was lying to me, would she?

Okay, I'm giving her money, but that's only to take care of her while she's in Thailand. It's all going to change when she gets to America. She'll be with me all the time then.

Extract from
CROSS-CULTURAL COMPLICATIONS OF PROSTITUTION IN THAILAND
by PROFESSOR BRUNO MAYER

The nature of prostitution in Thailand, involving a large number of tourists visiting the country in search of sexual experiences, means that the prostitute-client relationship in many cases is of a short-term nature, usually of a predetermined length of time. The farang arrives as a tourist, and the bargirl ascertains, often on the first meeting, the number of days he will spend in Thailand. The physical relationship therefore takes place within a set time frame, but it is in the girl's interest financially, and the farang's interest emotionally, to extend the relationship once the man has left. The man will perhaps telephone, but long conversations are expensive and the girl's English is probably not of a high enough standard to maintain a long conversation. Letters therefore become the primary mode of contact between the bargirl and her farangs. Indeed, a bargirl will often maintain several such long-distance relationships, writing to several farangs with whom she has had relationships. The letters often contain veiled requests for financial support and declarations of love. It is a delicate balance. On the one hand the girl knows it is important that she doesn't appear to be only asking for money, but on the other hand she has to maximise her earnings.

Generally the girls who work in the bars are not able to write in English, and the vast majority of the farangs with whom they are involved with cannot read or write Thai. A third party therefore enters the relationship, a 'scribe' who works for the bargirl, reading the farang's letters and helping the girl write her reply. In many cases, the letters the farang receives are written by the scribe, though in some cases the girl copies the scribe's letter in her own handwriting. The scribes are generally Thais who can read and write English, or long-time farang residents of Thailand who need to earn extra money.

The scribes play an important role in the maintenance of the long-distance relationships. The farang often seeks reassurance that his 'girlfriend' is 'being good', especially if he is sending her money on a regular basis. He also needs to feel that the girl loves him, that she is conforming to his Western ideal of a girlfriend. In many cases the scribe will know the girl, and if he, or she, is aware that the girl is still working as a prostitute, will join in the deception of the farang, often suggesting phrases and sentiments to be included in the letter to allay the farang's suspicions. In some cases, the girl will leave the entire contents of the letter up to the scribe. With the arrival of the internet, the scribes have become an even more important link between the bargirls and their clients. One only has to look through the window of any of the many internet cafes close to the red light areas to see pairs of girls sitting at keyboards, sending emails to customers and sponsors around the world.

VERNON

The thing that Pete just doesn't get is that Sunan is different. She's not the same as Joy and she's not the same as the rest of the girls who work in the bars. Sunan hates being a bargirl; all she wants is the opportunity to leave that life behind. I know that if I give her the chance, she'll be a good wife. She's told me that so many times. "Vernon," she'll say, looking at me with her heart-melting eyes, "I love you, only you. I be good wife for you. I take care of you, I love you for ever." Pete just doesn't get that. He's been in Thailand too long, he's become too hardened by it all. I can see why he's so upset at the way Joy's treated him, if what he says is true. And I have my doubts about that, to be frank.

He seemed so intense on the phone, and I began to realise that it wasn't so much that he was trying to rescue me from the clutches of Sunan, but more that he wanted to punish the family. He kept telling me that I was stupid to keep sending money to Sunan, but hell, from the sound of it he's given Joy way more than I've given Sunan.

I wish there was some way I could fly over and talk to Sunan myself, but it's just not possible. I only get three weeks vacation a year, and I used that up when I went over to marry Sunan. I'm sure that if I could sit down and talk to her face to face, I'd know if she was lying or not.

Could she be lying? Could she be as hard-hearted and calculating as Pete says? I find it almost impossible to believe that a human being could be so unfeeling and callous. And yet Pete was right about it being strange that so many members of Sunan's family didn't attend the wedding. And the business of the wallet and the watch still worries me.

I decided to get in touch with the private detective that Pete had recommended. I figured it couldn't hurt. At least I'd know the truth, and if Sunan was lying to me, then I'd walk away. Guaranteed.

PHIRAPHAN

Pete had already sent me an email that an American guy called Vernon might get in touch, so I wasn't surprised to get the call from San Diego. Don't these farangs ever learn? This guy, he flies over to a country he's never been to before, proposes to a bargirl he's never met, pays a four-thousand-dollar dowry to marry her, and then flies back to America. Then he asks me to check whether or not she's being faithful. I could have told him the answer to his question without even meeting the girl, but the farang obviously has more money than sense so I said I'd take his case. We agreed on a fee of twelve hundred dollars. For that he wants to know if she's working and if she's already married. Easy money. He also wanted to know who else was sending money to Sunan. That's a harder job because it means getting access to her bank account but I know people in most of the big banks so it won't be too much of a problem. I asked him why he wants to know and he said he wants to warn the other farangs. He's wasting his time, of course. The world is full of stupid farangs more than willing to send money to bargirls. But who am I to argue? Twelve hundred dollars is twelve hundred dollars, after all.

PETE

Nigel rang up to say that he'd quit and was having a leaving do at Fatso's Bar. "Leaving your job?" I asked.

"The job, Thailand, everything," he said. "I'm heading back to the UK, for a few months anyway."

Bruce was asleep on the sofa so I gave him a shake and brought him up to speed.

"I'm not surprised," said Bruce, scratching his chin. "He wasn't getting anywhere, was he?"

I didn't know. I'd rarely discussed Nigel's work with him. He sold advertising for an internet company, Web pages and stuff like that. I know he was paid by commission and that he was always short of money, but he'd always sounded fairly upbeat. He was always planning some business venture or other—setting up a bar, launching a magazine for expats, guided tours of the red light areas, mostly pie in the sky stuff because he didn't have any capital. Like Bruce, I reckoned he spent too much time in the bars to get any serious work done.

Bruce showered and by the time we got a cab to Fatso's Bar, Nigel was already well pissed.

Jimmy had Big Glassed him with Singha beer and the boys were egging Nigel on as he drank it. Half of it seemed to have spilled down his chest but at least he'd given it a go. I got Big Glassed at least once a month with gin and tonic and always drank it in one. Bruce always avoided it. He'd tip the wink to the girls and they'd whisk it away while no one was looking. Chicken, huh? Pretends he can hold his drink but I've never seen him knock back more than half a dozen beers without getting rat-arsed.

It wasn't that a great an evening, to be honest. Nigel was obviously unhappy about having to go back to England. He'd submitted a business plan to his bosses in Bangkok and they'd turned it down flat. I got the feeling there was more to it than that but I didn't want to pry. He didn't have a job to go to and he'd rented out his flat in the UK so he was going back to stay with his mother. That seemed like a hell of a come-down to me. I mean, he didn't have that great a lifestyle in Bangkok, he lived in one room in a run-down block in a shitty area close to Soi Nana, but he had enough money to barfine a girl once or twice a week and I couldn't imagine he'd have much luck with women back in the UK, what with his missing eye and all.

We piled out of Fatso's Bar at midnight, me, Nigel, Bruce, Jimmy and Rick, and went along to Nana Plaza. Bruce persuaded us to go to Zombie, but I think he only did it to wind me up.

Half a dozen of Joy's friends came over, asking where she was. I said I didn't know.

"Why Joy not live with you?" asked Wan.

"Because she's got a husband," I said. Wan started to deny that Joy was married but I wasn't listening to her. I looked across at the DJ's booth. Park wasn't there. I didn't know whether that was a good sign or not. I didn't want to be anywhere near him, but at the same time I couldn't help wondering where he was. Maybe he was with Joy. Maybe she'd run away with him. The thought made me sick to the stomach. How could she love him? How could she love a man who allowed her to dance naked, to sleep with men for money? What sort of love was that?

Rick and Jimmy were talking to a long-haired katoey, patting her on the backside and nodding at Nigel. Nigel was staring glassy-eyed at the stage nearest our table. I could see what Rick and Jimmy were planning. Nigel was vehement in his dislike of katoeys, but in his present state he probably wouldn't be able to tell the difference. I shook my head at Jimmy but Bruce put a hand on my shoulder.

"Come on, let the boys have their fun," he said.

"You wouldn't like it if they set you up," I said.

"I wouldn't get as pissed as that," he said. "Besides, look at the state of him, he's not going to be able to get it up anyway. He'll probably just get a blow job and that'll be it. It'll be his swan song."

"What do you mean?"

"Come on, you know as well as I do that he won't be coming back. No one will give him a job, he's got no money. I've been lending him cash hand over fist for months and he's never paid me back. He's a sad fuck, all right."

I bought Wan a drink and she clinked glasses with me. "You get my letter, Pete?" she asked.

"Letter?"

"Last month, Joy asked me to write a letter to you."

I couldn't understand what she was talking about, then I remembered the letter Joy had given me, the one that hadn't been in her handwriting. I nodded.

"What you think?" she asked. "Is my English okay?"

She was like a schoolgirl seeking approval from her teacher, and I felt I should be awarding her marks out of ten. "It was really good," I said. "Did Joy tell you what to write?"

Wan shook her head fiercely. "No, she just told me to make it sweet. She said you like sweet. Was it sweet, Pete?"

I felt like I'd been kicked in the stomach. Joy had made such a big thing about the sentiments being hers, that she'd told her friend what to write, and here was Wan telling me that it was all her own work. Why had Joy done that? She'd written to me on numerous occasions and she was more than capable of expressing her thoughts in English. There was no need for her to have asked Wan to write the letter. Laziness, maybe? I felt as if I'd been used. Manipulated. Make it sweet, she'd said. Pete likes it sweet. Was I that easy to predict? Did Joy know how to press my buttons so efficiently that she figured she could even do it by remote control? I felt used, but I just smiled at Wan and complimented her on her English.

"It was a good letter, Wan," I said. She beamed. I paid my share of the bill and headed home. I don't think the lads noticed; they were too busy persuading the katoey to sit on Nigel's lap.

On the way out of the Plaza I met Dit. She gave me a big smile and asked me if I'd seen Joy. I said I hadn't and that I didn't know where she was. Dit was wearing a white T-shirt with Snoopy on it and blue flared jeans. She looked so like Joy it was scary. I asked her if she was going to work and she shook her head. She said the police were in the Plaza, and because she was only seventeen, she wasn't supposed to be in the bar. She'd always claimed to be eighteen before. Was everything I heard in the bars a lie?

On a whim I asked Dit if she'd come back to the apartment with me.

She looked hesitant, so I said I'd give her a thousand baht. All I wanted to do was to talk, I said. I meant it, too. I wanted to ask her about Park, and if Joy was still seeing him.

We got a taxi back to Soi 23 and we sat on the sofa for almost an hour. I told her about the private detective and I explained how betrayed I felt. "Do you think she loved me?" I asked.

Dit nodded seriously. "Sure. She love you too much."

"So why did she have a Thai husband?" I asked.

Dit shrugged. "I don't know."

I asked Dit if she had a boyfriend and she nodded earnestly. "He very good looking," she said. She opened her wallet and showed me a photograph of a young Thai man, bare chested and smiling at the camera. I wondered if Joy still had my photograph in her wallet, or if it had been replaced.

"Doesn't he mind that you work in Zombie?" I asked.

"He not care. He know I only work. I not love farang."

I felt suddenly tired, physically and mentally. I gave Dit a thousand baht like I'd promised and I stood up.

"Two thousand?" asked Dit, holding up her hand.

I shook my head. "Come on, Dit. I said one thousand."

Dit smiled and looked across at the door to my bedroom. She looked back at me and raised an eyebrow.

At first I didn't understand what she meant. When I did realise, I thought she was joking, but she kept on smiling at me. She meant it. Or was she testing me?

"How much?" I asked.

"Two thousand," she said.

"Okay," I said.

As she walked to the bedroom, I kept on thinking that at any moment she'd burst into giggles and tell me that she couldn't. But she didn't. She went into the bedroom and undressed. Even as I took off my clothes I still didn't think she'd go through with it. She was Joy's step-sister; if she thought that I meant anything to Joy, there was no way she could sleep with me. Even if she wasn't afraid of hurting Joy's feelings, surely she'd be worried about what Joy would do if she found out.

I got into bed with her and she put her arms around me and kissed me full on the lips. She felt and smelled just like Joy.

Did the fact that she was prepared to sleep with me mean that she knew that Joy no longer cared about me? That Joy had never cared about me, that I was just a farang customer to be handed from girl to girl?

She spent an hour in my bed, and there wasn't a second when I didn't think about Joy. Everything Dit did reminded me of Joy. She even made love like her, the same facial expressions, the same noises. She even covered herself up when she dressed, the same as Joy. And when she went, after I'd given her the money, she kissed me on the cheek and whispered that she loved me.

DIT

I knew Pete always liked me. I could tell from the way he used to look at me when I was dancing. Pete's like most farangs. He likes young girls with long hair and big breasts. My breasts are bigger than Joy's and my hair's longer, so maybe he likes me more than Joy.

All the time in his apartment he kept talking about Joy, but I knew he wanted to screw me. I didn't think he'd pay me so much, though. Three thousand baht. That's the most I've ever been paid.

He cried afterwards. He turned away so I couldn't see him but I know he was crying.

Was I worried about what Joy would say? Of course not. She'd know that I only let him screw me for the money. Think about the money, that's what Joy always says, and that's all I was doing, thinking about the money.

Afterwards I went to see my husband. He works as a tout outside the Rainbow Bar. I took him for dinner. Great food. We ate so much we could barely walk.

PHIRAPHAN

The Sunan investigation was a piece of cake. I sent around one of my girls to the apartment block where she lived, pretending to be doing market research for a cable TV company, offering free cable in exchange for participating in a survey. She got a list of who was staying in the room, with ID card numbers, the works. Vernon had told me that Sunan's brother Bird often stayed with her and that he drove her around in a Toyota pick-up truck that her father owned. All a lie, of course. Sunan owned the truck, she'd obviously paid for it with the money she'd made from the bars. She had three bank accounts with more than half a million baht on deposit. And every month a Norwegian guy transferred forty thousand baht into one of the accounts.

But the really bad news so far as Vernon was concerned was that Bird wasn't Sunan's brother. He was her boyfriend. In fact, two weeks after Vernon went back to America, Sunan and Bird were married in Si Saket. The wedding hasn't been registered with the authorities yet, and there's a good chance it won't be because Sunan's marriage to Vernon has already been registered, I suppose she's serious about wanting to get a visa to join him in America. I sent a full report to Vernon, along with an invoice for the rest of his bill.

PETE

I called Vernon to see if he'd heard from Phiraphan. He said that Phiraphan had sent him a report but he didn't believe it and was refusing to pay his bill. It seems that Phiraphan had discovered that Bird was Sunan's boyfriend, not her brother. I can't say that I was surprised, but Vernon kept saying it was impossible, he'd seen the two of them together and they didn't act like boyfriend–girlfriend. When Vernon had first met Sunan, he'd slept in her room with her. And while he was in bed with Sunan, Bird had slept on the floor.

I tried to explain that Bird wouldn't care because he knew that

Sunan loved him and that she was only sleeping with Vernon for the money. Vernon wouldn't have that, he accused me of lying and getting Phiraphan to lie, too.

I asked him why on earth I'd do that and he said it was because I was angry at Joy, that I was trying to break him and Sunan up to get back at Sunan's sister.

I was stunned. Gob-smacked. There I was trying to save him from himself, to point out the dangers of getting involved with a hardened hooker. I told him what a liar Sunan was, I told him that she was one of the hardest-working hookers in Nana Plaza, and I told him about the Norwegian guy who'd been supporting her for years. He just wouldn't listen.

He told me that Sunan was different, that she loved him, and I said that couldn't possibly be so: he couldn't speak Thai, her English was basic at best. They could barely communicate, so how could she love him? Did he think he was that special?

He wouldn't listen. There was nothing I could say that would sway him from his conviction that he'd found the love of his life. He was a lost cause. A sad fuck.

Eventually I slammed the phone down on him. I was fuming. He'd accused me of lying, he'd believed Sunan over me. He'd believed her despite the evidence that Phiraphan had provided.

What really annoyed me was that the things that I'd said to Vernon were a virtual replay of what Damien had told me about Joy. And the phrases that Vernon had used to defend Sunan were almost word for word what I'd said to Damien. She's different. She loves me. She knows I'll take care of her. No matter what she's done in the past, she'll change once she knows she can trust me. If I can take her out of her environment, she'll change.

I decided that if Vernon was so determined to throw his life away, I wasn't going to try to stop him, and then I wondered if that was how Damien had felt about me.

I wanted to get back at Joy, I wanted to show her that she hadn't won the game. I went back to Zombie and tried to barfine Dit again. She kept saying no, that she was scared of what Joy would do, but after half an hour or so she said it would be okay if Cat went as well. I was fine with that, I'd be having sex with Joy's step-sister and her friend, too. That would show Joy that I didn't care any more. Dit made a big play of shouting across to Cat and asking if she wanted to "bai gin khao", to go and eat, and Cat agreed. They'd obviously both rehearsed the little double act because there was no question of going to eat—we went straight back to the apartment.

Again, there was no shyness on Dit's part, or Cat's either. If anything, they were even more enthusiastic. I'm not sure how I felt about it. The sex was great, but knowing that it was purely a business transaction took a lot of the enjoyment out of it. And it was also becoming obvious that they didn't care whether or not Joy knew what I'd done.

They stayed for almost two hours—I gave Dit six thousand baht and Cat four thousand. That was way over the going rate but I wanted Joy to know that the money didn't matter.

I fell asleep, but about half an hour later I was woken up by someone knocking on the door. It was Bruce. I asked him what he wanted but he kept repeating "are you alone?" I was still half asleep so I wrapped a towel around myself and opened the door. He was grinning like a masturbating chimp, pissed out of his skull. "You got anyone in there?" he leered, trying to peer around the door. When I said I hadn't, he gave me a drunken thumbs up. "That's lucky, 'cos I've got someone who wants to see you." He scurried down the corridor like a demented gnome and reappeared with Joy. It was three o'clock in the morning.

BRUCE

I couldn't believe it when I saw her. I was on my way out of the Plaza, slightly the worse for wear, when I hear someone calling my name. It's Joy, too much make-up as usual, running along the pavement and waving. She was wearing a huge Garfield shirt that I think Pete used to wear and blue jeans, and big black clumpy shoes. She was out of breath, and started telling me that she'd just arrived from Si Saket and didn't have anywhere to stay. I said she could stay with me and we got into a taxi.

"I not care if Pete have lady, I sleep on sofa," she said. She showed me calluses on her thumbs that she said she'd got from planting rice for the past month.

"Why did you leave Bangkok?" I asked.

"Pete tell me to go," she said. "He say he not want me work Zombie, he say he want me go Si Saket."

I don't get Pete, I really don't. This bloody girl has done everything he's ever asked of her. He tells her to go to Si Saket, she goes. He tells her not to dance, she doesn't dance. He tells her to call him, she does. She showed me the tattoo on her left shoulder, a red winged heart with his name in it. Does he think she'd do that if she didn't love him? I've told him time and time again he should give the girl a chance, let her live with him so that he can keep an eye on her twenty-four hours a day. He'd soon know if she was serious or not. I mean, look at what she did to her wrist, for God's sake. She carved his name into the flesh with a piece of broken glass.

I told her that Pete thought she had a Thai boyfriend, but she shook her head earnestly. "No have, Bruce. You must tell Pete I have him only one." I believe her, but Pete just keeps on wanting to test her. It's like he wants to test her to destruction, you know? I think he'll only be happy if she kills herself.

Anyway, when I opened the door to the apartment, there were no girl's shoes to be seen so I was pretty sure he was alone. I knocked on the door and told him Joy was there, then left them to it. Regular little Cupid, aren't I?

PETE

I didn't know what to say to her. Totally lost for words. I mean, she'd been gone for almost five weeks. She was wearing the Garfield shirt I'd given her almost a year ago.

We spent the best part of two hours talking, but it was the same old routine. I told her I knew that she'd been with her husband all the time she'd been working as a waitress. She denied it. I told her that I knew her barfine had been paid, that she'd left the bar with at least one farang. She denied it. She in turn wanted to know why I'd barfined Dit and Cat. I told her why, because I wanted her to know that they weren't really her friends. And because I wanted to talk to them about her, and her husband.

"Why you give them money too much?" she asked. "You give Dit six thousand baht. Why, Pete? I don't understand."

The conversation went nowhere. I asked her where she was staying and she just shrugged. "I go see my friend," she said. "Maybe I can stay with her."

I asked her where her clothes were, and she said she kept some with her friends and some with Sunan. All she had with her was a small bag containing her make-up and her bright red wallet. My picture was still there. After everything that had happened, she still carried my photograph in her wallet.

I told her she could stay with me that night and she hugged me and kissed me. We made love, twice, and I fell asleep holding her.

We didn't wake up until after midday. We started talking again, and within minutes we were covering the same old ground, the same old accusations. It was as if I couldn't stop pushing her, trying to provoke a reaction, like sucking cold air into a tooth cavity, knowing that it's going to hurt but doing it none the less. She kept repeating that she had split up with her husband, that she hadn't told me that he was working in Zombie because she hadn't wanted me to worry, and that she had never, repeat never, let a customer pay her barfine while she'd been working as a waitress. I wanted to believe her, God I wanted to believe her.

She went into the bathroom while I dressed. When she came out, she had a wad of toilet tissue pressed against her left wrist. "Pete," she said haltingly. "You not believe me. So I give you my blood." She took away the tissue and held out her left arm. Two deep razor cuts ran across her wrist, and blood dripped on to the carpet. She smiled. "I love you, Pete. I not have husband."

I sat her down on the bed. The cuts were deep, but she'd only cut the skin leaving the muscles underneath untouched. She'd cut her wrists many times before and clearly knew what she was doing, but that didn't make what she'd done any less horrific. I got more tissue and held it against the cuts to stem the flow of blood.

I kept asking her why she'd done it. "Because I love you," she said. "I want you know I love you."

I put some antiseptic on the cuts and covered them with sticking plaster. I didn't know what to do or say. I gave her two thousand baht. I wanted her out of the apartment, but at the same time I wanted to ask her to stay with me for ever.

I asked if she was planning to work in Zombie again but she said she didn't want to go anywhere near Nana Plaza. "I want to be good girl for you," she said. I asked her what she wanted to do. She said she wanted a room where she could stay on her own, and then maybe she'd try to find a job in a restaurant or a shop. I knew she wouldn't be able to support herself, not if she was planning to live alone. Her wages as a waitress in a restaurant wouldn't even cover her rent and before I knew what I was doing, I heard myself offering to pay for her room and her utilities.

She threw herself at me and gave me a big hug. "I love you too much," she said. "I give you key to my room, you can come see me when you want. You can check me every day."

I sat on the bed with her until the bleeding stopped and then I bandaged her wrist. The cuts didn't appear to bother her at all, she seemed to be far more interested in where she should live and how much I was prepared to pay for her rent. We decided on a maximum of four thousand baht a month.

BIG RON

Pete came in with a big sloppy grin on his face like he'd won the lottery. "Joy's back," I said, and his face fell like I'd spoiled it for him.

"How did you know?" he asked, like I was with MI5 or something.

I just shook my head and called him a sad fuck. He just doesn't get it. Joy's a hooker, a hard-bitten professional who's only interested in one thing, his money. I reckon every farang has a weak spot, no matter how long they've lived here, no matter how much they think they know, and Joy is Pete's Achilles heel. You've only got to look at her to know how she feels about him, you can see it in her eyes. An ATM, that's all she thinks he is, a fucking money machine. She presses the right buttons and money comes out, and one ATM is pretty much like any other.

There's a guy I know, Squeaky they call him on account of his high-pitched voice. Squeaky got himself a Thai wife, pretty little thing that used to dance in Soi Cowboy. He buys a house in her name and for a few months he's as happy as Larry. Then his wife says that her father isn't well and that he has to come and live with them. No problem, says Squeaky, there's plenty of room. So then his wife says that her father is going to have to sleep in her room. That means Squeaky is relegated to the spare bedroom. The old man arrives, though actually he isn't that old, as it turns out. Squeaky's wife says that her father was still in his teens when she was born, that he was quite a bit younger than her mother. Squeaky still doesn't smell a rat, and she fucks him regularly in the spare room, but I ask you, what the hell does he think's going on? He came in here last week and told everyone that he'd bought his wife a four-baht gold necklace but that her father was now wearing it. "Why would she give it to her father?" he asked. Because it's not her fucking father, it's her fucking husband, I wanted to say, but I didn't. Sometimes there's no telling people. You have to let them make their own mistakes.

That's how it is with Pete. He'll find out eventually. I learned my lesson years ago, I got ripped off big time and it'll never happen again. You've just got to start with the premise that everything you hear in the bars is a lie. I pay their barfines, fuck them, and then send them packing. That's the only way to treat them. I won't ever let them stay the night. Ever. That's a rule. They're hookers and hookers don't stay the night. Once I've come, they're out. I'll kick them out if I have to, but out they go. Receptacles for jism, that's all they are, and to treat them as anything else is just asking for trouble.

"She cut her wrists," he said.

"So?" I said.

"So I think she loves me."

Bollocks. Bollocks, bollocks, bollocks. I've known dozens of slappers slash their wrists. It means nothing. They never kill themselves that way, it's just a form of self-mutilation brought on by low self-esteem. It's not even a cry for help. If a slapper wants to end it all, she'll hang herself, or she'll throw herself off a tall building. I didn't say anything because I didn't want to burst his bubble. But what a sad fuck.

ALISTAIR

Pete's work went from bad to worse. He was way behind with the travel-cookery book, and he hadn't done anything about the photographs. Head office were going apeshit. They were trying to get the autumn catalogue out but without the photographs they weren't even able to mock up a cover. And we'd had only half the recipes we needed. The travel writing wasn't up to snuff, either. There was no sign of any Cambodian copy, though he'd already put his expenses in. Head office were furious about that, too. There'd been countless calls to Thailand from his hotel room, amounting to hundreds of dollars in all. They'd emailed him for an explanation, but he'd yet to reply. I tried to speak to him, but he was never in when I called. I spoke to his flatmate several times, Bruce I think his name is, and Bruce said Pete spent most of his time with Joy. Jesus H Christ, I thought he'd gotten that hooker out of his system. Pete's appointment was rapidly turning into a disaster, and I told him so in a memo. It was a final warning, in effect. If he didn't pull his socks up, we'd have to let him go.

PETE

Joy found a room within a couple of days of getting back to Bangkok. It was in a block on a road called Soi Disco, off Sukhumvit Soi 71. It was several miles away from my flat in a busy area packed with shops and restaurants, and I took it as a good sign because it was a long way away from Nana Plaza. It was a pretty ground floor room with a Thai-style bathroom and a small patio. It was four thousand baht a month and I went with her to pay three months rent in advance. The only furniture was a double bed, a cheap teak veneer wardrobe and a small dressing table, but it was clean and the paintwork was fresh. I went shopping with her and we bought sheets, pillows, a portable colour television set, an electric kettle, plates and cups and stuff for the bathroom. Joy bargained for everything, getting discounts in every shop we went in. We saw a plastic plant in a pot, four feet high with long green leaves and yellow flowers, and we bought that, too.

There was a telephone in the room and Joy wrote down the number on a scrap of paper, and presented it to me with a key to the door and a key card to get into the building. "Now you can come see me every day,". she said.

VERNON

I spoke to Sunan and told her what Phiraphan had said, that Bird wasn't her brother. She asked who Phiraphan was and I said he was a private detective, the same man that Pete had used to check up on Joy in Si Saket. Sunan started laughing and said that I shouldn't believe anything he said. She said that Pete wanted to divorce Joy and that the private detective was lying so that Pete could get a divorce without giving Joy any money. Phiraphan lied about Joy having a husband, he'd lied about everything. Sunan said Pete didn't like her and he was probably paying Phiraphan to say bad things about her.

Sunan said that she loved me. "If I didn't love you, Vernon, why I marry you? Why I say I come to America to live with you?"

It was a good point. If she had a Thai boyfriend or a husband, she could stay with him and go back to working in the bars. She could earn more as a dancer than I was paying her.

"Pete want you not believe me," said Sunan. "He not good guy, Vernon. He not same you."

I think she's right, I think Pete was trying to split us up to get back at Joy. And I think he was jealous of the relationship that Sunan and I have. Sunan's much softer, much more caring than Joy, and prettier too. Joy always seemed to me to have a hard face, cold eyes, you know? She always had this calculating look about her, as if she was trying to work out how much money you had and how much you'd be prepared to spend on her. She's unbalanced, I think, you can tell that from the scars on her wrists. Sunan's never done anything like that to herself. She's a sensible, level-headed young woman, and she's going to make a great wife. She's my soulmate, and Pete's not going to split us up.

JOY

Sunan thinks I'm crazy. She says I should start working again because Pete's never going to take care of me properly. I told her that I wanted to give him a chance. Park was living with Daeng, I hadn't seen him since we'd had the argument in Zombie. What was I expected to do? To start dancing again, to have all my friends know that I'd lost Park and Pete? It's all right for Sunan, she's got Vernon and she's got Toine in Denmark. And she's got Bird. Who've I got? No one. Pete's giving me money again, and he's paying for my room and my electricity and for the phone, and he bought me a television and he's promised to get me a fridge. I think he'll take care of me this time. Maybe he'll take me back to England with him. I hope so because I'm bored with Thailand. I'm bored with everything.

I do miss the bars, though. It's difficult to explain why. There's something about the excitement of the bars. All the people, the noise, having your friends around. I used to enjoy going out with the girls after work, drinking and singing karaoke. I can still do that, of course, but Pete won't like it. He expects me to stay in the room twenty-four hours a day, like a dog.

DAMIEN

The big mistake that most farangs make is that they think the girls don't like being hookers. Well, they do, they bloody love it. For a start, there's the sex. Most of these girls lose their virginity before they're thirteen, and then it's to their father or their brother or one of their brother's friends. I mean, they're peasants, they see the animals doing it around them and it's a case of monkey see, monkey do. Sex to them is as natural as eating or shitting. I'm not saying they like it, I'm not saying that they have a thumping great orgasm every time a big, sweaty German climbs on top of them, but having sex is no big deal, it really isn't.

They like the dancing, too. They always dance, even when work's over they'll go to a disco or a restaurant and get tanked up on Thai whiskey or heroin or whatever their thing is, then they'll dance, dance until they drop. The DJs know what music the girls like, and they're all dancing together, so for them it's fun, not work. And they like the adoration, too. The fact that dozens of guys are staring at them with hard dicks, wanting them, willing to pay money for what they used to do for free back on the farm.

I tell you, there's girls get married from Zombie, they go back to Germany or Denmark or England, they live with the farang for a few years and then they say they have to come back to visit a sick relative or something. Sure, they go up country for a few days, but then they're back here, up on the stage flashing their tits and arses. Why? Because it's a turn-on, that's why. They've got guys staring at them, wanting them, lusting after them. Sure, men come in the bars and have women hanging all over them, but deep down we know it's for the money. With the girls, it's different. They like to be wanted. It's an aphrodisiac. It's power. It's a feeling they never get from a husband and a family, and it's something they miss. Something they need. That's why guys like Pete are never going to win. He's never going to be able to give Joy anything that comes even close to what she gets from dancing naked.

The other big mistake that farangs make is that they think there's a shame in working the bars. They think they're going to come in here and rescue the girls from a life of vice, that the girls will do anything to escape. They don't understand that there's no shame attached to being a hooker. None at all. Okay, some of the more educated Thais might look down on the bargirls, but basically the whole Thai social structure is built around the acquisition of money and the building of relationships that will lead to the acquisition of money. For the educated Thais or those born into rich families, it's all about forming and maintaining links with the army, the government and the police. With working class Thais it means getting on with your boss and with your opposite numbers at organisations you do business with. With hookers, it's getting a farang to fall in love with you so that you can take them for everything they've got. The Thais understand that, they know that the hookers are only doing a job.

But farangs think about it in their own terms. Back where they're from, being a hooker is a sinful thing, something to be ashamed of. Okay, so a bargirl doesn't go around broadcasting the fact that she's a prostitute, but she's not shy about walking around Robinson department store hand in hand with a guy twice her age. If anything she's proud of the fact. Look at me, she's saying, I've got a rich guy who's taking me shopping, who'll buy me anything I want.

There's a village in Isarn, right at the end of a dirt track in one of the poorest parts of the country. You come around a bend and you're confronted by dozens of big, expensive houses. They call it Swiss Village. Nothing to do with the style of the homes, it's because the whole damn village was built from Swiss money. About fifteen years ago, a girl from the village went to work as a hooker in a Zurich bar. She made a fortune in Thai terms and came back and built a house for her parents, bought a pick-up truck and a couple of motorcycles for her brothers. Word soon got around how she'd made her money. Do you think the villagers started pointing their fingers and shouting "shame, shame, shame"? Did they hell. The girls from the village were queuing up at her door, asking how they could go and work in Zurich, too.

So a few more local girls go over to the same bar. They make money, more money than your average Thai farmer would make in a hundred lifetimes. They come back, they buy land and a big house, and within a few years practically every girl from the area is on a plane to

Switzerland. These days it's a bloody business. As soon as a girl is old enough, and assuming she's not pig ugly, she's approached by an agent. The agent sends her to Bangkok for six months where she goes to a language school to learn French or German. Then she goes back to a sort of finishing school where girls who've been to Switzerland teach them to smoke, drink, touch up the guys. By then most of the girls are already experienced sexually, but if there are any virgins then a representative of the company that runs the bars, a farang, breaks them in.

Once they're ready, the company arranges their passports and visas and flies them over. They're moved around from bar to bar, never spending more than a month in any one. That makes it look as if the bars are always getting new girls, you see. Smart move, that. Punters don't realise the girl's been around for a while. They think she's fresh off the plane from Thailand. The girls dance, and they persuade the customers to drink champagne at God knows what price. They get a commission, and they can earn up to a thousand quid a month. There's no barfine system because the company is legit and obeys the law religiously, but after hours the girls are free to make whatever arrangements they want. And they do. Eight months later they fly back, their tour of duty over. Shame? Don't talk to me about shame. The only shame in Thailand is being poor.

I've lost count of the number of farangs who've written to me asking if their 'girlfriends' are being faithful, or if they're still going with customers. Usually they're sending the girl money every month but the girl has told them they want to keep working in the bar so that they can be with their friends. The letters go straight into the bin. The fact is, if the girls are dancing in the bar, they have to go with customers. Have to. We build it into their wages. If they have their barfine paid seven times in a month, they get their full salary. If their barfine is paid six times, we dock them three hundred baht. No barfines in a month and we take two thousand baht off their wages. It has to be that way. The barfines are a big slug of our income and if a girl isn't hustling, we're not earning and we'd be better off without her. So if a bargirl tells her farang boyfriend that she's dancing in the bar and not going with customers, then she's lying. In fact, if a bargirl tells her farang boyfriend anything, she's lying.

That's the golden rule when dealing with bargirls: if their lips are moving, they're lying.

The waitresses don't have the same pay structure as the dancers, but most of them will go short time with customers. But we don't dock their pay if they don't—it's their choice. Waitressing is one of the ways that the girls get into prostitution, it's sort of a halfway stage. They get to improve their English, they hang around with farangs, and they see how the dancers operate. Then one by one they succumb, and if they've anything about them they'll be up and dancing around the silver poles within six months.

A few days after Pete came into the office, I went looking for Joy. Server 127. She didn't look that special, I have to say, but cute in that Khmer way. Long hair, dark skin, upturned nose. I took her into the short-time room for half an hour and gave her one. Nothing special in that department. Wouldn't take it up the dirt-box but was up for everything else. Bit too old for me, truth be told.

PHIRAPHAN

I was in the Emporium department store in Bangkok just before Christmas and I saw a couple of Americans chatting. 'Have you met my wife,' says one, and introduces a girl probably ten years younger than he was, holding a small baby. A nice enough girl, but clearly a former bargirl. Showing her midriff, a bit too much make-up, probably a tattoo hidden from view.

I couldn't help wonder what had gone through the American's head before getting hitched to a prostitute. Doesn't he know the dangers of getting involved with a bargirl? And leaving aside the sheer futility of expecting a marriage to a hooker to have a happy ending, doesn't he realise that every Thai who sees them together will know that she was a bargirl? Every time they go out together, every restaurant they eat in, every cinema they go into, every shop they visit. And it will stay like that for the rest of their time in Thailand. No Thai he meets is going to take him seriously. If he works for a Thai company, his bosses will lose all respect for him. His Thai co-workers ditto. Why would anyone respect a man who has married a prostitute? Taking her overseas won't be any easier. Most people he will meet will assume, rightly, that he married a hooker. Why would any man put himself through that?

That got me to thinking about farangs who marry Thais. It seems to me, based on almost twenty years experience as a private detective, that the vast majority of farangs who marry Thai girls are sex tourists. And most of the Thai girls who marry Westerners are bargirls. This is a fact, no matter how unpalatable that is.

Now, most sex tourists wouldn't think of describing themselves as such. They see themselves as men of the world, visitors to an exotic country where young, beautiful girls treat them as gods. But in my view, ninety-nine per cent of men who visit Thailand without a female companion are sex tourists. And marriage between a sex tourist and a prostitute will always end in disaster.

Why? Because virtually without exception, bargirls are damaged goods. Addicted to booze, drugs or gambling. Probably with a Thai husband or boyfriend in the background. A child or two up country with the relatives. A box full of photographs and business cards. A mobile phone full of telephone numbers of men she's slept with. A jaundiced view of farangs in general and sex tourists in particular.

And what of the sex tourist? He's paid for sex with how many young, sexy girls. How likely is he to settle down? In a way, sex tourists and bargirls deserve each other. But one thing is for sure – the relationship won't last. Guaranteed.

The next group who tend to marry Thai girls are expats who say they live here. You'll meet them all the time in the bars of Bangkok and Pattaya. They sit there with a thick gold chain around their thick neck and a mobile phone clipped to their belt and talk about Thailand being their home. But when you get to know them, you discover that the bulk of them are actually long-term sex tourists, working at jobs that do little more than cover their living (and screwing) costs. English teachers, bar owners, website designers, scuba instructors. Anyone serious about any of those professions wouldn't be working in Thailand. A teacher of English as a foreign language can earn several times a Thai salary working in the States or Europe. Website designers abroad make a good living, here it's thirty or forty thousand baht a month at best. Magazine sub-editors here earn a fifth of the salary they'd get back in the States. Freelance journalists have to live like paupers to survive. These men aren't here for the money, they're here for the sex.

The same goes for most of the men here on retirement visas. They're not here for the cheap food and the temples. Ask yourself why so many live in Pattaya or within walking distance of Nana Plaza or Soi Cowboy. They are long-term sex tourists, nothing more, and personally I look forward to the day when the Government here bites the bullet and sends them all packing. Let's see how they get on paying for sex with girls a third of their age back in their own countries.

As in the case of short-term sex tourists, the long-term variety of sex tourist has no chance of getting close to a decent Thai girl. When they do marry, they almost always marry bargirls. Often they'll lie, claiming to have met the girl in Robinson's Department store or at a temple. Rubbish. Spend any time talking to the wife of a long-term sex tourist and you'll soon see her true colours. Often these men end up marrying a succession of prostitutes before returning penniless to their own country. Let's repeat: you cannot have a successful relationship with a bargirl. Anyone who thinks they have a loving, caring, sharing relationship with a (former) bargirl just hasn't discovered the truth yet. Get yourself a decent (honest) private detective like me and get the facts before you throw more good money after bad.

A growing percentage of marriages to Thai women involve sad men who can't find wives in their own countries. Strange as it may seem, there are probably more success stories among this group than any other. Usually they are middle-aged men, often with at least one failed marriage behind them, who decide that they want a Thai wife. What saves these men from disaster is that they don't go through the sex-tourist phase. Instead they use an agency to find them a partner. Providing the agency doesn't fix them up with a hooker, and providing the girl/woman is serious about wanting a farang husband, and providing she moves with him back to his country, these marriages do have a surprisingly high success rate.

They also tend to be marriages of equals, which makes them more likely to succeed. Plus marriages through agencies tend to be less for sex and more for companionship. That's where the sex tourist usually comes adrift. The Thai girl who looked so attractive dancing naked around a silver pole isn't quite so alluring wrapped up in a duffel coat against the chill winds of north east England. And it's amazing how quickly the slim, sexy bargirl figure (probably due to heavy Yar Ba consumption) turns to fat on an American diet. Men who use the agencies tend to be looking for companionship rather than sex, so they are less likely to be disappointed if they don't get fixed up with a sex goddess. Or if their sex goddess metamorphoses into a heavy-set lump, albeit one with a charming smile.

The last group of men who tie the knot with Thai girls are the long-term expats. These men are totally different from long-term sex tourists. They have real jobs and earn salaries comparable with what they would get back in their own countries. Often they are not here by choice, but have been sent to Thailand by their companies. These are not men you will ever see in a go-go bar, unless they are entertaining a visitor from overseas who wants to see sleaze. These are not men who would go near a bargirl and who would be contemptuous of any farang who did. More often than not, such men will already have families. Of those that are single, most would not want to marry a Thai. Those that are single will know all the pitfalls of marrying across a cultural divide, and will not enter into it lightly. And if they do marry a Thai girl, she'll be from a good family, either with a career of her own or rich enough that she doesn't have to work. It won't be a girl he met in a bar, working at Robinsons department store, dancing in the Hard Rock Cafe or prowling the various Thai internet chatrooms.

One thing you will notice about long-term expats who marry Thais— generally the age gap isn't much greater than it would be back in their own country. Generally five years, probably ten, in some cases fifteen. But what you won't see is a long-term expat marrying a decent Thai girl young enough to be his daughter. Or his grand-daughter. I don't care what the sex tourists say about Asian girls appreciating a man of senior years, there is something grotesque about a fifty-year-old man walking hand in hand with a twenty-year-old unless he is a blood relation. A thirty-year age gap is simply ridiculous. Forty is sick. My own wife is just two years younger than I am and she often tells me that I am too old for her.

It is not true to say that Thai girls prefer older men. Men with little or no hair. Men with beer guts. Thai girls like girls the world over prefer young, fit good-looking men. This is where the average sex tourist says, 'yes, but I make them laugh. They like me. I'm different.' Sadly, they're not. I've never yet met a sex tourist who I've found the least bit entertaining or interesting. Generally they're working class in a dead-end job from a minor provincial city. If they're British they're wearing sandals and socks and have probably got a shaved head and a couple of tattoos. If they're Americans they're from some mid-West town you've never heard of wearing a Harley T-shirt stretched over a massive beer gut and a goatee beard disguising a weak chin. These are not attractive people in the main, but even the good-looking ones fall down in the IQ department. You do not find New York bankers or London company directors hanging around the bars of Nana Plaza and Patpong. Sex tourists in the main are taxi drivers, butchers, plasterers, plumbers, low-grade office workers. Men who would find it difficult to get a half-decent girl back in their home towns.

You think that just because you've sat in the economy section of a long-haul flight for a day that you've suddenly become a fascinating person? Think again. Bargirls are not hanging on your every word because you are the life and soul of the party, but because she is a sex worker and you are a sex tourist and you are getting what you are paying for. Nothing more, nothing less. Long term expats know this and would no more dream of getting into a relationship with a bargirl in Bangkok than they would with a hooker in New York. They meet decent, 'real' girls and go through a proper courtship process before proposing and settling down.

So, do relationships between long-term expats and Thai girls from good families work? An unequivocal 'yes' to this one. They do work, with probably a better success rate than marriages generally in the States or Europe. That's because more effort is made on both sides to choose the right partner. And because the girl's family will also play a crucial role, both in whether or not they give their permission (and without it no decent Thai girl would get married) and the support they give after the marriage. Never forget, when you marry a Thai girl, you marry her family, for better or worse.

So, to sum up, here are the rules that I would suggest a farang follows if he is determined to marry a Thai:

1) If you want a Thai wife, don't become a sex tourist. Find a Thai girl in your own country, or join a respectable agency which can provide you with checkable references. And if you do find the girl of your dreams through an agency, get her checked out by a trustworthy private detective. It's the only way you will ever be sure that there isn't a Thai boyfriend or husband around.

2) If you decide to come to Thailand to look for a wife, do not go into a go-go bar or other places of prostitution. You wouldn't go looking for a hooker to marry in your own country so don't do it here.

3) Do not, under any circumstances, marry a bargirl. Marriages to bargirls do not work out. Anyone who has married a bargirl and thinks that he has a successful marriage just hasn't discovered the truth yet.

4) If you do marry a bargirl, don't complain when it goes wrong.

5) If you are a sex tourist, you will never have a successful long-term relationship, with any girl. Accept that and continue being a sex tourist.

6) Treat any Thai girl you meet on the Internet with suspicion. Ask yourself why a good Thai girl would go looking for a Western boyfriend on the Internet. The answer is simple, a good Thai girl wouldn't.

7) Marry a girl as close as possible to your own social, financial and educational standing. And the closer you are in ages, the better.

8) If you do marry a Thai girl, only stay in Thailand if you can earn more here than in your home country. Or if her family is a positive asset. Outwith those two provisos, your marriage will have more chance of working outside Thailand.

9) If you do stay in Thailand, learn the language. Learn about the country's history and culture. Watch local TV and local movies. Listen to Thai music. The only way you are going to have even a chance of

understanding how a Thai thinks and feels is to understand their culture.

Those are my nine golden rules. Follow them and you stand a reasonable chance of having a happy marriage. But if you do decide to enter into a relationship with a bargirl and want me to check her out for you, my number is in the phone book.

BIG RON

Pete's going from bad to worse. He spends hours sitting in the bar, drinking himself stupid. I've tried to talk to him but he won't listen. And when he's not here he's with Joy, sitting in some crappy room in Soi 71 watching Thai game shows on a portable TV. He keeps telling me that he's not sure if Joy's being honest with him, and asks me if I think she could still be lying to him. I want to grab him by the throat and shake him. Of course she's lying to him. Why would he expect anything else? Everybody lies, right? It's just that bargirls have it down to a fine art.

What are the three big lies? Someone told me ages ago. Something like: the cheque's in the post, I won't come in your mouth, and of course I'll respect you in the morning. Heard that years ago and it's so fucking true. Everybody lies. Period. Sometimes they're small lies, white lies if you like, and sometimes they're big lies, but only children expect to hear the truth. And what do we tell kids? We tell kids that on Christmas Eve a fat man in a red suit is going to climb down the chimney and leave presents for them. And we tell them that the fat man won't come if they've been naughty. Fucking stupid.

I tell you, if I had kids I'd put them straight about Father Christmas, and God, too. I mean, we tell them about Father Christmas, then as soon as they're old enough to understand, we tell them that in fact we were lying, there is no fat man in a red suit and reindeers can't really fly. "What about God?" they say. You said God watches over us and protects us and that if we're good we'll go to live with him. Is God like Father Christmas? That's when parents get all evasive and say that no, they were lying about Father Christmas but everything they said about God was true. Bollocks. Kids should be told the truth from day one. There is no Father Christmas. There is no God. And Thai bargirls don't fall in love with farangs.

I don't know why Pete keeps testing her. He sends her to Si Saket and finds she's got a husband. He pays for her to work as a waitress and she still screws customers. What more does he want? Why can't he just accept that she's a lying hooker and leave it at that?

PETE

Alistair sent me a memo by email threatening me with the sack if I didn't get the copy for the Cambodian book to him within seven days. The memo was already three days old when I got it because I'd been staying with Joy and I couldn't plug my laptop computer into her phone socket to pick up my messages. I didn't know what to do. I'd be hard pushed to finish it in four weeks, never mind four days. He'd been pestering me for weeks, but I'd been so caught up with Joy that I was way behind schedule. I sent him a short reply, just saying that it was on its way.

ALISTAIR

I gave Pete every opportunity to get back on the straight and narrow, but he just wouldn't get his act together. There was nothing I could do: if I didn't cut my losses then I'd get dragged down with him. I had to show head office that I was in control, and there was only one way I could do that. I had to let him go. I tried to get him on the phone but he was never in. I spoke to his flatmate, but he said Pete was probably with Joy and he didn't have her number.

In the end I had to do it by letter. I couriered it to him so that he wouldn't be able to deny receiving it. In the letter I asked him to hand over his notes and computer discs to his replacement, a guy who'd been working for us in Taiwan, an American Mandarin-speaker called Chuck.

I'm going to have to do the travel-cookery book myself. I told him I'd give him the editing credit because he had done a fair amount of work, but he hadn't sent any pages for the Cambodian guide so the new guy would have the credit for that one.

I don't know what it is about Thailand, but it seems to destroy people. Sucks the life out of them. I don't know if it's the climate or the bars, but there's something that seems to magnify the faults of the people who go there. It happened with Lawrence and it happened again with Pete. I'm not going to take the risk with Chuck. He's going to stay in Taiwan and edit the Thai books from there. I've learned my lesson. I just wish I could say the same about Pete.

PETE

I didn't like having to check up on Joy, but let's face it, her track record didn't exactly inspire trust. I left it a week, and then one evening, after we'd had dinner at a restaurant in Soi 71, I told her I had to go to Fatso's Bar to see Bruce. That much was true, I'd arranged to see him, but just after midnight I picked up a motorcycle taxi in Soi 4 and went back. The light was on in her room and I used the keycard and stood outside her door for a while. I could hear the television, but that was all. I felt suddenly guilty for suspecting her. I knocked on the door. Nothing. I knocked again. Silence. This didn't make sense. She wouldn't have gone out and left the light and television on. I took out my key and tried the lock. It turned, but the bolt was on so she was obviously inside. I rattled the door. "Joy. It's me."

There were whispers but I couldn't hear what was said. I couldn't even be sure if it was Joy or not. I pushed the door harder. "Come on, Joy. Open the door. It's me."

"Wait, wait," she said.

Maybe she wasn't dressed, I thought. Maybe she had a girlfriend with her, maybe the room was untidy and she wanted to clear up before letting me in. I was trying to persuade myself that everything was all right but in my heart of hearts I knew it wasn't. I knocked on the door.

"Joy, I want to come in now," I said.

No reply. I put my shoulder to the door and pushed, hard. It was a cheap bolt on the door and it only took a couple of shoves to break it. Joy was standing in the middle of the room. She smiled, but she looked scared. She was wearing the same clothes she'd had on when I'd left her, a small tank top and tight jeans. Sexy. "Sawasdee ka," she said, her forehead creased into a frown.

I pushed the door open. There was somebody else in the room, standing next to the television. It was a Thai man. In his twenties, slicked back hair and a muscular chest over which was stretched a black net T-shirt so that he could show off his body. He smiled at me. "Sawasdee krap," he said.

I glared at Joy. There was a game show on television and the audience was clapping and laughing. She said nothing. There was nothing she could say.

I turned around and walked away. I went outside, but as I did the anger flared inside me. It was my room, I'd paid for it. The sheets on the bed, the pillows. The television. It was all mine, and she'd taken a man back there. She was probably even making love to him on the bed when I knocked on the door.

I went back. She was standing in the hallway, staring at me through the plate glass door, a look of dismay on her face. I slotted in the key card but the lock wouldn't open. I kicked the door. The Thai man came over to the door as if he wanted to help open it. I swore at him, told him to get the fuck away. I kicked the door, pushed it with my shoulder. Joy backed away. She wasn't crying, she just looked shocked. I would have preferred tears, some sign of remorse, some indication that she was sorry. I tried the key card again. The lock buzzed and I threw the glass door open.

"Pete, kao mai ben fan. Ben puen." Pete, he's not my boyfriend. He's a friend.

I punched her on the chin. Not too hard, but hard enough. She staggered back, a look of disbelief on her face. There was no blood, I'd hit her on her left cheek, away from her lips. Crazy. I wanted to hit her, but I didn't want to hurt her.

I turned to look at the Thai guy. He stood there, smiling. Any sign of aggression, anything, and I'd have laid into him. He looked down, still smiling. I felt nothing but contempt.

I grabbed Joy by the hair and pushed her into the room. I kicked the door closed. "Why?" I asked her. "Why did you do it?"

"Mai ben fan. Ben puen."

I slapped her, open handed. She didn't cry out. She just kept staring at me, a look of dismay on her face. I looked around the room. There was more inane laughter from the television. Joy had betrayed me again, she'd brought a man into my room, into the room I'd paid for. I picked up the television and dropped it on to the tiled floor. It didn't break. I couldn't believe it. The laughter continued. I kicked the screen, hard, but all I did was hurt my foot.

"Pete, no!" Joy shouted.

I ignored her. I bent down, picked up the TV, and threw it down, harder this time. It crashed on to the floor, but still it didn't smash.

I heard the door open and shut behind me. Joy had gone, but I didn't care. I was mad, I was mad as hell, and all I wanted to do was to smash the room, to break and destroy everything I'd given her. I picked up the TV and carried it to the bathroom, pulling the plug out of the wall. The laughter ended abruptly. I lifted the TV above my head and dropped it, screen down, on to the bathroom floor. I expected an explosion, but the screen didn't break. It isn't like it is on the movies. God knows what they make the screens from, but take it from me, they're practically indestructible. I knocked everything off her bathroom shelf.

There was a glass of some red liquid, a soda maybe, on the bedside table. I threw it over the sheets. I pulled the clothes from her wardrobe and threw them on the floor. I screwed up the books she was writing and shoved them down the toilet. The Garfield watch I'd brought for her went into the toilet, too, along with her laser keyring. I overturned her table, kicking and stamping on anything breakable. I pulled out the cupboards from the wardrobe and tossed them on to the floor. Her wallet was there. She kept her wallet in the top drawer, and all the time she'd been in the room she'd never taken it out, not even when she went shopping. I'd come to realise that the wallet was something she only had with her when she was in the bar. It was part of the costume that went with the tight T-shirts and the eye-shadow. The fact that she had my photograph in her wallet didn't actually mean anything.

As I was pulling her clothes out, I saw an envelope at the back of the wardrobe. There were photographs inside. Pictures of Joy and her sisters, a young Joy with her mother, Joy with her father. There were other photographs, photographs taken in Zombie. Photographs of Joy with farangs. They'd obviously been taken fairly recently because she was wearing her waitress uniform. In all of them she was in the same pose, smiling at the camera with one hand resting on the guy's thigh. I wasn't special. I was one of many. I tore the photographs up, all of them, and threw them into the toilet.

I tossed my set of keys and the key card on to the bed, to show her that I'd never be back. I stood there for several seconds, staring at the keys, panting from the exertion of trashing the room. Then I picked up the keys and put them into my pocket. I don't know why I did that. Actually, that's not true. I do know. Despite everything, despite catching her with another man, despite tearing her room apart, I still wanted to be able to go back to her.

I went outside. She wasn't there. The Thai guy was there, still smiling. He pointed out to the street. "She go that way," he said.

After I left Joy's room, I went to Fatso's Bar and got drunk. Big Ron was there and I told him what I'd done. "Drop her," he said. "She's been lying to you from Day One."

I couldn't argue with him. It seemed that no matter what I did, no matter how I tried to help, no matter what allowances I made, she always let me down. I have a friend in New York, Mary's her name. We were at university together but she's been in the States for almost twenty years now. Anyway, Mary lives in this apartment block on 57th Street, on the tenth or eleventh floor, I forget which. One day she finds this stray kitten, probably wasn't more than a few months old, and she takes it in.

She loves this cat, and she really looks after it. Dotes on it. Then one day the cat climbs out of the bathroom window and falls all ten stories. Or eleven. Splat. Except that the cat's not dead, it lands on a sloping roof or something which breaks its fall. Mary rushes the cat around to the local vet and it's good news, bad news. The good news is that he can save the cat, the bad news is that it's going to cost a small fortune, several thousand dollars. The cat's got a broken leg, a fractured spine, internal bleeding, most of its nine lives are out of the window, literally. The vet suggests that the best thing to do would be to put the cat down, a simple, painless injection, total cost ten bucks or thereabouts.

Mary thinks about it. She doesn't have money to throw away, but she loved that cat. "Do what you have to do to save her," says Mary.

The vet does his stuff. The cat spends almost a month in the vet's surgery, then another two months in a body cast, lying around Mary's apartment being hand-fed like a bloody princess. Eventually the cast comes off and the cat's as good as new. And Mary's stuck with a hefty overdraft.

A week after the cast came off, Mary gets a phone call at her office. It's the vet. Seems the doorman discovered her cat lying on the ground and had brought it in. Mary remembered that she'd left the bathroom window open. The cat had fallen out of it again.

"Severe injuries again, I'm afraid," said the vet.

"Massive internal bleeding, both front legs broken, several ribs cracked. We can save her, but it's going to be expensive ..."

Mary didn't hesitate. "Kill it," she said, and put down the phone.

That's how I felt about Joy. I'd done everything I could, but it seemed that it was never enough, she'd always go back to her old ways, she'd always revert to type. I had to walk away.

I went home and slept. Bruce woke me up at about six o'clock in the morning. Joy's friend Wan was on the phone. "Pete, Joy want see you," she said.

"I can't," I said.

"You not understand Joy," said Wan. "That not boyfriend Joy. He sell yar mar."

Yar mar was the local name for amphetamines. I'd read about it in the Bangkok Post. Yar mar translated as horse drug, so-called because of the energy it gave users. The police got so fed up with the drug's sexy image that they rechristened it yar ba, crazy drug. It's a big thing among the bargirls, it helps give them the energy to dance all night, and helps them overcome their shyness. Many are addicted. Joy had always denied that she took drugs. But as I'd already discovered, Joy and the truth didn't exactly have a close, personal relationship.

"I'm sorry, Wan, I don't believe her."

"She speak true, Pete. Joy love you, only you. She say she want to kill herself."

I hung up.

BIG RON

Pete looked like shit when he came into the bar. He kept talking about "the game", as if what he was doing with Joy was some sort of abstract competition. He's fooling himself. She's destroying him and he can't see it. The sad thing is, he thinks he's winning whatever game it is he's playing. He says the tattoo shows that he's winning the game, because whatever happens she's going to go through the rest of her life with his name on her shoulder. Bollocks. She doesn't give a fuck about that. She's a Buddhist, the body means nothing because next life she'll be back as somebody else anyway. In fact, she probably reckons that she's winning the game because he's behaving so badly: he'll probably return as a fucking cockroach. Life to a Buddhist is all about earning merit in this life to improve your lot in the next. And nothing Pete has done since meeting Joy has earned him any merit, that's for sure.

He's like a fucking marlin taking on a game fisherman. I bet the marlin thinks he's winning the game as he thrashes around in the water. "Look at the boat I've caught," the marlin probably thinks. He gets pulled in, and as he's hauled on to the boat he's fucking thrilled to bits. "Yeah, look at me, I'm taking over the boat." Yeah, right up to the minute he's clubbed to death, the fucking fish probably thinks he's winning the game.

Pete just can't see it, but he's taken the bait and she's hauling him in. What a sad fuck.

PETE

I was lying on the sofa watching television when Bruce came in, red-faced and practically foaming at the mouth.

"I've fucking had it with you," he said.

I was shocked, because he's usually the most easy-going of guys. "What do you mean?" I asked.

"Joy's dead," he said.

I went cold. Like my blood had turned to ice in my veins. Time stopped. It seemed like an eternity before I could speak. "No way."

Bruce's face was red and his eyes hard. "She hanged herself. I'm fucking fed up with you, you've played one mind game too many with that girl."

"Why do you think she's dead?" I was stunned. I couldn't believe that Joy would kill herself. It was impossible. Unthinkable.

"Tukkata called this afternoon, while you were out. You're a bastard, Pete. She never did you any harm."

"And Tukkata said Joy was dead?"

"She said Sunan had called her. One of Joy's friends had phoned Si Saket and said that Joy had hanged herself. Sunan called Tukkata wanting to know where you were."

"It doesn't make any sense, Bruce. There'd be no point in Joy killing herself. It's all about money, and there'd be no profit in her killing herself. It's impossible."

"I'm only telling you what Tukkata told me. I've had a fucking shitty day, Pete, all because of you. First I get the phone call from Tukkata, then I go to Fatso's and everyone's talking about you beating Joy up."

"I slapped her, I didn't ..."

"And you trashed her room, smashed her TV."

Big Ron had obviously told everybody. That was my own fault. I'd always known that there are no secrets in Fatso's, everything said there is for public consumption.

"And now she's dead." He walked away. I sat at the table, too shocked to move.

So here I am, sitting in a taxi waiting for a traffic light to turn green, staring with unseeing eyes at three fat tourists feeding bananas to an elephant. I can't think straight. I just keep hearing Bruce's voice rattling around my head. "Joy's dead."

Part of me didn't believe it, didn't want to believe it, but she'd cut her wrists before and she'd talked about killing herself and coming back to haunt me. Maybe this time she'd done it for real. Maybe she'd done what Mon had done. I closed my eyes and prayed that she wasn't dead. But what if she was? What if she'd hanged herself and what if she'd left a note? She had my name tattooed on her shoulder, for God's sake. She was living in a room I'd paid for. And less than twenty-four hours earlier I'd hit her and trashed her room. What if she'd really done it, where did that leave me? How would I be able to live with myself? How could I?

Bruce had been right, Joy had never done anything to hurt me. She'd never pretended to be anything other than what she was, a bargirl, and if I'd resented the fact that that was what she was, then that was my problem, not hers. I'd had no right to try to change her life, to try to fit her into a mould of my making. I'd pushed her, I'd pushed her and I'd hit her and if she was really, truly dead then I deserved to be dead, too. I couldn't go on living, not with the knowledge that I'd killed her, that I'd pushed her too far, over the edge.

The amber light blinked below the red light but it seemed to do it in slow motion and it felt like an eternity before the green light went on. The traffic ahead of us crawled as if it were driving through water. I wanted to shout and scream, to tell the driver to put his foot down, to drive like the wind, but there was nothing I could do other than fight to stay calm, to hold on to what sanity I had left.

We went by the elephant. "Chang," said the driver, nodding and pointing. He had a small gold statue of a priest on the dashboard, an impassive, bald old man in a loincloth. What goes around comes around. If she was dead then I was damned, for this life and God alone knows how many more. I was tainted. Black. I didn't deserve to live. Joy had never tried to hurt me, never done anything to harm me. Whenever she got angry at me she'd always turn it inwards, she'd hurt herself. I was the one who'd shouted, who'd sworn. I was the one who'd lashed out. Who'd hit her.

The cab jolted to a halt. We were at the corner of Soi 71 and the soi where Joy lived. On the way to Joy's room I passed Wan. I was so caught up in my own thoughts that I didn't recognise her at first. I called after her and she came back. "Joy?" I said. I was so muddled I couldn't even form a sentence.

"Big problem," she said. She'd been crying.

The blood seemed to drain from my head. She was dead. Joy was dead.

I don't know why but I took her hand and together we went to the apartment block. As we got closer, I saw a figure on the balcony, bent over a washing-up bowl. It was Joy. I hurried towards her. She looked up and glared at me but her expression didn't worry me, so strong was the sense of relief that flowed over me. "Thank God," I said.

She turned her head away and concentrated on the pair of jeans she was washing.

JOY

Was I surprised that Pete came back? No, it was just a matter of time. He was always arguing with me and then making up afterwards. Hot and cold, loving and angry, Pete switches back and forth all the time. He's not consistent. Most farangs I've met have been like that. You never really know where you are with them. One minute they say they love you, the next minute they say they never want to see you again.

Thai men don't behave that way. Thai men say what they mean, and stick to it. Thai men hardly ever say that they love you, they show that they do and that's all that counts. But if a Thai man does say he loves you, it means he wants to stay with you and take care of you. If a farang says he loves you, it just means he wants to fuck you.

Pete didn't hurt me when he hit me. Not physically, anyway. I mean, it hurt for a little bit but there wasn't a bruise or anything. Men have always hit me, ever since I was a child. My father used to hit me if I didn't do what he wanted, my teachers used to hit me at school, my brothers used to hit me if they thought I was lazy at home. Park used to hit me when he was drunk. So I wasn't surprised that Pete hit me. That's what men do to women. My father used to hit my mother, too. I used to hear her crying at night. Mon's husband used to hit Mon, and Bird hits Sunan. That's just the way it is in Thailand. Well, that's the way it is in our family, anyway.

What really upset me is that I hadn't done anything wrong. The guy wasn't a boyfriend, he was just selling me some drugs. I was bored and I wanted a buzz. I called his pager number and he said he'd come around with the stuff. He'd only been there a few minutes when Pete broke down the door. Pete wouldn't listen, it was as if he'd already made up his mind that I was a bad girl and there was nothing I could do or say to convince him otherwise. When he started trashing my room, I ran away. I wasn't scared, and I didn't really mind him breaking the TV and all the rest of the stuff. After all, it was his room, he was paying the rent and other than the clothes, Pete had pretty much paid for everything. So if he decided he wanted to destroy it, well, that was his business.

That's not to say I wasn't upset, I was. I was angry that he didn't trust me, and that he felt he could control my life. It's like he thought I was a dog, and that because he fed me and gave me a place to live, he could treat me any way he wanted.

I went around to Wan's room and we drank beer. I kept crying and Wan told me that I was being silly, that I should just forget Pete and go back to Zombie. I could earn more money working in the bar than Pete gave me, and I wouldn't have to worry about what anybody thought. I tried to explain that I was tired of working and that I just wanted someone to take care of me. I was tired of supporting my family, tired of all the demands they kept making on me, tired of my friends asking for money. I wanted to leave Thailand, I wanted to start my life again.

I went back early in the morning. The flat was a mess. He'd broken everything that could be broken and he'd thrown my clothes on the floor. He'd even torn up the pictures of my family, including the photographs of Mon. I sat in the middle of the room and started crying. What he did wasn't fair. He had no right to tear up the pictures, they were the only ones I had of Mon.

I heard Wan outside the room, shouting my name. She must have followed me. I went into the bathroom and wrapped a towel around my neck and tied it to the shower, then I dropped to my knees. Was I trying to kill myself? I don't know. I wanted to die, but I didn't want to kill myself. Does that make sense? I wanted Wan and everyone to know how upset I was, but I don't think I really wanted to be dead. I often wondered if Mon really wanted to kill herself, whether she thought we'd realise what she was doing and cut her down before she died. I knew Wan was outside, and I knew she'd come to my room, and the towel wasn't very tight around my neck, so I suppose I wasn't really trying to kill myself. Not really.

Wan had a key to my room so she let herself in. I'd left the bathroom door open and she started screaming when she saw me. She was with two other girls from Zombie and they untied the towel and helped me down. Wan was crying. I told her I was all right but then I must have fainted.

The girls took me to hospital but I was all right really.

Wan stayed with me while the doctor examined me, but the other girls went away. I guess one of them must have phoned Sunan because when I went home Sunan called me. She said she and our father were in the pick-up with Bird and that they thought I was dead. I said it was all a misunderstanding and that they should just go back to Si Saket but Sunan said no, she wanted to see me. She was really angry but I wasn't sure if it was because she thought I'd killed myself or because she'd driven all that way for nothing. You never can tell with Sunan.

PETE

At first she wouldn't let me touch her, but eventually she put her head against my chest and slipped her arms around my waist.

"Pete, he not my boyfriend. He my drug-dealer. I not have anyone, only you."

I rested my chin on the top of her head. She smelt fresh and clean as if she'd just gotten out of the shower. At first what she said didn't register, then the words sank in.

"What? What do you mean?"

"He come here to sell me yar ba. Have police too much so he come my room. He not my boyfriend, Pete. I not have Thai boyfriend. I love you too much."

"Why, Joy? Why did you need yar ba?"

"Because I think too much. I not want to think too much."

I sat down on the bed with her. She started crying and I kissed her wet cheeks. "You don't need drugs."

I looked around her room. A half-packed bag stood by the door. She saw me looking at it. "I go back to Si Saket," she said. "Sunan come to get me. Then we go Si Saket. My father worry too much."

"Why?"

Her hand went up to her neck. For the first time I saw the red mark there.

"What happened?" I asked.

"I want kill myself," she said flatly.

"Why?"

"Because you not want to see me."

"What did you do?"

"Same Mon." Mon had hanged herself. I stroked the mark on her neck.

"Where?"

Joy nodded at the bathroom.

"You're crazy," I said. She was wearing a brown halter top with a teddy bear on it. I ran my finger around the tattoo on her left shoulder. She really was crazy. Had she really tried to kill herself? It didn't make any sense. She had nothing to gain and everything I knew about Thais suggested that they didn't do anything unless there was a pay-off.

"Why, Joy? Why did you want to kill yourself?"

She shrugged. "Bored," she said.

"Bored with what?"

"With my life. With everything."

"With me?"

She looked up at me and smiled. "I never bored with you, Pete. I love you too much."

I kissed her on the lips. Hard. She pulled me back on to the bed.

DAMIEN

A lot of the girls take drugs, but I won't allow them to bring them into any of my bars. Any girl caught with drugs is sacked on the spot, and the mamasan usually gives them a clout around the head for good measure. The cops are hard enough to deal with without bringing drugs into the equation. Having said that, most of the girls take drugs. Amphetamines, mainly, but some are on heroin and cocaine. We even have a few on Ecstasy but I try to discourage that. For one thing, it affects the way they dance, and for another, they get all lovey dovey and forget to ask the guys for money. Bloody dangerous, is E, shouldn't be allowed. Bad for business.

If they're on heroin, the mamasan makes sure they don't inject. No point in marking the merchandise, and a line of scars on the arms isn't exactly a turn on, is it? Some of them inject between their toes or under their fingernails, and that we let go. What the eye doesn't see, blah, blah, blah. The drugs keep them working, you see, and that's all that I care about. A girl with a habit to feed is going to go with as many customers as she can, sometimes several times a night. Every time she leaves the bar with a customer, the bar gets five hundred baht. The girl gets a hundred baht at the end of the month, and we keep the rest. So if a girl is bought out every night, the bar pulls in twelve thousand baht. Good money, huh?

Usually the girls start on amphetamines. It gives them the energy to dance all night. And the rest. When the girls first come here, they've probably never had sex with a farang. They hear stories about how well endowed we are compared with Thai men and it scares them to death. So the older girls give them yar bar, Dutch courage if you like. Then they don't give a shit who they make love to. Some of them smoke it, others just swallow the tablets. So long as they do it outside the bars, I don't care.

PETE

After we'd made love she fetched me a glass of water and sat on the edge of the bed as I drank it. I reached up and stroked her neck. The red mark seemed fainter. "Why did you want to buy yar ba?" I asked.

"I think too much. If I smoke yar ba, I not think too much."

"Smoke? You smoke it?" I'd assumed that she swallowed the pills.

She smiled coyly. "You want to see?"

My jaw dropped. "You have some?"

She nodded. "You want to see?"

I wasn't sure. I was interested, but I'd always steered well clear of drugs. And what if the police should find me with drugs? They'd love to put another farang behind bars.

"You want to see?" she pressed.

What the hell, I thought. I nodded.

She stood up and went over to the wardrobe and put a hand into a shirt pocket. She came back and held out her hand as if she was offering sugar lumps to a horse. "Yar ba," she said.

There were two small pills wrapped in foil in the palm of her hand. I picked one of them up and unwrapped it. It was smaller than an aspirin, a brownish-pink in colour.

"And you smoke it?"

She nodded.

I handed it back to her. "Can you show me?"

"You want?"

"Sure."

She grinned and took an empty cigarette packet, a cheap cigarette lighter and a pair of nail scissors from her dressing table drawer. She pulled the silver paper from the inside of the cigarette packet and wrapped it around the base of the lighter to form an oblong container. She twisted the end of the paper to make a handle, then pulled out the lighter. She held it up and proudly showed it to me. It was like a miniature pan. She flicked the lighter on and carefully burned off the paper, leaving only the foil, then she blew on it to cool it and put it on the bed. All the time her forehead was creased into a frown as she concentrated on what she was doing.

She used the scissors to cut an oblong of cardboard and then she rubbed it between the palms of her hands until it formed a tube. She licked the open end and rubbed it again.

I watched, entranced. Joy was clearly taking pleasure from the ritual, as if she were preparing to make an offering at a temple. When she'd finished, she crumpled one of the tablets into the foil pan and slipped the cardboard tube between her lips. She flicked her lighter and held the flame under the foil. The pieces of tablet began to smoulder and she sucked the smoke through the tube. She inhaled, and took the lighter away, then blew plumes of smoke through her nostrils, her eyes on mine.

"You're crazy," I said.

"Crazy for you, Pete," she said. She leaned forward and kissed me, blowing the last of the smoke into my mouth. I pushed her down on the bed and she slipped her legs around me.

Afterwards, I asked her what she wanted to do. She said she wanted to go back home, back to Si Saket. Sunan was driving down with Bird and several other members of Joy's family and Joy wanted to stay with them for a few weeks. I asked her if she wanted to move into the flat with me but she said no, she didn't think Bruce would want her there. She said she'd already spoken to the manager of the building and he'd agreed to give her most of the deposit back. I said I wanted to give her some money to take back with her but she shook her head. "I not want your money, Pete," she said. "I only want you love me."

I lay in the bed with my arms around her and told her that I wanted to give her money so that I wouldn't worry about her.

"Pete, I not go Si Saket long time," she said. "I come see you next month, okay?"

I wanted to ask her not to go, to stay with me, to tell her that even if it meant moving out of Bruce's flat and getting another place to live, I wanted her with me. But I knew that it'd be better for her to spend some time out of Bangkok. There were too many temptations in the city: the bars, her friends, the drug dealers. A few weeks back in Si Saket would be good for her, and it'd give me time to find somewhere else to live. I was fed up with living with Bruce, anyway, with or without Troy.

I told Joy I'd get some money from the ATM and arranged to meet her at the German restaurant at eight o'clock.

SUNAN

I was furious when I found out what Pete had done to my sister. How dare he hit her? How dare he? What does he think gives him the right to come to our country and slap around a girl half his age? Would he behave like that in England? Of course he wouldn't. The police would put him in prison. I told Joy, I told her straight, Pete was jai dam, black-hearted and she'd be better off without him. She kept saying no, she kept saying he was okay and that he hadn't really hit her hard but that wasn't the point and I told her so. He'd been manipulating her for months, using her, taking what he wanted from her without giving her what she was entitled to.

If he wanted to treat her as a bargirl, he shouldn't have made such a fuss about her working. He could have paid her barfine as often as he wanted, slept with her, taken her on holiday, but at least she'd have been earning money. And if he didn't want her to be a bargirl then he should have married her. It's not as if he had a wife or anything. He wanted to have his cake and eat it, whatever that stupid farang expression is.

Just look at what Joy's done to herself over Pete. She cut her wrists, she had his name tattooed on her shoulder, and now she's tried to hang herself. She doesn't seem to realise the damage she's doing herself. I don't just mean the scars, though they're bad enough, I mean the damage she's doing to her value. Her worth. The bars want pretty, young, fresh girls, they don't want girls with scars or tattoos. Farangs don't like scars or tattoos, they like their girls to have good skin. They don't even like scars from insect bites on our legs.

I've been trying to get Joy to apply for work in Japan or Hong Kong, or maybe even Canada, but who's going to want to employ a girl with the sort of scars she's got? She's crazy, but it's Pete that's made her crazy. Before she met him she had Park and she worked and she made good money. Okay, she spent a lot on drink and drugs, and she was always too generous with her friends, but at least she was sending money back to Si Saket for our family. Once Pete got his hooks into her, she stopped sending money to Si Saket, so our whole family suffered. When Mon died it was me that had to support the family, me. I had to work harder, hustle more, and I got no help from Joy. Now that wouldn't have been so bad if Pete was going to marry Joy and support her, be it in Thailand or in England. Then at least he'd be taking care of her and she could get him to give money to the family. But he left her in a limbo, and our whole family was suffering because of it. And on top of all that, he hits her. He hits her and abuses her so much that she wants to kill herself.

I thought Joy was dead, I really did. One of the girls from Zombie rang our village and left a message with the old woman who answered the phone, saying that Joy had hanged herself. As soon as I heard what had happened I telephoned Joy's room but there was no answer, so of course I got Bird and my father and our brother and his wife and we all got into the pick-up truck and drove to Bangkok. I was in tears, I was sure she was dead, it'd be just like Joy to kill herself the same way the Mon had done. Mon and Joy were so similar, they looked alike and behaved alike, and I know that Joy came close to killing herself after our mother died. Father was pale with anger, he kept saying he'd kill Pete with his bare hands, and I knew he meant it. Joy was always his favourite, he made no secret of that.

I didn't tell him about the private detective, that Pete had tried to split up Vernon and me. How dare Pete do that? What goes on between me and Vernon is nothing to do with him. Nothing. What does he think gives him the right to try to screw up my life? Just because he's in a mess, just because he can't handle his own life, he wants to make it difficult for everyone else. I can handle Vernon, so it wasn't a major problem. Same as I can handle Toine in Denmark. I bet Toine will still send me money when I'm in America. I'll just tell him that I'm there studying. It'll all work out fine. But no thanks to Pete.

All the way to Bangkok I was using my mobile phone, calling everyone I knew until the batteries went dead. No one knew for sure what had happened, though several of the girls from Nana had heard that she had hanged herself.

About two hours outside Bangkok I made Bird stop at a callbox and I rang Joy's room again. She was there. I was so relieved I almost fainted. She explained what had happened, and I told her not to go anywhere. Father started crying when I told him Joy was all right.

When we got to Bangkok, we all hugged Joy and told her she had to go back to Si Saket with us. She said that she had to see Pete, that he'd promised to give her some money. Father said he wanted to go with her, but I knew that he wanted to do something to Pete, so I said that he mustn't go. I'd already decided what I had to do. Joy always carried a photograph of her with Pete in the purse she took to work, and while she was in the bathroom I took it. Bird saw me but he didn't say anything. He knew what I was going to do and he just smiled. I told Joy I was going out to buy some medicine and told Bird to make sure she stayed in the room until I got back.

PETE

I went back to the flat. Bruce wasn't there and he didn't turn up while I showered and changed so I left a note for him, just to say that Joy was okay. I went to the Bangkok Bank and withdrew eight thousand baht on my Lloyds TSB Bank Visa card and another seven thousand baht on my Standard Chartered Visa card. Fifteen thousand baht. I wasn't sure how much money I had left in my bank accounts, but I figured I had enough to cover it. Without a regular pay cheque, it wouldn't take long for both accounts to run out, I'd always pretty much spent everything I'd earned. I was going to have to do something about getting a job, especially if I was going to get a place for me and Joy. I'd need a deposit and a month's rent in advance and deposits for the utilities and stuff. I figured I was going to need at least fifty thousand baht up front.

I had an hour to kill before I was due to meet Joy so I went to Fatso's Bar and had a couple of gin and tonics. Big Ron rang the bell and so did Jimmy, so that was two free drinks, but I didn't return the favour because I was going to have to take care of my money.

Nobody mentioned Joy's suicide attempt but I knew it'd only be a matter of time before Bruce started spreading the word. There were no secrets in Fatso's Bar, it wasn't just the bar where everyone knows your name, it was the bar where everyone knew your secrets, from Big Ron's genital warts to Jimmy's cocaine habit.

The guys were talking about death wishes, and I tried to explain how I'd always had an urge to throw myself off tall buildings. Always had, ever since I was a kid. It wasn't that I wanted to kill myself, that's definitely not the case, but whenever I was high up I always wanted to lean forward and imagine what it'd be like to plunge to the ground.

When I was at university I joined the parachuting club, just to see what freefalling was actually like, but I'd hated it, hated everything about it, the flight up, the sensation of falling, the landing. But I never lost the urge to jump. Weird. I guess it's a compulsion, but damned if I can explain what it means. I tried explaining it to Big Ron, and he kept nodding and agreeing with me.

He said that he knew exactly what I meant. Then he said that whenever a girl lay on her back and opened her legs, well, he just had the irresistible urge to dive right in, then and there. He laughed like a hyena and I realised he was taking the piss, as usual.

I went to the German restaurant to wait for Joy. She was late, but I didn't mind, it gave me the chance to have a few more drinks and get my act together. I'd call Alistair and see if I could convince him to give me my job back. I was sure I could get him to see my point of view. I was a good writer, one of the best, and I had a hell of a track record. I could be an asset to the company, and with Joy back in Si Saket there wouldn't be so many distractions.

BIG RON

Pete was in a right state when he came into the bar, knocking back the gins like there was no tomorrow. He kept rambling on about Joy loving him, that she was different from all the other girls who worked in the bars, that she'd proved that she loved him and that he was going to marry her and take her back to England. Then he started telling us about how he liked to stand at the top of tall buildings and imagine what it was like to throw himself off. It sounded as if he was thinking of killing himself but didn't want to come right out and say it. You know, like calling the fucking Samaritans and talking about the weather. That's what it felt like, anyway. Like he was on the edge and all it was going to take was one small step or push and that'd be it.

I guess part of the problem is that he's lost his job and doesn't have any money coming in. He hasn't told anyone here that he was sacked, but Bruce filled us in a while back. Doesn't look as if he's looking for a job either, he spends most of his time in the bar or over at Nana Plaza. He looks like shit, he hasn't shaved for days or showered by the look of it. He's a mess, and unless he pulls himself together no-one's going to employ him.

Thailand can do that to farangs. It lures them in with promises it fails to deliver, beautiful, sexy women, long, hot days, exotic food, smiling faces, but it's all a mirage, it doesn't really exist, and by the time you find that out it's too late, you're heading for the rocks and there's nothing you can do to change your course.

The guys who survive, guys like Jimmy and Rick and me, we see through the mirage early on and we accept it for what it is. We adapt. Guys like Pete, they believe the illusion, and they keep believing it right up until the moment it destroys them. That's where Pete's heading. Destruction. And Joy's the siren whose song is pulling him towards the rocks.

PETE

Joy was more than an hour late. She said that Sunan had arrived in Bangkok with her father and that they hadn't wanted her to come to see me. "They very angry you, Pete, but I tell them no problem, I tell them I love you, only one."

She looked stunning. She was wearing black Levi jeans and a black T-shirt and as usual she was tottering on chunky high-heeled shoes. I ordered her an orange juice, and when it arrived the waitress looked at the razor scars on Joy's left arm with wide eyes. Joy didn't seem to notice. She never made any attempt to cover up the scars and if anything appeared to want to flaunt them, because more often than not she wore short-sleeved shirts.

I asked her if she was hungry but she shook her head and said she'd already eaten. I realised that was probably why she was late, she'd gone out for dinner with her family. I felt a flare of anger but just as quickly I decided that I was being unreasonable. She hadn't seen Sunan or her father for some weeks, it was only natural that she'd want to spend time with them.

I told her what I planned to do, that I'd move out of Bruce's apartment and get a place for just the two of us, and she grinned. "Ching ching?" she asked. Was I serious?

I told her that I was, that I wanted to marry her and take care of her.

"Maybe I not go to Si Saket," she said. "Better I stay in Bangkok with you."

I told her no, that it'd be easier if she was away for a few weeks, plus I thought that it would be good for her to be with her family for a while.

"Okay," she said. "I do for you."

I told her the story of Mary and her cat. She listened seriously, from time to time asking me to explain words that she didn't understand. When I finished she reached over and held my hands. "Pete," she said, "I not same your friend's cat. I not need a second chance."

I was so pleased she'd understood the moral of the story that I didn't point out that it wasn't a second chance she was getting, she'd used up her second chance months ago.

I paid the bill and we went outside. I held her in my arms and she looked up at me with her big, trusting eyes. I kissed her and then buried my face in her hair and hugged her, so tightly that she gasped. I loved her more than I'd ever loved anyone in my life. She was my life. Right there and then I'd have died for her. I tried to tell her how I felt, I tried to put the feelings into words, but Joy just laughed.

"Pete, you drunk," she said, but I wasn't.

I said I'd get her a taxi but she said I should go first. She kissed me again and said that she loved me. I told her I'd phone her in Si Saket the next day. And the next. And every day until she got back to Bangkok. Tears welled up in her eyes and trickled down her cheeks. I suddenly remembered the money and I took it out of my back pocket and gave it her. Then I waved down a motorcycle taxi and negotiated a price to get back to Soi 23.

Joy stood on the pavement watching me go. As I turned the corner, she blew me a kiss.

SOMCHAI

Poonsak already had the engine ticking over when the farang came out of the restaurant. Sunan had given us a photograph so there'd be no mistake, but I didn't need to check it. It was him all right. I tapped Poonsak on the shoulder and he nodded. We were both wearing full face helmets just in case we were seen. Poonsak had stolen the bike and put false plates on, and once the job was done we'd dump it and set fire to it.

I'd worked with Poonsak more than a dozen times, he was reliable and never panicked. I was with one guy once, much younger than Poonsak, and when the gun went off he damn near crashed the bike. Poonsak's as solid as a rock.

The farang and Joy stood together in front of the restaurant, talking. Joy stood on tiptoe and kissed him on the cheek and he stroked her hair.

How romantic. Poonsak said something but I couldn't hear what it was over the noise of the traffic.

The farang gave her something and she put it in her pocket. Probably money. Farangs are always giving money to Thai girls, but I've never understood why. Do they think they can buy love? Impossible. If a girl loves you, she'll give you money, right? Not the other way around.

The farang flagged down a motorcycle taxi and spoke to the rider. It was hard to see clearly from where we'd parked the bike, but it looked as if Joy was crying. I wondered if Sunan had told her what we were going to do. She hadn't said, and I hadn't asked. But Sunan had insisted that Joy wasn't near by when we did it.

I've killed twenty-three people, but this would be my first farang. Because it was a farang, I'd raised my price, to ten thousand baht, double what I normally charged. Sunan had agreed to pay without any bargaining, half in advance, half when the job was done.

The farang climbed on to the back of the bike and waved goodbye to Joy. I tapped Poonsak on the shoulder. He put the bike in gear and headed down Soi 4 to Sukhumvit Road. We knew where the farang was going. Sukhumvit Soi 23.

I put my hand inside the jacket and touched the butt of my gun. There were six cartridges in the clip, but unless something went wrong I'd only use three. One to bring him down. One in the heart. One in the head.

VERNON

I couldn't believe it when I heard what had happened to Pete. Unbelievable. I know how bad the traffic is in Bangkok and how dangerous it can be using motorcycle taxis, but you never expect it to happen to somebody you know. At least he didn't suffer. According to Sunan it was all over in a matter of seconds and Pete probably didn't even know what hit him. It was a cement truck, Sunan said, and the driver was high on amphetamines. The guy ran a red light and hit Pete's motorcycle side on. Joy was totally distraught, of course. Hasn't stopped crying since, Sunan said. The family hasn't left her alone because apparently Joy keeps threatening to kill herself, says she can't bear to live without him. I wanted to go over to the funeral, but Sunan said he'd been cremated and his parents had taken the ashes back to England. There was no autopsy or inquiry or anything, but Sunan said the driver would probably be charged with manslaughter.

If nothing else, it made me realise how precious life is, how we have to grab everything we can in the all too brief time we're alive. One minute we're here, the next we're not. I'm going to make sure that I pack as much as I can into my life.

Sunan's arriving next month, and Joy's coming with her. Both their visas have been approved and I've paid for their tickets. It's going to be a whole new life for both of them. It'll be good for Joy, being here will help her get over what happened to Pete. They'll both be able to enrol on English courses, and I've already found a great place for a restaurant. It's a short walk from my apartment, with a bar on the ground floor and a small eating area upstairs. I reckon that by taking the bar out we'll be able to get another dozen tables in. The kitchen'll need fitting out but I think I can get everything straightened out for twenty thousand bucks. I've already sent photographs to Sunan and she's really excited.

Moving to San Diego is going to be the making of Sunan, I know it is. It'll get her away from bad influences of Bangkok, the bars and the bar girls. She'll have to settle down, and I'll know where she is every hour of the day. Okay, I'm not a hundred per cent sure that she loves me now, not totally, not in the way that I love her. But I know that once she's here, once she has a business to run and a real home, she'll grow to love me.

She's so excited about the restaurant. She's already planning the menu and the table settings and stuff. As soon as she's over here and got everything ready, we're going to bring Bird. Apparently he used to be a chef, and he'll be company for Sunan and Joy. It's going to be great. We're going to be one big happy family.

BIG RON

Was I surprised at what happened to Pete? Of course I fucking wasn't. He was on the road to ruin as soon as he let her get to him. A lost cause. A sad fuck. The whole saga was like a fucking fairy tale. Grimm.

Extract from
CROSS-CULTURAL COMPLICATIONS OF PROSTITUTION IN THAILAND
by PROFESSOR BRUNO MAYER

Relationships between farangs and prostitutes rarely reach a satisfactory conclusion by Western standards. There is always a level of mistrust, based on the fact that the girl is an active prostitute when they meet and the fact that their initial sexual encounter is, almost without exception, paid for. The farang is thus never sure of whether the girl loves him, or his money, and while this is not a problem from the girl's cultural perspective, it is not something that the man can accept from his Western viewpoint. The farang who does take a bargirl as a regular partner, to the extent of living with, or even marrying, her, often fears that she will return to a life of prostitution. This remains a constant source of unease. The girl, too, remains in a state of jealous tension. She knows that she met her farang protector in a bar and she is all too well aware how easy it would be for him to visit another establishment and meet a younger and prettier girl. The combination of mutual suspicion and mistrust, coupled with unending requests for money to support the girl's family, leads more often than not to arguments and the break-up of the relationship.

In an attempt to distance the girl from her previous life as a prostitute, a farang might decide to take the girl back to his own country. The radical change in the girl's environment almost always results in unhappiness and the eventual dissolution of the relationship. Unless she has travelled she will be ignorant of the man's country and customs, and will have only a rudimentary understanding of his language. This, coupled with the loneliness resulting from the forced separation from her family and friends, leads to tensions and conflict, resolved only by the girl returning to Thailand.

Either way, once the relationship has ended, the girl will almost certainly return to the bars and to prostitution. This is accompanied by an initial period of depression as the girl accepts that she has lost the reasonably comfortable life that comes of having the support of a farang and has to revert to the relatively unstable lifestyle of a bargirl. This period is quite short, however, and after a week or so she will once again be content in the disorganised and dissipate way of life, drinking bouts, drug-taking and card-playing, funded by sexual encounters with strangers. Until, of course, she finds herself another farang provider.

BRUCE

It's like the Buddhists say, right? What goes around, comes around. I was never happy with the way he treated Joy, making her jump through hoops like a trained animal. If he'd done the right thing by her at the beginning, if he'd just let her live with him, then I don't think any of this would have happened. Serves him right. Funny thing was, day of his funeral I found the watch. It was in the pocket of the jacket I'd been wearing when I got back from Nong Khai. I must have put it there without thinking, then hung the jacket up in the wardrobe. I still don't know what happened to the business cards, though. Right bloody mystery, that. Don't expect I'll ever find out where they went.

JIMMY

The guys from Fatso's went to the funeral and there was a piss-up afterwards but it wasn't much of a send-off. There was a rumour going around that Pete had left everything to Joy but I don't know if it's true or not. I decided to pop into Zombie, and bugger me but who should I see dancing stark bollock naked but the girl herself. First time I'd seen her dancing in a long while, she was always waitressing when Pete was around. There was a girl who looked just like her dancing a couple of poles down and I figured it was her sister. When their dancing shift finished I waved them over and bought them colas. Within minutes the sister, Dit her name was, had her hand on my thigh. I asked if I could barfine both of them and ten minutes later we were back in my apartment.

I always get a kick out of sisters, you'd be surprised how many there are working the bars. Joy and Dit had obviously worked together before: Dit stuck her tongue down my throat while Joy gave me a blow job, then they switched places. I wanted them to do a lesbian show for me and they balked at that, but I put a lesbian video on, and after watching that for a few minutes they got into it. Lesbian Lust, it's called, I got it in Hong Kong a couple of years back and it's never failed me yet. Joy and Dit started kissing each other out while I played with myself, then I screwed Joy while Dit kissed her. Did them both without a condom. Hate the things, they take all the fun out of screwing. They started moaning about wanting me to put one on, but I told them to fuck off, I know full well that they don't make their Thai boyfriends wear them.

It was a hell of a night, screwed them in all sorts of combinations, and by the end of the evening they seemed to be enjoying the lesbian thing, too. I went to shower and when I came back they were at each other like dogs on heat, fingering each other and kissing. I was too knackered to join in so I gave them a thousand baht each and kicked them out. I figured it was the sort of send-off that Pete would have appreciated.

EPILOGUE

Sunan arrived in San Diego in December 1996, just in time for Christmas. Bird arrived soon after, with Joy. Vernon and Sunan were married on St Valentine's Day the following year. Plans for the Thai restaurant were put on hold when Sunan fell pregnant. Bird couldn't settle in the United States and decided to return to Thailand in the summer of 1997. He asked Sunan to go with him, but she told him that she wanted to make her life with Vernon. She gave Bird a hundred thousand baht that she'd saved over the years. Bird wished her well and never saw her again once he returned to Thailand. Vernon introduced Joy to several of his friends in the hope that she would find someone she could settle down with, but she never really felt comfortable in America. She returned to Bangkok in the spring of 1998 and started dancing in Zombie again. In October an Australian walked into the bar who was the spitting image of Pete. Joy paid her own barfine to go with him and they haven't spent a night apart since. They were married in 1999 and his parents and brother flew from Melbourne for the ceremony. The Australian returned to Melbourne in 2000 to take up a new job and Joy went with him. She's pregnant now with their second child. The tattoo is fading, and the Australian never mentions it.

Vernon and Sunan have three children, all boys. If Vernon's family and friends have noticed that the eldest boy looks nothing like his father, they've never said anything.

Bruce was sacked from the handbag factory. He tried to get another job in manufacturing but word had gotten around that he was an unreliable employee and he wasn't able to convince anyone to take him on. He got together a small group of investors and set up an English restaurant down the road from Fatso's. He even poached one of the chefs from Fatso's and two of Big Ron's waitresses. He spends twelve hours a day in the restaurant and is putting on weight.

In 1999, Big Ron met the love of his life in a go-go bar in Nana Plaza, married her and has two beautiful daughters both of whom, thankfully, take after their mother.

Alistair moved to Bangkok in 1998 to take over the production of the guide to Thailand. He refused to even set foot in a go-go bar for the first year he was in Bangkok, then eventually relented and went to the Long Gun Bar in Soi Cowboy with three squash-playing friends. A girl from Surin who was dancing naked around a silver pole smiled at him and three months later they were married. He bought her a house, a pick-up truck and set her up in a small beauty parlour in Sukhumvit Soi 24 before discovering that she was still married to her childhood sweetheart, a motorcycle taxi driver who worked at the Asoke end of Soi Cowboy. Alistair quit his job and moved to Pattaya and in the autumn of 1999 was found dead at the bottom of a high-rise hotel. Police closed the case as suicide brought on by depression.

Somchai was arrested in 1997 after fleeing from the scene of his twenty-sixth murder for hire. He was using a new driver, a student at Assumption University who needed the money to finish his studies. The driver accelerated too quickly and Somchai fell off the back of the bike. He woke up in hospital surrounded by half a dozen police officers. Somchai asked for all twenty-six murders to be taken into consideration and in October 1997 he was sentenced to life imprisonment. He was released in August 2004 along with 25,000 other prisoners to mark the 72nd birthday of Her Majesty The Queen. The wife of the Prime Minister gave each freed prisoner two hundred baht to pay for their trip home. Somchai spent his money on whiskey and carried out his twenty-seventh contract killing two weeks later. The student who was driving the motorcycle was never caught. He finished his studies and now practices as a dentist in Soi Thonglor.

Professor Bruno Mayer was killed in a traffic accident in September 2003 when Pam tried to answer her mobile phone while driving him to a craft festival in Chiang Mai. Their vehicle ploughed into a cement truck and they were both killed instantly. Professor Mayer's wife refused to pay for what was left of the body to be shipped back to Germany and suggested that he be cremated in Thailand. She did not attend the funeral.

Nigel set up an import–export business with a Thai businessman in the summer of 1997. The company was amazingly successful and by 2002 was turning over several million baht a month, mainly exporting Thai foodstuffs and furniture to the UK, and bringing fire extinguishing equipment from the UK to Thailand. The company moved to new offices in a prestigious block in Wireless Road and Nigel moved into a four-bedroomed apartment a short walk from Nana Plaza. His apartment was raided by two dozen police officers on Christmas Eve 2002. Nigel was discovered with two underage prostitutes in his bed and four kilos of pure heroin hidden behind an air-conditioning unit. Nigel proclaimed his innocence (of the drugs, but not of the girls) and declared that someone must have set him up. The Thai businessman promised to do whatever it took to have Nigel freed, but despite his best efforts Nigel was found guilty of possession of Class A drugs and was sentenced to ninety-nine years in jail. Nigel hasn't seen or heard from the Thai businessman since, but by all accounts the company (of which Nigel is no longer a director) is prospering.

Jimmy started to get sick in 2003. It started with night sweats and headaches, then flu-like symptoms that he couldn't shake off. He was diagnosed as HIV-positive at the end of 2003 and in the summer of 2004 he developed full-blown Aids. He went back to the UK to throw himself on the mercies of the National Health Service. He died just before Christmas 2004, denying his illness to the end.

Also by Stephen Leather

Two-timing bargirls, suspicious spouses and lesbian lovers—it was all in a day's work for Bangkok Private Eye Warren Olson.

For more than a decade Olson walked the mean streets of the Big Mango. Fluent in Thai and Khmer, he was able to go where other Private Eyes feared to tread.

His clients included westerners who had lost their hearts—and life savings—to money-hungry bargirls. But he had more than his fair share of Thai clients, too, including a sweet old lady who was ripped off by a Christian conman and a Thai girl blackmailed by a former lover.

True stories based on Warren Olson's case files, retold (to protect the innocent, and the guilty) by bestselling author Stephen Leather.